# BLAZE OF GLORY

## ROSANNE BITTNER

OUTLAW HEARTS SERIES

*OUTLAW HEARTS* SERIES IN ORDER OF PUBLICATION:

OUTLAW HEARTS (Sourcebooks)

DO NOT FORSAKE ME (Sourcebooks)

LOVE'S SWEET REVENGE (Sourcebooks)

THE LAST OUTLAW (Sourcebooks)

A CHICKADEE CHRISTMAS (Short story in an anthology titled CHRISTMAS IN A COWBOY'S ARMS (Sourcebooks)

BLAZE OF GLORY (An Amazon publication)

This book is a work of fiction. All characters and their names, and all incidents in this story are a product of the author's imagination and meant only for entertainment reading. Contains violence and adult content.

Copyright © 2021 by Rosanne Bittner. Any reproduction of this book, in whole or in part, without the author's permission is deemed copyright infringement and grounds for criminal charges.

Cover Design: Amy Anderson

*Dedicated to Glenda Kinard, who was the kind of person no one ever forgets or sets aside in distant memory. Glenda was more than just a devoted fan. She was a good friend who loved me like a sister. I will never forget when she helped me dress for the part of an "Old West" prostitute for an event at a national writers' conference in Atlanta. We had so much fun, and a lot of laughs!*

*Glenda was a big fan of my hero Jake Harkner in my Outlaw Hearts series, and even her e-mail address included the words "outlawjake." I hope to go to Heaven when I die, and when I get there, I have absolutely no doubt that Glenda will be there, too, and we can sit and visit for hours.*

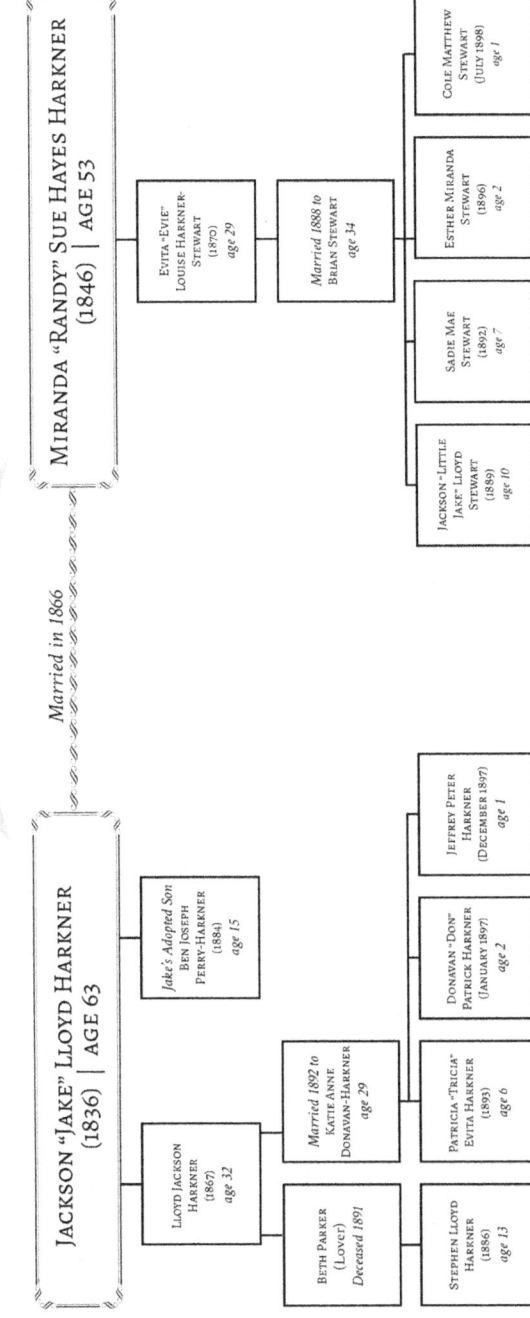

# PART I

For he will command his angels concerning you to guard you in all your ways . . .
 *Psalm 91:11*

# PROLOGUE

*Mid-May, 1899 . . .*

*His daughter calls him an avenging angel.*

Chicago reporter Jeff Truebridge paused to oil a key on his Remington typewriter, then checked to be sure he had plenty of ribbon left. Sighing in thought, he leaned back, remembering his chance of a lifetime—several days of riding with U. S. Marshal Jake Harkner in Oklahoma Territory. Parts of that territory were still called No Man's Land, and who better to go after the worst criminals in such dangerous territory than Jake, who once led a life just as criminal as the men he hunted down? He was probably one of the best shooters still alive in what was becoming the Old West, but he could also be ruthless. The criminals he chased down either gave up or ended up dead. Jake was not known as a patient man.

Jeff still had the notepad he'd used on his adventure, some of the notes hard to read because when Jake said, "Let's go," you grabbed what you could and hoped you could keep up. Those notes led to a best-selling book titled *JAKE HARKNER: THE LEGEND AND THE MYTH*. By some miracle, Jake had allowed Jeff the privilege of writing his story, *and what a story it is,* Jeff thought . . . a little boy from Texas who'd suffered at the hands of a brutal, alcoholic father who'd beaten Jake enough times as a child that he shouldn't have survived. At only eight years old, and too little to help stop his father, Jake witnessed the man murder his mother and little brother. To this day, the memory fed Jake's need to protect and defend those he loved.

Jake was raised off and on by prostitutes, many of whom risked beatings to protect him from his father. At the tender age of fifteen, Jake finally shot the man to death to stop him from raping a twelve-year-old girl.

For the next fifteen years, Jake led a ruthless, outlaw life that left him wanted for a slew of charges, some warranted, some false. Known as the "handsome outlaw," Jake's face showed up on WANTED posters all over the South.

"And then came Miranda," Jeff muttered, grinning. The story of how Jake met his wife was Jeff's favorite part of the man's story. *She's the air I breathe,* Jake had described her in his first interview with Jeff. Jake and his "Randy" were still desperately in love after over thirty years together. Few women would put up with what Miranda had gone through to stand beside a then-wanted man who lived by the gun—a man haunted by his own past, and to whom Miranda had to teach the meaning of the word "love."

Since the publication of THE LEGEND AND THE MYTH, Jake's infamous behavior hadn't stopped. Jeff continued to write monthly articles about the him. A special plaque hung on the wall across from Jeff's desk that had been presented to him by the *Chicago Daily Journal* for his investigative reporting on a legendary character who still lived.

And now Jake was coming to Chicago, the first pleasure trip he and Randy had ever taken. Jeff scooted closer to his desk and began typing again, composing a new column about Jake's visit. Right now it was more a matter of notes he would have to edit and rearrange later.

*Jake Harkner is a man of stark contrasts,* he typed. *The bad is as bad as bad can get. But the good is astoundingly deep for a man who can walk right up to someone, put a gun to his head and pull the trigger. That's what Jake did in Denver a few years ago, after an old enemy snuck into a cattlemen's ball and shot Jake's son. Thank God, Lloyd survived. Jake was constantly at his side, and he avoided prison because of the incredibly devoted love and support of his family and even some of the witnesses. And that family is surprisingly big for a man who was once a wanted outlaw. Jake has a son and daughter and an adopted son, plus eight grandchildren, with more on the way.*

*Jake would give his life in a second for any member of his family, and sometimes, even for a stranger. Two summers ago he risked his life in Mexico to rescue a fifteen-year-old girl who had been captured into unspeakable slavery. He'd never even met the girl, but she lives a free and happy life today because of Jake's sacrifice. The wounds he suffered took months to heal, and left Jake missing and thought dead for several months. A broken leg that was never set correctly gives him pain to this day.*

Jeff paused again, thinking about Jake's reasons for his actions. He'd risked his life in Mexico as a favor to the most notorious prostitute in Denver, Gretta MacBain. The kidnapped girl was Gretta's daughter, a sweet girl raised by adoptive parents. Jake had an affinity to befriending women like Gretta because of how he was raised, and Miranda understood that. Now Gretta was married to one of Jake's ranch hands, and they lived on Jake's sprawling ranch in Colorado. Gretta's daughter was going to finishing school in Denver.

*I met Jake when I went to Guthrie, Oklahoma to see if I could write a book about his life,* Jeff continued typing. *When I first met the dark, dangerous, and distrustful Marshal Jake Harkner, he scared me to death. I was a young city boy with thick glasses, and a shrimp of a man compared to Jake. But I came to learn that the man had a heart as big as his six-foot-four-inch frame and the booming guns he wears. Riding with Jake and his son, Lloyd, who served as a Deputy U. S. Marshal, was an experience I will cherish forever. Life could not have been more exciting. Lloyd can be just as ruthless as his father, but because he was raised in love, he doesn't have that down-deep mean streak Jake has.*

*The Harkner family owns the J&L Ranch in the foothills of Colorado, a one- hundred-fifty-thousand-acre horse and cattle spread.*

*At sixty-three, Jake is still hard as a rock, strong, healthy, and damn good with his famous .44's. He turns women's heads even though he bears scars from a very rough life. His wife, Miranda, ten years younger than Jake, is a sophisticated, well educated woman from Kansas, and despite the hardships she has known, she is still beautiful. Different as she and Jake are, their love story is like a romantic storybook. Miranda Harkner is a foot shorter than Jake, and she barely weighs a hundred pounds, but she can lead that man around like a puppy dog. He is totally devoted to her, and watching them together is nothing short of entertaining. They have a unique relationship, and Miranda has a way of subtly controlling her big, tough husband without him realizing it.*

Jeff grinned.

The real test of friendship would be when one of the richest men in Chicago, Attorney Peter Brown, hosted Jake and Randy's visit. Peter befriended Jake and Randy years ago in Guthrie, when, as a grieving widower, he'd moved his practice there. Miranda worked for Peter in order to keep busy when Jake was gone for days or weeks on the job. To this day, Jake's and Peter's friendship was dicey. As an attorney, Peter helped keep Jake out of trouble more than once, but not for Jake's sake. He'd done it for Miranda. Peter loved her, and Jake damn well knew it.

Still, there was trust and a rather surprising but cautious friendship between Jake and Peter, and Peter's unspoken affection for Miranda remained just that – unspoken. Now re-married, Peter Brown lived in a mansion on Lake Michigan in North Chicago.

*I'll never forget the first day I met Miranda Harkner,* Jeff continued writing. *It was that first day this nervous reporter arrived in Guthrie. Jake rode into town with four criminals in tow—one dead, the other three looking like they wished they were dead. He gave out a whistle, his signal to Miranda that he was back.*

*And then, there she was . . . running up the street to greet him. The minute Jake set eyes on her, the ornery, mean, dangerous man changed to a loving, attentive husband who greeted his wife with a gentle kiss, after which his ornery side walked over to a hefty young man who was threatening to kill him and*

*slammed a rifle butt into the young man's chest, cracking his breastbone. Jake then threw him into the street as though the young man weighed a mere five pounds. Jake's brute strength for his age surprised me. Later, he walked back to his wife, put an arm around her, and took her home, as though bringing back four criminals and then throwing a tough young man into the street was just an every-day matter.*

*That, folks, is the man who is coming soon to visit our fair city.*

Jeff paused again to stretch his arms and back. He rubbed his eyes, then returned to his typing, determined to make this particular article as exciting as possible.

*I'm sure the public imagines Jake as a dangerous, weathered old man, but I can assure you, you will be surprised by his winning looks and very affable persona. Harkner can be pleasant and accommodating. He has a surprising sense of humor and is deeply loyal to those he trusts as true friends. With a man like Jake, you are either his worst enemy, or his best friend. Few people fall between.*

*Be sure to watch this column for news of when Harkner will arrive in Chicago. I will list the events where you might be able to meet him, or at least get a look. Don't be surprised by anything Harkner says. He wastes no words when it comes to speaking his mind, and believe me, he always speaks his mind, and he always means what he says.*

That last comment made Jeff laugh out loud. He'd never met a more blatantly honest and opinionated man who seldom worried about offending someone.

*Hold on to your hats, folks. Jake Harkner is coming to town.*

CHAPTER 1

Late May 1899...

"What the hell? It's like the sonofabitch has nine lives. Is he part feline?" Grizzly Smith handed the old newspaper article back to Brady Fillmore.

Brady grinned through yellowing teeth. "If I have my way, Harkner will have used up his last life. After nine comes ten, and by then even a *cat* has to die." He sniffed. "I can't believe I've come across somebody who knew him back in the day. You say he rode shotgun for the owner of a Colorado gold mine?"

Grizzly nodded. "Long time ago." He picked at food stuck in what was left of his teeth – a few on the bottom – an eye tooth and two back teeth missing on top. "Once Harkner started guardin' the gold shipments, nobody was able to rob from the Yellowjacket. He was like a goddamned legend, 'til his past finally caught up with him and he moved someplace else. I jumped for joy when I heard he went to prison a few years later. Around thirty years ago, I tried to rob a Yellowjacket shipment. One of Harkner's bullets got me through the throat, and I ended up with this voice—kind of like a boot scrapin' over gravel mixed with steam hissin' from a train engine. At least that's how one whore put it to me. She told me not to talk while I was pokin' her 'cuz my voice took the romance out of it."

Brady grinned. "I didn't know whores even cared about romance. But I don't blame her. Hell, that voice of yours is bad enough, but that weathered old face and tangled beard would cause even a whore to hesitate."

Grizzly took no offense at the remark. He was used to such joking insults. "Yeah, I'm like an old grizzly bear that will likely go to sleep some winter and never wake up. It was that same whore that told me that, too. She's the one who gave me the nickname Grizzly. It just kind of stuck."

Both men laughed.

Brady ran a hand through the too-long strands of his thinning hair. "Just whores? Haven't you ever been married?"

"Nope. Never wanted to settle that way." Grizzly frowned. "Why in hell did you perk up when you heard me braggin' to Carl Ellis about once knowin' Jake Harkner?"

A darkness moved into Brady's brown eyes. "Because I hate the man, and I'm looking for anybody else who hates him and would love to see him dead. Both him and his son. I thought, since Harkner shot you in the throat, maybe you had a grudge against him."

Grizzly grunted a mock laugh. "Oh, I hate him, all right. I suffered an awful lot over that bullet—nearly died—lost my voice completely for a while. It was a long time ago, and I lost track of Harkner after he went to prison for all the killin' and gun runnin' and robberies he'd committed before hidin' out under a different name and workin' at the Yellowjacket." He leaned in, resting his arms on the table in the small restaurant he frequented near a Denver warehouse where he worked with Brady. "Tell me somethin'. Back in the day, they used to call Harkner the Handsome Outlaw. Leastways, the whores did. Since you saw ole' Jake up close not that long ago, is that bastard finally all crippled and toothless like me? We're about the same age. I'm sixty-one. How's a sixty-somethin' Jake Harkner look? He's led a hell of a rough life, and that news article says he had a bad time of it rescuin' that young girl down in Mexico."

Brady shook his head. "Haven't seen him since then, so I can't say as to what might have happened. But I knew him and his son right before all that. I was farming near their ranch. At that time, the fucker hardly looked a day over forty. Had all his teeth and a smile that turned women to pudding. Thick, dark hair showing streaks of gray. Some men seem to get even better looking as they age, and that sonofabitch is one of them. It isn't fair, I'll tell you that. He's stronger than a bull, hard-edged, and I'm betting as good as ever with those .44's. And what irks me even more is that wife of his is still beautiful—long blond hair and a shape that makes a man want to strip off those clothes and have at what's under them."

"I'll be goddamned." Grizzly squinted through faded blue eyes and leaned back in his chair. "Far as I can remember, his wife was eight or ten years younger than him." He scratched at his beard. "Maybe Mexico did ole' Jake in and his age is startin' to show." Frowning, he wiped his nose across his shirtsleeve. "You said you hate Harkner. Why? What the hell did he do to you?"

Brady folded the news article and leaned back to shove it into his pants pocket. "That bastard and his son stole my land and cost me my family. I intend to get the land back. What I have in mind could lead to a range war, but I don't give a shit. I intend to goad Harkner into a trap where he finally meets his Maker. Or more likely finally meets the

Devil, who'll lead him straight into Hell itself. That's where he belongs."

"I gotta' agree with you there." Grizzly lit a cigar. "How'd Harkner get your land?"

"It's government land I settled rightfully, but Harkner and his son took over my claim after a little feud we had." Brady slugged down what was left of his whiskey. "I had a bad year farming and asked the Harkners for help a time or two. They loaned me a few tools I couldn't afford, but later accused me of stealing those tools. Then they accused me of rustling their cattle."

"*Did* you steal from them or shuffle any cattle onto your place?"

Brady shrugged. "Hell, I had to support my family. And I meant to give the tools back. I needed them to build a barn to store my crops, but things went bad, and I didn't have any crops to store. The family was starving, so I stole a calf—one calf, mind you—to feed my wife and kids. I was taking it to my place when I, well, I dropped my smoke, and it was extra dry that summer. The valley caught fire, and it spread too fast for me to put out. Burned all the grass the Harkners were saving for the winter. Some neighboring rancher saw it all and accused me of setting the fire on purpose. Jake's son, Lloyd, he wanted to hang me."

Lips pursed, Grizzly studied his cigar. "Why didn't he string you up? He had the right."

"The hell he did! It was an *accident*! I tried to tell him that."

"Taking that calf was no accident."

"Well, they should have been generous enough to realize I needed it for my family. Hell, I would have paid for it."

"And where's your family now?"

Brady looked at his empty glass. "Gone. My wife took

the kids to her ma's in New Orleans and filed for divorce. Jake told me the only way keep from getting my neck stretched was to give my land to the J&L. Said if I did that, he'd make sure his son didn't hang me. But then that bastard whacked me upside my head with his rifle. That wasn't necessary. Did that out of pure meanness. He has the devil in him. A man can't rid himself of somethin' that evil. Harkner doesn't have an ounce of goodness in him."

Grizzly shook his head. "I'd say a whack on the side of the head is a site better than getting hung. Seems to me Harkner saved your hide. You said his *son* wanted to hang you."

Brady waved him off. "Yeah, the apple didn't fall far from the tree there. And I know damn well Jake would have gone along with it if a couple of his grandsons hadn't been there that day. He just didn't want them to see something that ugly. Most old men mellow with age, but not Harkner. Don't believe for a minute that that whoring outlaw has softened one bit. He's got his own form of justice, and you can bet that even when he was a marshal in Oklahoma, he didn't follow any laws."

Grizzly grunted a laugh. "He sure dealt his own justice when he rode shotgun for the Yellowjacket. I owe that sonofabitch for this voice and the pain I went through when he shot me. I wonder if he'd remember me if he saw me again."

"I doubt it. It was over thirty years ago. I'll bet you didn't even have that beard."

Grizzly fingered the wiry black hair on his chin. "You're right."

"There you go. Harkner won't know you, which could help in some of the plans I have."

Grizzly met Brady's glowering gaze. "Like what?"

"I told you. I intend to get my land back. I'll register a complaint with the State of Colorado. And I heard the law here is looking for men to serve as Range Detectives, ride around looking for rustlers and such. I aim to volunteer. That would give me a legal way to be on J&L land any time I want. It's kind of like being a lawman, and it's a good way for me to keep giving the Harkners headaches, and they won't be able to do a damn thing about it. Could be that a Harkner man gets shot—or Jake himself—mistaken for a rustler. See what I mean?"

Grizzly nodded. "By God, you've got a good idea there, Brady. I just might join up with you. I'd purely enjoy makin' trouble for that man."

"Getting a job as a Range Detective is a good start. It'll take more, though, to bring down Harkner and the J&L. Jake doesn't fold easy. Down in Mexico he was left for dead in the desert, but damned if he didn't show up alive a few months later. Still, like I said, he's been in enough gunfights and taken enough bullets and such to have used up those nine lives. And he's getting older. Older means slower."

Grizzly frowned. "I wouldn't count on him being slower. I witnessed how good he is with those guns." He thought a moment longer. "Still, I wouldn't mind the reputation of bein' the man who shot down Jake Harkner."

Brady chuckled. "You'll have to get by me first, but if it ends up being you, I guess that's okay, as long as Harkner is good and dead."

"Well, then, we'd better stock up on guns and ammunition. We'll have to quit our jobs here once we get enough men together. And we need a plan. Since Harkner ain't a man to deal with lightly, I don't like the thought of goin' up against him and his son without bein' sure how we'll do it."

"That's the best part. There's a settler meeting tomorrow night. I heard about it from some men in the Silver Heels Saloon - farmers talking about how hard it is to claim public land under the Homestead and Desert Land Acts. It's the same problem that caused the Johnson County War up in Wyoming."

"Yeah? Well don't forget that ended pretty bad."

Brady leaned in closer. "But these farmers figure to do pretty much what the Cattlemen's Association did in Wyoming. They'll get a lot of *their* kind together, ride onto open Colorado range and start claiming land - stake out sites and settle as fast as they can by putting up homes and barns, then gather as many more settlers as they can. They will make it impossible for the big ranchers to go after all of them. *They* will be the ones ganging up on the *cattlemen*. They will plow up the land and chase off the cattle and horses – do all they can to rile up the cattlemen and then look like the innocent ones."

"I'll be damned," Grizzly said in a near whisper.

"And they're planning to hire real sharp-shooter gunmen to help them if and when the big ranchers start coming for them," Brady continued. "I intend to join them and start trouble over the forty-thousand acres Lloyd Harkner bought from the government that's contingent with the hundred thousand he already had. Then he added my ten thousand. I aim to reclaim my land. If I can make trouble for Lloyd over that other forty thousand, that's fifty thousand acres I might be able to erase from the J&L. We'll see how many cattle can graze on what's left. That should knock the Harkner men down a peg or two."

Grizzly nodded. "Sounds like something that could work."

"Sure it could. Want to help? You could end up getting a piece of Harkner land and just maybe get a chance to bring down Harkner. The man who shoots him down— legally, mind you—would make a name for himself. That's how these farmers are finding paid gunmen. There isn't a shootist alive who wouldn't like the reputation of besting

Jake Harkner. And the farmers are reminding them that if they join up, they could claim themselves a good piece of land and make some money from it."

Grizzly leaned back in his chair. "Sounds like a lot of planning went into this."

"Sure did. And when you said you didn't have much use for Jake Harkner, I knew you might be interested."

"I sure as hell am."

Brady motioned for Grizzly to lean in again. "If I can pin on a Range Detective badge, I can ride right onto the *J&L* and start harassing Jake," he said, lowering his voice. "I'll warn him he stands to lose land to homesteaders, whether he likes it or not - give him something to worry about. He's on thin ice with a judge here in Denver because of that shooting at the Cattlemen's ball three or four years ago. Shot the man in the head, right in front of everybody at that ball. Lucky he wasn't hung, so now he'll have to be really careful how he responds to a visit from a Range Detective."

Grizzly chuckled low in his throat. "I'd like to be there for that. I'll do what I can. Maybe work on ways to *keep* making trouble until the homesteaders make their move. I could maybe take a couple people along to pose as new settlers, try stakin' out a spot-on *J&L* land. I wouldn't mind seein' ole' Jake's reaction to that. And because of the law, he wouldn't be able to do anything about it."

Brady nodded, then finished his coffee and rose. "Learning that a man I work with hates Harkner as much as I do is a damn good sign, Grizzly." He patted the pocket where he'd placed the newspaper article. "Let me see about that Range Detective job. I'll get things started, then you can move in and make even more trouble."

"Be real careful," Grizzly warned. "It doesn't take much to set off Harkner's temper. I wouldn't do too awful much on my own. Wait for those farmers to get organized before you go too far with that man."

"I know what I'm doing. Harkner owes me. So does his son."

Grizzly rose, a darkness moving into his eyes. "He owes me, too, for this voice . . ." He yanked off his neck scarf. "And for this *scar*."

A woman dining nearby sucked in her breath in shock, and Brady curled his lip in disgust. "Damn, that looks bad. I'm sorry for you."

Grizzly retied the scarf and glanced at the woman. "Don't worry, lady. I don't bite." She looked away, and Grizzly turned his gaze back to Brady. "Feel sorry for *Harkner*, not me. When this is over, he'll be *dead*. Maybe even his son, too. Count me in on that meeting tomorrow night."

"Sure thing."

The two men walked outside together.

"Don't tell anyone about this just yet," Brady warned. "And don't do too much too soon. Wait until the farmers make their move. We'll hit other ranchers, but the real prize is Jake Harkner himself!"

Grizzly shoved a wad of tobacco into his mouth between his gum and cheek. "He's a prize, all right. I expect he thinks every man from his past is either dead or has forgot about him. He'll find out different."

Both men laughed again as they headed back to work.

# CHAPTER 2

Early June . . .

Jake bent his legs behind his wife's and pulled her close against him, her back pressed against his chest. He moved his left arm between the warmth of her cleavage, enjoying the soft fullness of her breasts beneath her flannel gown.

"Don't even think about it," Miranda told him.

Jake nuzzled her hair, thinking how the little bit of gray there hardly showed amid her long, blond tresses. "Think about what?"

"About something I'm too tired for. I spent a long day baking bread and catching up on things that got ignored while you and the men spent the last month working the stock. I'm always glad when roundup and branding are over."

"You think *I'm* not tired? I'm getting too old to wrestle down calves. And, woman, you should be happy you're still so beautiful that I can't keep my hands off you. The day is coming when I might not be able to be a man for you in all the right ways."

Randy chuckled. "*You?* I'll believe *that* when it

happens." She turned to face him, smiling. "At the moment, I think we should talk instead."

"About what?" Jake kissed the side of her neck.

"Stop that. You know what kissing my neck does to me."

"You bet I do." He kissed her ear.

Randy laughed again as she shoved at him. "Jake, we need to talk about our trip to Chicago."

"We can talk about it after I'm done with other things."

Randy put fingers between her mouth and his just as Jake tried to kiss her. "You don't usually talk after sex. You roll over and go to sleep. If we don't talk now, we'll just be putting it off even longer."

Jake moved a leg over both of hers. "Only a woman would want to talk *before* sex. Is this another rule of yours?"

"Rule?"

"If I remember right, you once told me you didn't think it was right to have sex before you went to church. Not that it would matter to a sinner like me, because my stepping foot into a church is an insult to God Himself. Either way, I've always thought that's a silly rule. Thank goodness there isn't a church for miles around."

"Only *you* would say something like that."

This time he managed a kiss.

"At least we have our beautiful Evie to say prayers and sing hymns at our family dinners on Sundays," Randy added.

"And I still say you cheated on me, because that girl can't possibly have a drop of my ornery blood in her."

"It's impossible to deny her heritage. You've said yourself she's a replica of your mother. She's too beautiful to *not* belong to you. And stop thinking God wants nothing to do with you, Jake. Evie thinks you walk on water, and your little granddaughters do, too."

Jake chuckled low in his throat. "Those little troublemakers keep trying to goad me into helping collect eggs again, so they can watch that devil rooster attack me. Then they can tattle to their mothers that grandpa used bad words. That damn rooster is the bane of my existence." He moved on top of Randy.

"Big, bad, ruthless Jake Harkner, afraid of a chicken." Randy put an arm around his neck.

"I'm not afraid of that Satanic demon. What I'm afraid of is what I might *do* to him someday in front of those girls. They sure wouldn't think I walk on water if they witnessed me wringing that devil's head off."

Randy grinned and moved her hands down his muscled torso, then sucked in her breath. "Jake, you're *naked*! I never noticed you take off your underwear."

"You were facing the wall when I came to bed." Jake grinned and kissed her again. "I've decided this is the most comfortable way to sleep in case of an emergency, like suddenly needing sex." He studied her by a shaft of bright moonlight that shone through the window. This woman he loved beyond measure needed no paint or fancy hairdos or jewels to be beautiful. She radiated beauty, both physically and spiritually. "Now, you wanted to talk, Mrs. Harkner, so *talk*." Another kiss.

"With my handsome, naked husband on top of me?" Randy pushed at him again, and he moved slightly to her side. "What I wanted to say, my dear husband, is that roundup is over. Calves have been branded, bulls castrated and otherwise abused and humiliated by the mean things you men do to the poor things. You've separated bulls and steers and cows and calves and whatever all you have to separate, and those to be sold have been herded to Denver for shipment to their awful deaths, just so men can eat steaks."

Jake burst out laughing and moved on top of her again. "I never knew you looked at it that way."

"Well, I do, but this ranch is Lloyd's dream, and I'd never tell him how much I hate the branding and all of that."

"Hell, woman, *I've* branded *you*."

Randy smiled. "Yes, but in a much more pleasant way. Don't think I'd accept it if you wanted to press that J&L brand on *my* rear-end."

Jake laughed again and kissed her eyes. "I *love* your rear-end. It's beautiful and round, and it fits my hands perfectly." He moved one hand under her bottom. "I'd never permanently ruin this pretty butt."

Randy gave him a scolding look. "I'm not done talking."

Jake kept massaging her bottom as he answered her. "Go ahead. I'm listening."

Randy closed her eyes and sighed. "Quit that. I'll forget what I wanted to say."

Jake moved his hand to her side, running a thumb over her hip bone. "Say it quick, before this hand starts exploring other places."

"Honestly!" Randy traced a finger over his full lips. "The Twisted Tree cookout is in a few days, and Jeff and Peter need us to give them a date for our arrival in Chicago. It's time we decided on that. After all, this trip is the Christmas present you promised me. And I can tell by Jeff's letters that he and Peter are both excited to show us around their fair city."

"*Fair? No* big city is *fair*. They're all noisy and dirty and dangerous. And we both know why lawyer *Peter* is excited about us coming there. The man's been in love with you since back in Guthrie." Jake kissed her throat again. "Once he gets you to Chicago, you'll be in his web of fancy restaurants and theaters and museums and spending time at his castle of a home. On top of that he'll be extra lonely, what with his wife gone to France again."

"The point is, he *does* have a wife, and Treena is beautiful and sweet. And *she's* totally taken with *you*, I might add. She *did* call you magnificent, if you remember. And she compared our son to a Greek god."

"Yeah, well the only thing magnificent about me is I'm a magnificent sonofabitch."

Randy leaned up and kissed his chest. "Most men your age have big bellies and balding heads. But not my Jake."

"I'd rather have that big belly and balding head if it meant erasing everything this family has suffered because of my past. And my dear, you're avoiding the fact that Peter Brown loves you."

"And is a faithful husband and a gentleman. Besides, Heaven forbid Peter should suffer Jake Harkner's wrath! He's not crazy, you know. And don't forget that he literally saved your neck from a noose in Denver."

"How could I forget that? It's the only reason I let him live."

Randy snickered. "You don't fool me. You like Peter, and you know what a loyal friend he is, to *both* of us."

"The fact remains that everything Peter does for me is because of *you*, but that's okay, as long as he loves you from afar."

"Afar? Is that why you're putting off going to Chicago?"

"Maybe." Jake grinned as he moved his hand to push up her nightgown. He trailed his fingers over her belly and inside her panties, pulling them down a little to massage her bottom again. "The reason I've put off this trip is because you are going see how Peter lives and the genteel life you could have had married to a man like that. It breaks my heart to think of what you've been through being married to me."

Randy sobered as she traced her fingers along his eyebrows, down the long, thin scar on the left side of his face. So many scars, and each scar had a violent story behind it. But the scars didn't detract from his dark eyes and square, cleft chin. "You know very well I'd not trade life with you for all the wealth in the world. You're my Jake, at least as far as I know, what with all the prostitutes you've called friends over the years."

Jake grinned. "Friends is all those women are, and you know why." He grasped the waist of her panties and pulled them farther down. "I'm married to the most beautiful woman in Colorado. Why would I look at any other?"

"Even though I'm getting older?" Randy bent her legs and let him pull her panties all the way off.

"When I look at you, Mrs. Harkner, all I see is angel-gold hair, beautiful gray-green eyes, perfect breasts, a nice round bottom, and a smile that says, 'kiss me.'" He gently tasted her mouth again. "Besides that, you're ten years younger than I am."

"I only see a man who's still hard as rock – and able enough for a twenty-year-old, or a *thirty*-year-old, like Gretta MacBain."

Jake smiled sadly. "You know Gretta's just another of those good friends, and she's Cole's wife now. And some days I feel a *hundred* years old, so you'd best take advantage of the times I still feel good enough to do this. *Quiero hacerle el amor a mi esposa hermosa.*"

"You know all the tricks, don't you?"

"Like speaking words of love to you in Spanish?"

"You're a devil."

"That's a given."

Randy smoothed strands of hair back from his face. "Jake, when I think of what happened in Mexico, I just cry. I know that leg bothers you constantly."

Jake sobered. "I've grown used to it."

"No one gets used to constant pain."

"You do when you grow up with it as a child. Besides, when a beautiful woman is lying mostly naked under a man, he tends to ignore pain." Jake nuzzled her neck again and moved between her legs. "Go ahead and write Jeff and tell him we'd like to come in July. Tell him to have Peter make the ticket arrangements for around the fifteenth. Peter will know what station he'd want us to arrive at in Chicago. Another six weeks or so gives us time for the July 4$^{th}$ cookout at the Twisted Tree and for things to settle down from roundup and branding and all that." He gently moved his fingers into her depths, drawing forth sweet juices that told him all he needed to know. "Do you have any idea how much I love you?"

Randy breathed deeply from his touch, and Jake met her lips again, invading her mouth while toying with places private to everyone but him. He never wanted this woman he loved to feel one second of pain, so he always made sure she was ready, always waited for the climax that meant he could be inside her for her pure pleasure. Their conversation stopped as he continued gentle kisses, enjoying her groans of pleasure.

Too many times they'd been apart for weeks, months, even years . . . shootouts . . . four years of prison . . . weeks on end of worry and anxiety when he rode as a lawman . . . then Mexico . . . apart for nearly a year . . . the surety he'd been killed. For a time, even *he* thought he'd never see his precious Miranda again.

He felt her pulsating climax and quickly entered her, pushing deep and hard, always making sure she knew whose bed she belonged in, always fighting the secret fear that somehow he'd lose her, if not to death, then to a final ugliness from his past that would drive her away forever.

He'd even *tried* to make her leave, for her own good,

but it never worked. She refused to leave his side for a better life, and if he was the one who left, he always came back to her because he simply couldn't live without her, and that was the hell of it. Until Miranda had come along, he hadn't a clue as to the meaning of love.

He invaded her deeply, and she took him eagerly. "Who do you belong to?" he whispered. He always asked the question, and she always answered, "Jake Harkner, always and forever," just as she did now.

Years of shared experiences resulted in an intimacy far deeper than most couples knew. He'd tasted all her secret places, and she'd done the same for him. Each was familiar with every inch of the other's body, and there wasn't one inner heartache the other didn't know about. Miranda Harkner kept him sane. She was the only light in his darkness.

He raised up, grasping her bottom and moving inside her with a gentle rhythm. This was where he belonged - where they both belonged – in this bed in their big log home in the Rocky Mountain foothills – and in each other's arms.

He stayed on top of her when he finished, resting on his elbows to keep his weight off her tiny frame. "Now, what else do you want to talk about?"

Randy laughed. "You want to roll over and go to sleep now, don't you?"

"Well, you *do* have a way of wearing a man out."

"You insisted on this, so don't be saying I wore you out." Randy leaned up and kissed his chest. "How's that leg?"

"Hurts, like always, but I'll live."

That desperate look came into Randy's eyes again—the look he hated to see—brought on by too many years of wondering when the next bullet would end his life.

"I never again want to go through what I did when you

left for Mexico," Randy told him. "It was awful thinking you'd been killed. I still don't understand how you survived. I can't stand to think about what you went through, Jake. Maybe we can find a doctor in Chicago who can help the pain in your leg."

Jake sighed and rolled onto his back. "I know I promised you and Lloyd I'd see a specialist, but I don't like the idea of some sawbones I don't know experimenting on me. Brian told us it could involve breaking my leg all over again, and I'm not going through that."

"Oh, Jake." Randy moved to lie across his chest. "Brian loves you like his own father. He didn't mean to upset you by telling you that. As a doctor, he was just being honest, and he told you there might be an answer beyond something that drastic. That's why he suggested a specialist, and where better to find a doctor like that than in a big city like Chicago?"

"We'll see. Right now let's talk about something else - like the fact that the men are coming along on that chapel they are building for Evie. Evie thinks she can get them to go there Sundays—probably thinks they all need saving as much as her father does—but they love and respect her, so, they'll probably go. Most of them already attend her services in the barn. Before you know it, we'll have a whole town growing here, with Evie a preacher, her husband the town doctor, Lloyd running everything like a damn mayor, Katie and her brood running some kind of childcare so the men can get married and keep families here. You and Evie could open a little school for all the kids. I could be a gunsmith and—"

"My goodness, have you been planning all this without telling me?" Randy leaned over and kissed his shoulder.

"I'm just thinking about how this ranch and the family are both growing, and ways to get by if the government and all the new laws about open rangeland ruin cattle ranching. I sure never dreamed meeting you back in Kansas all those years ago would lead to all of this." Jake kissed her once more, then turned to sit on the edge of the bed. "I don't deserve any of it."

Randy moved behind him and kissed his back . . . his back so badly scarred from his father's beatings . . . more scars from being bull-whipped in Mexico. "Jake, when we get back from Chicago, let's go up to the line shack on Echo Ridge again."

He nodded. "Sure. Maybe we can go *before* we leave. The men are up there right now finishing that road so it's not so dangerous getting up that steep slope."

"I'd love to go sooner! That line shack is where I have you completely to myself." Randy embraced him from behind. "Promise me that place will always be just ours, Jake. I want to be buried up there together, just you and me, with the eagles and the angels, where no one can ever, ever take you away from me again."

Jake turned and grasped her arms. "No more such talk." He pulled her up to rest her head on his pillow. "We'll go to that cookout at the *Double T* on the 4th, and then spend a few days at the line shack before we head for Chicago. How's that?"

"Perfect!"

"I think you'll enjoy the train trip from Denver to Chicago. It sure as hell will be more comfortable for you than the way we first traveled out here in that damned little covered wagon, half lost in the middle of nowhere."

"Oh, but the things we did in that wagon made it enjoyable."

"Yeah, well, you'd have been better off if I'd left you at Fort Laramie and let you go the rest of the way with a wagon train, never to set eyes on me again."

"But what a boring and unfulfilled life I would have suffered."

Jake sighed. "You're a hopeless romantic and a glutton for punishment, Mrs. Harkner, and I love you so much it hurts." He kissed her again and stood up. "Once we get to Chicago, Jeff and Peter can show you the kind of life you could have been leading all this time if you'd left me and married Peter."

"I have all I want right here."

"You might change your mind once you see how Peter lives," Jake teased. "You know you'd fit right into high society." He reached for his long underwear and pulled them on. "I'm going downstairs to have a cigarette. Make sure I wake up early enough to wash up. I promised Sadie Mae and Trisha I'd take them for a ride with their ponies in the morning." He headed toward the door.

"Promise you'll stay inside the house and come right back up here?"

"Promise." Jake knew it would take a while for them both to get over what had happened to him in Mexico, but her mood just then was a momentary return to the Randy he'd lost mentally for several months after an old enemy, Brad Buckley, had so horribly abused her. "I'll just be downstairs, and I'll come right back." He opened the bedroom door.

"Do you know how indispensable you are to this whole family?" Randy called to him before he could walk out.

"Randy, just think about Chicago right now and the good time we'll have." He gave her a smile. "I want you to shop at the most expensive stores there. Think about *that*. Dresses—hats—shoes—handbags. Maybe even a diamond necklace. Maybe you can buy some fancy underwear or a sexy negligee."

That got a smile out of her. "I'll buy something only the

most wicked, seductive harlot would wear. I'm sure you'd love that."

"Oh, yes, ma'am. Just don't let Peter Brown see you in it."

Randy threw a pillow at him. "Get out of here!"

Jake headed down the winding wooden steps to the great room on the main floor. Randy kept an oil lamp lit on a nearby table at the bottom of the steps, so the house was never completely dark. The downstairs bedrooms were often full of grandchildren who loved staying overnight, and Randy never wanted them to wake up to complete darkness.

Jake glanced at his ivory-handled .44's, where they hung high over the front door so children couldn't reach them, and where they were handy in time of trouble, and trouble seemed to be his middle name. Making it to Heaven was going to be a major- and pretty unlikely - accomplishment.

He sighed from too many regrets. Randy deserved some final peace, as did the rest of the family, but he was who he was. As Evie would say, it was all in God's hands, and his own relationship with God was mighty questionable.

## CHAPTER 3

Morning brought the sounds of birds, neighing horses, lowing cattle, and the occasional whisper of a gentle wind in the pines behind the house. Jake leaned against a support post of the wide veranda that was built on the front and both sides of the house. Enjoying the much-needed peace they had been blessed with the last few months, he and Randy sat out here often, just talking, listening to the grandchildren play, and to the sounds of the animals, of the men breaking horses in distant corrals, the clang of the stable master's hammer beating a horseshoe into shape against his anvil.

Lloyd and Evie and their families lived in their own log homes on either side of the main house, and a new, small log home sat on the far side of Lloyd's house, where his wife's parents lived now. Patrick and Clare Donavan had moved from Guthrie and were a great addition to the growing J&L, and a big help to Katie, who was pregnant again.

Jake noticed the rose bushes surrounding the porch were loaded with blossoms. He could smell them, and that fragrance always reminded him of the woman who'd devoted her life to him. Randy loved roses and had planted them everywhere they'd lived in their years of hiding, and everyplace they'd lived since. She pressed and saved oil from her roses and used it to add a lovely scent to the soap she and the housekeeper, Teresa de Jesus, made together. She also used it when making candles and had learned to make her own body oil with it.

His heart ached to think of how much she must have hated leaving her roses behind every time they'd had to move, always because of him. And he wondered if the yellow roses were still blooming around their little yellow house back in Guthrie. Guthrie . . . where so many awful things had happened – Evie's awful ordeal at the hands of men who hated her father – the scare they'd gone through thinking Randy had cancer – and the many times death stared him and Lloyd in the face when they rode as U. S. Marshals.

His thoughts were thankfully interrupted when granddaughter Sadie Mae came running toward him, ready for the horseback ride he'd promised her and Tricia. His precious Sadie Mae was seven, a replica of her dark and beautiful mother, Evie, who looked very much like his Mexican mother, Evita, whom she was named after.

Blessed, trusting Evie refused to see any of the bad in her father, even after the horror she'd suffered back in Guthrie, *because* of her father's dark past. Somehow she'd risen above all that and was a sweet, forgiving, Christian woman who sang and prayed at Sunday dinners. Jake, on the other hand, would never forgive himself for what happened to her in Guthrie. Never!

Evie's kind, devoted husband, Dr. Brian Stewart, waved at Jake from the front porch of his and Evie's house. Jake waved back, always grateful that Evie had married such a good man. Brian was always neatly dressed, usually in a suit or at least a vest. Doctoring on a big ranch kept him busy which was fine, because Brian was a gentlemanly, educated man who did not fit the demeanor of most of the rugged cowboys on the J&L. He and Evie had three other children besides Sadie Mae. There was Esther Miranda, two-and-a-half; Cole Matthew, one; and their oldest, his own namesake, Jake. Young Jake was growing fast and was tall for ten years old, anxious to be as "big and strong" as his grandfather. The boy rode toward him now on a good-sized sorrel mare named Sandy. All the Harkner children learned to ride early, and young Jake was bringing with him the Pinto pony his little sister would ride today. Sadie Mae loved that horse, which she called Salty, for no particular reason.

"Wait, Jake!" Sadie Mae called to her brother. "Put me on my pony!" Young Jake obliged her.

"Big" Jake lit a cigarette as six-year-old granddaughter Tricia came out of Lloyd's house holding her mommy's hand. Behind her was thirteen-year-old big brother Stephen, Lloyd's son with his first wife, Beth. After losing Beth, Lloyd met Katie Donavan in Guthrie. A red-haired beauty, Katie was a good mother to Stephen, and to her and Lloyd's three children—Tricia, Donavan, and Jeffrey.

Katie was seven months pregnant with her and Lloyd's fourth child, and Lloyd suffered a lot of wry jokes about him keeping his wife almost constantly pregnant. Jake couldn't help smiling over the fact that Lloyd deserved the love Katie gave him, and he deserved this ranch, the dream he'd put off when he rode with Jake as his deputy. At thirty-two, Lloyd was the most loyal, loving son a man could ask for. He understood his father's dark side, and for a time, that dark side had come between them and had almost claimed Lloyd, too. But father and son had come to an understanding, and too many times back in Oklahoma they'd saved each other's lives in dangerous shootouts.

Young Stephen rode out of the barn they'd built in '96.

. . after the fire set by old enemies. Jake took another deep drag on his cigarette, then bent to tie his holsters to his thighs. He struggled to bury yet another bad memory - Randy's ordeal at the hands of one Brad Buckley, who'd made off with her while Jake, Lloyd and the other men fought the barn fire. The thought of Randy's suffering made him want to vomit.

"Damn it," he whispered, hating it when old horrors tried to steer his thinking. He straightened to see Stephen trotting a black gelding his way. The horse was called Coal, and Tricia's pony was called Star. Jake didn't much care about naming horses, but the women and girls insisted on it, so pretty much all the animals had names, even the damn rooster Jake hated. He'd been very properly named Outlaw.

Katie walked closer, still leading Tricia by the hand. In the distance, Lloyd led his Palomino gelding, Cinnamon, and Jake's big gray gelding, Thunder, out of the barn and past the chicken coop.

"Grampa, look at me!" Sadie Mae shouted as Young Jake led her pony to the house. "You'll still take us riding, won't you?"

Jake finished his cigarette and stepped it out. "You bet, Sunshine."

Just then, Tricia ran onto the porch, reaching up her arms. Jake picked her up. "You still going, Button?"

"Yes, Grampa!" Tricia was as different from Sadie Mae's dark looks as could be. She had her mother's coloring—a mass of red curls and eyes green as grass. She always wore a wide-brimmed hat to shade her fair-skinned, freckled face.

Randy came out the front door as Jake carried Tricia to her pony and plopped her on it. He began buckling straps leading from a belt around her waist to the base of the saddle, an invention by Jake's best hand, Cole Decker, to keep the girls from falling off.

"I don't need that anymore, Grampa," Tricia objected. "I ride good now."

"Maybe so, but I'm not taking any chances. I have enough things to answer to your mother for, Tricia, and Sadie Mae's mother, too. I don't need to add a riding accident to the list. When your parents say it's okay to ride without this belt, and when Brian and Evie agree to the same for Sadie Mae, then you won't have to be strapped to this saddle anymore."

"Aww, Grampa!" Tricia pouted.

"You just remember that you must do exactly as I say when we go riding, all right?"

"Okay. You won't have to use your loud guns, will you?"

"I certainly hope not." Jake leaned in to kiss her cheek, then walked over to check Sadie Mae's belt and straps. "You did a good job with these," he told young Jake.

His grandson smiled proudly. "See? We said we'd be ready. Uncle Lloyd saddled your horse and his. Me and Stephen saddled the others."

"Jake, be careful," Randy told him.

"Always am," he answered. Jake walked back up the steps and grabbed his wife close, planting a long kiss on her mouth. Stephen and Young Jake grinned, and the two little girls giggled.

"Jake Harkner, you never stop, do you?" Katie joked.

Jake gave Randy a quick hug and faced his daughter-in-law. "From the looks of you, Katie-girl, it's my *son* who never stops. That belly of yours is growing fast."

"All right, Pa, get the hell out of here." Lloyd handed him Thunder's reins.

"Just saying it like it is." Jake mounted, wincing from the pain in his leg.

"I put biscuits and jelly into that potato sack on your saddle," Katie told Jake as Evie hurried to join them.

"There is fried chicken in a paper bag in Stephen's leather satchel," Evie told her father, "so you can have a picnic with the girls and nobody will be hungry. And here are some cupcakes." Evie tied a potato sack to young Jake's gear.

"I made sure there is plenty of water in those canteens," Lloyd told his father. He glanced at the girls, then back at Jake. "You want me to go with you?"

"Hell, no! I'm not riding into a gunfight or off to No Man's Land. We'll be fine. Get going. You're a busy man with plenty of chores just running this place, and I'm a big boy, remember?"

"You know what I mean, Pa."

Jake frowned. "I have two good men with me—Stephen and young Jake. Both can use their rifles and are plenty dependable. We'll be fine. I have my guns and rifle and, if memory serves me right, no man has ever got past either one."

"God knows that's true." Lloyd turned his horse and trotted up beside Thunder. "At least tell me where you're headed."

"I figure we'll ride up toward Echo Ridge. If the girls get tired, Stephen and I can take them onto our horses. I want to see how the men are doing cutting a better road up to that cabin where your mother and I like to go."

"You be careful, Daddy," Evie told him.

Jake shook his head over the fact Evie always called him daddy, even as a grown woman. "Evie, do you really think it does any good for all of you to keep telling me to be careful?"

Lloyd grinned. "Pa, you can't help finding trouble where you never expect it. You never look for it. It just comes to you. That's what worries me."

"Well, Lloyd, let's be thankful things have been peaceful since Mexico. All of you quit behaving as though I'm taking my grandchildren into outlaw country. We're on J&L property and it's a beautiful day, so go on about your business and enjoy it."

"I've heard those words before, Pa." Lloyd removed his hat and shook his hair behind his shoulders. He left it long because Katie liked it that way, but Jake worried that someday someone would shoot him from a distance, thinking he was a renegade Indian. "You always say you'll never live to be a really old man," Lloyd added. He put his hat back on. "Those words worry me. God knows you don't *behave* like an old man, or even *look* like one yet, so I figure you have some good years left. I just don't want anything to happen that might shorten those years."

"I have my good days and my bad days."

Thunder snorted and tossed his head, as though to agree.

"And you're still sometimes meaner than a snake whose nap in the sun has been interrupted," Lloyd reminded him.

"Thank God you didn't inherit the mean part." Jake shared a look of understanding with his son. "Stop worrying."

"Stop worrying?" Lloyd looked around. "I have a wife and four kids, another on the way, a mother, sister, stepbrother and four nieces and nephews to look out for. Not to mention a bunkhouse full of rough, half-outlaw men, a hundred-fifty-thousand acres of cattle and horses, and never-ending nesters and rustlers to keep watch over. Oh, and then there is *you*. What is there *not* to worry about?"

"You damn well love all of this," Jake goaded. "Don't pretend it's all too much for you. You're one hell of a good man, Lloyd—a hundred times better than me. And I, of all people, should be the least of your worries."

Jake glanced at Randy. "We will probably be back for supper. But if we *don't* get back, it will be because the girls are tired, and we decided to camp or stay up at the line shack overnight. They would love that. Just don't panic if we don't come back till morning."

"Well, *I* will," Lloyd remarked before Randy could answer. "Don't forget someone stole some of those mustangs we had fenced in out that way. If it hadn't rained so hard, we wouldn't have lost their tracks and we could have found the culprits. If you aren't back by dark, Pa, I'll be high-tailing it to Echo Ridge to make sure why."

Jake shook his head. "This is *me*, Lloyd, remember? Nobody gets through me or young Jake or your son, especially when my beautiful little granddaughters are with us. The girls will be fine. I'll try to make sure we get back before dark, but you damn well know me and what I can take care of, so relax." He kicked Thunder into a gentle trot.

Stephen and Young Jake followed, Sadie Mae and Tricia riding beside their respective brothers.

Lloyd glanced at his mother. "He okay? I know how moody he gets."

Randy sighed. "He's not real thrilled about leaving you and the family behind when we go to Chicago, but I think it would be good for him to get out of here. In thirty-three years together, we've never taken a trip of any kind."

"I agree, Mother," Evie added. "And if you go by train and then spend your time with Jeff and Peter in a civilized place like Chicago, what can go wrong?"

Lloyd turned his horse to face his sister. "Are we talking about the same man? Jake Harkner? I think that's his name, isn't it?"

Evie grinned. "I prefer to think positive, big brother.

God brought Daddy home from Mexico. Nothing much worse could happen to him than what happened there."

"Evie, if Pa goes to heaven, he'll find trouble *there*, too."

Evie grinned and shook her head as Lloyd turned his horse and headed back to the barn, where one of his many dependable ranch hands, Terrel Adams, was saddling a horse.

"Terrel, I know I told you to go move that bull, Old Lucifer, to the south pasture, but I'd rather you followed after Pa and the kids. He can sure as hell take care of himself, but he's taking the girls extra far today, and I've been uneasy since those mustangs we rounded up and left in the north pasture went missing. Somebody's out there making trouble."

Terrel cinched the saddle tight. "Sure, Boss. If I stay in the foothills, I'll be able to see them without them seeing me."

Lloyd lit a cigarette. "Maybe, but you know Pa. Eyes in the back of his head. Let's just hope somebody else isn't lurking out there that he *can't* see."

Terrel mounted up. "You sound like Jake now—always on the watch. God knows you sure *look* like him."

Lloyd grinned wryly, ducking his head as he rode from the barn and up to his mother. "Rest easy. Terrel's going to tail them."

Randy took a deep breath. "Good. Thank you."

"Mom, those girls are having the time of their lives," Evie reminded Randy.

"I know." Randy watched Terrel ride off to follow Jake. "It's just that this country's still so big and so wild."

"Like Pa?"

Smiling, Randy met her son's gaze. "Yes, like your father. And you look just like he did when we first met, except he was a filthy, bearded outlaw."

"And you shot him."

"Oh, dear God, yes, I shot him." Randy covered her eyes, laughing lightly. "He scared me to death. Thank God I used that silly little pistol I carried. It didn't do much damage. I still have that thing. It looks almost comical next to your father's .44's."

"Well, you'd better keep the pistol. You might want to shoot Pa again. Lord knows there're times when he makes you mad enough."

Randy waved him off and reentered the house.

Lloyd headed out to check on a pregnant mare, which reminded him of Katie's current pregnancy. She hadn't been feeling well with this one, and that worried him. He couldn't go through another wife dying in childbirth.

Losing Beth had put him into a spin of depression that took a long time to get over.

He glanced in the distance to see Terrel disappear into a stand of aspen trees and breathed a little easier knowing one extra man was trailing Jake.

Jake Harkner was physically the strongest man he'd ever known, and the fastest with a gun, but he loved almost *too* much, and if anyone he loved was threatened in any way, that meant trouble. It was a gut reaction Jake could seldom control, and Lloyd knew his mother worried that the day would come when Jake fell off that high, narrow ledge he walked mentally—love and joy at the top —hell and damnation below.

## CHAPTER 4

"This is fun, Grampa!" Sadie Mae trotted her pony between Jake and her brother, who always sat taller in the saddle when on a mission he considered especially important. Jake suppressed a grin at the proud look on young Jake's face. The boy took his role as an heir to the J&L and protector of his little sister very seriously, as did Stephen, who rode to his grandfather's left. He held onto his sister Tricia, who had fallen asleep on her pony. Jake had taken her from her horse and gave her to young Jake, who now held onto her with one arm.

"You sure you're okay, Sadie Mae?" Young Jake asked his own sister. "You should probably take a nap after that big picnic meal you ate."

"I'm okay. I took just a little nap after we ate, but look at Tricia. She's asleep again. She can't ride a long time like I can."

Jake glanced at Tricia. Her head bobbed rhythmically as Stephen held her tightly.

"Need me to take over, Stephen?" Jake asked. "Even a girl little as Tricia can start feeling pretty heavy after a while."

"I'm okay. Just watch Sadie Mae. She might think she's doing fine, but I saw her nod off a couple times."

"I did not!" Sadie Mae objected.

"Well, if you get sleepy again, Sunshine, don't be too proud to tell your brother or Grampa." Jake glanced over at the tree line to his left. Damned if Lloyd hadn't sent Terrel to trail them. He'd recognized the ranch hand's Pinto in one glance before the man deftly disappeared into a stand of Aspen, the glittery green and silver leaves creating good cover.

"I see Echo Ridge up ahead now," Jake told the boys. "Some of the men are clearing a road up to the cabin. We'll eat Evie's cupcakes when we get there."

"Why do you and Grandma like to go to that line shack?" Young Jake asked.

"Don't you know?" Stephen answered before Big Jake could. "'Cuz they've been through a lot of bad things and sometimes they just like to be alone."

"You don't know *everything*, Stevie," Young Jake bit back.

"Your grandmother just likes to get me all to herself once in a while," Jake told the boys. "I think she figures when she gets me up to that cabin, it's a way of keeping me out of trouble."

They all rode silently for several yards. "You really, really love Grandma, don't you?" Young Jake asked.

Jake halted Thunder, lit a cigarette. Took a deep drag. "Yes, I really, really love her. She breathes me in, and then I breathe her in. That make any sense to you?"

Young Jake shrugged. "Kind of."

"It'll make more sense when you love a girl yourself, Jake." Big Jake kneed his horse into motion.

"I won't ever find somebody like Grandma," young Jake lamented.

"Oh, you might. Lloyd found Katie. And your own

mother is as close to an angel as a woman can get. She and your father are happy. There are lots of good women out there in the world, Jake, and when the right girl comes along, you'll know it. You and Stephen both."

Just then, Jake saw two riders ahead. He knew every man and every horse on the J&L. These men did not belong. He halted Thunder. "Stephen."

"Yes, Sir?"

"Hand Tricia over to Jake. And Sadie Mae, you stay right beside Jake and let him hold Salty's reins, understand? No arguments."

"What's the matter, Grampa?" Sadie Mae asked.

"Probably nothing. But doing what I say will help me." Jake turned to his namesake. "Stephen and I will ride ahead and talk to those men. Stay with the girls, behind and to the side. That's a big responsibility, so I'm depending on you, Jake. If I tell you to take them farther away, you do it, and fire that rifle several times if that happens. The J&L men up ahead will come running."

"Sure, Grandpa. You think they're trouble?"

"All I know is they aren't J&L men, and horse thieves stole some of our mustangs a few days ago. Stephen, take out your rifle and cock it, but leave the safety on."

"Yes, Sir."

Sadie Mae sniffled. "Are you gonna' shoot your guns, Grampa?"

"Not if I don't need to, Sunshine. Don't you be worried about a thing. You stay right here with your brother, and if he tells you to ride the other way with him, you do it, no matter what. Promise me."

The girl sniffed again. "I promise."

Jake glanced at young Jake again. "Relax. I think Terrel has been dogging us this whole time, so you have help if you need it."

"Okay, grampa."

Jake kicked Thunder into motion. "Follow me, Stephen."

Jake glanced back to see Terrel riding out of the woods along the foothills. *Damned if you didn't get it right, Lloyd.* As the strangers headed toward him, he pulled his rifle from its boot and cocked it mid-air with one hand. A man couldn't be too careful this far from a town or any sort of law.

They drew closer, and Jake realized one of the riders looked familiar. "Get that rifle in a shooting position," he told his grandson quietly, "and keep it there."

"It's already aimed at the man in front," Stephen answered.

Anger rose in Jake's soul at recognizing one of them. "Jesus," he muttered before shouting at the man he'd recognized. "Brady Fillmore! What the hell are you doing on the *J&L*?"

Brady looked around. "Well, now, I don't see that fucking son of yours, so maybe I'm okay, seeing as how you saved my ass when Lloyd wanted to hang me."

"Don't count on me being so generous again. I asked what you're doing here!"

Jake heard hoofbeats behind him. That would be Terrel, riding hard to catch up.

Brady raised his chin, a cocky look in his eyes. "Well, now, Jake, I can ride on your land all I want." He pulled one side of his wool jacket open, showing off a badge on the vest underneath. "Seeing as how I took the job of Range Detective a few days ago. I explained to the U. S. Marshal, Hal Kraemer, as to how I know this part of the country pretty good, so I know what to watch for. This here is Hardy Judd." Brady indicated a rather meek looking cowboy who sat his own horse beside Brady. "And another friend of mine, name of Grizzly Smith, might also be putting in for Range Detective. Ever hear of him?"

"*Should* I?"

"You think about it. His real name is Frank." Brady closed his jacket. "You looking to chase a range detective off the *J&L*? That wouldn't look too good to Marshal Kraemer."

"You're a thief and a liar," Jake accused bluntly. "Hal Kraemer would never hire somebody like you for Range Detective if he knew the truth. I'll make sure he *does*, and let him know the reason why you know this country so well. Rustlers *need* to know all the places to hide out."

Brady grinned. "Kraemer said you were offered this job a while back and that you turned it down, on account of that wife of yours don't like you to be gone from her bed. Or something like that."

"Shut your filthy mouth!" Jake raised his rifle. "When I tell Hal Kraemer you set fire to the *J&L's* best grazing grass, he'll rip that badge right off you."

"You never told Hal about that fire? Hell, Jake, what else haven't you told the good marshal? You afraid that judge in Denver will find out you nearly hanged a man on the *J&L*? Or there might be some men buried out here the judge doesn't know about. Am I right? Would that judge have known about *me* if you'd let your son hang me?"

"I would have told him. Gladly!"

Brady chuckled. "You won't use that gun. Not with them little girls watching. And considering your reputation, that judge might not take too kindly to the news, not after you barely missed getting hanged in Denver when you blew that gunman's head off at the cattlemen's ball. Shoot me, and you might get arrested and hanged after all. You can't be shooting a range detective. I'm a whisper away from being a Marshal."

"You're a whisper away from being *dead*." Jake fired, and Brady's hat flew off.

"Shit!" Hardy Judd put up his hands. "I've got no quarrel with you, Harkner!"

Jake kept his eyes on Brady, who's own eyes widened with shock when Jake's bullet whispered through his hair. Using only his legs and feet to control Thunder, Jake urged the horse closer. He shoved the still-hot end of his rifle up under Brady's chin.

Brady sat still, swallowing. His defiant look faded to terror.

"Pick up his hat," Jake ordered Judd.

Judd cautiously retrieved the hat and re-mounted, backing his horse away. "Come on, Brady. Let's get out of here."

Brady's dark eyes burned with rage, Jake's rifle under his chin keeping him frozen. "You fucking bastard!" he growled through gritted teeth. "I'll have you arrested!"

"*Try* it!" Jake pushed the barrel up, forcing Brady's head back. "Be glad I only parted your hair, Fillmore. I'd hate to blow your brains out in front of my grandchildren, but I by God will if it's called for. And when you try to get me arrested, you can explain to the state authorities how you stole *J&L* cattle and set that fire." He rammed the rifle swiftly upward, knocking Brady off his horse.

"Get off the *J&L*! *NOW*!" he warned.

The sound of Tricia's crying incensed Jake even more, but he forced himself not to climb down and lite into Fillmore. Men from Echo Ridge, upon hearing the gunshot, were riding toward them now, and Terrel rode up behind Jake and the boys.

"Mount up and ride, or you're a dead man!" Jake told Brady.

Hardy Judd charged away, still carrying Brady's hat, but Brady remained on hands and knees beside his horse, choking and coughing. When he managed to get to his feet, blood poured between the fingers he held under his chin. It dripped onto his jacket.

"You sonofabitch! You . . . broke my jaw!"

"Get on that horse and get off *J&L* land before I break your *skull*!"

"You'll pay for this, Harkner." A red-faced, bloody mess, Brady managed to mount his horse. "Damn you!"

"I was damned to Hell a long time ago, Fillmore, by men far more formidable than you! Now get going before I tell my men to do whatever they want with you. Most would have hanged you back when you burned Fire Valley, so they wouldn't mind burying you where no one would ever find you."

"I'll tell Hal Kraemer you said that. I've heard talk, Harkner! I've . . . heard talk about that Brad Buckley fellow who threatened you back in Denver. How come nobody has ever heard from him lately?"

Jake fired into the air, causing Brady's horse to rear then take off at a gallop. Fillmore clung to the horse's mane, struggling to grab the reins. As he charged past the *J&L* men, they turned their mounts and pursued, firing into the air and whooping to keep his horse at a run.

Lowering his rifle, Jake turned to see Terrel sitting on his horse beside Stephen.

"Keep your rifle on safety and eject that bullet from the chamber," Jake ordered his grandson. "You won't be needing it."

Stephen obeyed. "I was ready to shoot him, Grampa." His voice shook with nerves.

"I'm sure you were, but that's the last thing I want you to have on your conscience, Stevie. Killing a man is a hard enough burden on a grown man." Jake shoved his rifle into its boot. "Take it from me." *Especially when it's your own father you killed.* He rode up beside Terrel. "Can you believe that sonofabitch actually got a job as a range detective?"

"You'll set Hal Kraemer straight on that, Jake."

"You bet I will." Jake lit another cigarette and glanced at a still-sobbing Sadie Mae, now joined in tears by Tricia. The rifle fire had waked her up.

Jake turned again to Terrel. "Lloyd sent you, didn't he?"

Terrel grinned and nodded. "Ain't a man on this ranch wants to see you hurt, Jake. We'll always have your back."

"Appreciate it, but I don't like what Fillmore said about Brad Buckley." He met Terrel's gaze. "That name had better never come up in front of my wife."

"She'll never hear it from any of us." Terrel lit his own cigarette. "Lloyd will be angry about this. He *hates* Brady Fillmore."

"The worst part is, I'm the one who said not to hang the bastard. But the boys were there, and I didn't want them to see that."

"I understand. I think Lloyd does, too."

Jake removed his hat and ran a hand through his hair. "You might as well stay with us. We're going to see how the road up to the line shack is coming. Then the girls will ride with you and me on the way back. I want to make it back home before dark, so I'll have one of the other men bring the ponies back at a slower pace. They'd never be able to keep up. This little holdup didn't help things."

"Sure."

Jake trotted Thunder over to his granddaughters, who were still beside themselves in tears. He pulled both girls in front of him on his saddle. He glanced at the line shack high on Echo Ridge, calming the girls with a story about why it was special to him and their grandmother.

*It's special, all right.* He and Randy had made love there too many times to count, slept in each other's arms, shared the fireplace warmth on chilly mornings, gone for walks, talked, held each other. He struggled against an inner fury at Brady Fillmore and told himself to stay calm for the girls' sake.

"Grampa, you're feeling mean. I can tell." Sadie Mae wiped at her tears.

"Not toward you, Sunshine." Jake kissed both girls' heads. Behaving civilized after a confrontation with a man he'd like to kill was hard. He felt like two different men, wished he could separate the mean one from the good one and let the former go off on a killing spree that would end every last bit of his ugly past.

"You girls remember something. When you're with me, you're always safe. Your grandma tells me all the time - that she always feels safe with my arms around her. You should feel the same. I just wanted to make sure that man knew he'd better not draw his gun or try to hurt my precious granddaughters."

Both girls turned sideways and hugged Jake around the middle.

"We were scared he'd shoot you, Grampa," Tricia cried.

"Don't worry about that," Jake assured them. "I've been shot at before, and here I still am. Now, both of you, give me a pretty smile. I want to see which one of you has the deepest dimples."

Always in competition for their grandfather's attention, the girls looked up at him with the biggest smiles they could muster.

Jake shook his head. "I can't decide. You will both have to practice smiling all the way home."

They giggled, grinning at each other. Terrel rode up beside Jake as they headed toward Echo Ridge.

"Terrel, you ever hear of that friend Fillmore mentioned? Grizzly Smith? Fillmore said his real first name is Frank."

"No, sir. Never heard of him."

"Apparently Fillmore thought I might have. That worries me."

"We all have names from the past that worry us. There's still a husband out there somewhere who'd like to blow me away."

The remark helped ease Jake's thoughts. He glanced at Terrel. "A *husband*?"

"Yup." Terrel stared straight ahead. "Don't worry, though. I won't try to steal *your* wife."

Jake broke into hearty laughter. "Where's the woman now?"

"Don't know. We had one night together, and she ran off on me, too, so I expect her husband's after more than just me."

Jake laughed again and picked up the pace, heading for Echo Ridge while reminding his granddaughters to keep practicing their smiles.

# CHAPTER 5

It was nearly dark when the group reined in at Lloyd's house, Jake with Sadie Mae and Terrel with Tricia. Both sleepy girls sat with their heads slumped against the shoulder of each man.

Lloyd rose from his chair on the porch. "Pa, when you say by dark, you cut it pretty damn close. We were all getting worried."

"Grandpa couldn't help it," Stephen told his father as he reined in beside Jake. "That neighbor you chased off a couple years ago, Brady Fillmore, came along and tried to make trouble. Grandpa took care of it."

"*Brady Fillmore?*" Lloyd moved to take Tricia from Terrel. "I *knew* there'd be trouble. I felt it because of those stolen horses."

"Well, I sure as hell didn't *invite* the sonofabitch to pay us a visit," Jake pointed out.

Lloyd carried his still-sleeping daughter up the steps and handed her to Katie. He leaned down and kissed his wife reassuringly before she took Tricia inside.

"Hi, Dad!" Young Jake said to Brian as his father came down the steps and walked toward Thunder. "You should have seen what happened today! Grampa really gave Brady Fillmore what for!"

"I have a feeling I'm better off *not* seeing." Brian took Sadie Mae from Jake, looking him over as he did so. "You okay?"

Jake glanced at Lloyd. "Thanks for asking. My son never bothered to."

Lloyd tossed his hair behind his shoulders as he came back down the porch steps. "Of course, I didn't ask. Why would I worry whether you're okay when facing a sniveling coward like Brady Fillmore, who, I might add, you should have let me hang a couple years ago. Men like that can't hold a candle to you."

Jake dismounted. "Well, I suppose I could have hung him *for* you this time, son, or maybe shot his head off - all in front of those little girls. Would you have preferred that?"

"What is going on?" Randy hurried over from the main house to join the little confrontation. "Jake, did something go wrong? Are the girls okay?"

"Those girls are just fine." Jake leaned down and kissed her forehead. "Go inside. I'll explain when I come in."

"I'm staying right here until *you* are ready to go inside," Randy told him.

Jake knew better than to argue. He turned to his horse and untied his bedroll.

"Apparently there was trouble," Lloyd told his mother. "And don't tell me that surprises you."

"Relax, Boss," Terrel said. "It was nothing we couldn't handle. I happened to be along, but Jake didn't really need me. And Stephen and young Jake here, they handled it real good. Those girls were never in any danger. You ought to know that better than anybody."

Lloyd shook his head. "I'm sorry, Pa, but those rustlers have me on edge. And Katie isn't handling this pregnancy well. She's been sick a lot. After what happened to Beth, I'm a damned nervous wreck."

Jake handed his bedroll to Randy and pulled his rifle from its boot. "Understood. God knows how fast I lose my temper when I'm worried about somebody in the family."

Brian handed Sadie Mae over to Evie. "Daddy, are you really all right?" Evie asked Jake.

"*Yes!* All of you know better than to worry about me. I'm fine. The *boys* are fine. Sadie Mae and Tricia are fine. Now take my granddaughter home and put her to bed."

"Well, I want to know more later." Evie turned with Sadie Mae and headed for her house.

"What the hell actually happened?" Brian asked Jake.

"You should have seen it, Dad!" Young Jake blurted out excitedly. "Grandpa shot Brady's hat off and scared the hell out of him!"

"Watch your language, Jake," Brian warned. "You know your mother doesn't like you talking that way."

"Sorry, Dad. Grandpa busted Brady Fillmore's jaw! Brady was bleeding like a stuck pig by the time he rode off."

"Oh, good Lord," Brian muttered.

Terrel proceeded to explain the entire incident.

Lloyd turned to his father with an all-knowing look. "And this all happened in front of the girls, of course."

"Couldn't be helped," Jake answered. "Naturally, I made them cry—something *else* I'm good at. But afterward, I had them smiling in no time. And, by the way, they are now in a contest for which one has the deepest dimples. I'm sure they'll be practicing tomorrow, smiling their biggest smiles."

Lloyd snickered and turned, muttering, "God help me." He leaned his head back and sighed again. "So, Fillmore's trying for the job of Range Detective, is he?"

"Apparently so. But that won't last when I talk to Hal

Kraemer. In fact, once Kraemer sees Brady's busted chin, he'll figure it out."

Lloyd faced his father again. "You'd better hope this doesn't backfire on you and you find *yourself* arrested."

Stephen spoke up. "Grandpa didn't do anything wrong, Pa."

"Stephen, you and Jake and Terrel take all these horses to the barn and get them unsaddled and rubbed down," Lloyd ordered. "They look like they've been ridden pretty hard."

"Yes, Sir," Stephen answered. "A couple of the men will be coming in later with the ponies – maybe not till morning. Grandpa knew the ponies couldn't keep up." He took his and Jake's horses' reins, then paused, looking back at his father. "Don't be mad at Grandpa. It's right what he did. And *J&L* men chased Brady Fillmore and the man with him clean off our land. They won't be back."

The boys and Terrel walked off with the horses, and Jake faced Lloyd.

"Those girls are fine, son. I had them giggling in no time. You know damn well I'd give up my life before I'd let anyone threaten them. If I thought for one minute there would be trouble like that, I'd have called off the ride in the first place. They had fun. They loved the picnic, then napped, and at their age, the whole thing will end up as just an exciting memory. You explain that to Evie and Katie."

"You know I will." He looked his father over. "You really all right?"

"Nice that you finally asked. And hell yes, I'm all right. It's *Fillmore* who's hurting. And the man with him just might *still* be kicking up dust. He ran so fast he was out of sight in no time. He's probably over the Rockies and into Utah by now."

Lloyd couldn't help a grin. "Go home and go to bed,

Pa. We'll talk in the morning. We *all* need some sleep." He started inside, then paused. "I hope you know I sent Terrel along, more for you than the girls, and not because I don't trust your abilities. It's because I can't get over how it felt thinking you'd died in Mexico. Maybe my overprotectiveness is an insult to a man who's been handling things like this mostly on his own for fifty years, but having someone watch your back when I can't do it makes me feel better."

"I know that," Jake told him. "Go inside and keep Katie calm. That's all that's important right now."

As Lloyd nodded and went into the house, Jake looked down at Randy. "I hope *you* aren't going to scold me, too. I'm damn tired and want some sleep."

"Just sleep?"

Jake grinned. "Just sleep, believe it or not. I wear out a little easier than I used to."

Randy smiled and took his arm, heading for the house. "Lloyd loves you beyond words. He worries about you."

"He shouldn't." Jake paused and looked down at her again.

" I guess not," Randy answered. "After all, just the other day Sadie Mae told me you were the biggest, strongest man ever, ever ever, ever, ever." Randy chuckled. "I might have missed an 'ever.'"

"Not another word. You're making me cringe." Jake led her to the house, where he paused at the steps to the veranda. "Go on inside and get ready for bed. I need a cigarette and a few quiet minutes alone." He handed her his rifle. "Put this away for me."

Randy took the rifle and looked up at him. "This was not your fault, Jake."

"I know, but this isn't the first time those boys have seen me be violent . . . or even the girls. When I made Young Jake hang back with them, Tricia asked me if I was going to shoot my 'loud guns.' That kind of broke my heart, you know?"

Randy smiled sadly. "I know. But those 'loud guns' as she calls them, haven't always been used for bad. For years now they've been used for good. And this time you used your head, not your guns. Lloyd sees that. So do the boys, so don't get in a mood."

Jake leaned down and kissed her. "That's why I'm having a cigarette out here alone. I need to take a deep breath and calm down."

Randy patted his chest. "If you say so. I love you, Jake."

He put a hand to the side of her face. "Well, now, that's the one sustaining strength I have. *You*. Now, go to bed. I promise I'll be right there myself in a bit." He kissed her again.

*Thou art my rock and my salvation.*

For some reason Jake remembered the Bible verse Evie had read at a Sunday dinner. He had no idea why it suddenly came to mind, but this woman truly was his rock and his salvation.

His chest ached. No one, not even Randy, knew how terrified he'd been that Brady Fillmore would get off a stray shot and accidentally hurt one of the kids. If that had happened, Fillmore would have regretted the day he was born.

Randy went inside, and Jake walked up the steps to lean on a porch rail to smoke quietly, listening to nothing but crickets and some laughter coming from the bunkhouse. He heard Stephen and Terrel's parting words as they exited the barn, watched Stephen's shadow as he headed for home. In the distance Billy Dooley whistled softly to some cattle, and somewhere a horse nickered. Again, Jake wondered at how he'd ended up this way, wondered if the ugly memories of his father's drunken beatings and watching the man murder his mother would ever stop bringing out the old anger and need to defend.

He threw down his cigarette and stepped it out, shaking his head. It was so hard for him to stave off things better left deep, deep in the past and in his soul. He turned and headed inside, removing his boots and hat and vest, hanging up his guns. He headed upstairs and quickly undressed, went into the washroom and splashed the plains dust from his face and hands, ran wet fingers through his hair. He lifted the blankets and climbed into bed, pulling his sleepy wife into his arms. "I changed my mind," he told her. "I need my wife." To his surprise, Randy was naked.

"How well do I know you?"

Jake grinned. "Apparently, all too well. *Yo te amo, mi quiero.* Being inside you soothes my soul."

Randy sucked in her breath as he entered her with no foreplay. It was seldom this way, but whenever painful memories flared up, or something happened that, in Jake Harkner's mind, risked him losing someone he loved, he always came to her this way. He grasped her hands I a reassuring grip and held them gently as he pulled her arms toward the headboard in the possessive way we had of taking her when he thought about the hard times they had been through. "Who do you belong to?"

"Jake Harkner."

*"Tu eres, mi vida."* Jake released his pent-up need much sooner than he would have liked to. He kept her close as he moved to her side. "That was too quick and demanding," he said softly. "I'm sorry. I'll make it better next time."

"I know you will," Randy answered. "You always do." The next thing she knew, Jake was asleep.

# CHAPTER 6

Jake studied the mix of ranch hands sitting around the bunk house and waiting for Lloyd to show up for a meeting. Every man on the J&L was loyal to the family, and many had worked for Jake and Lloyd for years. Most had pasts no one talked about, and Jake well knew such men. They didn't talk, and he didn't ask. He could read a man's eyes and knew instinctively when a man could be trusted, in spite of questionable backgrounds. That was all that mattered.

Cole Decker came barging in at the last minute and limped over to sit down next to Vance Kelly. Cole and Vance were two of the best men on the J&L.

Cole had gone to Mexico with Jake and had to leave Jake behind in order to get young Annie MacBain across the border after Jake rescued her. The man had never quite gotten over having to leave Jake with a broken leg and lying under his dead horse, shot down by Mexican outlaws as Cole fled with Annie. Jake was dragged away to the worst hell he'd ever known. The family and all these men figured Jake to be dead. Jake remembered, when he returned home months later, that Cole cried like a baby with joy and relief, and when a man like Cole cried, you knew it was genuine. The man was hard and brave. He had a limp when Jake first met him, and all he'd ever said about it was that it was "from the war." Jake had never asked for details.

"What kept you, Decker?" Vance Kelly asked teasingly.

The rest of the men laughed as Cole waved them off. The poor man was a source of endless razzing since he'd married Gretta MacBain, Annie's mother, who was once the notorious owner of the fanciest brothel in Denver.

"You boys need to lay off," Jake stated. "Cole's a happily-married man now, and Gretta's a good woman."

"We should *all* be so happily married," Charlie McGee offered.

All the man laughed again. Charlie was younger, in his thirties, as was Billy Dooley. Jake had sent Terrel to Brighton with their youngest hire, Tommy Tyler, to buy supplies and to telegram Marshal Hal Kraemer. Jake wanted to talk to the marshal about Brady Fillmore, who was the reason Lloyd had called this meeting.

New hires Calvin Malloy, Win Lee and Lou Younger had remained out at Echo Ridge to keep working on the new road to the cabin. Younger swore he wasn't related to the Youngers who'd ridden with Frank and Jessie James, and Win Lee had worked for the Union Pacific when it was first being built thirty years prior. Jake figured Lee to be at least in his fifties, though he didn't look it. The small-built man worked harder than any man on the J&L, and he never complained.

"How's Win Lee doing?" Jake asked the others.

"Damn good worker," Cole answered. "Quiet. Keeps to himself. Obeys every order with that way he has of bowing every time somebody talks to him."

Jake kept his cigarette between his lips. "Win Lee's

dependable and honest. Make sure all of you treat him with respect." He took a deep drag on his cigarette.

"Where's Lloyd?" Billy asked. "We're getting hungry, and some of us have chores to do."

"He'll be along soon. With Katie's folks here now, and Katie carrying again, things get hectic at Lloyd's house. The Donavans have been a big help, but Lloyd still worries about Katie's being so busy with that brood of theirs."

"Well, there's one way to fix havin' too many kids," Vance said wryly. "You spend more time riding the range and out of a beautiful woman's bed."

They all laughed.

"Beautiful don't begin to describe Katie," Charlie said amid the chuckles.

Jake waved them off. "Ease up. All of you should know Katie has had problems with this baby, so jokes about him and Katie are a touchy subject right now. If something goes wrong, I'm not sure how Lloyd will handle it. I might need your help because he tends to turn to whiskey when that big, soft heart of his is broken."

Jake took another drag on his cigarette, memories of his alcoholic father always making him sick inside. It was why he never drank, in spite of all his other past sins. Lloyd was a good, strong, caring man, but he had that weakness for turning to the bottle when he was hurting. He and Randy had a rough time with Lloyd years ago when Jake was sent to prison, and again when Lloyd's first wife died along with the baby she was carrying.

"We'll keep an eye out," Vance told Jake. They all quieted when Lloyd walked inside then.

He hesitated, eyeing all the men as he closed the door. "All right," he said studying the way they looked at him. "I'm not even going to ask what you bunch of no-goods have been talking about." He lit a cigarette and walked closer to his father, just as tall and broad as Jake. "I didn't figure you'd be up this early, Pa, after the long day you put in yesterday."

"I've been getting up by five am most of my life, rain or shine, tired or not."

"Yeah, well, I expect you're up for the same reason *I* woke up early. Because you hardly slept after seeing that goddamned Brady Fillmore again." Lloyd sighed and removed his hat, then leaned against a storage shelf and took a deep drag on his cigarette.

"Which is the father, and which is the son?" Charlie McGee asked in an obvious effort to clear the tension in the room. "If you two had the same haircut, nobody would know."

Lloyd faced Charlie and grinned. "Well, that's exactly *why* I keep my hair long. God forbid somebody should mistake me for Jake Harkner. I'd like to live to a ripe old age."

That brought a few more chuckles as Lloyd glanced sidelong at Jake.

"Can't blame you there," Jake answered. Their gazes held a bit longer, a silent sharing of love between man and son.

"At least you seem to have a way of coming back from the dead," Lloyd told him, "so, if we're lucky, you'll be around a while longer."

"I'm not so sure others would call that luck."

"You know better, Jake." Charlie McGee again. "That son of yours nearly beat the shit out of Cole when he came back from Mexico without you. We had to pull him off. Lloyd might pretend he don't want to be like you, but he sure as hell is, and he don't mind."

"Don't be speaking for me, Charlie."

"Charlie McGee from Tennessee," Jake joked, using McGee's nickname. "You're a fervent peacemaker. Unless, of course, you're holding your own Peacemaker in your hand, wanting to use it on somebody."

More laughter.

The tension in the room lessened as teasing remarks were bulleted back and forth until they all finally quieted again.

Jake set his hat aside, cigarette still between his lips. "So, why are we here, son, as if I didn't know?"

Just then, Jake's adopted son, Ben, walked in, his white-blond hair looking even whiter in a shaft of sunlight behind him. He nodded to the men.

"Have a seat, kid," Billy Dooley told him, moving over on his bunk.

Ben looked sheepishly at Jake and Lloyd. "Sorry I'm a little late. On my morning rounds I noticed that roan mare's acting restless. I think maybe she's gonna' drop her foal before the day is out."

"You'd better tend to her then as soon as we're done, little brother," Lloyd told him.

Jake felt a stab of pride at Lloyd's way of addressing Ben. Jake had come across a then eight-year-old Ben back in Oklahoma. Ben's father was beating him mercilessly with a belt, and Jake had lit into the man and nearly killed him. Ben's father, after declaring he wanted nothing to do with the boy, left. Jake took Ben with him and legally adopted him. He loved him like his own, and Lloyd and Evie considered him their brother in every way. Neither harbored one ounce of resentment over it.

"Have your say, Lloyd," Cole said. "I told Gretta I'd eat breakfast with the rest of this bunch this morning, and it smells like Rodriguez is cooking up some *huevos rancheros*."

Lloyd grinned. "I agree that it smells pretty damn good." He rubbed wearily at his eyes. "You all know by now what happened yesterday out near Echo Ridge. And you all know what Brady Fillmore did to Fire Valley. I take pride in the fact that few strangers make it onto the J&L, especially after what happened to my mother a couple of years ago. I swore nothing like that would ever happen again, and I hate that my father had to deal with Fillmore yesterday in front of the girls, so now that I've hired three new men, once that road up on Echo Ridge is finished,

I'm stationing five of you around the borders instead of just three. I want all five in high places with spyglasses. I'll rotate you so no one's out there alone for too long at a time, and your replacements will ride out to you, so no outpost is ever left untended. If one of you is bushwhacked and hurt, we'll know it right away when your replacement gets there, instead of waiting for you to show up back here. Do all of you understand?"

Affirmations filled the room.

Lloyd continued. "You men know the rules. When a stranger rides onto the J&L, you meet him, take his gun, and then accompany him the rest of the way in. Let me or Jake decide if he belongs here. If Pa and I aren't here, the decision goes to Cole or whoever's here at the homestead standing lookout. Ben or Stephen can also decide. They're old enough now to start taking on responsibilities like that." Lloyd smoked quietly for a moment. "Pa and I *both* have old enemies, mostly from our days as lawmen in Oklahoma. If an old enemy gets on this property and harms any of my family, whoever let him slip by will have to answer to me or Jake. Understood?"

"Damn straight," Billy answered.

Lloyd pulled his hair behind his shoulders. "That's all I had to say. All of you go eat breakfast."

The men scrambled out the door to head for the cook house. Ben paused in front of Lloyd. "Thanks for saying I can have more responsibility, Lloyd."

Lloyd reached out and tousled his brother's thick,

blond hair. "You've earned it. You're going to inherit part of the *J&L* someday, so you need to learn all the ins and outs. Go on to the house now."

"Which one?"

"Where'd you sleep last night?"

"Evie and Brian's."

"Well, take your pick. I'm sure Evie, Katie and Randy all have breakfast cooking. And they love you, so it doesn't make much difference whose house you pick."

"Seems like you belong to *everybody* around here," Jake told Ben.

Ben laughed with delight. "I'll go eat at our house, since that's where my bedroom is and you're my pa."

"Check on that mare first," Lloyd said. "Then go eat quick and get back out there. Keep me posted how she's doing."

"I will!" The boy ran off.

"He's a good kid," Lloyd commented to Jake. "Good thing you made his father give him up."

"I didn't have to *make* him do anything. The bastard didn't want his own son. Reminds me of someone else I once knew."

"Yeah. I guess some men just aren't cut out to be fathers. You, on the other hand, are a damn good man for the job."

Jake flicked his cigarette into a bucket of water that hung on a nearby post, put there for spent cigarettes. "And isn't *that* strange, considering how I was raised."

Lloyd shrugged. "For a man who started out the way you did, you sure do know how to love, Pa."

Jake shrugged. "That's all because of your mother." He sighed. "I'm sorry about yesterday."

"No need. I'm glad you were there. Don't think for one minute I don't trust those girls to the man who can handle himself better than any man here, other than me, of course."

Jake gave him a light shove. "So you keep saying."

"The day of reckoning is coming, Jake Harkner."

"And don't I know it?"

"I'm sorry it seemed like I blamed you for yesterday. I was just mad that Fillmore made it so far onto the J&L. And I hate for those girls to see violence."

"I wanted to make sure Fillmore thinks twice about coming onto the J&L again. The girls will be okay. They have Harkner blood."

They left the bunkhouse together, but

Jake paused before they parted. "Lloyd, Brady Fillmore claimed people were asking around about Brad Buckley, wondering what happened to him."

Lloyd looked away. "Shit."

"Yeah." Jake rubbed at his neck. "I think Fillmore was just feeling me out - trying to get me to react. Randy never talks about what happened, and I don't blame her, but I can tell she's not completely over it, even now. I don't think she remembers shooting Brad Buckley, but he sure as hell would have died by my hand, and it would have been a much slower, more painful death. She did him a favor, but she might not see it that way. Hell, I can shoot a man and go eat breakfast, but it's a whole different feeling for somebody like your mother."

"I know." Lloyd looked toward the main house to see Ben greet Randy on the porch. "Just take one day at a time, Pa. I'm proud of how you handled what happened with Buckley without riding off, thinking Mom's better off without you. She wouldn't have survived without you being there for her. I know how hard that was for you. If she remembers something that she's buried down inside, you let us help you with her, especially Evie. You aren't alone in any of it, and Evie has a way of working magic on people, even on you, God bless her."

"Pa!" Ben yelled. "Mom said to get in here before breakfast is no good anymore."

Jake grinned and turned to Lloyd. "The woman has spoken."

"Yeah, and she's the only person in your life who's been able to boss you around, all five-feet-four-inches and one-hundred-and-ten pounds of her." Lloyd grinned. "I told her to hang on to that little pistol of hers because she might want to use it on *you* again."

"And she would have every right." Jake turned and walked to the house, remembering that first day he'd set eyes on Miranda Hayes in a supply store in Kansas. Her beautiful eyes had gotten as big as a scared deer. She pulled that damned little pistol from her handbag and shot him. He didn't blame her one bit.

# CHAPTER 7

Brady Fillmore answered the door to his ramshackle, one-room cabin outside of Denver.

Grizzly Smith took one look at him and burst out in uproarious laughter, barging in without closing the door. "By God, you look like *shit*!"

"Shut up!" Brady lightly touched the bandage on his swollen, bruised chin.

Grizzly sat down to the table. "Jake Harkner did that, didn't he?"

"Fuck you," Brady mumbled, closing the door.

Grizzly laughed harder. "You stupid sonofabitch! You really were dumb enough to ride onto the J&L. I didn't think you'd do it."

"I had a right."

Grizzly slapped his knee, laughed again, then lit a cigar. He puffed on it for several seconds while Brady sat with his elbows on his knees, head hanging.

"I think a range detective is supposed to have a good reason to go onto a rancher's property," Grizzly told him. "If nothin' was wrong, and if Harkner wasn't under arrest for somethin', then you had no right to be there. Looks like he set you straight on that one." He shook his head. "I would have thought up a good reason to go out there and rile Jake, but what made it worse is ole' Jake *knew* you. I *told* you he ain't a man to mess with. You should have known that yourself."

Brady just sat there scowling.

"You give me your badge, Fillmore, and I'll go out to the J&L and stir up legitimate trouble. I ain't fuckin' stupid enough to be showin' my face on Harkner land without lookin' like a man of authority. And I'll take a woman with me to pose as a settler. Ole' Jake has a soft spot for women, so that'll probably make him hesitate. I also plan to scout around other ranches. The best way to start some trouble is to sniff out other homesteaders and nesters, create the unrest we talked about. Them nesters'll be the ones most willin' to make trouble, on account of they hate the big ranchers who chase them off their land . After goin' to that meetin', I can see how easy it'll be for them to start trouble. And that shootist they hired looked like a man who'd be right happy to be known for shooting down Jake Harkner."

"You'll end up on the wrong end of Harkner's gun yourself, and he won't care if you're wearing a badge or not," Brady warned.

Grizzly puffed his cigar. "Did Hal Kraemer fire you? He's a hard man, and I heard he's more Harkner's friend than he is out to catch him doin' somethin' wrong."

"He hasn't fired me yet." Brady winced in pain. "Said he'd talk to Harkner first."

"Good. Since you still have that badge, I can borrow it." Grizzly scratched the back of his neck. "I knew you'd get too cocky wearing that badge. What'd you do? Insult Jake's wife? Back when he rode shotgun for the Yellowjacket, I remember some man threatened to look up his pretty, young wife. Minutes later that man could hardly walk. And Ole' Jake's got even more family now. You gotta' be the dumbest man who ever walked!"

Brady pulled a gun from the holster hanging on his bedpost, cocked it, and aimed it at Grizzly. "Stop your laughing!"

Grizzly waved him off. "You ain't gonna' shoot me. Hell, I came over here as a friend."

Brady gently set the hammer back in place and holstered his pistol. "If you're here to help, then stop laughing. You don't have any idea how much pain I'm in."

"Oh, I think I do. The whole bottom of your face is purple and swollen, and I see blood all over that bandage on your chin."

"Harkner broke my jawbone right smack in the middle." Brady couldn't put his lips together, so his "m's" sounded like "n's," and his "b's" like "d's."

"How in hell do you eat?" Grizzly asked.

"Haven't been hungry. Too much pain."

"Well, then, I'll go over to the Chicken Delight and get you some broth, maybe some noodle soup. You sure can't be chewin' anything solid for a while." Grizzly paused. "Sorry about laughin', but Jesus, Brady, I told you to wait. If you want to make trouble, don't be showin' your face so soon. Now Jake's on the alert. Ten to one, they've put more men out guardin' the border. You made it harder for *me* to get to him."

Brady fisted his hands. "That bastard hasn't changed even a little bit."

""Was he alone?"

"No. Had a couple of grandsons and two little girls with him."

"Jesus Christ, no wonder he knocked you flat! If that was a few years ago, you would be buried on the *J&L*. I'm guessin' Jake don't let *nobody* get near his family. Boy, you're a slow learner, Fillmore."

"Yeah, well, I'm not going to let this go. No, sir."

"You'll get your revenge when those farmers get enough gunmen together to go after Jake and Lloyd."

Brady's expression was dark. "Riling up those farmers will be easy, and tempting men like Kyle Pendergrass with the chance to shoot Jake Harkner will make it even easier. Some men would willingly go to prison for killing him."

"I don't doubt that, but Harkner's goddamn famous with those guns, and I expect he's got a lot of friends. Some might claim they'd like to kill him, but most tend to change their mind once they come face to face with him. Harkner reads a man real good, and he tends to shoot first and ask questions later. It's kind of a bad habit of his. Remember that."

"Look, you bastard, I found out something that could help."

"Yeah? What?"

"The *Denver Post* prints that column from the Chicago papers that friend of Jake's writes – the guy who wrote that book about Jake. He says Jake and his wife are going on a trip this summer to Chicago. What better time to make trouble for the *J&L* than with Jake gone?"

Grizzly's eyes lit up. "Now you're finally thinkin' like a reasonable man. While Harkner's gone, we can stir up trouble that makes him come chargin' home, out for blood! He's a man who can't control his temper or his thirst for revenge once it sets in. When is he supposed to go?"

"It didn't say for sure – just that it would likely be sometime in July. I figure we have between now and two or three months from now to stir things up and have some real action going by the time Jake gets back home."

Grizzly nodded. "And that gives us time for a quick trip into Outlaw Country. We maybe can find some men there who'd like to bring down Jake Harkner."

Brady tried to smile but winced in pain. "Good idea.

Go get me some of that soup, will ya? Just the thought of Harkner getting killed has brought back my appetite."

"Sure." Grizzly stopped to press Brady's shoulder. "Don't you worry. We'll figure somethin' out. But just remember that Harkner don't make no bones about defendin' what's his. He gets them guns blazin', and they'll be pickin' up bodies all over the place."

"I figure that by the time we're through, they'll be picking up *Jake's* body – maybe even that son of his. We need to figure a way to make this look like a range war, so nobody can pin down our names as the instigators." Brady met Grizzly's gaze. "One thing is sure, once Harkner is buried, I intend to dance on his grave."

Grizzly just laughed and shook his head as he walked out to get Brady some soup.

# CHAPTER 8

Randy jumped at the gunfire, six shots coming in a matter of a few seconds.

"Honestly, Jake." She set aside the dish she'd almost dropped and removed her apron. She'd no more than put the dish away before a knock came at the front door. It opened before Randy could get to it.

"Mother?" Evie called out.

"I'm here." Jake's guns boomed again. "Apparently your father and brother are giving Stephen and Ben the shooting lessons they promised them."

Evie shook her head. "Daddy hates having to teach anyone to shoot a six-gun, but the boys are turning into men, and they've a right to learn, I guess. As for me, I hate all guns. I wish Daddy would give his up."

Randy hugged her daughter, thinking how neither Evie nor Lloyd looked as though they were hers. Both were tall and dark like their father. The top of her own head came to just above Evie's shoulder.

"I know you hate it, honey, but you can't live in back-country Colorado, with grizzlies and bobcats and rustlers and Heaven knows what else, and not carry a revolver, *besides* a rifle. It's just life." She leaned up and kissed Evie's cheek. "As far as your father, you might as well ask him to cut off both hands as to ask him to give up his guns. He worries too much about his past causing problems."

"I know. I worry about that, too. But I also worry about Little Jake. He's biting at the bit for Brian and me to let him take lessons, too, but he's still too young. And he's so brave and wild, just like Daddy. It scares me."

"Jake knows how to handle his grandson. You let him take care of that boy and quit worrying. Besides, who better to teach Little Jake the right and wrong of it?"

The air rang with more gunfire. Randy had grown used to the sound of Jake's guns and knew the last shots weren't his. And they came much slower. It had to be one of the boys.

"I know Lloyd isn't crazy about teaching them, either," she told Evie, "especially Stephen. But at least they'll learn how to *safely* use those guns. My problem is, the boom of Jake's .44's brings back memories I would rather keep buried. So would he."

"And don't I know about trying to bury memories?" Evie moved to set a tray of cookies on the table. "The one that really sticks in my mind is seeing the flash of Daddy's rifle up on that hill at Dune Hollow. Feeling that bullet whizz past my ear made me gasp. The next thing I knew, the man holding me hostage crumpled to the ground. Daddy told me he was terrified of pulling that trigger because he could have killed me instead of the man holding me, but I never doubted his ability. I just knew he would find me and get me out of that awful place. That's what helped me bear all of it. I never felt hopeless."

"I didn't mean to bring up something you shouldn't have to talk about," Randy told her.

Smiling through tears, Evie turned to her mother. "That isn't a bad memory, Mother. It's a good one. When daddy whistled from up in those hills, I knew everything was going to be okay. Next thing I knew, he was holding me like I was five years old. I never felt so safe in my life, and I don't mean that as anything against Brian. A woman couldn't ask for a better husband. It was just . . . that awful day. I *felt* like a five-year-old when daddy wrapped that blanket around me and just collapsed to the ground holding me."

"I know exactly what you mean about feeling safe in Jake's arms."

Evie grasped Randy's hand. "Oh, Mother, now *I've* been the one to bring up something I shouldn't. What you went through—"

Randy shook her head firmly. "No more talk of that. Why are you bringing me cookies?"

Jake's guns boomed again, and they heard a few men cheering.

"Lord, God, I think I'm in love!"

Randy and Evie both laughed. There was no mistaking those words came from Gretta, who always boldly spoke her mind.

"I'm gradually getting used to the way Gretta talks," Evie commented. "And that loud voice and laugh! She might be married to Cole now, but her bawdiness hasn't changed."

"And you can't help liking her." Randy chuckled. "I'm sure some of the neighbor women can't understand how I tolerate Denver's most infamous prostitute living here as a ranch hand's wife. God knows what kind of gossip they spread, but if not for Gretta's testimony after the shooting at the cattlemen's ball in Denver, Jake might be in prison – or worse."

"The gossips don't understand how Daddy feels about women like Gretta - why he'd do everything in his power to help them. No other man would have gone to Mexico after Gretta's daughter. I know Cole went, too, but it was daddy who stayed behind and was dragged away. I'll never forget how it felt to think he was dead." Evie shivered.

Randy hung up her apron. "Well, he's home now, and young Annie knows who her real mother is and they are close now. Annie seems to be doing well at that finishing school in Denver."

Evie took a deep breath. "I don't know how we ended up talking about all this." She hugged her mother again. "I brought the cookies over because I'm sure Sadie Mae and Tricia will be over here soon. Maybe even little Esther and Donavan. They both like to tag along with their sisters. Lord knows they love coming here to hang all over Daddy."

"And Jake loves it," Randy added.

"Hello! Hello!" Brian walked in, leading Sadie Mae and little Esther by the hand. "Katie's right behind me with Donny and Tricia. We both had a time of it keeping them away from Jake and the boys, so we figured bringing them here would keep them from running out behind the barn, around all that shooting." He kissed Evie and turned to Miranda. "I hope you don't mind me bringing the kids here."

"Not at all. Evie and I were just talking about that." Randy admired her son-in-law, always so patient and loving toward Evie. If not for his love and kindness, and his abilities as a doctor, his wife might not have recovered from her horrible ordeal back in Oklahoma. Amid all the turmoil that sometimes enveloped the entire Harkner clan, Brian remained rock solid and level-headed. He was always pleasant, a well-educated man whose skills were definitely needed on the J&L. Lord knew the kids' health and Katie's and Evie's pregnancies kept him busy, but there were dozens of ways ranch hands could be injured on such a big spread – lots of cuts and scrapes and broken bones.

Katie walked in with Donny and Tricia as the shooting continued in the corral. "I'm sorry, Randy, but these two wanted to come and see Grandma, since I forbid them to go out to where Grandpa and Lloyd are."

"I don't mind, dear." Randy studied her beautiful but very tired-looking daughter-in-law. "You need the break anyway." She grunted as she picked up Donny. "This little guy will be as big as his daddy in no time. Lloyd was a real chunk, too, when he was little."

Katie smiled. "And now he's a *big* chunk."

They all laughed.

"My mother is watching Jeffrey," Katie added, "so I'm going back to bed—Lloyd's orders."

"That's a good idea. No one would blame you if you *stayed* in bed until you have that baby," Randy told her. "It won't be that much longer."

"Oh, I feel so guilty. And so *fat*!"

"And Lloyd couldn't care less. He loves you and wants things to go right. So, if he tells you to stay in bed, you stay in bed."

"I can just hear what Jake would say about that." Katie chuckled. "He'd say that staying in bed is what got me this way in the first place." She kissed Tricia. "Be good for Grandma, and help her watch Donnie."

"I'll help, Mommy."

Randy noticed Katie's milky-white complexion was flushed, her bright-red hair damp with perspiration. She turned to Brian. "Brian, walk her back to her house, will you?"

"Sure. We'll both go with her." He led Evie toward the door and took Katie's arm.

"I'll check back with you later," Evie told her mother.

Randy stood at the door watching their progress across the yard.

The children ran off to the bedroom where their toys were kept, and Randy realized the shooting finally stopped. She saw Gretta walk from behind the barn and head toward the house. She was a lovely woman no older than Lloyd. Her story was a sad one – forced into prostitution by an uncle when she was only twelve. Annie was born when Gretta was only fifteen. She had no idea who Annie's father was, and she wanted her baby girl to have a decent life, so she adopted her out to a Christian family and went on to get rich on the only kind of life she felt she was good for.

"What's going on?" Randy asked Gretta when she got closer.

No longer wearing the makeup, fancy clothing and jewels she'd been famous for, Gretta wore a simple, blue-gingham dress, her long, blond hair drawn back straight and tied with a ribbon.

"That husband of yours sure can put on a show," she stated. "I've never seen anybody draw so fast and shoot so accurately. In fact, you hardly even *see* him draw. One second those guns are holstered, and the next, those cans on the fence go flying."

Randy smiled. "How'd the boys do?"

"They're getting pretty good. I came over to tell you that Vance told Lloyd he thinks some nesters are planning to settle on J&L land north of here. He, Lloyd and Jake are going out there now to point out where J&L land ends and free range starts. Jake and Lloyd are worried it's more somebody who wants to make trouble, rather than legitimate nesters."

Randy sighed and shook her head. "I don't like these sudden, strange incidents with settlers. Since that mess with Brady Fillmore, Jake thinks maybe we shouldn't go to Chicago."

Gretta came up the steps. "Oh, hell, Lloyd and the men can take care of things, Randy. Jake shouldn't worry. You two deserve that trip."

"I know." Randy saw Jake and Lloyd standing by the barn, talking. "It's just that things have been so good these last few months. Jake's been happy and more at peace, but that thing with Fillmore when Jake had the granddaughters with him has him feeling restless." She looked at Gretta. "He's used to dealing his own form of justice, as you well know. He can't do that if he wants to stay out of trouble, but it's hard for him to control that side of himself." Leading Gretta inside, she checked to see if Jake and Lloyd were still near the barn. "Gretta, there's something you should know about Jake," she said quietly. "When trouble comes, you just might find him on your doorstep. He tends to turn to women like you—I mean—that's not meant as an insult . . ."

"Don't worry about offending *me*. I have a hard crust, and this family's been incredibly kind. Cole told me a lot about Jake. You don't need to explain."

Randy sighed and leaned against the door jam. "It's just that despite how much Jake loves me and how many times I've told him he can talk to me when he's upset, prostitutes represent his comfort zone. They raised him, and because of his background and that part of him he thinks is no good, he believes only women who live that rough life would understand. It's why he turned to Dixie James back in Guthrie when Evie was kidnapped. He came close to killing himself from lack of food and sleep in his quest to find her. Dixie was the only one who could talk some sense into him." She suddenly felt like crying.

Gretta put a hand on Randy's arm. "No more

explaining. Jake can come to me any time, but I'll just tell him to go to the woman he *should* be talking to."

"He thinks he's sparing me by not burdening me with the hell he goes through on the inside. I swear he will never figure out that I understand every little thing about him."

Randy shook off her worried look when she noticed Jake coming toward the house. "It looks like he'll come talk to me before leaving with Lloyd and Vance."

Gretta joined her at the screen door as Jake passed the chicken coop. The rooster he hated crowed and spread its wings. Jake stopped to pick up a rock. He threw it at the rooster, then pulled his gun and shot the rock into little pieces, making the bird squawk and strut and spread its wings again.

Both women laughed as they walked out onto the porch.

"Damn black devil!" Jake swore. "He should have been named Lucifer!"

"Jake so very much wants to use that demon rooster for target practice," Randy told Gretta. "They had a little confrontation once, and the rooster won!"

Gretta laughed even harder as Jake paused near the porch steps.

"I don't like the looks on your faces," he told them. "And I don't like that laugh, Gretta Decker. Am I in trouble?"

"If your name's Jake Harkner, you're *always* in trouble." She stated, smiling.

"That's for damn sure."

"I just hope you're done with those guns," Gretta added, "My ears still hurt."

Jake pulled out one revolver and reloaded it as he came up the steps. "I hope I won't need them any more today. Lloyd and I are riding out in a few minutes to check on some nesters who seem to think they can settle where they don't belong." He studied Randy. "Woman, what have you been telling Gretta?"

"You don't want to know."

"That's a hell of a wife you have there," Gretta told Jake. "Take good care of yourself so you can love and protect her for a long time to come."

"You don't need to tell me that." Jake pulled Gretta into the crook of his arm and kissed her hair. "And Cole needs some lunch before chores. He said to send you home."

Gretta laughed and ducked out from under his arm. "I enjoyed watching you with those guns today. Between you and Cole, I'm feeling safe as a bug in a rug." She hurried down the steps, heading home.

Jake looked down at Randy. "Vance is saddling Thunder. Can you pack a couple of biscuits or something for me to take along?"

Randy put her arms around his waist and rested her head against his chest. "Jake, whatever happens, please let Lloyd and Vance take care of it."

"We'll be fine." He bent down to meet her lips in a gentle kiss. "Are there grandkids here?"

"There are *always* grandkids here. Evie brought over some cookies, and Katie brought Donny and Tricia, then went back home to lie down. She didn't look good. I'm worried about her."

Hugging her tighter, Jake sighed. "You and me both."

"I'm not going to Chicago until she has that baby."

"I agree." Another kiss.

Lloyd and Vance rode up, leading a saddled Thunder.

"How long have you two been married?" Lloyd called out. "Thirty-three years? Or thirty-three days?"

Jake kissed Randy once more. "Thirty-three *hours*." He gave her a smile and stepped off the porch to mount Thunder.

"Keep him out of trouble," Randy told Lloyd.

"Oh, no problem. We know how easy that is."

"Do you have food with you? Jake hasn't had breakfast or lunch."

"Rodriguez gave us fritters and dry-rubbed pork. I know he came here for something to take with him, but there's no need to bother."

"We will *make* him eat!" Vance assured Randy.

Jake tipped his hat and all three men rode off.

Randy wondered how many times she'd watched her husband ride away in all their years together - or heard that high-pitched whistle when he was coming back. She'd never forget hearing that whistle when he finally returned from Mexico, seemingly coming back from the dead. It was winter, and snowing, but she'd run out the front door to greet him—barefoot and with no coat. She never noticed the cold. She only saw her husband coming home. Everyone else was sure he'd died in Mexico … but she never gave up. Her Jake always found his way back to her.

# CHAPTER 9

"Take it easy, Pa." Lloyd reigned his horse to a halt and patted the horse's neck. "I told the men that if newcomers look like regular farmers, they should let me take care of it. Those people could just be confused as to where they are, so maybe there's nothing wrong here."

Jake studied the covered wagon below, and the supply wagon behind it. A kettle hung on a tripod over the flames of a campfire.

"Something about that camp doesn't look right," he told Lloyd. "Most newcomers have fairly good maps as to where they should be. And I don't see the kind of supplies farmers carry with them. That wagon looks half empty, just a little lumber, no farm tools. And where are the extra horses, or a milk cow?"

"Let's check it out, but you be careful. Remember the new laws and that judge in Denver."

"I will." Jake glanced at Lloyd. "You and Vance keep a good eye out." Jake nudged Thunder into a gentle lope, pulling his rifle from its boot as they rode toward what looked like homesteaders preparing to stake their claim ... on *J&L* land.

Lloyd shook his head and followed his father. All three men paused again when they came closer.

"Okay, I agree," Lloyd told Jake. "That man on the left is no farmer."

"Keep him in your sights. Vance, you watch the driver of that supply wagon."

"Yes, Sir."

A young woman in a slat bonnet and blue gingham dress straightened from stirring the cookpot. She stepped back as the men rode closer, then moved to stand beside a man who looked about Lloyd's age. He wore a common cotton shirt and pants held up by suspenders, a floppy farmer's hat, and mid-calf boots. Jake noticed a handgun stuck in the farmer's belt - a belt he didn't need because of the suspenders.

The man to Jake's left stood near his horse. Bearded, he wore scuffed but shined knee-high boots, the kind worn in a city, and dark pants threadbare at the knees. A dark-gray frock coat over a striped waistcoat and a string tie completed his outfit. His gray felt hat had a narrow brim, not the wider brim of most farmers' or ranchers' hats in high plains country. Dark, curly hair stuck out from under it. The sun hit him from the side, casting a shadow that made it hard to figure his age. Jake guessed in his sixties.

One thing he'd learned as both outlaw and lawman was to observe everything about a stranger and go with his gut feeling. He closed in on the couple while Lloyd moved toward the bearded man, who held a rifle but didn't raise it. Vance approached the supply wagon and its driver, who looked more like a cowboy than a settler. Most farmers didn't carry or wear sidearms, but this one wore a gun in a holster.

The bearded man held Jake's gaze for a moment, then looked away, avoiding eye contact.

Jake shifted his gaze to the farm couple. "State your names."

"What's it to you?" the man asked.

*Wrong answer.* New farmers were generally friendlier. "I want to know because you're on private property."

Thunder snorted and tossed his head. The couple both took a step back.

"Whose property?" the bearded man asked in a raspy voice.

"*Harkner* land. The *J&L*," Lloyd answered. "I'm Lloyd Harkner, and the man on the gray there is my father, Jake Harkner. What are you doing here?"

The bearded man gave the couple a warning look. They looked up at Jake, silent.

"How about answering my first question?" Jake asked again. "State your names."

"Stella and Howard London," the farmer said, voice shaky. "We're here from St. Louis to claim our hundred and sixty acres under the Homestead Act. Fair and legal."

"You can't legally settle on someone else's property," Jake stated. "And even if you find available land, it's not really yours until you live on it and farm it for six months. But this is *J&L* land, and you're leaving today."

"It will be dark soon!" Howard objected.

"Sometimes cattle and horses get stolen after dark."

"Are you accusing us of being *rustlers*?" the supply-wagon driver asked.

"I'm saying bad things sometimes happen after dark," Jake answered. "So, no stranger is staying on the *J&L* after sunset."

The bearded man spoke up. "You can't make them leave."

"Yes, we can." Lloyd turned his horse so the settlers could see the holstered pistol on his right hip.

The raspy-voiced man raised his rifle slightly.

"I wouldn't, if I were you." Jake nodded at Lloyd. "My son's just as good as I am with that piece he's wearing, and I've yet to find the man who can raise a rifle or pull a handgun faster than either of us."

"Are you really *that* Jake Harkner?" Howard asked.

"Shut up, Howard!" the bearded man told him.

Jake's suspicions rose at this exchange, and he backed Thunder up a so he could keep all four people in his sight. "Do you have papers from the land office?"

"They're comin'," the bearded man answered. "These kind people came out here to build a farm. They wanted to see the land first, and I agreed to come with them to protect them from big cattle ranchers like you—men who think they own Colorado." He pushed his frock coat aside to reveal a badge.

Jake just grinned and shook his head. "Well, well, well. Another Range Detective."

The man stood straighter. "Yes. And if you bring me harm, or harm any of these innocent people, you'll be arrested."

Without warning, Jake charged Thunder at the Range Detective, knocking him over. The couple backed up farther when Lloyd dismounted, rifle in hand, and moved in while Jake dismounted to grab the detective's rifle. Jake tossed it several yards away before the man could get to his feet.

"You aren't arresting *anybody*, Mister," Jake growled. "And you're no range detective. Hal Kraemer would never hire vermin like you!"

Vance rode closer to the wagon. "Lift that revolver from its holster and throw it into the wagon bed," he told the driver.

The driver slowly obeyed as Jake yanked the supposed detective to his feet and shoved him toward the couple.

"You can't treat innocent settlers like this," Howard complained.

"You're rude and a bully," the woman declared, holding her chin high.

She backed farther away when Jake shoved the detective toward her, then went to the kettle hanging over the fire and looked into it. He spat, then went to her and pushed back her bonnet to reveal her face.

"She's a whore, Lloyd."

"How *dare* you!" She tried to slap him, but he caught her wrist.

"What's your *real* name, honey?"

"Pa?" Lloyd said with a frown. "You'd better be sure."

"Who knows prostitutes better than I do? And if you were as close to her as I am, you'd know, too. She reeks of cheap perfume, and there's makeup residue on her eyelids and cheeks. Farm women don't use make up unless they're going to a dance, and this is no dance."

"You have no right—" The woman started to protest.

"I have *every* right!" Jake interrupted. "And I asked your name. Your *real* name."

The woman raised her chin. "None of your business, you bastard!"

"I've been called a lot worse. I have also been around too long not to know when somebody's trying to fuck me over." Jake stepped back. "Tell me you don't know who Gretta MacBain is."

The quick light of recognition in the woman's eyes gave him his answer.

"That's what I thought. Except Gretta's one of the *good* ones." He turned to the farmer as he said, "Lloyd, keep your attention on the bearded sonofabitch over there. If he's a Range Detective, I'm a Harvard Professor."

Vance chuckled then turned to the wagon driver. "Climb down off there. What's your name?"

"Clem Logan." As soon as his feet touched the ground, Logan put his hands up and looked at Jake. "Look, Mister, I know who you are, and you should know that if these others have ulterior motives for you and yours, I don't know what they are, and I have nothing to do with it. I'm bein' honest. All I know is that bearded one over there—Mister Smith, he said he was a Range Detective. Said he'd pay me to haul lumber out here to help a couple of settlers he was accompanying. I didn't know this was *J&L* land or that anything was illegal about this."

Jake shifted his gaze to the bearded man. "That true?"

"Yes. And that cowardly weasel can leave if he's of a mind to."

Jake paused to light a cigarette, studying all four intruders closely as he took a deep drag, then exhaled as he spoke. "Let the driver go, Vance."

"Go on with you," Vance told Clem. "Go back where you came from, but as long as you're in my sights, you'd better not reach for that gun."

"Yes, sir!" Clem scrambled up onto the wagon seat and drove off.

Jake gestured toward the woman. "Did you pay her to pose as a farmer's wife?" he asked Smith.

"How'd you know?" The man's scratchy voice sounded like it might pain him to talk.

"There are men out there who want me dead and, Mister, I read men real good when my life depends on it. That driver called you Smith. Might that be *Frank* Smith? Maybe now you go by the nickname Grizzly?"

The man swallowed hard.

"Your friend, Brady Fillmore, mentioned you a few days ago," Jake told him, "hinted I might know you. That was before I busted his jaw. That's probably Fillmore's badge you're wearing. Am I right?"

Grizzly looked from Jake to Lloyd, then back to Jake. "Goddamn you, Harkner."

"God damned me a long time ago." Jake dropped his cigarette and crushed it under his boot heel. "How's Fillmore doing? Can he move that jaw yet?"

"Hey, what's *really* going on here, Grizzly?" Howard London asked. "You didn't tell us any of this. All you said was that you'd pay us to come out here and pose as settlers."

Jake glared. "Smith, you should have picked some poor, decent young girl off the street who needed the money for your little plot—not a whore. I can spot a whore from a mile away."

"I'm sure you can, you sonofabitch. God knows you've hung out with enough women like her."

Hands on hips, the woman in question faced Jake. She stuck her chest out and gave him her best smile. "Listen, Mister, why don't you just let us go? If you do, I'll give you a free lay in the back of that covered wagon."

Jake stared back impassively. "Honey, you could stand there buck naked and it wouldn't phase me. I've been around women like you way too long, and my son and I have wives waiting for us back home." He looked up at the still-mounted Vance. "How about you, Vance? Got an itch that needs to be scratched?"

"No, Sir. I have a woman in Brighton."

"That so? You've never talked about a woman in Brighton."

"That's because she has a husband."

Grinning, Jake shook his head. "You and Terrel seem to have a hankering for other men's wives. Maybe I'd better keep a closer eye on Randy."

"Shit, Jake, I value my life enough to stay away from *that* kind of trouble."

"Are you gonna' let us leave or not?" Grizzly Smith asked, irritation in his voice.

"You and I have some talking to do first," Jake said. "You stay put." He turned to the woman. "I asked your name."

She sniffed. "Stella. Stella Flynn. This man here really is Howard London. He's a gambler at the Aspen Saloon in Denver. I work upstairs there." She tossed her head a little and stepped closer. "If you ever change your mind about that free lay, come see me. Maybe you're getting tired of the wife. A man needs some variety sometimes."

"Get the hell out of here," Jake ordered. "You and your gambler friend. I've never hurt a woman, but if you ever make a remark about my wife again, I'll be tempted."

Stella stepped back farther as Jake asked Howard, "What's really going on here?"

Howard swallowed. "I . . . Grizzly there, he plays cards at the saloon where I work. Said he'd pay me to come out here and pose as a farmer. Didn't say why." He glanced at Grizzly. "You didn't say anything about maybe runnin' into Jake Harkner." He looked back at Jake. "Can we go?"

Jake glanced at Stella again. "I'm apologizing. Not because you deserve it, but because I believe Smith didn't tell you the whole story about why he brought you out here. Just don't let me ever hear that you've insulted my wife again."

Stella smiled slyly. "My. My. I guess it's true what one of Gretta's girls told me about you. You have a real soft spot for women."

"Not if they threaten my family, so don't count on that. Get off the J&L!"

Howard eagerly helped Stella into the wagon, then climbed up beside her, picking up the reins. "You aren't going to shoot me in the back as I leave, are you?" he asked Jake.

"Mister, I've done a lot of ugly things, but shooting a man in the back isn't one of them."

"No," Grizzly spoke up. "Ole' Jake here prefers putting a gun right to a man's forehead . . . sometimes in his mouth . . . and *then* pulling the trigger."

"Shit!" Howard drove off.

Seeing the look in Jake's eyes just then, Grizzly started to mount up.

"Stay put!" Jake told him. "We're going to have a heart-to-heart, Smith."

"Like hell! You'd better let *me* go, too, Harkner. Don't forget there's a judge in Denver who wouldn't mind hangin' you. Those three that just left can testify as to me bein' left here alone and never heard from again. Everybody knows what you're capable of, so don't be thinkin' you're gonna' bury me like a dead prairie dog."

"I should!" Jake stormed up to Grizzly and backhanded him.

Grizzly stumbled sideways and fell. He reached inside his vest, but Jake's .44 was against his temple before he could draw.

"Toss that gun and get up!"

"Pa, be careful," Lloyd warned.

Grizzly got to his knees and threw the gun aside. He put a hand to the side of his face. "Goddam you, Harkner! Do you make a habit of bustin' peoples' jaws?"

Jake jerked him the rest of the way to his feet. "Did Fillmore send you out here, or did *you* send *him* the other day?" When Smith tried to turn away, Jake jerked him back around. "Fillmore said I knew you, and I have a damn good idea you're someone from my past. Someone who's holding a grudge and decided to do something about it. Is *that* it?"

Grizzly's cheek was already growing purple. "I should kill Brady Fillmore for leakin' my name. Stupid sonofabitch!" He sneered the words through clenched teeth. "I know you from when you worked for Ike Jones, that gunsmith up in Virginia City. Rode under the name Jake Turner back then because you were *wanted!* Then you foiled a bank robbery, and folks figured out you was real good with them guns."

The memory hit Jake hard. He shoved Grizzly away and stepped back.

"Pa? You okay?" Lloyd asked.

Grizzly grinned. "He's rememberin', that's all. The Yellowjacket Mine owners hired him to ride shotgun for gold shipments. Imagine that, a thief, gunrunner, murderer and bank robber guardin' gold shipments! He had a wife and kid by then. I expect *you* were the kid. Your pa needed money to support you and your ma. Life gets expensive when you're always on the run, don't it, Harkner? Wanted men have a hard time findin' decent jobs. By the way, are you still married to that pretty little golden-haired gal of yours? Or did she *leave* your sorry ass?"

"You're here to make trouble Smith, plain and simple, and you just might get more than you planned on!" Jake roared the words. "Now get off this ranch!"

Grizzly breathed heavily with anger.

"You bet your ass I'm here to make trouble!" He yanked down his shirt collar to show the ugly scar across his throat. "Your *pa* did this to me," he said to Lloyd. "We got in a shootout when I tried to rob one of them gold shipments. He killed three men and put a bullet across my throat that took out most of my voice box and left me with this ugly scar and this ugly *voice!*"

"*Now* I remember you!" Jake exploded. "Apparently, I should have put that bullet through your **heart** instead of your throat, but I was too busy fending off five other men to look where I was aiming."

Lloyd stepped in front of his father. "Just let him go, Pa, or Hal Kraemer might come out here asking the wrong questions. You know you can't keep taking care of things like this yourself anymore. It's just a fact of life."

Jake glowered at his son. "This fucker is making trouble because of *me*, and something that happened thirty *years* ago! It's not fair to you."

"And nobody's been hurt. Just wait and talk to Kraemer about this and about that incident with Brady Fillmore. We'll report both, and then you need to take Mom to Chicago like you planned and just get the hell away from the *J&L* for a while. This isn't like in Oklahoma when it was just you and me."

Jake fingered the butt of his gun. "Get out of my sight!" he demanded of Grizzly Smith.

Grizzly grinned. "Glad to oblige." He started to pick up his rifle and handgun.

"Hold on!" Jake told him. He walked over and ejected all the bullets from the man's rifle, then dumped cartridges out of the handgun. He shoved both against Grizzly's chest. "Leave now, and I won't use you for target practice on the way out," he growled.

Grizzly backed away, then walked to his horse and shoved his rifle into its boot and his gun into his belt. He mounted up, then grinned. "I'll likely be back, Harkner."

"*Try* it!" Jake warned. "Whatever you and Fillmore have planned, you might as well give it up, unless you like the thought of being fertilizer for daisies!"

Grizzly's smile vanished. "I'll leave – for now. I reckon' me and Brady have a little more plannin' to do if we're gonna' be known as the men who brought down Jake Harkner and lived to talk about it!" He turned his horse and rode off.

"I'll tail the bastard for a ways to make sure he keeps going," Vance told Lloyd.

He rode off, and, hanging on to Cinnamon's reins, Lloyd kept his father's gaze.

"Pa, when you get tangled up in these things, disaster tends to follow, so go home and plan that trip to Chicago. Let Mom see you're okay. And make sure Katie knows *I'm okay.*" Cinnamon pranced nervously in a circle, and Lloyd kept a tight hold of the horse's reins. "And be careful. It'll be dark soon." He turned and mounted Cinnamon. "I'm going to catch up with Vance and make sure all four of those no-goods leave the ranch. Don't follow me." He charged after Vance.

Jake watched after both men. He didn't trust what had just happened, especially not about Grizzly's last words. . . . *if we're gonna' be known as the men who brought down Jake Harkner* . . .

"Go ahead and try, you bastards!" he muttered. "But if the little finger of any one member of my family gets hurt because of it, you're *dead* men!"

# CHAPTER 10

Jake didn't get back to the house until well after dark. He asked Tommy Tyler to put up his horse, then walked inside to find Evie, Gretta, and Randy all sitting together near the fireplace, Randy in her nightgown and curled up in his big, red, leather chair. The other three looked up at him as though relieved to see him home, but Randy looked away.

"Jesus," he whispered under his breath.

"Don't use the Lord's name in vain, Daddy," Evie told him.

Jake removed his hat and hung it on a hook near the door, then faced Gretta and his daughter. "I'm not even going to ask what you've been talking about, or why you all look so worried. I told Randy I might be gone all night because of distance. Fact is, Lloyd and Vance won't be back 'til morning. They went on farther northwest to make sure troublemakers we came across are completely off the J&L."

Evie rose and walked up to him, speaking quietly, "Daddy, we weren't worried about you coming home. We decided to sit here with Mother until you got back, even if it meant waiting all night. Something's wrong."

Jake frowned. "What are you talking about?"

Gretta stood up and moved to Randy. "We're here if you need us, honey." She glanced at Jake with deep concern in her eyes as she passed by him to leave. "We're here for you, too, if you need to talk. But you take care of your wife first."

Jake felt a dark foreboding. "What—"

Gretta patted his shoulder. "It'll be okay, now you're here. Work your magic, Jake." She gave him a wry smile and left.

He turned his attention to Evie. "What the hell was that about?" He glanced at Randy, who simply sat quietly staring at a small fire in the fireplace. Jake realized that she'd said absolutely nothing since he walked in. "What happened?"

Evie grabbed his hand and pulled him out onto the porch. "Daddy, I came over earlier to help Mom cut dough for noodles like we'd planned," she told him, keeping her voice low. "But she was quiet through it all, and when we finished, she started crying. When I asked her what was wrong, all she said was, "I remembered something. I need to talk to Jake."

Jake turned away. "*Damn* it! It must have something to do with Brad Buckley!"

"Stay calm, like you were when you first found her after she was taken. She doesn't need you upset and roaring mad about Buckley. It's all about *her* right now. You go in there cussing and swearing and blaming yourself, you'll just make things worse. She needs the gentleness you showed her after it happened."

Jake put his hands against the front wall and sighed. "How do I control this rage first?"

"You control it by thinking about how much you love

Mother." Evie rubbed her hand over his back. "Hold her and listen to her and love her, like you did with me at Dune Hollow, and like you did with her after you found her and took her to the cabin on Echo Ridge. When I realized she was brooding about something, I sent for Gretta, just to sit and make small talk, and so she wouldn't be alone with her thoughts. But It's *you* she needs, Daddy."

Jake turned to Evie. "It's as hard for me to talk about what happened as it is her. I'm afraid I'll say the wrong thing – trigger the wrong memories."

"Staying calm will help her. I think all she needs is to talk. Just let *her* talk. You need Mother to be strong just the same as she needs that from you. You feed off each other's strengths. Lloyd would tell you the same thing. Remember how he helped you when it first happened? I wish he was here right now. Is he really okay?"

"He's fine. Not much gets past Lloyd. You know that. I thank God that when I'm gone all of you will still have Lloyd to look after you. He'll be here come morning."

"Then I'll go reassure Katie. She was worried about him. In the meantime, let Mother talk. If she's remembered something, let her get it out."

Jake reached down and untied his holsters, then straightened to unbuckle his gun belt.

"Please tell me you didn't have to use those guns earlier," Evie asked him.

"I didn't – but not because I didn't *want* to."

Evie patted his chest. "You are hopeless. Go take care of my mother."

She leaned up and kissed his cheek.

"I'm going over to Katie's now."

She left, and Jake went inside, his heart racing with worry over the woman who sat in that big chair – the woman who was his reason for living – the woman who had gone through so much and now had to deal with ugly memories because of who she was married to. He stood there fighting the urge to throw his gun belt as far as he could and then start bashing everything in sight. He forced back his anger. Randy didn't need him to be angry right now. He turned and hung his guns high over the door like he always did, then locked the door.

Randy sat watching him silently.

He ambled to where she sat and leaned close, bracing his hands on either side of her. "I'm here, baby. Tell me what's going on."

Randy touched his face. "First tell me Lloyd is okay."

"Lloyd is fine. And no, there wasn't any shooting. I'll tell you about it after you tell me what happened today."

"You have to promise not to get upset, Jake. I don't want you blaming yourself."

He kissed her lightly. "I won't get upset. I already promised Evie, and I hate breaking promises to women I love."

"You hate breaking promises to *any* woman."

Randy put her arms around his neck and Jake wrapped her in his arms and lifted her out of the chair. He turned and sat down in the chair himself, pulling her onto his lap.

"Talk to me."

Randy rested her head on his shoulder. "After you left this morning, I gathered the eggs I needed to make the dough for noodles. As I was coming out of the hen house, Charlie McGee saw a coyote sneaking out from under the shed nearby, and he shot it. It startled me. One of the other men—Terrel, I think—cheered, and then he picked up the coyote and said something like, 'Should we bury the sonofabitch or just throw him out in the foothills for the wolves?' It hit me then - this vague memory of one of our men saying that about Brad Buckley." She swallowed and wiped at her eyes. "I … killed him … didn't I?"

Jake ordered himself to stay calm. He stroked Randy's hair, which was brushed out long. "Baby, you don't need to suffer any guilt over killing that man. Understand? After what he did to you, there isn't a judge or jury in this country who'd blame you for it. If you could have found a way to shoot him before we got there, you still would have done it in self-defense. And you had every right." He kissed her hair.

"But you *were* all there. You had him down, but I walked out of that horrible little shack they had me in, and I shot him anyway, before you realized what I was going to do."

"All you did was spare him a lot of misery. I never would have ended his life that quickly. And now that shack is burned to the ground and Buckley and those other two are buried deep on the *J&L* where they will never be found. And no one who was there will ever talk about it to the outside world."

Randy wilted against his chest. "But so many men were there. And Lloyd. Stephen and Ben - even Little Jake. I took Vance's gun right out of his holster." She curled tighter against him.

Jake felt like tearing the room apart. "Those men love and respect you as much as I do. There isn't a one there that day who wouldn't die for you. As far as they're concerned, they didn't see a thing, understand? Even those boys, as young as they were, understood. They cried because they blamed themselves for not being able to protect you from the men who took you. I damn well understand how that feels. Lloyd and Brian and I had to do a lot of talking to those boys to make them understand it wasn't their fault."

"Oh, Jake, they got hurt trying to help me. I . . . remember. And I ... Jake, how could I forget something as awful as walking up and killing a man?"

"Look at me, Randy."

She met his gaze, and Jake wiped tears from her cheeks. "You didn't remember because the goodness in you didn't *want* to remember. I know what that is like, better than most. I *struggle* with ugly memories day and night, so any time you need to talk about it, then *talk* about it. You're always the one telling me that. And remember that I don't pretty things up. When I tell you how something is, that's exactly how it is, and I'm telling you that I don't ever want to see shame or embarrassment or sorrow in those beautiful eyes over this. Not ever. Understand? Remember Echo Ridge? We healed there after what happened—both of us. So please don't fall back into being the woman I hardly knew after that. You're stronger than that. I lost you emotionally for a long time."

Randy settled against his shoulder again. "You were so patient with me. I was afraid you wouldn't be able to love me anymore."

"*Nothing* could make me stop loving you. How could you ever doubt that? And as rough and lawless as some of the men on this ranch can be, they live by a code that doesn't allow hurting a woman, whether she's some man's wife, or if she lives over a saloon. They honor and respect you too much to ever give Buckley's death and how it happened another thought."

Randy kissed his neck. "All those years ago, after you got out of prison and we went to Outlaw Country to find Lloyd and rescue him . . . I had to shoot two of those men with that shotgun you gave me. That never bothered me because it was truly in self-defense, and to save my son. I had no choice. But with Brad Buckley . . . " She hesitated.

"Honey, the reason doesn't matter."

"To me it does. I shot him because I *wanted* him to die. I have never felt that way, before or since. And I shot him because I didn't want that judge who'd almost hanged you in Denver to hear you'd killed Brad Buckley. I shot him so no one could say Jake Harkner killed him."

"Baby, you had been through hell and you weren't even in your right mind. You hardly knew what you were doing. All the outside world needs to know is that Brad Buckley left Denver after my trial and was never heard from again."

"I just . . . I don't know how to feel about it." She closed her eyes. "Do you think God will forgive me for shooting that man without any feeling?"

Jake couldn't help a silent grin. "You're asking *me* about forgiveness and regrets? Pray with Evie about it, Randy. Lord knows I can't help you in that department."

"She prays for you, too, you know. And don't tell me you have no regrets."

"The only thing I regret is thinking I had the right to fall in love with you and marry you. I knew damn well how hard life would be for you – like just now – you having to remember something awful."

"I made the choice to marry you, Jake. I was completely aware of what could happen. You were still a wanted man, but look how it all ended up. Whether you like to admit it or not, God has blessed you."

Jake kissed her hair. "And the way it all turned out is thanks to you. Not me. You, *mi esposa,* are the only light in that tunnel I live in—the only thing that's soft and good and calm in my life. I need my strong, bossy wife to keep me in line, so don't fall apart on me again."

"I won't, as long as I have these arms around me. It helps to talk about it, so *you* need to talk to *me,* too, Jake. And don't think you don't deserve Evie's prayers. I know you believe, because you've kept your mother's Crucifix all these years, and sometimes you even wear it under your shirt."

"Sure I believe. I just don't think I have a right to bother God with the messes I make out of life."

"You don't cause those messes. Others bring them *to* you. Which reminds me – " Randy sat up straighter and faced him. "What happened out there today, with Lloyd and Vance?"

Jake pulled her closer. "It doesn't matter. No one got hurt, including the trespassers we ran off."

Randy sighed and ran her fingers through his hair. "You've had a long day. Let's go upstairs so you can get undressed and go to bed."

He put a hand to the side of her face and kissed her. "You sure?"

"Yes. I'm sorry you had to come home to this."

"I'm not, because now I can stop worrying about when you might remember things you shouldn't have to remember. I was afraid this day would come." He stroked her cheek. "You sure you're okay?"

"Now that you're home safe from Mexico, and I have these arms around me every night? I'm all right." She settled into his arms again.

"This is such a safe place, right here in your arms. Nothing bad can happen to me when these arms are around me."

"Did you ever stop to think that you are *my* safe place?" Jake asked her softly.

What would he do without her? Thank God tonight hadn't taken her back to that lost, frightened woman he hardly knew just after her abduction. He loved her for her strength, for the way she understood him, for the way she loved him in spite of all his unforgiveable faults.

"Tell me who you belong to, *mi vida*."

"Jake Harkner," she answered softly.

"You bet. And nothing will ever change that, or change

how I feel about you. And no man will ever touch you wrongly again. Understand? Not ever."

"I understand."

They sat there quietly, until Jake felt her breathing softly in sleep. He fell asleep himself for a while, then roused awake and kissed her hair. *I do pray sometimes,* he wanted to tell her. *I just don't see why God would listen to a man like me. I lost my chance at Heaven a long time ago.*

"*You're* my heaven," he whispered. He managed to pick her up as he got out of the chair, then carried her up the stairs to bed.

## CHAPTER 11

Jake came down from the bedroom for a cup of coffee, moving to where Randy stood in front of a coal cook stove. He embraced her from behind. "You okay?"

"Yes." She turned her head slightly to let him kiss her. Randy smiled lovingly. "Just *be* with me. That's all I need."

Jake pulled her close and kissed her hair.

"Just so you're okay with what we talked about last night."

"I am."

Jake glanced at a coo-coo clock on the wall. "My gosh, it's nearly eleven. I can't remember the last time I slept this late."

"You had a trying day yesterday, what with going after those nesters and then coming home to an upset wife." Randy met his gaze. "Have you told me everything about yesterday?"

"We chased off some people who just wanted to make trouble, and that's that."

Randy pulled away and grasped his hands. "You didn't shoot anyone?"

He grinned and shook his head. "Hell, no." He kissed

her again. "I'm more worried about the condition you were in when I got home." He pulled her close again, and she hugged him around his middle. "Tell me true, Randy."

"I am all right. Evie was already over this morning, asking if we're going to have our normal family dinner, or if we needed more time alone. She's concerned because we didn't show up this morning at the barn for her worship service." She looked up at Jake. "I told her we worked things out, and that I wanted to have everybody over like always."

Jake leaned down and kissed her forehead.

"Good. And I'll be glad when the men finish building that chapel for Evie. She deserves a better place than a barn to hold her services. They complain that nine o'clock on a Sunday morning is too early, but they respect her so much that they always show up, even if some of them got a little too drunk the night before."

Randy smiled. "She holds those services early because she wants to get home in time to help cook Sunday dinner. And maybe those early services will cure some of them from downing too much whiskey on Saturday night." She leaned back and touched his arm.

"I think Chicago will be good for us. We've never taken a trip like that together, and it's been a long time since it was just the two of us, except for when we go to Echo Ridge." She ran her hands over the hard muscle of his arms. "You didn't get hurt yesterday, did you?"

"Do I *look* hurt? Just pour me some coffee and quit worrying."

Randy turned to pour the coffee, and Jake looked past her at the stove. "I don't see you doing much cooking – not like you normally do."

"Evie is cooking the chicken, and Katie's mother is making potatoes. I'm just responsible for pies and bread, and both are already made." She poured herself some coffee. "Our sweet daughter didn't want me to have to do too much today. She said they've all decided we'll have dinner this way from now on, so no one of us has to do all the work. This family is getting too big." She poured a second cup and set both on the kitchen table. "We'd better sit here a few minutes and enjoy the peace and quiet before the whole brood comes barging in."

Jake watched her lovingly as she took some homemade butter from the ice box and set it on the table, along with three loaves of bread. "It wouldn't matter to me if all we ate was that bread of yours. Nobody in Colorado makes better bread."

Randy sat down across from him. "Well, thank you. You've talked about my bread the whole time we've been together. It's almost a joke among the family – how much Jake Harkner loves his wife's bread."

"And that's not all I love about you." Jake looked her over lovingly.

"By the way, I like the idea of sharing the cooking. You're right about the family getting too big. When we go to Chicago, I want you to do absolutely nothing but enjoy yourself. I'm sure Lawyer Peter will help me there."

Randy shook her head. "Don't start, Jake. I'm sure Jeff and Peter will be wonderful hosts, and Peter will be a pure gentleman, like he always is."

"He'll be all of that, but I know what he *really* wants, and what he really wants belongs to *me*."

Randy sipped some coffee. "Peter is our good friend. Besides, I'm the one who will have to stay extra alert in Chicago. Some of those fancy, refined women there have never met a man like you . . . all rough and rugged and handsome. They probably read those dime novels about men like you. They will be stumbling all over themselves for your attention." She threw her head back and put a hand to her forehead. "Oh, save me! Save me!" she mocked.

Jake couldn't help laughing.

Randy gave him a look of mock scolding. "You just might find some of them hard to resist."

Jake shook his head and laughed again. "Right now, I just want to come over there and save *you*, and you know what I mean. Too bad the family is on their way over. He got up and walked around to pull her out of her chair. "Grab your coffee and come sit with me by the fireplace until everybody gets here. You look like you're still tired. Come sit on my lap and put your head on my shoulder and get some more rest."

Randy took both cups into the great room of their large log home, where Jake sat down in his leather chair and pulled her onto his lap, then drank a little more coffee. Randy settled against his shoulder as he moved his arms around her, creating that safe, safe place she loved. "Do you know how much I love your smile?"

"You *make* me smile. I didn't do a lot of smiling before I met you."

"Yes, well, it's that smile that got me into all this trouble. You're quite irresistible, you know."

Jake chuckled. "Lord, woman, you sure know how to ask for trouble."

Randy smiled and closed her eyes. She slept lightly as they sat there enjoying a quiet house - until they heard the clamor of footsteps on the front porch. The front door opened.

"Mother?"

It was Evie, followed by Brian, who carried a huge pan of fried chicken. Evie noticed her parents relaxing in her father's chair. "Oh! Did we come too soon?"

"Of course not." Randy sat up and smoothed a piece of

hair behind her ear. She and Jake both rose, and Randy hurried over to help Brian with the food.

Jake gave his daughter a hug. "We were just resting. Yesterday was a long day, but I don't mind being interrupted when it's because of my beautiful daughter." He leaned down to kiss her forehead.

Evie grasped his wrists. "Is everything okay with mother?"

"Everything is fine."

"I'm glad of that, but what about you? Lloyd says he had to warn you not to go too far yesterday. I know what you're like when you're angry and think you're defending us, so you must have come home upset, and then you had to deal with Mother."

"Evie, I'm used to dealing with your mother, and she's used to dealing with me. *That's* the hard part. As far as yesterday, I managed to keep my temper in check. Now, go help your mother."

Evie left to help in the kitchen. Jake picked up his coffee and stood by the fireplace, safely away from the ensuing procession.

Young Jake came in next, carrying Cole. Esther toddled behind, and Sadie Mae came bounding in last. She ran up to Jake and reached up. Jake set his coffee aside and picked the girl up, giving her a kiss on the cheek. She put her arms around her grandpa and rested her head against his chest as more family members came in.

Lloyd was next, carrying a big bowl of mashed potatoes and followed by Katie, leading Jeffrey by the hand. Katie's mother, Clara, carried Donavan and Katie's father, Patrick, carried Tricia.

Last of all was Stephen, carrying a pan that he announced was the gravy. "Where should I put this?"

Bedlam took over. Every grandchild clamored around

Jake, while Lloyd fussed over Katie, insisting she sit down and do nothing.

When Young Ben came in, he announced he'd stayed overnight at the bunkhouse.

"The *bunkhouse?*" Lloyd shook his head. "You won't learn anything over there but dirty jokes, womanizing, drinking, cards, and cussing."

"Sounds like the perfect upbringing," Jake called out from the fireplace.

Everybody snickered, and Ben's face turned red. "Heck, Lloyd, all I did was work with Charlie McGee," the boy answered. "He taught me some stuff about blacksmithing. If I'm gonna' help out around here, I have to know all of it, don't I?"

Lloyd grinned. "I expect you do."

"Jake, I heard about that mess that happened yesterday." Patrick Donavan told Jake, walking closer. "Lloyd got back just in time to clean up and change for Evie's worship service."

"Well, Patrick, we have to handle things like that, or we'll end up in a range war," Jake replied. "These new laws for settlers are a big problem for free-range grazing." He kept an eye on Randy, who hated talk about anything that meant danger for him or Lloyd, but she didn't seem to hear.

She was in her most joyous mood when surrounded by family.

Vance showed up with a block of ice for the ice box. Jake set Sadie Mae on her feet and walked to the kitchen. "Stephen, open the bottom of the ice box for Vance."

"Smells good in here," Vance said when he finished. He tipped his hat to the women and bowed to Randy when he passed by. He then glanced at Jake. "I still can't figure out how an old outlaw like you managed to end up with the most beautiful woman in Colorado."

"Because she's smart enough to know that men like you are like that black devil rooster out there," Jake answered. "They can't pick just one hen to stay with."

That brought laughs from everyone.

"You'd better look out, Jake," Vance warned, grinning. "There's not a man out there who wouldn't be clamoring to marry Randy if you broke her heart. So be good to her."

"That thought keeps me on the straight and narrow."

More laughter.

"Daddy, come sit down," Evie told him as Vance left.

Jake gave Randy a supportive hug before sitting and gesturing her to do the same. "Let Evie and Clara do the work."

"Thanks a lot, Daddy," Evie told him.

The day turned into a typical Sunday, except the main topic this time was Jake and Randy's upcoming trip.

"You can fool everybody in Chicago into thinking you're a distinguished, rich cattleman and a gentleman, pa," Lloyd joked. "But we all know better when it comes to the gentleman part."

"Your father *is* a true gentleman when he needs to be," Randy stated.

"Gentleman isn't quite the correct adjective," Katie added.

Randy smiled. "It is around women. The average woman wouldn't guess he had a mean bone in his body."

Lloyd nearly choked on his coffee. "I'm not going to touch that one."

The main course ended, and Clara Donavan set a piece of apple pie in front of Jake as dishes clattered and dessert was laid out.

Lloyd touched Jake's arm. "Is Mom okay?" he asked, lowering his voice.

"I think so. I'll talk to you outside later."

"Randy, you look so tired, dear." Clara patted Randy's hand.

"Jake got home late, and I always wait up for him. Which means we didn't get much sleep last night."

Sadie Mae, always loving her grandfather's attention, climbed onto Jake's lap.

"You make sure you visit a specialist while you're in Chicago, Jake, and see if there's anything that can be done about that leg," Brian told him. "And maybe they've come up with something better than Laudanum for pain. If so, I want to know about it. I'm tired of having to get those cowboys out there drunk before I set a bone or stitch up a gash."

Jake whispered something into Sadie Mae's ear. She covered her mouth and giggled. "Grampa told me a secret!"

"Yes, we all know about you and Grandpa's secrets," Evie answered, "and how you never *keep* them a secret."

"Yes, I do, sometimes," Sadie Mae said, chin in the air.

"I'll bet you can't keep this one any more than you keep the others." Randy came to Jake's side. Folding her arms across her chest, she looked down at her granddaughter. "What did Grandpa just tell you?"

Sadie Mae glanced at Jake, then leaned her head back and looked up at Randy. "Grampa said you aren't really the boss. He said you just *think* you are."

Randy looked at Jake. "Is that so?" She leaned down and kissed him. "We need to have another talk so I can set you straight, Mr. Harkner."

Young Jake snickered. "Grampa thinks Grandma's the prettiest woman there ever was. I do, too."

"Well, thank you, Jake," Randy told him. "Coming from Big Jake, I'm prone to take those words with a grain of salt. But from you, I know they're genuine."

"I mean it, Grandma."

Jake finished his pie and got up from the table. "When you're done cleaning up here," he told Randy, "Go get some rest. That's an order from the *real* boss." He glanced at Lloyd. "Come on outside with me. I need a cigarette."

Both men walked to a nearby corral and leaned against a railing.

Jake lit a cigarette and took a deep drag.

"So, tell me my mother isn't going to slip back into that awful depression she suffered after that mess with Brad Buckley," Lloyd told his father. "Evie told me about last night and that she thought it had something to do with that." He lit his own cigarette.

Jake watched some of the children playing on the porch. "She remembered shooting Brad Buckley."

Lloyd closed his eyes. "Shit."

"I convinced her Buckley was already dying, and all she did was put him out of his misery. God knows I was ready to kill the sonofabitch myself. A few seconds later and he would have been dead." Jake drew on the cigarette again. "She knew it. She said she did it so no one could tell that judge in Denver that I did it." Jake watched a bird land on the chicken coop roof. Squawking, the devil rooster chased it away. "I think she was more upset about the condition she was in at the time. She was half out of her mind. It bothers her that you and the men were there and all she had was that blanket around her."

Lloyd pulled his hair behind his shoulders. "She's my mother, so I don't even count. And all the men choose to remember is helping capture Buckley and those other two and burying them good and deep. They all love mom and want to protect her."

"That's what I told her. Part of me is glad she remembered, so I don't have to worry every day about what it might do to her. I was afraid she would pull back into that world again of being afraid all the time, but I think it brought us closer together," Jake said quietly. "It also made me remember how wrong I was not to be there for her other times when she needed me most. When it comes to being the perfect husband, I'm sure not the best man for the job."

Cinnamon trotted over to nudge at Lloyd's shoulder. The horse whinnied softly, and Lloyd reached behind him and petted its nose. "Mom loves the hell out of you, and you know it. She understands everything you do and how you think. I'm glad you two are making that trip to Chicago. She needs that. She's excited about it."

"I know. I don't like leaving you and the J&L with trouble maybe brewing, and I'm not much for big cities, but Randy will enjoy it. That trip will be like a long, long overdue honeymoon."

Lloyd grinned. "Long overdue is no exaggeration. And don't worry about what's going on here at home. The trouble doesn't apply to just the J&L. The government is selling off free range, and that affects *all* the ranchers, so I won't be alone in whatever happens." He turned around and scratched Cinnamon's ears, then kissed his nose. "I don't want you and Mom worrying while you're gone. I'm a big boy now, remember?"

Jake smiled sadly. "You're also my son."

Father and son stood there, practically twins in looks, smoking quietly and watching a couple of the men herd some mustangs into a corral in the distance. From inside the house, they could hear common family chatter and laughter, the clinking dishes. Donavan came running out of the house then, and Stephen charged out to catch him.

"Come back here, you little devil!" Stephen yelled.

"Donavan runs like a damn deer on those chubby little legs." Lloyd grinned. "It's part of the reason Katie needs help. She can't keep up with him."

Both men laughed, but Jake sensed Lloyd's worry. "How is Katie, *really?*"

Lloyd sighed "I'm not sure. She's so tired all the time, and she wasn't that way with any of the other babies. Stephen and I and her parents help all we can with the little ones." Lloyd drew deeply on his cigarette, then added haltingly. "I can't lose her, Pa." He cleared his throat and swallowed. "I just can't."

Jake watched Stephen chase Donavan around a watering trough. "Lloyd, your mother and I aren't going to Chicago until the baby is born. We're going up to Echo Ridge after the Twisted Tree cookout, so you can send for us there if you need us, but we aren't going any father until we know Katie and the baby are okay."

Lloyd nodded and took the cigarette from his lips. "She's so goddamn beautiful, isn't she?"

"She's the prettiest woman on this ranch, and that's saying a lot when you think of how beautiful Evie and your mother are. And she's a great mother. You picked the best when you married her. That's at least one good thing that happened when we lived in Guthrie."

Lloyd wiped at his eyes with his shirtsleeve. "Yeah." He shook his head. "You and I sure had some wild times hunting down men in No Man's Land, didn't we?"

"I couldn't have done it without you."

Katie came out of the house. "I'm going to go take a nap, Lloyd," she called to him.

Lloyd straightened and sighed. "See what I mean?" he told Jake. "She sleeps all the time. That's not like her, even in the latest months of pregnancy." He stepped out his cigarette. "I'd better go with her." He started off, then turned. "You sure Mom's okay?"

"I'm just taking it one day at a time. Your mother is my job. You just go take care of Katie."

Lloyd rushed over to take Katie's arm, and Jake

thought what a handsome couple they made, and such a stark contrast—Lloyd's nearly-black hair hanging well past his shoulders, and Katie's as red as desert rocks. She'd come into Lloyd's life at just the right time.

He watched as Lloyd put an arm around her shoulders.

"Jesus," Jake muttered, this time using the name in prayer. "Don't take that woman from my son."

He thought how strange it was that a man could be so big and strong and able and brave but fall to pieces over a woman. He was no different. Without Randy, he might as well end his life and blow away in the wind.

# CHAPTER 12

Late June .. .

"Well, if it isn't the esteemed Attorney Peter Brown." Jeff stood up from his desk at the *Chicago Journal* and put out his hand. "To what do I owe this honor, as if I don't already know?"

The debonaire Peter grinned as he shook hands with the reporter. "Jeff, you know better than to treat me like royalty. We're too good of friends for that. Sit the hell down." He took a chair at the other side of Jeff's desk as Jeff took his own seat. "How are the wife and little ones?" he asked Jeff.

"They are all fine." The fact that Peter lived in a mansion in the wealthiest part of Chicago, and ran with the city's elite lawmakers, councilmen, and even the mayor, did not make Jeff feel uneasy. Peter was one of those rare men of wealth who was relaxed and easy around any man, wealthy or not. "Let me guess," Jeff added, "you're here to talk about Jake's up-coming visit. And more to the point, *Miranda*'s visit."

Peter removed his top hat, and Jeff wondered how the

man managed to keep his hair looking perfect, even after taking a hat off and on all day.

"Yes," Peter answered. "I thought we should talk about that. Is there any news from Colorado . . . of the wild shootout kind we sometimes hear about Jake?"

Jeff laughed. "No. Things have been quiet, as far as I know, but then I never know what will be in Randy's next letter, or in tomorrow's headlines, for that matter."

Peter shook his head. "With Jake, the story *never* ends. But my memories are a little different from yours. I never got to ride with him like you did, but I sure remember the ruckus and the crowds of Guthrie citizens who gathered every time Jake came back dragging outlaws behind him —more often dead than alive."

"And every time he returned, he'd give that whistle, and Randy would run up the street to greet him."

Peter sobered. "And every time he left, Randy worried over whether he'd make it back alive. I watched the hell she went through. It was the only reason she worked for me back then—to stay busy and keep her mind off Jake and Lloyd's dangerous work."

Jeff studied the change in Peter's demeanor. He knew how much the man loved Randy Harkner. "Have you heard from Treena?" He deliberately changed the subject to Peter's wife.

Peter nodded. "I got word that she made it to France just fine. It's just too bad that the reason she had to go was because her mother is sick. She would have loved to entertain Jake and Randy."

"I believe her term for Jake is 'the Magnificent' Jake Harkner."

Peter grinned. "The Magnificent Jake Harkner is why I'm here. Jake and Randy will arrive in a month or so, and you and I need to make plans. I want Randy to see museums, art galleries, the opera and live theater. And the way she tends those roses of hers, she'd love the Lincoln Park Conservatory. I also want to arrange for some of Treena's women friends to take her shopping. And I think I'll have a gathering at my house, a *big* one – a regular ball, dancing and an orchestra and all. A lot of important people want to meet Jake, including the mayor."

"I've a feeling Jake would rather see the stock yards - see where J&L cattle end up when they're shipped east," Jeff added. "I can't quite picture him at an opera. As far as a ball, you know how he hates any kind of public attention, although he won't have much choice once he's here. He is able to make the best of things if he has to, but sometimes he has to grit his teeth to do it. A ball sounds like something Randy would love, so he'll put up with it for her sake."

"The man does have a way of rising to the occasion." Peter stared at his hat. "Put him in an expensive suit, and the high society women will turn their heads and giggle behind their lace fans when he's around. Like you said in your book, the man walks into a room, no matter how big, and just fills it up." He rubbed at his eyes. "I was going to put them up at the Palmer House, but I've decided they can stay at my place instead. It's quieter there, and they can have some privacy, sit and watch the lake, things that would keep Jake a bit more out of the limelight and away from **situations** that might light his fuse and get him in trouble. God knows he needs a relaxing getaway even more than Randy does."

"Good idea. Those two will experience as much luxury at your castle of a home as they would at the Palmer House. Maybe more. And I'm sure you're worried more about Randy's comfort than Jake's."

Peter shrugged. "I can't deny that."

Jeff adjusted his round-rimmed glasses and felt a little

self-conscious in his plain tweed suit. Peter was pure, slick money, but amazingly kind and easy to talk to. They had remained friends since coming home from Guthrie. Both had been at Jake's hearing in Denver, where Peter acted as Jake's defense attorney, and both had gone to Mexico to search for Jake when he didn't return from rescuing Gretta MacBain's daughter . . . and both mourned when they were convinced Jake had been killed there and lay in some unknown grave.

"Jake and Randy have never taken a trip together, not for enjoyment, anyway, so this will be a very different experience for them. Denver is growing, but it doesn't compare to Chicago. We have nearly a million people now. It's going to be quite a contrast to living in a remote area of Colorado with only family and cowboys and cattle and horses around."

Peter nodded. "That's certain. I want to make sure they enjoy this trip without problems."

Jeff grinned. "Sometimes that's a tall order where Jake is involved." Both men snickered as Jeff leaned back in his chair. "Just don't forget my description of Jake in my book, Peter . . . Nitroglycerine. Shake it up just a little, and the explosion can devastate. I've no doubt that down deep inside Jake thinks about what a good life Randy could be leading if married to someone like you and living in luxury."

Peter leaned forward and rested his elbows on his knees, staring at the floor. "I'm no fool, Jeff. I've seen that nitro explode, but Jake knows how I feel. We've been through enough together that he trusts me. Besides, not only am I a married man, but there isn't a man alive who would even *think* about trying to come between Jake and Randy. I resigned myself to that a long time ago, which is why I married Treena."

Peter couldn't help thinking about when he left

Chicago all those years before to practice law in the fast-growing city of Guthrie, Oklahoma—a way of dealing with the memory of his first wife's death. Then Jake Harkner came to town as a U. S. Marshal, sentenced to service by a judge who figured the gunman was perfect for helping bring law and order to the most dangerous territory in the West. "An outlaw chasing outlaws," was how the judge had put it. Who knew better how to track the worst no-goods in the country than someone who had been in their shoes?

And track them Jake did—with a vengeance. If risking his life in No Man's Land was the only way to stay out of prison and be with his wife and children, he was willing to do it. But it had been so hard on Randy, who'd taken a part time job working for Peter. And what lonely widower would *not* fall for such a kind, beautiful woman as Randy Harkner?

"Jake is by no means poor," Peter told Jeff. "Thanks to his share of the royalties from your book and that reward he got for stopping that bank robbery in Boulder. Of course, Lloyd's inheritance from his first wife didn't hurt either, and the *J&L* has done well."

"Jake gave most of that reward money to his kids," Jeff reminded him. "He didn't feel right taking it, since he used to rob banks himself. He's a surprisingly humble man when you get down to it."

Peter leaned back in his chair. "He's a hard man to figure. Damned unpredictable for the most part. And although I have some family trust documents Jake will need to sign while he's here, the real reason for this trip is to show Randy a good time. So, I am wondering if you have any other ideas besides the obvious for entertaining our famous friends."

Jeff ran a finger over his chin. "So far, I think your

plans are fine." Removing his glasses, he cleaned them with a handkerchief as he spoke. "Entertaining Randy will be easy, but Jake's interests couldn't be more removed from his wife's. Besides the stockyards, he might like going to the shooting range at the Chicago Armory. Given his reputation, some of your friends would probably like to see him shoot."

"Probably so, but Jake doesn't like being singled out in a way that looks like he's showing off," Peter replied. "He's humble about that, too, and he's not proud of his past. I have to think about a way to convince him to display his shooting skills without him feeling like he's being asked to put on a show."

"Why not have your friends ask Jake for some tips? Rather than just having him to show how he draws and shoots, they could make it look more like a teaching experience. Jake takes those guns pretty seriously, and he trained Lloyd in a way that he respects guns and the right way to use them. He's doing the same with his grandsons."

Peter shifted in his chair then glanced at his gold pocket watch. "I like your idea about the shooting range and the stockyards." He took a cigar from an inside pocket of his suit jacket. "Want a smoke?"

"No, thanks. And I'd offer you a drink, but all we have around here is pitchers of water, although I know of a few reporters who hide bottles of something else in their desk drawers. And I might be able to find some coffee somewhere."

"That's okay." Peter lit his cigar and puffed on it a moment, then set it in an ashtray on Jeff's desk. "Actually, I have an appointment in about an hour. With the traffic building in this city, and horses and buggies getting tangled up with more and more automobiles and street cars, it will take me a good half hour to get to my office, so I'll have to leave pretty soon."

"I suppose you're driving that Columbia Motor Buggy of yours."

"No. I'm actually using horse and buggy today. Just thought I'd stop here first to see what you thought about an itinerary for Jake and Randy. They had one of their men ride to Brighton and wire me – said to go ahead and make train reservations for ten days or so after the Fourth of July. I think they go to a big shindig at some other ranch on the Fourth, and they hope Lloyd and Katie's new baby is born not long after that. I've set things up so that, barring any delays, they'll arrive at Grand Central July fifteenth around four p.m. Jake's wire asked me to reserve a Pullman, which tells me he wants to make things as comfortable for Randy as possible."

"I'm sure he does. And once he gets here, I want to be present for everything he does. My readers will want a blow-by-blow report. They love that column I write about Jake. I'll wait with you at Grand Central on the fifteenth. I don't want to miss Jake's arrival, as it's bound to be an event. How long are they staying?"

"Three weeks, give or take. I didn't buy return tickets because I figured I'd let them decide when they're ready to leave. I think it will depend on how much Randy is enjoying herself."

Peter rose, and Jeff stood up to walk to the door with the man. "This is Jake's Christmas present to Randy, so yes, he'll let her stay as long as she wants," he told Peter. "Their visit should be very interesting. Jake is a lot more famous than he realizes. He has no idea the kind of reception he will likely receive. The family doesn't even see a newspaper until it's at least a week old, but at least they have electricity now."

"And a beautiful home," Peter added. "It's certainly

rustic compared to life here, but in spite of all the luxuries I have, I admire that beautiful location of theirs, nestled against the Rocky Mountain foothills. The West is just about the prettiest country in the world, and I've *seen* other countries."

"And things are growing out there on the J&L – the family – the ranch. Randy wrote in her last letter that Evie is having the men build a little chapel at the homestead so she can hold Sunday services there and use it as a schoolhouse during the week."

Peter kept the cigar between his teeth as he spoke. "Evie is quite the woman of faith – hard to believe, considering what she went through back in Oklahoma. It's amazing how well she recovered from that. Her eyes are usually glowing with joy and prayer."

Jeff nodded. "She and Katie and Evie all take turns teaching the children now. Randy helps, too. She's the one who schooled Lloyd and Evie, and those two seem just as educated as if they'd gone to school their entire youth."

Peter took his cigar from his mouth and smiled. "She taught Jake, too. He told me he could barely read when he met Randy. His father never let him go to school."

Both men sobered. "Yes, well, that's a pretty sore subject I hope no one brings up while Jake is here." Jeff put on a smile. "But . . . it's time to put the past behind us and look forward to a visit from the infamous Jake Harkner."

Peter extended his hand. "I'll see you on the fifteenth." He put on his hat, picked up his cigar and started through the door, then turned. "And God help us," he added.

Jeff burst into laughter. "I've already thought that same thing. A visit from Jake is enough to make this Jewish man pray to Christ Himself that all goes well."

This time the laughter came from Peter, who continued laughing all the way out the door.

Jeff walked to a window to study the busy street below.

"Yes," he muttered. "God help us." He was glad, though. He missed Jake. Questionable reputation or not, a man couldn't ask for a better friend, once he managed to break through that wall Jake built around himself.

## CHAPTER 13

"I love these rare moments when roundup and branding are over, and things quiet down for a few days." Randy leaned back to enjoy a breeze across the shaded veranda, while several grandchildren played near a watering trough, splashing water on each other to stay cool.

Jake drank some lemonade she'd poured for them, then leaned back in his own chair. "Quiet makes me nervous," he answered. "That calm before the storm feeling."

"Well, maybe for once it will *stay* calm," Randy suggested.

"Always optimistic, aren't you?"

"I *have* to be where you are involved."

Jake watched dust billowing in the distance. "Speaking of calm before the storm—someone's coming." He stood up and waited, giving a whistle he knew would bring Lloyd from behind the barn, where he and Cole were urging a new bull to mate with one of several "chosen" cows.

In minutes Jake recognized Tommy Tyler's horse. Randy also stood up as the young man reached the house and reined to a sliding stop.

Jake stepped off the veranda and grabbed the horse's bridle. "Whoa, there, Tommy! You've worked this bay up to a lather."

Tommy dismounted. "I was headed out to relieve Charlie, Sir, when Rodriguez came riding up, all excited. He rattled off to me in Spanish, so I had to calm him down and get him to speak English." He removed his hat and wiped sweat from his forehead. "Rodriguez said to tell you Marshal Kraemer and a couple of his deputies are headed this way."

"Oh, no," Randy said softly.

Jake looked past Tommy to see riders far off on the northern horizon. "Go put up this horse, and don't let her drink or eat yet."

"Yes, Sir."

Tommy hurried off, and Jake stepped up onto the veranda. Lloyd was already headed their way, Terrel right behind him.

"Pa, what's going on?"

Jake leaned against a support post. "Hal Kraemer and a couple deputies are coming."

Lloyd tossed his hat onto a chair. "Damn. Fillmore probably got to him and told him a dandy story about what happened between you and him."

"Yeah. I don't think Grizzly Smith and that bunch have had time to reach Kraemer with their own bullshit story, but he might have – and you *know* Fillmore has." Jake glanced at Randy. "Don't be upset. I'm sure he's just checking out Fillmore's story."

"But that judge in Denver is always asking Marshal Kraemer to check up on you," Randy told him. "I'm afraid he'll come up with some excuse to arrest you."

Jake laid his cigarette in an ashtray and walked over to grasp her arms. "Make sure there is plenty of lemonade and stop worrying. Everything will be fine. I've been expecting this after that run-in with Fillmore when the girls were with me. Bring the lemonade and some glasses out here. Let's be cordial to the marshal. I haven't done anything wrong."

Randy gave out a big sigh and went inside while Jake leaned against a support post and waited, smoking quietly.

"Katie gets upset, too," Lloyd told him. He lit his own cigarette. "I'm not exactly always a good boy myself." He yelled to Stephen, who was dunking Young Jake in the watering trough. The two boys were always tussling, and today they had no chores. Both boys, shirtless, came running over. "Stephen, go tell Katie that Marshal Kraemer is coming in—just to talk and catch up on things. Tell her to stay inside where it's cool and not to worry. I don't want her getting upset in her condition."

"Sure, pa." Stephen ran off, and Young Jake watched the horizon.

"Is there really nothing to worry about?" Jake's namesake asked.

"Far as I know," Jake answered. "If he asks about that day we took the girls riding, you just tell him the truth, Jake. Don't be worried and don't try to hide anything."

"Don't you want your guns?" Terrel asked Jake.

"Hell, no. Seeing me standing here with guns on will only make Kraemer more suspicious." He glanced at Lloyd. "I see you aren't wearing a gun, either. Probably best."

"Yeah, well right now I feel pretty naked."

All three men grinned, and Jake noticed that practically every man working at the homestead was walking or riding up, armed to the hilt, and looking like a small army.

"Jesus, you and I sure as hell *don't* need our guns," Jake joked. "Just stand easy, boys," he called out. "Some of you go back to whatever you were doing. All of you standing around here will make me look guilty as hell. Kraemer might think I murdered somebody."

Some of the men laughed. "Terrel, you stay," Jake told him. "You were with me that day we took the girls for a ride."

Vance started to leave with the other men. "Vance, you stay, too," Jake called to him. "You were there the other day when that sonofabitch Grizzly Smith came around. I don't know if that's the reason Kraemer is coming, but we'd better be prepared."

Most of the men disbursed, but by then Cole and Gretta joined Jake and young Jake on the veranda.

Randy came out with the pitcher of lemonade, and after taking it from her, Gretta suggested they sit down.

"You can," Randy told Gretta. "I—I'd rather stand."

By then Evie had also arrived. "I heard," she told her father. "I was with Katie when Stephen came over. Mister and Mrs. Donavan are keeping the little ones inside."

"Good." Jake looked around, noticing Brian also approaching. "Everybody just stay calm and let me and Lloyd do the talking," he announced. "Sit down, like we're just friends and family sitting and visiting on a warm summer afternoon. Stop looking so worried."

Ben and Stephen joined them.

"Mom said she'd stay inside, but she's by the door watching," Stephen told his father.

"Okay. Okay," Jake told the family, holding out his arms defensively. "The more concerned all of you look, the more Kraemer will wonder if something is up." He chuckled at how Vance and Terrel stood at the corner of the porch with guns on and feet slightly spread.

"For God's sake, you two look like you're ready for a gunfight," Jake told them.

"*Should* we be?" Terrel asked.

"Hell no! I'm not even wearing my guns."

Vance and Terrel walked over to a hitching post and leaned against it casually, both men lighting cigarettes. Jake glanced at Randy, hating to see the trace of tears in her eyes. "Come here."

Randy moved to his side, and Jake drew her close. "I told you not to worry."

She put her arm around his back as Rodriguez rode in with Marshal Kraemer and two deputies. They reached the house and slowly dismounted as Rodriguez nodded to Jake. "It is the Marshal, *mi amigo*. I had no choice."

"Of course you didn't," Jake answered. "It's okay, Rodriguez," he told the man in Spanish. "Go put up your horse. Everything is fine."

"*Si, Senor.*"

Kraemer glanced at Vance and Terrel, then moved his gaze to Cole and surveyed the family members on the veranda, some sitting and some standing. He shook his head as he came up the steps. "Jake, in all my pursuits, I've never come across a ruthless sonofabitch who could drum up his own little army as quickly as you can," he joked. "Have I started a war?"

"Don't worry," Jake answered. "I won't let anybody waste his life defending the likes of me. You're safe, Hal."

Kraemer grinned. "Why am I not reassured by those words?"

Jake paused to light another cigarette. "Hal, of all my faults, I never lie." He took a long drag on the cigarette. "To what do we owe the honor of a visit from a United States Marshal?"

"You don't know?"

"I have my suspicions."

Gray hairs showed from beneath Kraemer's wide-brimmed hat. He was a tall, handsome, tough-looking man close to Jake's age. He wore knee-high boots, black cotton pants, a white shirt with string tie, and a lightweight suit coat, his badge pinned to the coat's lapel. He bowed and tipped his hat to Randy, the hundreds of wrinkles on his face from years of riding in the sun showing deeper when he smiled.

"Mrs. Harkner, you are just as beautiful as always." He glanced at Evie. "And you, Mrs. Stewart." He turned his attention to Lloyd. "And where is the lovely Katie?"

"She isn't feeling well," Lloyd answered. "She's resting, and I told her to stay inside. God knows if maybe you're about to say something to upset her."

Kraemer chuckled. "I always get such warm greetings from you and Jake." He turned to his deputies. "Gentlemen, this is the infamous Jake Harkner." He pointed at Jake. "My favorite outlaw." He indicated Lloyd. "And his son, Lloyd, whose reputation is just a tad more respectable than his father's."

"Nice to meet you both," one of them spoke up, nodding toward Jake and then Lloyd. "I think."

Kraemer extended his hand. "Let's break the ice here and shake hands, Jake."

Jake obliged.

"You introduced me as your favorite outlaw, Kraemer. Don't forget that I rode for three years as a Marshal myself. So did Lloyd. We aren't exactly unfamiliar with the law and how things are changing."

"Oh, I haven't forgotten your service, Jake, but I believe you've often referred to those years as one outlaw chasing other outlaws. You don't fool me. You're still an outlaw at heart."

Jake snickered as he laid his cigarette back in the ashtray. "Would you and your men like some lemonade? You must have had a long ride. Did you camp somewhere on the *J&L* last night?"

"I *think* it was *J&L* land," Kraemer answered. "This ranch is so big, it's hard to tell sometimes where it leaves off, and free rangeland begins. Of course, you know about that. Free rangeland, I mean. And you know a lot of it is up for sale and being settled by farmers and smaller ranchers."

"I damn well do know. Do you want some lemonade or not?"

"Thanks. One glass each will do. And we won't be here long. I just wanted my two new deputies to meet you, so they know what you look like." Kraemer nodded toward his deputies as Evie quickly poured three glasses of lemonade. "The man on the left is Robert Snelling," Kraemer told Jake, "And on the right is Bert Zent. They're both still learning the ropes, but they're good shootists and brave young men. They're also rightfully excited about meeting the one and only Jake Harkner. I just hope they never have to *shoot* you."

Jake kept an arm around Randy. "They'd be better off hoping *I* never have to shoot *them*."

Both young men laughed nervously as Evie handed them their lemonade, then handed a glass to Kraemer. "Thank you," Kraemer told her.

"Glad to meet you, Mr. Harkner," Snelling told Jake. "The marshal here has told us a lot about you."

"Has he?" Jake smiled wryly. "I'll bet he didn't make many glowing remarks."

Hal shook his head. "Oh, I praised your skills to no end, Jake, and I also gave them a long list of why you belong in jail."

"Well, hell, Hal, I can't think of one reason. Do you have some kind of new charges against me?"

The marshal took a thin cigar from his pocket and lit it. "Well, there's a man back in Denver by the name of Brady Fillmore who has a wicked-looking broken jaw. He tells me you're the one who broke it."

"I did, and he's goddamn lucky that's *all* he got. That

sonofabitch threatened to arrest me for no good cause. Worse, I had my two granddaughters and two grandsons with me. I wasn't going to let that weasel draw on me and miss, maybe hurting one of my grandchildren. Nor was I going to let him make up some excuse to take me away."

"Fillmore said he didn't do one thing to provoke what you did to him, Jake."

"His just *being* there was enough provocation. I clobbered him so I wouldn't have to shoot him in front of two innocent little girls. And like I said, if he'd gotten off a shot, a stray bullet could have hit one of the kids." Jake let go of Randy and gently pushed her toward Evie. "You should have investigated that bastard deeper before you gave him a badge, Hal. Lloyd came close to hanging Fillmore a couple years ago for stealing a calf and setting fire to some of the *J&L's* best grass. I stopped the hanging because the boys were there, and I didn't want them witnessing that. And instead of hanging him, we made Fillmore sign his land over to the J&L before we let him go. He should have been grateful I spoke up for him, but he's hated us ever since."

"You sure about him stealing cattle?"

"I'm sure. He stole from other ranchers, too. Ask any of them about it. Henry Till was there when we caught Fillmore running from the fire. Clyde Lacey was there, too. Some of *them* wanted to hang him, too. If he shows his face on the *J&L* again, he might not keep his neck out of a noose."

Hal sighed and looked around at the others. "You should have reported that, Jake. We have law and order in Colorado now, remember? Men can't exact their own judgment anymore."

"And you're talking to someone who doesn't give a damn."

"That's my point in coming out here. I understand how

you feel about it, but I'm warning you. That Denver judge still asks about you. Remember that when trouble comes around. Report it to the authorities instead of taking care of it yourself."

Jake pressed his cigarette out in the ashtray. "Lloyd is much better at obeying the law than I am, Hal. He tries to keep me in check, and he's a damned responsible man, a *good* man. And he wasn't there when I had the confrontation with Fillmore a few days ago."

"And I know Lloyd can sometimes tread a little too close to the other side of the law himself, just like you do. But I like you, Jake. We're more alike than you think, except I wear a badge and you don't anymore. You should have taken that job of Range Detective. You could use the badge as an excuse to break men's jaws."

"It's a thought, but my wife likes me around home. My being gone a lot would be too hard on her."

"Well, I can't blame her there." Kraemer nodded to Randy again before turning his gaze back to Jake. "Only God knows why she puts up with the likes of you. You have a beautiful family, Jake. Just keep in mind that they need you, so stay out of trouble."

"I'll do that. And since you said to report things, I'm letting you know something's awry. Something I can't put my finger on. That incident with Fillmore was followed by a visit from a man who knows him, Grizzly Smith. I dealt with him about the same way I dealt with Brady, and he'll probably come to you with his own story. Smith's first name is Frank, and he has a scratchy voice. He got that from me. I shot him across the throat years ago when I rode shotgun for the Yellowjacket Mine. He tried to rob a gold shipment."

"You guarded gold shipments?" Hal shook his head and chuckled. "Jake Harkner, the bank robber? The gun runner? By the way, what other crimes did you commit back then?"

"Too many to name, but what matters now is Grizzly Smith came around, out of nowhere, after years of hating me. He made friends with Brady Fillmore, and his old grudge came alive. I don't think either of them is done trying to make trouble, so keep an eye out."

He explained about Smith and the fake settlers.

"I know about the trouble that some settlers are trying to cause," Hal told Jake. "I've been to some of their meetings. You rest easy and let me take care of things."

Jake came more alert. "They're holding *meetings*? What the hell *else* do you know? Randy and I are leaving for Chicago in a couple of weeks. Should I call off the trip?"

"Absolutely not. I'm sorry, but your presence usually only makes things worse. Believe me, I'm watching this, and I damn well intend to see that things don't turn into some kind of battle. Let me do my job, Jake."

"As long as my family isn't threatened or harmed."

"You just remember that not everything is your fault, Jake. This is a matter of free range. As far as more personal dangers, life is life, and there will always be men who are worthless and men who would love to bring you down."

"You one of them?"

Kraemer laughed and shook his head. "No, thanks. I plan to live to a ripe old age." The marshal's eyes narrowed as he sobered. "Jake, this isn't just about you. It's about the Homestead Act and making sure new settlers don't tread on ranch land that doesn't belong to them. We have people in Denver taking care of things, and I'm making sure simmering water doesn't come to a boil. Understand?"

"All too well."

"Just don't go thinking this is a Harkner thing. It involves *all* cattlemen, and I don't intend for this to end up in a range war. Whether you like it or not, more people are moving into Colorado and have a right to settle on government land—grazing land you cattlemen have always used like your own."

Their gazes held in mutual challenge.

"You'd better be right about keeping things calm, Kraemer," Jake said in a low threat. "I'll do whatever's necessary to keep my family safe, law or no law."

"Most of those nesters don't even know how to use a gun, Jake. Remember that. I don't want innocent people getting hurt. Be fair to those who want to claim some of that free land and build farms the legal way. It's going to happen, and you need to stay out of it."

"We have every intention of accepting those who settle under the law," Lloyd told Hal. "We aren't the type to go hurting innocent people or destroying someone else's property. You know us better than that, Hal."

"I'm counting on that." Hal nodded to Jake. "Take that wife of yours to Chicago and get out of here for a while, Jake. She deserves the trip, and you might save a lot of people a lot of trouble. I think Lloyd knows what to do, but you—" Kraemer shook his head. "You have a way of complicating things."

"Are you ordering me off my own land?"

The marshal smiled sadly. "I'm not that crazy. I'm just warning you—for your own good. And speaking of orders, Judge Carter told me to ask you about one more thing. It's something I wish you'd satisfy for me, too. Tell me truthfully, one last time, that you don't know what happened to Brad Buckley."

Randy let out a little gasp, and Jake pulled her closer. "Why would I give a shit what happened to that man? I've told you that I don't have any idea where he went or if he's dead or alive."

Kraemer shook his head. "Mmm-hmmm. And every

time I ask about Buckley, you kind of dance around the subject. The way your wife just now reacted, I have no doubt you damn well *do* know what happened to him."

"Jake—"

He kept a tight arm around Randy and his gaze on the marshal. "Don't ever mention that man's name in front of me or my wife again, Kraemer. I told you—I don't know anything about what happened to him."

"*I* know!" Randy spoke up.

"Mom!" Lloyd moved beside Randy. "You should go inside."

Evie stepped closer. "Mother, come with me."

"No! I won't let this man keep trying to accuse Jake of something he didn't do!"

"Randy, don't," Jake ordered, keeping her close.

Randy pulled away and squared around on Kraemer. "Brad Buckley was one of the vilest men who ever walked this earth. Compared to him, my husband's a saint who sits at the right hand of God Himself. Gretta knows what kind of man Buckley was. And when a notorious prostitute believes a man is evil, he *is*."

Kraemer frowned and glanced at Gretta, who stepped forward, hands on hips.

"She's right. If I could have gotten away with killing Buckley myself, I would have."

"I won't go into details of how I know what an animal he is," Randy stated. "All I want you to know is that my husband did not kill him. *I* did!"

Jake grabbed her arm. "God *damn* it, Randy, don't do this!"

"She's wrong," Cole spoke up loudly. "*I* killed Buckley."

Everyone looked at him, confused. Vance and Terrel stepped up onto the veranda then.

"It wasn't Cole *or* Mrs.Hharkner!" Vance said. "And not Jake either. *I* killed the bastard!"

"No. It was *me*," Terrel put in. He turned and shouted. "Hey! Some of you men out there get over here!"

Randy covered her face with her hands as Billy Dooley, Charlie McGee and Tommy Tucker hurried over. Rodriguez came around from the side of the house and joined them.

"The marshal here wants to know who killed Brad Buckley," Terrel told them. "We can't figure it out. Randy there says she did it, but we all know that's not true, right? I told him I did it, but then Cole said he did, and then Vance said *he* did. Maybe it was one of you."

Oh, yeah, *I'm* the one who killed him," Billy Dooley insisted.

"No, *amigos*," Rodriguez spoke up. "*I* did it."

"Nah. It was me," Charlie told the marshal.

"The hell it was," Tommy said. "I didn't work for Jake then, but I thought it was that old guy you used to call Pepper."

"No, you idiot," Charlie answered. "He's the one who died in the barn fire when – " He caught himself before he admitted Randy had been abducted.

"I did it," young Stephen said. "Me and Little Jake had guns. We stole an extra handgun from Cole's gear. We both shot at Brad Buckley 'cuz he hurt Grandma."

"Well, if *I had* been there, I'd have *gladly* killed him," Tommy Tyler added.

"*I* did it," Ben spoke up.

"No. It was me," Lloyd told the marshal. "And if you knew what he did to my mother, you'd have shot him yourself. You'd have done *worse* than shoot him. You'd have made him suffer first, lawful or not!"

Jake pulled Randy close. She hugged his waist and wilted against this chest.

"My God," Kraemer muttered. He looked at Jake. "And *did* you make him suffer?"

"We *all* did," Vance answered.

Kraemer rubbed the back of his neck. "God damn it!"

"You going to arrest *all* of us?" Vance asked.

"I know you have a wife and daughter, Hal," Jake said. "What would you do if an old enemy of yours came along and—" Randy cringed against him. "I won't say what happened. Use your fucking imagination. U.S. Marshals make a lot of enemies, so I'm sure you've tallied up a few."

Kraemer sighed deeply and looked around. "Did you bother to bury the body?"

"He's buried, all right," Vance answered. "And you'd be wise not to tell that judge any of this."

Kraemer looked at Vance. "Is that a threat?"

Vance grinned. "Let's call it a request, out of respect for Mrs. Harkner."

Kraemer glanced at a trembling Randy, who still clung to Jake.

"Leave this alone, Marshal." Lloyd asked. "Go after *real* criminals. We'll be careful with the nesters, but my pa and I haven't done anything wrong. And my mother . . . Just leave things be. Tell that judge that as far as you know, Brad Buckley took off for parts unknown and just plain never came back. Pa paid his dues for his past a long time ago and almost died in prison. And he's done a lot of good since then. He risked his life in Mexico rescuing a little girl he didn't even know. And he did a lot of good work in Oklahoma. He cleaned up dens of filth most people can't even imagine. I know, because I was with him. He's done a lot of good and risked his life doing it. And don't tell me you haven't shot a few men you shouldn't have, because I know what your job is like."

Hal Kraemer glared at Jake. "You're not going to add anything to that?"

"I'm not saying a goddamn thing," Jake told him. "It's like Vance said. We *all* killed Buckley, so either leave it alone, or arrest *all* of us – all but my wife. She's innocent of any wrong-doing."

Kraemer sighed deeply. "Well, Jake, you've put me in a bad spot."

"No, I haven't. *Brad Buckley* put you in a bad spot."

The marshal glanced at Randy, still standing in Jake's embrace, her face turned away. He turned his attention back to Jake again. "I don't need to ask what that man went though. Sometimes you get the look of a demon in those dark eyes, Jake, and that's what I see now."

"Look around you," Jake answered. "You'll see it in the eyes of every man here."

Kraemer slowly nodded. "I know you well enough to know that backing you into a corner is a very bad idea. You just remember that I'm not your enemy. I like to think we're actually friends. I had no intention of forcing your wife to make a statement or do anything else. She's a beautiful, gracious woman who very obviously went through something traumatic. I suspect – *if* she shot Buckley – she was likely half out of her mind, and it was more a matter of self-defense. You should know me better than to think I would go so far as to arrest a woman like Randy for something like that." Hal met Lloyd's gaze. "Tell me we have an understanding about trouble with the settlers."

"We do. Just don't let me hear that you or either one of those wet noses with you have said a word against my mother—or mentioned Buckley's name again. This is *private!*"

The marshal glanced at Gretta. "I know you're married now, Gretta, but I remember your reputation in Denver. One thing was sure—you were blatantly honest. If you say Buckley deserved to die, I'll take your word for it."

"Oh, he *damn* well deserved to die," Gretta answered. "I wasn't a part of whatever happened to him, but I know the truth, and I had a very unpleasant run-in with that man myself. When a woman like me is offended by a man and pulls a gun on him, you know he's as low as a man can get. And I *did* pull a gun – not on him, but on a piece of scum he ran with. Buckley was just as bad, and I'm glad he's no longer on this earth."

Hal moved his gaze to Randy, who remained turned away. "I'm sorry for whatever happened, Mrs. Harkner. If I'd known—"

"Just go, Hal," Jake told him.

Kraemer looked around at the ranch hands, then back at Jake. "You know, Jake, few men can garner the kind of friendship and loyalty you have from these men and from your family."

"It wasn't loyalty to *me* this time," Jake answered. "It was how much they care about my *wife*."

Kraemer nodded. "Yes, I suppose so."

He quickly finished his lemonade and walked off the veranda, ordering his deputies to mount up. He tipped his hat to Jake as he deputies finished their lemonade and obeyed Kraemer's order.

"Are we still friends, Jake Harkner?" Kraemer asked.

Jake kept his arms around Randy. "Let's just say we understand each other, and as long as you respect my wife and never bring this up again, then yes, I'd just as soon be friends with you as your enemy."

Kraemer grinned wryly. "*Nobody* cares to have you for an enemy, Jake." He turned his horse and faced his deputies. "I advise both of you to keep this to yourselves, or you won't just answer to Jake, which is bad enough. You'll answer to me. You're going to learn in this job that sometimes the law is right . . . and sometimes a man has to interpret it his own way, especially in places where civilization hasn't quite settled in." He glanced at Jake again. "Take good care of that woman." He turned his horse, and all three men rode off.

Everyone breathed a sigh of relief.

"My God." Evie rushed over to put a hand on her mother's shoulder. "Mom, come inside."

Randy pulled away from Jake and wiped at silent tears. "It's all right. It's done now. I'm glad."

Jake grasped her arms and leaned down. "Jesus, Randy, why did you do that?"

"I just . . . I wanted it over with. I wanted the questions to stop. And I was . . . scared for you." She looked up at him. "I don't know what to say to all those men."

"You don't need to say anything. They understand."

Cole walked off the veranda. "Let's get back to work!" he told the others.

The men moved off toward the barns and paddock. Little Jake touched his grandmother's shoulder. "We love you, Grandma."

Randy turned and hugged him tightly. "I know you do."

"You okay now, Mom?" Ben asked, putting a hand to her back.

"I'm fine." Randy glanced at Gretta. "I'm so sorry, Gretta. I called you a notorious prostitute."

"Well, hell, I *was*." Gretta grinned. "No news there." She touched Randy's arm. "You showed some real courage, honey. Everything'll be okay now. And I expect those men admire you more than ever." She glanced at Jake. "Are you going to handle this without shooting somebody?"

"I'll handle it."

Gretta patted his arm. "Go on and take her inside." She stepped off the veranda and left with Cole.

Lloyd met his father's gaze. "Tell me what to do."

Jake shook his head. "Nothing. We'll be all right."

Randy reached out to pat her son's chest. "It's okay, Lloyd. Go check on Katie."

"Mom—"

"I'm fine. I'm just so touched by what those men did . . . and you and the boys."

Lloyd turned to Jake. "Pa, if you need me, you tell me."

"I will. Do like your mother said and go take care of Katie."

"Randy, I can give you something to make you sleep for a while," Brian told his mother-in-law.

"I'm all right. Thank you. Just take Evie and do whatever you can to make her feel better. God knows she has her own memories to deal with."

"You heard what Lloyd told you," Brian said to Jake. "It's the same for me. I'm right next door."

"I know."

Sighing deeply, Brian put an arm around Evie and urged her to come back to their house with him. Evie saw the devastation in Jake's eyes. She also saw tears there.

"Daddy, it's okay."

"No, it isn't! This brought up bad memories for you, too."

"I learned to live with them a long time ago."

Jake turned away. "God *damn* it," he muttered under his breath. He took Randy inside, where she turned and hugged him again. "It's you I'm worried about, Jake."

He grabbed her closer, holding her tight in one arm and wrapping her hair into his other hand. "I'm so damn sorry, baby."

Randy wept softly against his chest. "I'm just glad the truth is out and it's over."

Jake glanced at his guns hanging over the door. *Sometimes it seems like these things are never over.* He kept the thought to himself.

# CHAPTER 14

*Early July* . . .

"There's a lot of people here," Brady told Grizzly, smiling.

Grizzly leaned close to Brady's ear to be heard over the din of a room full of settlers and land agents. "I told you this was the best way to stir up trouble."

Brady scowled. "You might have a good idea here, friend, but you were just as stupid going out to the *J&L* as I was. I hope that was a lesson for you."

Shouts went up, arguments about how to claim public land.

Lester Bates, a graying, heavy-set Denver realtor, held up his hands to quiet the crowd. "I have paperwork here as well as maps," he announced. "I know which parcels you can claim and which ones you can't, so if you'll line up at my table, I'll help you pick out a claim."

The crowd stopped arguing and settled into a restless quiet. To Brady, it felt like a long fuse burning toward a piece of dynamite—a quiet sizzle leading to an explosion. The dynamite would probably end up in the form of one Jake Harkner.

Pushing long, thinning hair behind his shoulders, the farmers' self-chosen leader stood up on a chair and scanned the room. "My name is Edgar Mullins, and I've been wanting my own farm ever since I moved here to Denver from Illinois. But we all know how hard it is to go up against the big cattlemen. And we all know what happened up in Wyoming. In the eyes of the big cattlemen, small ranchers and farmers don't belong on those millions of acres of free grazing land - public land we're now allowed to settle on."

Men and women cheered their support, including Brady and Grizzly.

"Some of us have decided not to let what happened in the Johnson County War happen here." Mullins' hands fisted. "Instead of settling and then risking the cattlemen coming after us, we've decided to turn the tables and surprise them. *We* will go after *them*!"

More clapping and cheering. But as the crowd voiced their backing of Mullins, a dark-eyed man dressed all in black moved forward from the back of the room. He wore a gun on each hip. People quieted as he stopped in front of Mullins then turned to face them.

"That's him," Grizzly told Brady. "Kyle Pendergrass."

Brady studied Pendergrass. He looked about six feet tall. Broad in the shoulders, and young enough to be Jake Harkner's son. "He's a lot younger than Harkner. I think he could take him if he had to."

"Maybe he can take father and son both," Grizzly suggested. "You said Jake went at you with a *rifle*, not his six-guns. He never pulled his handgun on me, either. Maybe he's slower now. Maybe he's not near as good with those .44's of his as people think."

Brady shook his head. "I wouldn't bet on that."

Mullins stressed that the settlers needed to take the first step. He emphasized that the law—even the Federal government—was behind them. "It's time we settled on land that's rightly ours and turned a lot of free range into farms and homesteads and smaller ranches."

Amid the cheers, another man climbed onto a chair, waving his arms for silence. The crowd calmed again to listen.

"I'm Grant Seyres." He was shorter than average, with thick, sandy-colored hair that hung past his shoulders. His sun-weathered face made it hard to tell his age, but a solid, stocky body said he was in his prime. "I've got a wife, four kids, and a place outside of Denver in an area where I can't expand. So, I want to settle on public land, too. But there's one thing you're forgetting - the *J&L*. You all know that stands for Jake and Lloyd Harkner."

The crowd quieted even more.

"We've all come to know the Harkners as fair men," Seyres continued. "But fair or not, Jake Harkner's not a man to cross. So, I'm warning everybody not to get so anxious to go up against the big cattlemen that you make foolish decisions. The Harkners and some of the others will deal with you if you're honest with them. But if you don't plan to go to them first, better make sure the land agents you use know what they're talking about, so's you don't plunk yourselves down illegally on a big cattleman's land. Yes, it's legal to claim public land, but there are lots of shady land agents out there who will be here today and gone tomorrow, leaving you on your own to face some big rancher whose land you're squatting on."

"That's why *I'm* here." The man in black spoke in a deep, authoritative voice. "And I've got friends. Ain't one of them—nor me, either—who's afraid of Jake Harkner."

"You'd *better* be afraid!" another deep voice shouted from near the barn door.

Everyone turned to see Marshal Hal Kraemer. They stepped back as he moved through the crowd, his eyes on the obvious gunman in front. Kraemer stood a little taller than most men there and he didn't bother standing on a chair.

"Shit," Brady muttered. "Where'd he come from?"

"Word gets around," Grizzly answered. "He's heard about this meeting, and he means to keep the law."

"I know Jake Harkner about as good as anyone outside of his family," Kraemer told them. "He's not easy to get close to, but I know him well enough to tell all of you not to take him for granted. He walks a thin line between lawful and unlawful, so I'm warning all of you to be careful where you settle and where you graze your livestock. Like Mister Seyres there told you, Jake and his son Lloyd deal an honest hand, but if you go hiring men like that no-good standing up there wearing guns, and think he can go up against a man like Jake, you'd better think twice—especially if anybody in his family comes to harm. Jake might be getting older, but I for one wouldn't want to have to face him down."

"We don't mean anyone any harm," Mullins told the marshal. "And we've hired this man here to make sure the cattlemen don't try chasing us off land that will legally be ours. This here is—"

"Kyle Pendergrass," Kraemer interrupted. "I damn well know who he is. He's spent time in jail for all kinds of crimes, including being a gun for hire and shooting an innocent man. He managed to convince a jury it was an accident, but he still did for it. He's good with those guns, but I'm telling you that he doesn't give a damn about any of you. He's here to make a name for himself. But if he causes problems with the Harkners, it could turn into a bloodbath. You cross Jake Harkner the wrong way, and you won't find a gunman in this country who can bring him down. And I, for one, don't intend to let this get that far out of hand. As the marshal for this territory, I aim to keep the peace. You'd all better understand that."

"I can take Harkner any day." Pendergrass spoke in a slow Southern drawl. "Everybody in Kentucky knows my reputation. I've won every shooting contest there, and everyplace else." He put his hands on his hips in an authoritative stance. "And whether I can or not, there are plenty of men who'd like the reputation of taking down Harkner. You folks'll have plenty of help from men who know how to use a gun." He turned to the Hal. "Harkner's days are over, Marshal. He'll find that out if he gives these people trouble."

Kraemer faced Pendergrass. "*Your* days will be over real fast if you start a gun battle over this, Pendergrass," he warned. "And I'm telling you now, if I have to choose sides, it won't be the side of a two-bit wanna-be like you. Both Jake and Lloyd rode as U.S. Marshals in the most dangerous, lawless territory in this country. They might not be lawmen anymore, but I know them to be fair enough that if I get involved in this, I'll back *them*." He faced the crowd. "Not lawbreakers who try to make trouble for the cattlemen, and not the gunmen they hire. All of you had better understand that and think about it."

"Lloyd Harkner tried to hang me once," Brady shouted. "Does *that* sound like a fair and lawful man?"

The crowd mumbled.

"It does when the man being hanged is a cattle thief who set fire to valuable grazing land," Kraemer answered. "And Jake rightfully chased you off when you tried to start trouble with him. That's why I took away your badge. You had no right riding around as a range detective."

More whispers and gasps circulated among the crowd.

"And I was told," Kraemer continued, "that Jake himself saved your neck back when you set that fire. He wouldn't let Lloyd hang you, so don't talk to me about what's fair. You're alive because of Jake."

"Yeah, well not long ago he did *this* to me!" Brady pointed to his jaw, still purple with bruises. "Just for stepping onto his property. And maybe he didn't let me hang, but he and his son forced me to sign my ten-thousand-acres over to them before they'd let me go back when they wanted to hang me. Does *that* sound fair—or even legal?"

"Would you rather be dead?" Kraemer asked.

Some in the crowd snickered and shook their heads.

"That doesn't matter! It's not legal what they did. You're the law! You should have done something about it!"

"That happened just before I took over this territory," Hal announced. "Even so, I looked into it. You never had legal claim to that land. You never filed the right paperwork with the government or finished paying for it. The Harkners did, according to the note you signed giving up your supposed ownership."

"And there's a good example of how rich cattlemen can get away with whatever they want," Brady shot back. "These good people here only want to settle legally. Nobody here wants any real trouble."

"Is that why you hired this gunman?" Kraemer asked.

"We hired him just for protection," Mullins answered.

Kraemer eyed Pendergrass again. "You make one wrong move, and you'll be in prison. That's a promise."

Kyle straightened his shoulders and looked boldly at the marshal. "I can handle myself."

Kraemer shook his head. "You ever face a man like Jake Harkner?"

A slight hesitation, then Pendergrass said, "Every man has his last day, Marshal."

"And yours is coming." Kraemer looked around the

room. "All of you, get out of here and cool down. Talk to proper land agents and file proper claims, and there will be no trouble. The Harkners and the other cattlemen around here aren't going to cause trouble for legal settlers. If they have a problem with more public land being used for farms and smaller ranching—or with fences going up—they'll have to deal with the *government*, not with gunmen like Pendergrass here. Men like him have no legal authority in any of this. Things have changed out here, and most cattlemen I know don't want the kind of trouble that happened up in Wyoming. Law and order have come to the West, and you need to stop making trouble where there *is* no trouble. Now, go on home!"

People mumbled and milled about for a few minutes but gradually left. Kraemer eyed Brady Fillmore and the bearded man standing next to him, then walked closer. "Are you Grizzly Smith?"

"How do you know?"

"I was at the *J&L* recently. Jake told me about you."

Grizzly spit tobacco juice on the floor beside the marshal's feet. "Did he tell you he came close to shooting me for no good reason?"

"I heard the story, and I don't blame him." Kraemer turned to Brady. "You two had better warn that so-called gunman over there that he'd better go back to wherever he came from. If he follows through with making trouble for the Harkners, he'll never live to find out if he earned that fame he's after. If you two get mixed up in it, you'll be nursing more than a busted jaw. Mark my words. Stay away from the *J&L*, and especially from Jake Harkner." He turned and walked out.

Brady looked over at Pendergrass, who was shaking hands with Mullins. "This might not work out the way we planned," he told Grizzly.

"Sure, it will. All we need to do is find a couple more like Pendergrass and keep those settlers stirred up."

"How do you figure to do that?"

Grizzly shrugged. "The *Denver Post* society page said as how Jake Harkner and his wife are leavin' for Chicago around the fourteenth. They'll be gone a good two or three weeks, maybe more. That gives us time to hop a train south, then west to the Outlaw Trail. That only takes a day or two now. In outlaw country, it'll be easy to find a couple more gunmen who wouldn't mind joining up with Pendergrass to go after Harkner."

Brady frowned. "Maybe." Doubt filled his eyes. "Kraemer's right, you know. No one can take Jake lightly. He fought seven men in that gunfight back California. They all ended up dead. And I've heard stories about his days as a marshal. They aren't pretty. Jake Harkner got his reputation from *reality*. And the reality is that he's still damn tough, and still damn good with those .44's."

Grizzly shook his head. "You need to buck up, friend. I've a feeling several more gunmen are gonna' join us soon. All we have to do is leave word that we can be found at the Aspen Saloon. We get a few more like Pendergrass, and Harkner's days of fame are over."

"And I'm the one to do it," Pendergrass interrupted. He glanced at Mullins. "Keep gathering the settlers and keep them stirred up. Let's get at least one parcel of land titled—to me and those two over there. You, too, if you want. We'll quick build a place to stay in and use it as our vantage point for keeping an eye on the big ranches. If we start doing a little rustling, we'll ruffle some Harkner tail feathers and get their attention. I have other ideas, too. By the time I'm done, Harkner himself will be high tailing it to our little settlement and looking for blood. And blood is what he'll get. His **own**."

Grizzly grinned and glanced at Brady. "What did I tell you?"

Brady sighed and shook his head. "I'll believe it when it happens."

"*Believe* it," Pendergrass told him. "I know how to bring Harkner back from Chicago real fast and real mad and real careless. Because he'll be out for vengeance. A couple months from now, Jake Harkner will be dead. I guarantee it."

## CHAPTER 15

Jake leaned against a hitching post to watch the square dancing. Henry Till's men had built a large wooden platform to serve as a dance floor for the *Double T*'s annual cookout, and right now couples stomped and whirled and gave the platform a true test of its strength. It was located inside a corral that had been thoroughly cleaned for the occasion, with United States flags draped around the outside fence. Henry always combined his cookout with a celebration of Independence Day.

Tables donned with red checkered tablecloths and loaded with a variety of food and baked goods were set up in a nearby barn that had also been cleaned. Randy was there, helping set vases of wildflowers on the tables. Just outside the barn a side of beef, donated this year by the *J&L*, was turning on a spit over open flames.

Most of the Harkner family was present, as well as several *J&L* hands. From miles around, other ranch owners, their families and cowboys had also come to the *Double-T*, also known as the Twisted Tree, for the grand event, a nice break from roundups and branding.

A few arrived in automobiles, a new-fangled mode of transportation Jake and most other ranchers thought was a ridiculous replacement for horses, especially out here on the high plains of Colorado, where the landscape was not fit for such contraptions. The noisy things might be fine for cities, but a good horse remained far more reliable and a lot quieter. And a live horse was sure a better companion than a bunch of metal that produced smoke and sometimes backfired, which was what had happened only minutes ago.

Jake grinned and lit a cigarette. That damn automobile had given off a crack that caused several men to pull their guns, thinking someone was shooting. A horse hitched to a buggy nearby reared in terror, pulled loose from its hitch and took off at full gallop. One of Henry Till's ranch hands jumped on his horse and rode after it, and the entire event caused screams and laughter among everyone there. The general uproar and good feelings, combined with talk about "those damned automobiles" lingered, causing a lot of whooping and hollering and whirling among the square dancers.

Couples reeled to the crazy and confusing calls of Tex Sanders, one of Henry's men who liked to lead the dances. Some of the dancers ended up stumbling into each other as they tried to maneuver the ridiculous turns and partner exchanges Tex called. The music came from two banjos, a piano, two fiddles and a guitar, all six men playing their instruments in a fast-stepping rhythm, and not always hitting the right notes.

Randy finally came out of the barn and around the corral to stand beside Jake. She looked beautiful in a yellow dress with lace trim. Yellow was Jake's favorite color on her. He smiled and put his arm around her shoulders, loving the way her golden hair was twisted into a mass of curls with real flowers in them. Her bodice revealed a tempting peek at her generous bosom, and her gray/green eyes sparkled with joy.

"You having fun?" Jake asked.

"Oh, you know I am. And look at Evie and Brian! They look so happy, Jake. They love to square dance."

"It's always good to see Evie looking happy."

Randy clapped to the music as she laughed and pointed to one confused couple who just stood amid the dancers, looking bewildered. "I set out my bread and pies. Now we can dance, but we'll have to wait for a waltz."

"I know you love to square dance, but if I took part in all that foot-stomping, this leg would keep me up all night."

"I know." Randy turned. "You look so handsome, Jake." Reaching up, she adjusted the silver and turquoise concho slide that held his string tie together at the neck of his white shirt. "I've seen how some of the women have been eyeing you."

Jake just laughed, leaned down and kissed her, but she pushed him away.

"Not in front of all these people."

"Since when do I care if people see me kissing my wife? And since when do *you* care? You love giving the women something to talk about. Don't deny it."

"Well, I *am* with the most handsome man here. Other than Lloyd, anyway. But then he looks just like his father, so how can he help being handsome?"

Over the next several minutes, neighboring ranchers stopped to say hello, some commenting on Evie's having a chapel built on the *J&L*. She'd invited them to come some Sunday when it was finished.

"Friends are always welcome," Jake told Henry and Bessie Till. "You'll run into *J&L* men when you come onto Harkner land, but they'll let all neighbors through."

"And we have lots of room," Randy told Bessie. "I

know it's a long ride, and you'd probably have to come a day early to be there for morning worship. We have extra bedrooms, so you could stay with us. In fact, maybe we should start a rooming house like you and Henry have. It will be so nice to be able to stay there tonight before we head home."

"Well, we do a lot of entertaining like this," Henry told them, "And, of course, some people have to travel through the *Double-T* on their way to someplace else, so we figured to make some extra money with a place where tired travelers can stay." He smiled. "I see most of your family is here, Jake. You sure have a big brood."

"And soon to get bigger," Jake told him. "Lloyd's wife Katie is expecting soon."

"Katie stayed home because she isn't feeling well," Randy told Bessie. "She was afraid the day-and-half trip here by wagon would be too much. She insisted that Lloyd come, though. This is one of the few times a lot of neighboring ranchers are all together in one place."

"Oh, the poor girl. Katie is such a beautiful, sweet woman," Bessie told her.

"Her parents are there to help, so she's in good hands, but Lloyd is heading home yet tonight - right after the men have their meeting. I hope you both understand."

"Oh, of course," Henry answered.

A few others gathered to visit, always curious about the infamous patriarch of the Harkner clan. The square dance ended, and Brian and Evie joined them while Lloyd stood across the way talking to another rancher.

Jake smiled at the fact that every member of his family who'd come to the cookout today was involved in their own fun. Tricia, Sadie Mae, and the rest of the little ones, including Lloyd's children, were with a host of other youngsters of similar ages. They played tag and other games in a grassy area near Henry's house, where women took turns keeping an eye on them. Stephen and young Jake were out riding with some of the older boys, and Ben was helping baste the roasting beef with Bessie Till's home-made barbecue sauce. Everyone wanted her secret recipe, but she never gave it out.

"I hear you had a little run-in with Brady Fillmore," Henry Till interrupted Jake's thoughts.

"I did. He's trying to make trouble over all of us kicking him off his land, but I don't think he'll try coming back anytime soon. I left him in a bit of pain."

Henry laughed. "I'll just bet you did. He *is* still alive, isn't he?"

"Only because I'm trying to abide by all the new laws."

Henry laughed even harder. "Well, I understand why you didn't want the bunch of us to hang him back when he started that fire, but we'd all probably have been better off if we'd strung him up."

Jake took a pre-rolled cigarette from an inside pocket on his dress jacket. "Henry, nobody knows better than I do that when you let an old enemy live, you usually regret it. We had another run-in with a friend of Fillmore's a few days later. I think some trouble is up, and you all need to be aware of it. Lloyd wants to talk more about it at the meeting."

"Sure. We'll meet around five o-clock. Give everybody a chance to fill their bellies with all this good food and *J&L* beef first. And thanks for donating this year, Jake."

Jake struck a match to light his cigarette. "Be sure to thank Lloyd, not me. The *J&L* is about eighty percent his. He always wanted to ranch and be able to build something —stay in one place. When he and I earned the right to quit chasing scum around Oklahoma, we came out here, and here we intend to stay." He took a deep drag on the cigarette. "Land doesn't get much prettier than the Rocky Mountain foothills," he added.

"Damn right," Henry agreed.

The fiddlers started another snappy square dance, and the crowd broke up, several couples going back to the platform. Randy watched, tapping her feet to the rhythm.

Jake noticed Vance talking with some other cowboys and hailed him over. "You like to square dance, Vance. How about some two-stepping with my wife?"

"Oh, Jake, he doesn't have to—" Randy started to object.

"I know you want to dance," Jake insisted.

Vance removed his hat and bowed to Randy. "Ma'am. You look beautiful today, but then you *always* look beautiful."

"Lay off the sweet talk," Jake joked. "Randy loves square dancing, and this leg won't let me dance that fast. You like to dance, so do me a favor and help this woman have some fun."

"Jake, are you *sure*?" Randy asked.

"Yes. Vance here likes to dance with pretty women."

Vance grinned. "And Randy here is the prettiest of them all."

"There are several young, single girls here you could dance with," Randy pointed out.

"He prefers *married* women. Isn't that so, Vance?" Jake turned to Randy. "Vance and Terrel are both risking getting their heads shot off by a couple of husbands in Brighton."

"Vance Kelly!" Randy spun to face the cowboy. "Is that true?"

"Ma'am, the younger women just want to settle and marry, and I'm too old for that. The married ones come with no strings attached, except for you. You come with a *chain* attached, by the name of Jake Harkner. So, I only aim to dance with you as a friend. But if you were married to anybody else—"

"Just remember I'm watching," Jake warned. "You try stealing *this* wife, and I'll put you on the fence rail next time we practice shooting and use *you* for a target."

"All I'm sayin', Jake, is I don't want your wife thinkin' I'd dance with her just as a favor. It's because she's prettier than any other woman here, except maybe for your daughter, but heck, foolin' with her would be like foolin' with the Mother Mary herself."

Jake frowned. "Vance, you're real close to sitting on that target rail. If I were you, I'd stop talking and go dance."

Vance grinned. "Just let me take off my hat and gun." He walked over to a fence post to leave both items.

Randy stood on tiptoe to kiss Jake's cheek. "Jake —"

"Vance is a damn good friend. And don't tell me you don't want to join in the square dancing."

Vance returned. "Jake, what if your wife tells me she likes me better than you?"

"I've never shot a man in the back, but if he's running off with my wife, I might be tempted." Jake leaned closer. "Now, get the hell out of here before I change my mind."

Vance laughed and took Randy's arm.

He helped her onto the dance platform, where her attention instantly went to listening to Tex's calls.

"Drink up, Pa." Jake turned to see Lloyd to his left. He held a glass of punch in each hand, and Jake took one from him and sniffed it.

"How much whiskey is in here?"

"Just one shot. I've seen you drink that much, so don't worry. A man your size won't get drunk on a shot of whiskey."

Jake studied him a moment. Lloyd's smile didn't fool him. "How many shots are in *yours*?"

Lloyd shook his head. "Just one."

"Truth?"

"Truth."

Jake downed the punch in a couple of gulps and set the glass on the fence rail. "I know you're worried about Katie, but just be careful with that stuff. You don't have to stay for the meeting if you want to get back home. I can stand in for you."

"No, I'll do it." Lloyd downed his own punch. "And don't worry. This is all I'm drinking, other than water or coffee or more plain punch."

Jake rested an arm on the rail and faced his son. "It depends on a man's ability to handle just one shot. I've seen the worst of what that stuff can do, and I didn't raise you to be the good man you are only to see you turn into something else."

"Pa, I'm okay. We've been together night and day ever since you got out of prison, so you know I can handle whiskey."

"Except when something bad happens, like with Beth. And you didn't have a great big family and a ranch to run then."

Lloyd met Jake's gaze. "Quit worrying. You've told me enough stories about your father to scare me sober. I've just been so worried about Katie that a shot of whiskey sounded good. That's all."

"Mmmm-hmmm." Jake took another drag on his cigarette. "I know I smoke too much, Lloyd, but it's the only thing that keeps me calm enough to stay away from whiskey." He turned to watch the dancers. "Stick to cigarettes, and to that beautiful wife of yours. I tried drinking when I ran off after killing that sonofabitch whose blood runs in my veins, and it made me do things I'll regret 'til the day I die. But your mother turned off my need for whiskey like a water faucet. Let Katie do that for you."

Both men turned to watch the dancing.

"Hey, is that Mom dancing with Vance?"

"Yup."

"With *Vance?* Shit, Pa, he might throw her on a horse and take off with her. You know what a heartbreaker he is."

Jake grinned. "I figured it would be good for your mother to dance. I'm hoping it will help her get over feeling self-conscious around the men." He sobered. "It really touched her heart—what those men did the other day."

"It touched *my* heart. They're a good bunch."

"That they are."

The square dance ended, and Jake noticed Randy laughing. Vance hugged her, and Jake shook his head. "I think it's time I stepped in," he joked to Lloyd.

"I'd say so." Lloyd walked off laughing.

Vance and Randy stepped down from the platform, and Randy took a clean handkerchief from a pocket on her skirt and dabbed perspiration from her forehead as they walked up to Jake.

"You done trying to steal my wife?" Jake asked Vance. "I said you could *dance* with her, not hug her like she belonged to you."

"Hell, Jake, you can't blame a man for tryin'." Laughing, Vance, put on his hat and strapped on his six-gun. "It's not fair that every woman in your family is beautiful. If she's not your wife, she's your daughter or Lloyd's wife. None of us has a chance. And now even Gretta is taken, so she's off limits, too. Guess I'll have to keep lookin' up the married women in Brighton."

Jake put his arm around Randy's shoulders. "And someday you'll ride off to Brighton or Denver, and we'll never see you again because some husband will string you up by the heels. I won't mention what else he might do to you."

"Jake Harkner!" Randy covered her face with her hands.

Vance grinned. "Well, if that happens, I'll at least have the memory of havin' a damn good time up until then." He bowed to Randy. "Thank you, ma'am, for the dances. I hope you enjoyed it."

"Of course, I did. Thank you, Vance. Now go flirt with some of the single women here. And be careful with the married ones. You're needed on the *J&L*. I'm sure Jake and Lloyd would hate to lose you to some jealous husband."

"I'll keep that in mind, Ma'am." He glanced at Jake, and the two men exchanged a look of understanding. Vance damn well knew Jake thought the dance would be good for Randy. "You take good care of that woman, Jake."

Vance walked off, and the little group of musicians on the platform began a slow tune.

"You too tired to dance a slow one?" Jake asked Randy.

"With you? I'm never too tired."

Jake led her up onto the dance platform and pulled her into his arms. Smoothly, they joined the other couples turning to the slow strains of the fiddles.

"Did Vance offer to take you away with him?"

"Of course. We're leaving tonight, after you fall asleep."

"That so?" Jake drew Randy even closer.

"Oh, yes." She leaned her head back a little to look up at him as they danced.

"*Sabes quanto te amo,*" Jake told her softly.

"I love you more," Randy answered.

Jake lifted her off her feet and kissed her, both of them standing still in the middle of the dance floor. Men whistled and whooped. A few women gasped. Others whispered behind hand-held fans and more of them laughed in nervous twitters.

The kiss deepened, and Randy wrapped her arms

around Jake's neck. Both grinned and laughed in the middle of the kiss.

"So, which one is it?" Jake asked. "Vance? Or me?"

They began dancing again.

"You'll have to do much more than kiss me before I decide," Randy teased.

"Yes, Ma'am." Jake lifted her off the floor again, and Randy tightened her hold on his neck as he turned them to the music. "We'll leave in the morning and stop at Echo Ridge on our way home."

Randy deserved his full attention, deserved a vacation, but Jake needed the calmness of their favorite getaway, too. He hated the thought of possible trouble brewing. "We'll stay three or four days on Echo Ridge while everybody else goes home. Then we'll head for Chicago."

"I can't wait. I love having you all to myself." Randy noticed a few women staring at them. "But for now, Mister Harkner, we are dancing much too close."

"We're married."

"I know, but even married couples don't do this in public."

"Is that another new law?"

"I think it's been on the books pretty much forever."

"And who are you married to?"

"Jake Harkner."

"And since when does Jake Harkner obey the law?"

Randy laughed and kissed his cheek. "You can break the law with me any time."

"Then I'll be breaking all kinds of laws up at that cabin."

"Oh, my! I might have to arrest and punish you."

"I promise not to fight you. You can tie me up and do what you want with me—for punishment."

They danced to two more waltzes before the music sped into a square dance.

"We might as well go eat," Jake suggested. "I need to rest this leg, even if the next dance is another waltz."

"Oh, Jake, you should have told me."

"And miss dancing with the prettiest woman here?"

"Not if it hurts your leg."

Jake kept an arm around her as they stepped off the make-shift dance floor and moved toward the barn and the food tables. Just as they neared the barn doors, someone shouted loud enough to be heard above the crowd.

"Jake Harkner!"

Everyone quieted, and the small orchestra stopped playing. All eyes turned toward Jake, who stood watching a man astride a big roan gelding, a woman perched behind him on the same saddle.

"I'm here to kill you!" the man announced.

# CHAPTER 16

People began backing away.

"Jake, who is that?" Randy asked.

"I don't know. Get inside the barn."

"Jake—"

"Go!"

Randy hurried away, joined by several others just inside the barn door, while those still outside moved farther back, out of the way of possible stray bullets.

"Mister, I don't even know you," Jake said.

"Name's Chester Ainsley, and I'm right good with a gun!"

"Chester, get down off of that horse!" The words came from Henry Till. "You're *drunk*. And you'll die today if you don't get rid of that gun right now." Henry moved closer to Jake. "Ainsley worked for me for a couple of weeks, but he drinks too much, so I fired him."

Jake saw Lloyd approaching from his left. "Leave this to me, Lloyd."

"You sure, Pa?"

"It's one drunk man. Of course I'm sure."

"I ain't givin' up my gun, and I ain't backin' down!" Ainsley spouted, his hand on the gun at his hip.

"For God's sake, Chet, do you realize who you're challenging?" Henry turned to Jake. "I don't know who that woman is on the back of his horse."

"I do," Jake answered. "She's Stella Flynn, a whore from Denver. Came to the J&L a few days ago with a couple of troublemakers posing as farmers. Better step aside, Henry."

"This is ridiculous. I'm sorry, Jake." Henry stepped away.

"Mister, what's your beef?" Jake asked Ainsley.

Chester swung his leg over his saddle horn and slid down from his horse, stumbling a little as he landed. "That pretty little lady sitting on my horse there—I met her in Denver. She told me you and your son abused her when you ran into her on the J&L. So, I'm here to defend her honor!"

"That pretty little lady is a liar," Jake retorted. "And believe me, she *has* no honor. She came to the J&L pretending to be a settler's wife, and my son and I threw her and the other imposters off our land. Don't make me shoot you for no good reason, Ainsley."

"Get off the *Double T*," Henry shouted to Chester. "And take that woman with you."

"I have a right to be here," Stella said haughtily. She sat up straighter on the horse and raised one side of her skirt, baring her leg all the way to her hip. "Jake, honey, did you tell your wife how you beat and raped me that day you caught me on the J&L?"

"Nobody touched you," Jake answered calmly. "Besides, no man needs to force himself on *you*, does he? He'd end up having to *pay* for it, and I'm talking cash, not the law."

That brought laughter and whistles from most of the men, gasps and whispers from the women.

"You're a murdering, low-life bastard!" Stella shot back.

"And you're exactly right. So, you'd be wise to get down off that horse before I shoot at that drunken idiot in front of you and maybe miss."

"I've always been told that Jake Harkner *never* misses," Stella said, "not with a gun, and not with a woman."

"There's always a first time." Jake took a step toward Ainsley. "Somebody get the woman and that horse out of the way!"

One of Henry's men hurried over to grab the horse's bridle.

Chester glanced over his shoulder. "You leave my woman right there!"

"Let him get her out of there, Ainsley," Henry ordered. "Drunken fool. Even a man with all his senses wouldn't challenge Jake Harkner."

"I can shoot that gun right out of his hand," Jake murmured to Henry.

"Just make sure that's all you do," Henry muttered back. "I don't want Marshal Kraemer out here trying to make this more than it is."

"I don't' deliberately kill idiots, Hal."

"Get ready to *die*, Harkner!" Ainsley announced. He planted his legs apart as the *Double-T* man hurried away with the horse and Stella, the latter cursing Jake as they disappeared around the corner of a barn.

As soon as horse and woman rounded the building, Jake's gun boomed twice, the unexpected move startling everyone there. Women screamed. Men cursed. And a baby started crying.

"Jesus!" someone exclaimed.

Everyone stared dumbfounded as Chester Ainsley fell

onto his butt, looking down at his right thigh in shock. His holster had been shot off, and his gun lay nearby, blown in half.

"I never even saw him draw," someone in the crowd exclaimed.

"Jake!" Randy called from the food barn.

"I'm fine." Jake watched Ainsley a moment more, then holstered his gun.

Henry Till sighed and shook his head. "He didn't even get a chance to draw."

"Why drag it out?" Jake asked. "I never draw first, but if I'd given him a chance to fire, God knows *who* he might have hit. I figured I'd better get that gun away from him before any damage was done."

Henry chuckled. "I'll have my men throw him and the woman off the *Double T*."

One of Henry's men helped Chester up. Stella came back around the corner, leading Chet's horse and still cursing Jake.

Jake turned to Henry. "Like I said, trouble is brewing. Things like this keep happening. Just small stuff right now, but you'd better be alert to something bigger."

"And look who's *making* that trouble, Jake—Brady Fillmore, that no-good Grizzly Smith, and now a drunken cowboy carrying a grudge," Henry said. "They are all the kind of men any of these cowboys can take care of. Quit worrying."

"I'm just warning you to be aware."

"One hell of a shot, Harkner!" a man yelled, interrupting the conversation. He was helping Ainsley to his feet. "You didn't even scratch his leg. How in hell can you shoot that close to a man and not hit him?"

"Because I wasn't *aiming* for him. I was aiming for the holster. He's damn lucky I didn't aim just a little more to the right. He wouldn't be visiting the whores anymore."

That brought more laughter, along with a few feminine gasps.

"You're a murdering bastard, just like Stella said!" Ainsley yelled. "I'm not done with you, Jake Harkner."

"You'd *better* be." Lloyd stepped out of the barn with Randy by his side. "Next time you might end up facing more than just my father."

"I've never seen a shot that good," a *Double-T* man told Ainsley. "Not many men face Jake Harkner and live to talk about it. You oughta' be *thanking* him, not cussing him out."

There came a few more whistles mixed with laughter. A couple of on-lookers even clapped.

"Damn it," Jake muttered. He turned and walked over to Randy and Lloyd.

"I kept an eye open, Pa," Lloyd told him, "just in case some other drunken cowboy thought he'd make a name for himself while your attention was on Ainsley."

Jake scowled. "I hate being the reason some idiot might start shooting and hit innocent people." He put an arm around Randy's shoulders. "I'm sorry."

Randy wrapped her arm around his back. "I don't know why men can't leave you alone."

"You two go eat," Lloyd told them. "I'll talk to Henry about where to have the ranchers' meeting." He met his father's eyes. "Pa, it was nothing. Shooting at his holster was a good idea. Nobody got hurt."

Jake frowned as he walked away with Randy. Various guests stopped him on the way into the food barn, expressing compliments about the good shooting. Some praised him for how he'd handled Chester Ainsley.

"I hate this," he told Randy.

They put up with nearly twenty more minutes of interruptions and handshakes before being able to fill their plates and sit down.

"We'll get out of here first thing in the morning," Jake told Randy. "I'm anxious now to get you alone up on Echo Ridge and be away from all of this."

"That sounds wonderful." Randy rubbed his shoulder. "Try to eat something."

"You need food worse than I do. You're still too thin, ever since . . . "

Randy poked at some ham. "I know."

"Eat up while you can. If things like this keep happening, we won't be invited to any more cookouts," Jake added.

"Of course, we will. In fact, I already volunteered to hold the next one at the *J&L*."

Jake cut into a roasted potato. "Did you check with Lloyd?"

"Of course. He's fine with it."

Jake glanced past the crowd to see two of Henry Till's men running Chet and Stella off the *Double T*. *Good riddance,* he thought.

"You okay, pa?" Jake's adopted son Ben sat down beside his father.

"'Course I am."

"That man must be nuts to try a show-down with somebody like you."

"There is one in every crowd, Ben. You just remember that's no way to live, and the day is coming when it will probably be against the law to walk around with a gun strapped to you hip, so get used to living a better way. You know how I feel."

"Sure, I know. So do Stephen and Jake, but we still want to learn – just in case. We want to help Lloyd run this place when – " The young man paused. "I mean – "

"I know what you mean. It's a fact of life, Ben. I won't always be here, so you remember everything I've tried to teach you."

"Yes, sir. I'm sorry."

"Don't be." Jake cut a piece of ham. "It just means you're thinking about Lloyd and the future of the ranch. Nothing wrong with that." Jake finished his meat, then realized Ben was being oddly quiet. He glanced sideways at him and saw tears in the boy's eyes. He rubbed a hand across Ben's shoulders. "Ben, it's okay."

Ben sniffed. "I'm just glad to be your son."

"And I'm glad to be your father. Now, eat, and quit worrying about things. I'm damn proud of you – Stephen and Jake, too."

They continued eating, and Randy decided to lighten the moment. "So, you've met Stella before today?"

Jake grinned. "She was among those Lloyd and Vance and I took care of a couple of weeks ago, when we rode out of here to chase off nesters. I knew right away she wasn't any common farmer's wife."

"Of course you did. Did she make you an offer?"

Jake snickered. "You jealous?"

"Oh, I stopped being jealous years ago."

Jake wiped his hands and mouth with a checkered cloth napkin. "Well, she *did* try to get out of it by plying her trade right there in a wagon, but even Vance didn't want anything to do with her. She's the kind who would get a man drunk and then steal his stash as soon as he passes out."

"Not like Gretta, I suppose."

"*Nothing* like Gretta."

Randy raised her eyebrows in mock scolding. "And how am I supposed to take that remark?"

"Exactly like it sounds, Mrs. Harkner. Gretta is one of the good ones, and like you said, I should know. Now, finish that food. Let's get this shindig over with and head for Echo Ridge. What you are suggesting is just making me want to get you alone."

Ben giggled. "You and mom are funny," he told Jake.

Jake glanced at Randy, and they both smiled. Jake leaned closer and kissed her. "Your mother is one in a million, Ben," he told his son. "Any woman who puts up with me deserves some kind of medal."

Stephen and Jake hurried over to set down plates of food across from Jake and Randy. "Good shootin'," young Jake told his grandfather. "Boy, oh boy, you sure showed everybody!"

Jake just rubbed his eyes, wondering what he was going to do with his namesake. The kid couldn't wait to *"shoot a gun like grandpa can."* "All I did was show you that you don't need to kill or injure a man just because he's being stupid," Jake told him. "There is always someone who thinks he can make a name for himself the way Ainsley tried to do. The key is to never allow yourself to gain a reputation with a gun in the first place, Jake. You remember that. It's not like you think."

"Oh, I know. But shooting his holster off – wow! I can't believe your aim! You didn't even injure that man!"

"And that's what I want you to remember. Now, eat. I think the Tills have some kind of games planned for you kids. Both of you should go keep an eye on your sisters and brothers and help the Tills."

"Yes, sir," Stephen answered. He turned to young Jake and gave him a nudge. Both boys chuckled and dove into their food.

Jake glanced at Randy again. She smiled and touched his arm. "They will turn out just fine," she assured him.

Jake kissed her cheek. "Finish every bit on that plate. That's an order." He rose and stepped over the bench of the picnic table. "I'm going to have a smoke."

"Jake, you didn't finish all your food."

"I'm not that hungry." He glanced at young Jake. "You boys keep your grandmother company for a few minutes. And be sure to thank the Tills for all their work."

"Sure, Grampa," both boys answered.

Jake rose and walked aside to light a cigarette. He leaned against a support post near the entrance to the barn and watched the boys joking around as they ate, listened to Randy's laughter . . . a good sound. He remembered her running to him when he made it home from Mexico . . . running through the snow in nothing but stockinged feet, because when she heard his whistle, she didn't even stop to put her shoes on.

*I knew you would come back!* How many times had she told him that?

*I'll always come back for you, mi amor.*

## CHAPTER 17

"I could sit here with your arms around me and stare at this view forever." Randy leaned back against Jake's chest. "In fact, if heaven is like this, then I'm not afraid of death."

She sat between Jake's legs, his arms around her and his chin resting on the top of her head. From a grassy knoll high on Echo Ridge, they studied the magnificent scene below. The homestead was in sight, though the houses were just tiny dark spots against a wall of pine and mountain.

"I lost a fear of death a long time ago," Jake answered. "I've been too damn close to it too many times. I've witnessed it my whole life. In fact, instead of *waiting* for the Grim Reaper, sometimes I feel like I *am* the Grim Reaper."

Randy squeezed his arm. "Jake Harkner, you've been in a mood ever since the cookout. Don't let what happened spoil our time here. And, by the way, I am proud of how you handled that drunk. You know, sometimes humiliating a man in front of others can be just as satisfying as shooting him."

That brought laughter from Jake. "Baby, I thought you understood me."

"I do. Don't tell me you didn't take secret pleasure in shooting that man's holster off and making him fall on his rump."

"I guess I enjoyed it some, but if he had hurt someone innocent, he'd have ended up with more than a sore ass."

Randy grinned. "Well, the way you went easy on him impressed everyone there. So put it behind you and let's think of things to be grateful for, like the fact that we're here alone to enjoy this beautiful place we love, and that we have known peace and quiet since you got home from Mexico."

Jake sighed deeply and kissed her hair.

"All right. If you want to talk about things to be grateful for, I'm glad I was *able* to come home. To tell you the truth, Randy, I think I *did* die in Mexico, and somehow that old Mexican Indian who found me managed to bring me back to life. I suspect it was our daughter's fervent prayers back here at home that convinced the Man Upstairs to – once again – let me live."

Randy kissed his brawny forearm. "There. You see? God isn't ready for you yet."

Jake snickered. "Woman, I've always told you not to be so sure that once I'm gone from this earth, I'll go *up* instead of *down*. I'm amazed death hasn't claimed me already, but it will, and I figure it won't be pretty when it happens."

"Don't talk that way, Jake. I have never been able to imagine living without you."

"Yeah? Well be careful what you wish for, my darling wife."

Randy turned her head up so they could kiss. "I can take whatever comes, as long as I have these arms around me." She turned her attention back to the scene before them. "Look at the colors on the mountaintops way out to the right. I love when the morning sun lights them up. And down in the valley, Horse Creek sparkles like little diamonds. And Evie's Garden Valley is such a deep green. It's been a good summer so far. We've even had more rain than usual, and we have that wonderful trip to Chicago ahead of us." She snuggled closer. "This view is like Heaven. Tell me what you see, Jake."

He snickered. "I'm not poetic like you."

"Yes, you are. I've heard you say such lovely things about the children and the grandchildren. And the way you say words of love to me in Spanish is so beautiful. You have a surprising way with words sometimes. In Jeff's book you said I was the air you breathe. That's one of the most poetic things I've ever heard you say."

Jake kissed her hair again. "I remember when I said that. It was at that little yellow house we lived in in Guthrie." He paused. "Jeff asked me to describe how I felt about you. I was laid up with that leg wound at the time, and all I could think of was seeing your beautiful face and hearing you pretty much *order* me not to die when I was laying out there in the street practically bleeding to death. *Just keep breathing, Jake,* you told me. So, I kept breathing because my wife *demanded* it. And you were leaning so close, it was like you were putting your own breath in me." His voice broke a little and he took a deep breath, then cleared his throat as he stroked her cheek with the backs of his fingers. "I don't think in poetic notions. I just describe things the way I see them." He laughed softly. "Hell, I know a few men who'd have a good laugh if you told them I was poetic."

Randy grinned. "I'm sure of that. Now, tell me what you see right now, in whatever glowing terms you can manage."

"Why are women such romantics?"

"It's in our nature. And you don't even realize it, Mr. Harkner, but you are absolutely the most romantic man who walks the earth."

That got a heavier laugh out of him. "I wasn't very romantic when we first met. I was lost and lonely and running from the law. I never slowed down until I landed in your house with that belly wound you, of all people, gave me. I guess that God of yours figured the only way to make me see another way to live was to force me to stay in one place . . . and to watch a beautiful young woman cook and bake and nurse me and, I don't know, show me what peaceful means, I guess. When we parted ways after I got well . . ." He paused again. "God, I missed you, Randy. All I could see was that scared look in your eyes, but I was scared, too - scared of falling in love with a decent woman.

I knew you wanted me to take you to Nevada to find your brother, but I ran instead. It didn't take long to realize that I by-God couldn't go on without you, though, so I turned back around. When I found you at that filthy trading post dying from a snake bite, I knew I wanted to love and protect you for the rest of our lives, but—"

Randy felt his pain. "None of that, Jake. You didn't fail me, so stop going back to that. You're supposed to tell me what you see down in the valley."

Jake gave her a tug. "You won't give up, will you?" He sighed. "Okay, but don't take this too far. Talking about feelings is not one of any man's best qualities. When you're forced to shut off all feelings for half your life, it's hard to find them again."

"I know. But that's the *other* Jake, not the one I'm sitting here with now."

He remained quiet for several long seconds. Only the sound of a gentle wind through nearby pine trees and the distant cry of an eagle could be heard.

"Okay. You asked me to describe the scene before us. I

see life in the way Horse Creek meanders through Evie's Garden Valley . . . I see your eyes in the mixture of gray and green below." He paused and kissed her hair again. "I see glittering little birds fluttering about, kind of like how the aspen leaves move in the wind. I see power in the eagle that's circling up there . . . and I see a fragile woman when I see a doe grazing with her babies—a strong, protective husband in the buck nearby. I see a homestead that spells love for—" He hesitated and cleared his throat. " - love for a man who doesn't deserve it. And in those mountains, I see incredible strength. I see myself there, standing against anyone who dares to threaten those I love. Men don't appreciate the magnificent beauty of these mountains. They have been digging at them for years now, robbing them of their minerals, all for money. And yet there those mountains stand, refusing to crumble from mankind's onslaught." He sighed deeply. "There. Are you satisfied with my poetic abilities?"

Randy blinked back tears and drew a deep breath. "Jake, you never cease to amaze me. For all the ugliness you've been through, you can still speak like the best of poets. The way you were raised, I find that miraculous. It breaks my heart to think of what a smart, beautiful, soft-hearted little boy you must have been. How can any man mistreat such a beautiful child?"

Jake scoffed. "That little boy killed his own father, and by then he wasn't soft-hearted at all. That side of me died when I helped bury my mother."

Randy turned her head and saw his eyes brimming with tears. Again, she saw the boy who'd never once received love or a hug or a word of praise from his alcoholic father, only ugly, shouted words . . . and beatings.

"You know you couldn't help what happened when you were little," Randy reminded him. "And remember what you're worth to *me*—to the whole family - to the men who call you friend. I loved your description of the landscape, and I'm going to write it down before I forget the words." She knew he was teetering on the edge of going to that dark place she hated him to be in. "Jake, keep your mind on the present, not the past. Let's enjoy the here and now—this moment—the quiet. It's going to be a hot day in the valley, but up here it's cool and so beautiful."

They sat in silence for several minutes.

"I just realized how long we've been out here." Randy turned more to meet his gaze. "I'm getting hungry. How about you? Want some breakfast?"

He smiled sadly and shook his head, then grasped her face in his hands and gently kissed her. "No. I just want you." He grasped her arms and turned her, rolling her over onto the blanket they sat on.

Randy laughed. "You mean *here? Now?*"

"Here and now." He opened the blanket that was wrapped around her shoulders. "You know how lying with you always helps my mood. And we're leaving here in the morning. Once we're home, grandkids will be bursting out of all those extra bedrooms most nights. We won't have these chances to be alone."

Her eyes widened. "Jake, we're out here in the open! It's like . . . I don't know . . . like having sex in front of God."

He snickered. "You don't think God sees us when we have sex in our bedroom?"

"Well, I suppose He does, but—"

Jake laughed harder. "Good Lord, Woman. You have the strangest ideas when it comes to this. Is this yet another rule? We can't have sex on this beautiful, warm morning under the rising sun with eagles flying overhead?"

"Well, it just seems—"

"I'm putting my foot down."

Randy frowned. "What on earth does that mean?"

"It means you can't set any more rules as to when and where we have sex."

Randy thought a moment, then burst out laughing. "*You* are putting your foot down? What on earth are you going to do to punish me if I object? *Shoot* me?"

"I'll refuse to make love to you—for as long as it takes for you to stop making rules for when and where we can make love."

Randy laughed again. "*You*? The man who, according to Gretta MacBain, reeks of sex? *You're* going to hold out on *me*?" She pushed at him. "You wouldn't last a week, if that long. You *love* sex."

"And you don't?"

"Well, I mean, with *you* I love it."

"Then we should make love any time we feel like it. I've told you before that you can't count on how long I'll be able to keep this up. Why do you think so many old men ogle young women? They're wishing they still had what it takes to please them."

Randy reached up and ran a hand through his thick hair. "You, Mr. Harkner, will *always* have what it takes."

He chuckled. "You'd better pray you're right."

"And what if *I'm* the one who gets too old to handle a stallion like you?"

Snickering, he nuzzled her neck. "We'll figure it out." He began unbuttoning her dress. "I'll find ways to make it pleasant."

"I'm sure you will." Randy took joy in his changed mood. "Do you know how much I love your laugh? And that smile? All you need to do to get me under you is smile at me."

"Is that so? Most men would say that makes you easy."

"I *am* easy when it comes to you."

Reaching inside her dress, Jake gently massaged a breast as he met her mouth in a deep kiss.

Randy closed her eyes when his lips moved to her throat. "Jake, I love this, but we made love just last night, and Lloyd has men posted all over this ranch. Someone could be watching us right now. They all carry looking glasses so they can see things up close."

He leaned down farther and kissed her nipple. "I know where they all are. No one can see us in this spot. I'd never take that chance with you."

"What about Vance? He's down below somewhere keeping an eye out to make sure no one bothers us. What if he rides up here?"

Jake licked his way back up to her mouth for another deep kiss. "He'd go to the cabin first. And he knows I'd fire a warning shot if we needed help." He leaned lower and kissed her breast again. "And we sure as hell don't need any help right now." He ran one hand up her leg, over her thigh and hip, then grasped her bottom.

They'd dressed quickly to go for a walk, and up here Randy didn't wear the bothersome underthings Jake hated. No girdle, camisole or stockings, just a dress. No one was around. They could go for a walk naked if they wanted and, knowing Jake, he'd have no qualms about doing just that if she let him.

The conversation ended. Jake's butterfly kisses along the inside of her thighs led to secret places that brought on a climax. He moved inside of her before it was even over, filling her to her very depths. The shirt he'd never buttoned when they first dressed was still open, and Randy leaned up to kiss his solid chest, then laid her head back and watched the eagle soaring above them now. Jake said he saw power in the eagle. She did, too, but that power was Jake himself.

He moved in sweet rhythm, and she took him with

matching thrusts, luxuriating in the way he had of turning her into as wanton a woman as those he used to visit above the saloons.

In these intimate moments they drew strength from each other. More than that, when Jake made love to her, it soothed his ugly memories . . . memories that often took him away from her and into dark places where she could not reach him.

He finished with powerful thrusts mixed with deep, erotic kisses then lay there breathing deeply for some moments. He moved slightly off her, his lips near her ear. "Want more poetry?"

His sincerity surprised her. "Of course."

"It's going to sound pitifully melancholy coming from someone like me."

Randy kissed his chest and ran a hand along his arm. "I'd never take lightly anything you say, nor would I think it was pitifully melancholy. I love that side of you."

Jake pulled the extra blanket over them.

"Okay. Here it is. When we came up here, I saw a pine tree with an extra thick trunk. A vine was growing up the trunk, and I thought that was kind of like us. I'm the solid tree, and you're the vine—wrapped around me, taking life from me. The vine had flowers on it, and to me those were our children and grandchildren. The vine seemed to keep the *tree* alive, like you keep *me* alive."

They lay there quietly until Randy's body jerked slightly.

"Are you crying?" Jake asked.

"Yes."

"I didn't' mean to make you cry."

Randy kissed his chest again and wiped at tears. "Jake, that was incredibly beautiful."

"Just don't tell that story to Jeff. If people read that in

an article about me, they'll laugh themselves out of their chairs."

"I don't think so. They'd sit with their mouths hanging open, wondering how a man like you could have such beautiful thoughts." Randy leaned back to meet his gaze.

He kissed her tears. "Was that pitiful enough for you?"

She gave him a watery smile. "You know it was a perfect comparison to us." She rested her head against his chest and wrapped her arms and legs around him. "And I love being the vine. And you *are* hard and strong like a tree."

Jake rolled her onto her back again. "And the tree and the vine share roots, kind of intermingled, like when I'm inside you."

"I love the feel of you inside me," Randy told him softly.

"I thought you were hungry."

"I am. But not *that* hungry. I can wait."

They made love all over again.

The following morning was sweet and quiet as they made their way down the wide path the men had recently cut into the side of Echo Ridge. A cool breeze wafted down from the mountains, but the sun was bright. Randy could tell it was going to be much hotter later. She hated leaving, but their four-day stop here was over. Up here, she had Jake all to herself. Here they fed off each other's strengths. Here, Jake was calm and happy, where he expressed feelings he never expressed otherwise. Here, they made wild, passionate love right out in the glory of Mother Nature. And here, they knew only peace. But now it was time to get back to normal life, as well as pack for their trip to Chicago.

They reached the bottom of the steep trek down when they saw a rider coming.

Randy rode up beside Jake. "Who is it?"

"Looks like Cole."

Randy's stomach tightened. "If he's coming to find us, maybe something's wrong."

"Maybe. Stay beside me." Jake urged Thunder into a gentle trot, and Randy kept pace with him.

"Yeah, it's Cole," Jake said as they drew closer.

When they reached him, Randy noted the look of sorrow in Cole's eyes. *Dear God, what's wrong?*

Cole adjusted his hat.

"What's happened?"

"Well, Jake, I don't like bringin' bad news when you two are enjoyin' some peace up here, but it's Katie . . . She lost her baby."

Removing his hat, Jake looked away. "Shit," he muttered.

"Oh, no," Randy lamented. "Is Katie all right?"

"Far as I know. Her ma is with her, of course, and Evie. You know Evie. If anybody can pray Katie out of her sorrow, Evie can. And from what I'm told, Katie didn't lose a lot of blood or anything like that. The baby was full developed but wasn't breathin'. They tried everything, but I guess it just wasn't meant to be. In fact, Brian thinks the baby had already been dyin' inside Katie. That's why she felt sick and was so tired all the time. I think she suspected somethin' wasn't right." Cole rubbed at the back of his neck. "I swear, though, it seems like it was worse on Lloyd than on Katie. That's why I came to get you."

Jake closed his eyes. "Whiskey?"

"We all know he's had a drinkin' problem in the past, and Randy and Evie had to work real hard to keep him from turnin' to the bottle again when you went missin' down in Mexico. We decided it was best you get home and talk to him, on account of he usually listens to you on things like that. He sat up all last night at that little grave and drank."

"Oh, no," Randy said softly.

Jake put his hat on. "Cole, you bring Randy home. I need to high-tail it back and I don't want her riding that hard."

"Jake!" Randy called as he started off.

He turned Thunder, and Randy rode up beside him. She reached out and squeezed his arm. "You stay strong, not just for Lloyd, but for you and me. If Katie's okay physically, they'll get through this. I love you."

Jake leaned over and kissed her. "I'll be all right." He turned Thunder and whipped him into a hard run, heading for the homestead.

Randy turned to Cole. "Things like this are so hard for him to handle."

"I know. Gretta thought about goin' up to that grave and talkin' to Lloyd, but she figured maybe she should let Jake do that. She wasn't real sure what Lloyd would be like drunk."

"He can get pretty angry. He took a swing at Jake once after Beth died. But minutes later he fell right into Jake's arms like little boy."

"Jake's a good father—probably better because of wantin' his own kid to have what he never got as a kid. I ain't never seen a man love his pa as much as Lloyd loves Jake."

Randy smiled through tears, feeling achingly sorry for Lloyd and Katie, but proud of the kind of father Jake was.

# CHAPTER 18

Gretta wiped her hands on her apron as she opened the front door to see Jake standing there. "I heard you ride up."

"Have you seen him? Talked to him?"

"No. It's not my place."

Jake closed his eyes against the tears that wanted to come. He leaned against the door jam and lit a cigarette. "I just thought . . . I don't know."

Gretta smiled. "Randy told me that in times like this you sometimes turn to women like me. It's okay." She took hold of his hand. "Lloyd is up on that grassy knoll north of the barns. Cole told me that's where the family planned to start a burial plot, but nobody expected there would be a grave up there this soon." She squeezed his hand. "Just go to him, Jake."

Jake took a drag. "Sorry to bother you. I just thought I'd, uh, see how things are first. I don't want to talk to Evie yet. I know her heart, and she's surely grieving, too."

"She's with Katie, helping take care of her . . . and praying for her, of course. Your daughter's a pillar of strength, very much like her father, I might add. She'll be fine, and she'll make sure Katie gets through this. Lloyd, too."

"Times like this I don't *feel* like a pillar of strength, believe me." Jake sighed. "Cole is bringing Randy in. They are probably about an hour behind me. I rode pretty hard - wanted to get here as quick as I could." He swiped his shirt sleeve across his eyes, then met her gaze. "How bad is Lloyd?"

Gretta patted his chest. "I'm not sure. I only know he sat up there by his baby boy's grave all night nursing a bottle of whiskey. He's probably feeling like hell this morning—in every way. Remind him that he should be hugging **Katie**, not a bottle of whiskey. You are more than most with what alcohol does to a man."

Jake adjusted his hat. "I'm familiar, all right." He stepped away and smoked quietly for a moment. "Jesus," he muttered, before turning back to Gretta. "I don't want my son to be dependent on that demon drink like my father was."

"You just remember one thing, Jake." Gretta put a hand on his arm. "Your reasons for not drinking are linked to what you went through with a mean sonofabitch for a father, and with believing you aren't worth a shit. It's different for Lloyd. He has a damn *good* father, and he drinks because he loves *too* hard, just like you. He'll come out of this—for Katie—and for you, because he hangs on your every word."

Jake tossed the cigarette. "You can't grow up like I did and then know how to be a decent father who always has the right words. It was easier when he was little."

Gretta stood on her toes and kissed his cheek. "Just love him, Jake. You have a wonderful son." She stepped back then, putting her hands on her hips. "Go out there to Lloyd now, and just be there for him – and for Katie and for you *wife* when she gets here."

Jake took hold of Thunder's reins and mounted up. "Times like this, a man feels torn in about six different directions."

"You just zero in on what's most important at the moment, and that's Lloyd. Everything else will fall into place, Jake. Don't think you need to be everything to everybody all at once. *Nobody* can do that. Go talk to your son for now."

Jake nodded. "Thanks." He turned his horse and headed for the spot Lloyd had fenced off last fall for a burial plot. He and Randy would be buried on Echo Ridge near the line shack they loved, but a family the size of theirs needed someplace to bury everyone else—a thought that tore at Jake's heart. He hoped he never saw another grave on that knoll before he died himself.

Aspen and pine surrounded the high, quiet, grassy area where the earth was soft, unlike the hard, rocky ground found in most of the foothills. Thick, green grass grew here, and Jake could see Lloyd sitting near a fresh mound of earth. His heart tightened. He hated to see his son grieving.

Lloyd watched him as he rode closer, and Jake could see his eyes were bloodshot. Jake dismounted and smacked Thunder's rump, knowing the horse would return to the barn on its own. He removed his hat and walked through the gate to the still-unmarked grave, then stood there quietly a moment, head bowed.

"It was a boy," Lloyd told him, his voice flat. "We named him Gabriel, because he'll never be more than an angel." He snickered sadly. "Gabriel Lloyd Harkner. How's that for one of Jake Harkner's grandsons? Named after an angel."

Jake removed his gun belt and dropped it to the ground. Pain from his bad leg made him wince as he managed to sit down in the grass beside Lloyd. "Well, Evie calls me an avenging angel, so I guess that's a good name for a grandson of mine. And it's good you gave him your name, too."

A gentle wind blew some of Lloyd's long hair into his face. He brushed it back with his fingers. "It's strange, Pa. All the awful things I saw when we rode together in Oklahoma, all the blood and guts, the shootings, the fist fights, the stabbings, women beat up, the Indian massacres we came across . . . I could handle all of it. But when I held that dead, bloody little body in my arms—" He let out an odd gasp and wiped at his eyes.

Jake put an arm around Lloyd's shoulders. "I'm no Evie, son. I don't have the words of faith and all that, but if I do get to Heaven, I'll get to meet Gabriel Lloyd Harkner, and I expect he'll be healthy and smiling. Maybe God will let me in just long enough to get to know him before I'm kicked out. Either way, it's a good bet I'll meet him long before you do. So, if I stay in Heaven, I'll be sure to look out for your son until you get there."

Lloyd laughed softly, then turned away, his shoulders shaking.

Jake struggled to find the right words. "Lloyd, I figure Evie would say this was God's decision, not yours, and not Katie's. Something went wrong, probably days or weeks before he was born. You know that from how Katie was feeling. That little boy might be happier where he is now than he would have been on this earth. You have to accept that." He rubbed at Lloyd's shoulders again. "I see that broken flask of whiskey lying over there against a pine tree. You're smart enough to know whiskey just makes things worse, and I don't need to remind you that you need to fight the urge. You know what it did to my father, and why I won't drink that stuff."

"I know." Lloyd sat up straighter and again wiped his eyes and nose on his shirtsleeve. He pulled a cigarette from a shirt pocket, as well as a match. He flicked his fingernail over the match to light the cigarette, then handed another smoke and a match to Jake. Jake cupped his hand to keep the wind from blowing out his match and lit up. Both men sat quietly smoking for a few minutes.

"You know you need to get down there to Katie, right?"

Lloyd inhaled deeply. "I know."

"And you know even I don't mind downing a shot of whiskey now and again, but not when I'm angry or depressed. It's the same for you, Lloyd. It wasn't easy keeping you sober after we found you on the Outlaw Trail. And especially after Beth died. You've had your own hard times, but whiskey can never be the answer."

"I know that, too."

"Alcohol will always be a temptation, so you have to see it as the enemy. I put up with my leg pain because I won't use Laudanum. It's nothing more than whiskey with some other shit in it, and a man can get hooked on it just like on whiskey. So, I stay away from both and bear the pain."

Lloyd took his cigarette from his lips. "I want you to keep your promise, Pa, that when you go to Chicago you'll look for a good doctor, a specialist, who maybe can give you something to help your pain."

Jake looked out toward the homestead below. "I promise."

"Brian's a damn good doctor, but he can only do so much. He feels bad that he can't do more for you."

"Hell, the man has saved my life more than once. He has nothing to feel bad about."

Lloyd rubbed at his eyes. "He's a good man – the best. He's perfect for Evie. I'm glad she found him while I was off drinking and shooting my way along the Outlaw Trail.

I'll never forgive myself for abandoning Mom and Evie while you were in prison." His voice broke.

Jake sighed. "Lloyd, my list of things to be forgiven for would take hours to read. But one of the worst is betraying you by concealing my past when you were growing up. That came back to kick me in the teeth."

"And I'm the one who did the kicking."

"You reacted out of shock and hurt. And now you're a father—to three beautiful sons and a beautiful daughter. Remember that. You've just buried a fifth child, but those other four all need you. And they need you clean and sober. More than that, *Katie* needs you. Go down there and help her through this. Stay away from the goddamn whiskey."

Lloyd nodded and met his gaze again. "You know, Pa, I'm usually the one telling you to straighten your ass out and go to Mom. Since when are you the wise one?"

Jake smiled. "Hell, I just came down from four days on Echo Ridge with your mother. If that can't mellow out a man, nothing can." He gave Lloyd a light shove. "Give me a few days back here, and I'll be the sonofabitch I usually am."

Lloyd grinned. "I don't doubt that."

Jake sobered. "Katie loves you to the ends of the earth, Lloyd, and right now she needs you more than ever. Go take care of her."

Lloyd sighed deeply and wiped at his eyes again. "You're still going to Chicago, aren't you?"

"Only if you're all right. I'm not leaving if you need me around, son."

Lloyd shook his head. "I'll be okay."

"Good. I don't want to have to worry about you. The next time something bad happens, turn to Evie, not a brown bottle of demons. Your sister can help you a lot more than that devil-juice can."

"Yes, sir."

"Stop at our house and clean up before you go to Katie. Don't let her see those bloodshot eyes and that day-old stubble. My shirts fit you, so get a clean one of mine instead of wearing a shirt you've been in since yesterday."

"Yes, sir. Any other orders?"

"Yes. When I go to Chicago, promise you'll wire me right away if you need my help with *anything* on the J&L. You have plenty of men, but by God, there's nobody like your own father to deal with those who decide to make trouble for you."

"Yeah, well, I don't need my father back in prison."

"I have my ways."

"So you say." Lloyd got to his feet and reached down to help Jake up. "We'll be okay, Pa. Marshal Kraemer will keep an eye out, and the men will watch for trouble. Every rancher in the area knows it's brewing, so this isn't just a J&L matter." He met Jake's gaze. "You just have a good time in Chicago."

Jake picked up his gun belt. "Yeah, well, I'm sure Lawyer Peter Brown is also excited about our visit. Your *mother's* visit, I should say."

Lloyd grinned. "Don't worry. You couldn't pry Mom from your side with a crowbar. And Peter's a good man. He's a better friend than you think. He'll show *both* of you a good time, and there's no doubt Jeff is excited to see you, too. "

"Yeah, we had some pretty wild times with Jeff in Oklahoma, didn't we?"

"Hell, it's a wonder we're all still alive."

They shared a laugh that was more of a release of sadness than happiness. Lloyd suddenly threw his arms around his father, and Jake embraced him in return.

"Life can hand you some pretty awful things sometimes, Lloyd. I know better than most." Jake glanced past Lloyd at the broken whiskey bottle. "I've just got meaner blood in me than most men. That helps me ignore the ugly stuff and be glad for the good . . . like having a son like you. I'm proud of you, Lloyd."

"You might not believe it, but I'm proud of you, too," Lloyd answered.

They embraced for several silent seconds before heading downhill, but Lloyd stopped part-way to look back at the fresh little grave. "I never thought the first grave there would be one of my own kids." He wiped at more tears.

Jake grasped his shoulder with a reassuring squeeze. "Just remember your baby isn't in that grave at all. Consider him the lucky one. He got to heaven before any of us did. For now, I'm glad for all the beautiful *living* grandchildren I have."

They headed downhill again. Jake wanted to weep over his lost little grandson, and over Lloyd and Katie's sorrow, but he didn't want to show that weakness in front of Lloyd. He could not wait to hold Randy again. *She* was his whiskey.

# CHAPTER 19

*July 11 . . .*

Evie insisted on an early-morning prayer meeting at her new chapel, located on the rise near the family burial plot. The service had three purposes—to celebrate the completion of the little pine-log church, to pray for Katie and Lloyd and their little lost son, and to pray for Jake and Randy to have a safe trip. Everyone was there, including the hands not out on patrol or working the ranch.

This was the day Jake and Randy would leave for Denver to catch a train north to Cheyenne. From Cheyenne, they would travel east to Chicago.

The heavy mood over prayers for the lost baby lightened when Evie turned to prayers for Jake and Randy.

"Please keep my father out of trouble in Chicago," she prayed aloud.

That brought a few snickers.

She prayed the trip would be a wonderful experience and thanked God for the beautiful weather for traveling. She thanked Him for the law and order Marshal Hal Kraemer represented and asked that he be able to keep the peace as the free rangeland was settled.

"Protect my brother and my father, and all the men of the *J&L*," she prayed.

Randy grasped Jake's hand when he shifted restlessly at the words. She knew he was uncomfortable just being inside the chapel and that he was worried about trouble for Lloyd while he was gone. As though to read his mind, Evie asked God to "help my father understand that he can't protect the whole world, and that not everything that happens in this life is his fault. Bless the goodness in him, and send him and Mother on this lovely trip with Your blessings."

As Evie led a hymn, Jake let go of Randy's hand and leaned forward to rest his elbows on his knees. He hung his head in thought as Gretta's daughter, Annie, accompanied the hymn with piano music. She was visiting from Denver, and the arrival of the piano two days ago had caused pure bedlam for the whole family as they figured out a way to get it into the chapel. Evie had ordered it months ago from a catalogue, and the "gloriously beautiful" piano, as Evie called it, became the center of joy and attention ever since, especially since Annie knew how to play. It was part of her lessons in "becoming a lady."

Jake glanced at her now, remembering how he'd found her in Mexico, a terrified girl too young for what her abductors had planned for her. Seeing her now in a pink, frilly dress with a big pink bow in her lovely blond hair, told him the pain in his leg was worth what he'd gone through to get her back home. She'd grown into a beautiful young woman who had one more year of finishing school left.

She loved visiting the *J&L* whenever she could, and, Jake noticed, she'd taken a liking to Ben, which pleased him greatly.

Evie, having poured over books about theology and

religious studies the past two years, gave her first short sermon. She kept it more personal, talking about forgiveness and "loving those who've wronged us," another subject that made Jake restless.

Forgiveness was not something he was any good at, and he still could not fathom how Evie could forgive the men who'd so horribly abused her. He still felt rage at the memory.

More prayers.

The service was over.

A huge outdoor breakfast followed. Then everyone pitched in to load luggage into the buggy. Jake would ride Thunder while Vance drove Randy and the luggage to Denver. Charlie would follow on horseback with an extra buggy horse in case one might be needed, and Cole would also accompany them.

Randy smiled at the thought of being surrounded by four good men on the trip. Leave it to Jake to make sure she never went anywhere unprotected, although Lloyd joked that he was only sending extra men along to make sure his father boarded the train in Denver without incident.

Leaving was bedlam. Lots of hand shaking with the men—hugs from every single grandchild, from Brian, Evie, Gretta, Lloyd, Katie, Annie and from Ben.

"We'll go hunting when you get home, won't we?" Ben asked Jake. "I want to use my new rifle."

"Yes, Son. We can go hunting by then."

"Don't stay away too long, Grampa," Young Jake told him as they hugged. "We don't like it when you're gone."

"Just remember this is a trip for fun, Jake. We aren't going into any danger," Jake told the boy. "We're visiting Peter and Jeff, and your grandmother will be treated like royalty. I'm sure we will have lots of stories to tell when we get back, if I can even get grandma to *come* back. She might like life in the big city a little too much."

"Oh, Jake, don't be silly." Randy laughed. "How could I ever stay away from this big, beautiful family?"

More hugs.

Annie cried. "Even though I'm safe in Denver now, I'd be scared if something happened to you, Uncle Jake. Who would come to help me if I needed it?"

Jake held her close. "Well, let's see. There are ten or twelve men on this ranch who'd help. Your mother would help. Your adoptive mother would help. And you know damn well Cole would be right there for you. He's the one who got you back to Denver, not me."

"But you couldn't help that. I'll never forget how I felt when those awful men dragged you away. I thought sure you would be killed. I'm still so sorry – "

"No more of that. It's in the past, Annie."

Tricia and Sadie Mae began crying just because Annie was crying. They begged their Grampa to come back "tomorrow."

"Everybody quit acting like we are riding into No Man's Land!" Jake joked. "We are going someplace safe and fun, not going after outlaws. We will be back before you know it." Jake embraced Katie. "You doing okay now, Katie-girl?"

"I'll be all right."

He kissed her hair. "Keep an eye on my son. If he even looks at whiskey, go get the men. They'll rope and tie him and find ways to talk some sense into him."

Katie smiled. "I can handle Lloyd."

"Now you sound like Randy."

They both laughed, and Randy finally climbed into the buggy. Jake gave Katie one more hug, then mounted Thunder. He had packed away his gun belt, extra .44, and another revolver but kept his second .44 in his belt under his suede jacket.

As they started down the drive out of the homestead, Randy was excited, yet sad. She blinked back tears when she looked back from the rise leading away from the family. Every one of them was still waving.

Vance drove the buggy over the rise.

"Hold up a minute," Jake said. He reached out to Randy. "Get out of there and climb up here with me for a while."

Randy gladly obeyed. She reached up, and Jake easily hoisted her in front of him.

He put his arms around her. "You okay?"

She dabbed at tears. "Yes." She met his gaze. "Jake, we've never been away from them. Not the two of us together."

"Not easy, is it?"

Randy detected tears in his eyes, too. "No, it isn't. How did you manage when you left for Mexico?"

He kissed her cheek. "An innocent girl needed help. How could I not go? At least this time, we know we're coming back, so don't be sad." Hugging her close, he urged Thunder into a moderate gait. "You'll be okay when we get into that Pullman car. We'll even spend a couple of nights on the train. We've never made love on a train before."

Randy grinned and leaned against him. "Leave it to you to be thinking about something like that."

Jake leaned to kiss her cheek. "I want you to enjoy every bit of this. Lloyd and I had a long talk last night - about the fact that he has to get used to me not being around because the time's coming when I won't be. You and I both need to unload some responsibilities and have some fun."

"Stop talking about when you won't be here. I refuse to think that way."

"It's just a fact of life."

Vance headed out front with the buggy, an extra horse tied behind it. Charlie rode on the left of the buggy, and Cole rode on the right, a little behind Jake and Randy.

"When we get near land being settled by strangers, I want Randy in the buggy," Jake yelled to all three men. "Cole and I will ride on either side of the buggy and all of us surrounding it. I still feel trouble brewing, and I don't trust Brady Fillmore or Frank Smith. They are still a threat."

Randy thought how strange it was that this was the first trip they had ever taken together just for fun and relaxation. They had spent so many years on the run, lived so many different places –then prison – then Guthrie. Now they were going somewhere to celebrate being free and together. It had taken thirty-three years to reach this moment . . . thirty-three years since they'd met . . . back in Kansas . . . a frightened, lonely young widow meeting up with an ornery, dangerous wanted man.

How could that have been so long ago? Sometimes it seemed like yesterday.

# PART II

*A true friend sticks closer than a brother ...*
*Proverbs 18:24*

## CHAPTER 20

*July 14 . . .*

"Jake, this is beautiful!" Randy sucked in her breath as she scanned the private car that would be theirs for the next two nights. "The hotel room in Denver was lovely, but this is even better than that!"

"I told Peter I wanted the best, and God knows he'd know about such things," Jake replied. "He probably travels this way all the time."

Randy walked around the Pullman, touching the velvet-textured upholstery of the sofa and two large wing-backed chairs. The chandelier, tightly secured to the ceiling with rods, obviously wouldn't sway. The entire car was plush, decorated with heavy brocade curtains at the wide train windows, gold etching along the ceiling, beautifully carved, dark wood trim everywhere, Tiffany lamps, paintings with gold frames, thick carpeting with mosaic designs, everything plush.

"I feel guilty traveling this way." Randy turned to Jake. "Are you sure we can afford this?"

"Sure, we can. I robbed a couple of banks while I was down in Mexico."

Randy laughed and walked up to hug him.

"Actually, you can thank my notorious reputation for this," Jake said. "The money from Jeff's book and the articles he keeps publishing about me are paying for this, and Lloyd insisted on giving me some of that reward money I got for stopping that bank robbery in Boulder. When was that? Two years ago? Four? I'm losing track of time lately."

"But you gave all that money to Lloyd and Evie."

"And they both gave back a little of it – transferred it to our bank account without telling us. They both insisted they wanted us to have it for Christmas last year. They are the ones who suggested we take a trip together."

Randy leaned up to kiss his cheek. "You deserved that money. For heaven's sake, you were shot doing something the town sheriff should have done."

"You and Tricia were in that bank. I had no choice. But it didn't seem right that a former bank robber should take reward money, so I let Lloyd and Evie have it."

Two porters brought their luggage into the car, and Jake gave each a large tip.

"How and when do we eat?" he asked.

"Sir, behind that partition is a buffet with sweet rolls, cold meat, water and wine," one of them answered. "Name's Frank. This other man here is Lou."

Jake nodded to both.

Frank had red hair and spoke with an Irish accent, and Lou was a black man. They both stared wide-eyed at Jake.

"You really Jake Harkner?" Frank asked.

"I really am, and don't make something of it. I'm nobody important, believe me."

"Oh, you're important, all right," Lou stated.

"Oh!" Frank suddenly appeared to have woken from a trance. "A bedroom and private washroom are also behind the partition. Keep the door that leads to the platform at the other end of the car locked. We'll ring the electric bell when we're outside the door. If you need anything, the red button beside the door rings us from your end.

"You and the Mrs. can go out that door any time," Lou added. "There are two passenger cars and a dining car ahead of this one. But this car gives you complete quiet and privacy. And no smoke or soot gets in here. And, unlike trains from years ago, it's warm in here."

"I know about how cold trains can get," Jake told them. "I used to *rob* trains." Jake meant the remark as teasing, but both porters stepped back a little. Jake chuckled. "Don't worry. I haven't robbed a train in over thirty years."

The two men laughed nervously.

"Well, if you were going to again, this would be the one," Frank said.

Lou grabbed his arm. "Hey, you ain't supposed to tell people about that," he warned.

"Tell people about what?" Jake's protective nature kicked in. "Look, I used to be a U. S. Marshal. I know when something is up. Is there something about this train I should be aware of?"

Lou and Frank looked at each other.

Frank swallowed before answering. "Don't tell anybody I said anything, but the mail car's carrying gold from the Denver Mint. An overflow, you might say."

"It's nothing to worry about," Lou cut in. "These trains carry gold all the time, to San Francisco, Philadelphia, New Orleans—all over. They keep those shipments real low profile, know what I mean? The public usually never knows about it, and there hasn't been a robbery on this route for years."

"Oh, Jake, the food!" Randy exclaimed from the other side of the ornate partition. "Sweet rolls, grapes, little meat rolls—and hot coffee! And the bed back here has a beautiful velvet quilted cover."

Jake wrestled with alarm at the idea of gold on the train.

"You won't tell anybody what we just told you, will you?" Lou asked. "I mean, you joking about robbing trains just kind of stirred up our excitement."

"We could lose our jobs if the U. P. found out," Frank added.

"I won't say anything, not even to my wife." Jake gave them a smile. "She's so wrapped up in this fancy car, she probably wasn't even paying attention."

"Thank you, sir!" Both men spoke in unison.

"You – you won't try robbin' this train yourself, will you?" Lou asked cautiously. "Now that you know what's on it?"

Jake couldn't help laughing. "Lou, that was another life, one I don't care to revisit. Besides, I'm getting too old for things like that. Right now, my wife and I are both tired. It's been a long day and two overnight stays just getting to Denver, so if we have food and coffee, we won't need either of you 'til early this evening, maybe not even 'til morning. We might walk to the dining car for breakfast, just to get some exercise and check out the rest of this train."

Both men nodded and backed away.

"It's an honor to meet you, sir," Frank said.

"Thank you very much."

"Thank *you*, sir, for the generous tip," Lou told him. "I'll come back around six to see if you need anything."

Jake nodded and thanked them again.

"We can go out the back door here and walk around outside to the kitchen car," Frank explained. "This train will be underway real soon. Have a good trip, Mr. Harkner."

"With good service like yours, we'll be fine."

Both men left, and Jake closed and locked the rear door. He walked around the partition to see Randy nibbling at the buffet offerings.

"Have some," she told him. "It's all so delicious."

"Quite a setup, isn't it?"

"Oh, Jake, it's wonderful," Randy answered with her mouth full.

Jake loved seeing her so happy . . . and eating. She never ate enough as far as he was concerned. "I hope you know we're going to make full use of that bed."

Randy chuckled and stopped eating long enough to unpin her hat. "How well do I know you? The bed's not big enough, though. Your feet will hang over the end, and we won't be able to sleep without touching."

"And that's supposed to upset me?"

Jake pulled her close and kissed her. "We'll be touching all right . . . a lot . . . and we won't be sleeping when we do."

Smiling, Randy reached around his neck. "Jake, this is far beyond what I expected."

The train lurched a little, and stumbled together. They could hear the muffled sound of the steam engine's horn as it let out three blasts. The train started forward, and Jake pulled Randy over to a love seat next to a bedroom window to look out at the platform. Due to a curve in the track, they could see heavy volumes of steam pour from the sides of the huge engine.

"Mrs. Harkner, we're on our way north to Cheyenne, where they will hook this Pullman to a different train and take us to Chicago."

Randy huddled closer. "I can't believe we're doing this. How long will it take?"

Jake shrugged. "I think we get into Cheyenne

tomorrow late, then it's three more nights to Chicago. We get there the eighteenth."

Randy leaned to look out the window again. "This is so exciting!" Her joyous excitement told Jake he was doing the right thing. He'd promised her this trip, and God knew he'd broken too many other promises. He wasn't about to break this one, but he couldn't help feeling uneasy knowing there was a lot of gold on this train.

# CHAPTER 21

Randy finished brushing out her hair and walked over to sit beside Jake on a loveseat he'd turned toward the large side window. Wearing only the bottom half of his knee-high long johns, he put out a cigarette in an ashtray stand and put an arm around Randy. She snuggled against him, and they watched out the window as the train rumbled through desolate, rugged country.

Wearing only the bottom half of his knee-high long johns, he sat smoking quietly, but he put out his cigarette in an ashtray stand when Randy sat down.

"I like watching the colors change as the sun sets," Jake said.

They were high in the Rockies. They both leaned closer to the window to see below, where a river ran through a deep, deep valley, looking like a silver ribbon in a shaft of evening light. It twisted through rocky terrain, sometimes disappearing into shadows then reappearing as the train meandered along, sounding its whistle in a lonely wail.

"Do you realize we're going right through Outlaw Country?" Jake asked. "We probably traveled some of this on horseback while looking for Lloyd all those years ago."

"Oh, my! Jake, we've lived so many places, most of them wild and lawless. Our trip to outlaw country seems like a hundred years ago now." A rocky bank blocked the view of the river for a moment, then they could see it again when the train rounded a curve. "Jake, look! Wild horses."

Jake watched a herd of mustangs running alongside the river far below. "Pretty picture, isn't it?"

"Yes, but we're awfully high. Makes me nervous."

"It's Colorado. You like Echo Ridge. *That* doesn't make you nervous."

"Yes, but when we're up there, we aren't in a big, heavy train snaking around the side of a mountain." Randy glanced at him. "And we *did* go through country like this looking for Lloyd. My God, Jake, where on earth have all the years gone?"

He kissed her forehead. "For a while it will be just you and me again, like when we first came out here."

Randy leaned closer to the window again. "I can almost see the two of us riding together down there." She turned to see pain in Jake's dark eyes.

He smiled sadly.

"I'm so damn sorry, Randy, for everything you've been through."

Randy wrapped her arms around his neck. "Don't ever, ever be sorry. I wouldn't change any of it if it meant not being with you."

Jake scooped her up, carried her to the bed and laid her on it. He stretched out beside her as the train whistle wailed into the mountain air, echoing in distant canyons and against rock walls.

The view that rushed past outside darkened more as the sun settled behind the highest peaks, and for a few seconds all went black as the train moved through a tunnel. It slowed a little then as it climbed a steep grade.

Jake kept Randy close in his arms.

"I have to confess something."

"Oh? *Now* what have you done?" Randy smiled and traced her fingers over his dark brows.

"The day I rode out of your life back in Kansas was the loneliest day of my life." He kissed her deeply. "But I wanted to get away and raise some hell, figuring that would help me forget you."

"You should have come back and raised hell with *me*," Randy teased, smoothing some of his hair away from his forehead.

That brought the smile she loved. "Would you have *let* me raise hell with you?"

"Probably."

"Even though I was trying to make you hate me, so I'd have an excuse to leave again once we reached Virginia City? I left because I didn't want to make your life miserable by forcing you to stay with me."

Randy sobered. "I have always stayed of my own free will, and It hasn't been miserable at all. It's been hard, but never miserable. Miserable would have been you never coming back for me and never touching me again."

She breathed deeply when he ran his hand under her gown and smothered her with another deep kiss. He lightly ran his fingers over her thigh and on into her love nest, touching her in that way he had of bringing forth the sweet juices necessary to enjoy being a part of each other. He nuzzled her cleavage through the soft gown as he worked his magic.

Randy leaned up and kissed his chest as she ran her hands along the hard muscle of his arms, loving all that was lonely, hard and manly about him, yet he was so devoted to her, iron on the outside, soft sand on the inside.

Her gown came off. His underwear came off. He grew more demanding, hands and lips touching and tasting everywhere, her breasts, her neck, her belly, down her legs to her ankles, moving to that secret place only he had ever claimed. She caressed him in return, feeling and tasting everything male about him, letting the woman in her enjoy the man in him in ways they both teasingly referred to as wonderfully disrespectful.

She kissed her way from the vee-shaped path of hair at his belly, up over his flat middle and solid chest and to his lips. He moved between her legs and pushed his hardness inside her, claiming, branding, adoring, filling her deeply as they held hands and Jake gently moved her arms above her head.

"*Siempre requerdes cuanto te amo.*"

Randy felt a catch in her heart. *Always remember how much I love you.* Why had he said that? She knew his moods. Talking about his loneliness when they first parted had stirred something deep inside. Too many times he'd referred to leaving her one day for good, hinting that it would not be willingly. He was sure death would come in a blaze of bullets.

She wondered if that was what he was thinking about now. He moved harder, deeper, faster, as though to make *sure* she would remember. When he finished, they both lay perspiring, silent until he leaned over her and lightly fondled her breasts, kissing the nipples.

"And now, Mrs. Harkner, after all these years, we've had another first-time experience." He massaged her breasts as he moved his kisses to her throat. "We've made love aboard a train." He smiled down at her.

The darkness she'd seen a moment ago evaporated, and she wanted to keep him smiling. "Well, let's see," she answered. "We've made love in a covered wagon, in cheap hotels, rooming houses, in the open air . . . under the stars, at a fort, and once, even, in a brothel that put us up for a night. If I remember right, about a thousand times in our own big bed at home, in our barn, in a fancy hotel in Denver . . . and now on a Union Pacific passenger train . . . in an expensive Pullman car, no less." She ran a finger over his full lips. "What a wonderful way to travel. Thank you so much for all these comforts, and the food and the privacy—"

Jake cut her off with another kiss, then stretched out beside her. "I'm not crazy about another first that's coming —making love in one of Peter Brown's bedrooms."

Randy gasped and gave him a shove. "Oh, Jake, we can't make love there!"

Jake snickered. "Why. You afraid Peter will hear us?"

"No! But . . . I don't know . . . it just doesn't seem right. We're his guests."

"And that means we can't make love?"

"I don't know."

"Baby, we will be in the home of a man who'd steal you from me in ten seconds flat if he could. I'll need to make sure you remember who you belong to. After all, you might look around that castle of his and start thinking what a nice life you could have if you lived there."

"Oh, stop! You know better. I couldn't live without you. I've been without you too many times, and it's awful."

Jake kissed her and pulled her on top of him. "Right now, it's your turn to do the work."

Randy straddled him and ran her hands over his broad chest then leaned down and kissed him. "I should remind you that not a few rich and fancy women will be enamored with the infamous Jake Harkner when we get to Chicago. You think *I'm* the one to worry about? It will more likely be the other way around."

Jake grasped her hips as she raised up and guided him into her.

He groaned with pleasure, rocking her gently. "And

my eyes will be on *you*, and you alone." He reached up and grasped her hair, arching himself into her as he drank in her nakedness before he rolled her back over to make love to her all over again. *"Yo te amo, mi quiero."*

"And you know how much I love you in return."

His closeness, his scent, this intimacy they shared was wickedly beautiful, familiar yet somehow always new and exhilarating. He always seemed to know when to be gentle and when to be wild . . . when she was too tired, and when she wanted much more than intercourse. He knew what pleased her and what she was uncomfortable doing, even with this man who brought out her wildest needs.

She loved when he tasted her intimately, but he knew she had trouble returning the same intimacy, so he never asked. Despite all these years together, he still cared what she did and did not like, cared that he pleased her, cared if he might do something that would hurt or offend her. His lovemaking was always patient and deliberate.

She climaxed a second time, a deeper, desperate second climax that came from somewhere only Jake could find. Her body pulled him deeper as she felt his life surge into her depths. She told herself not to worry about his comment that she should always remember that he loved her. She could only assure him how much he was loved and needed in return.

Right now, she felt like the most beautiful, pampered, adored, privileged woman on the face of the earth. He kissed her deeply, then put his arm around her and curled behind her, pulling the covers over them both.

"We'll wash up later," he murmured. "I just want to lie with you like this for a while."

Randy kissed the forearm across her chest. "Jake?"

"Hmmm?"

"Let's eat breakfast in the dining car. I want to see who's on the train and what the dining car is like."

"Whatever you want, *mi querida esposa*. I wouldn't mind seeing who else is on this train myself, especially since we'll take on more passengers in Cheyenne. This is still wild country, you know. Lord knows who might climb aboard."

Randy kissed his arm again and snuggled closer. The memory of actually riding with Jake in this wild country after he got out of prison, both searching for their then-wayward son, caused her to relish the feel of Jake's arm around her.

Safety. That's what he represented for her. Safety and bravery and determination. If he was bent on saving someone he loved, nothing stopped him. Fear had no meaning. Death itself had no meaning. That was what worried her.

The wail of the train's whistle against canyon walls sounded lonely, reminding her of how unbearably lonely she would be without this man at her side.

## CHAPTER 22

*July 15 . . .*

Randy stirred awake and looked at a ticking alarm clock next to the bed.

"Oh, my gosh! It's nine am!" She turned to wake up Jake, only to see him sitting in the love seat by the window, fully dressed. "Jake! How long have you been up?"

He took a cigarette from his mouth. "An hour or so."

"You should have waked me. We never, *ever* sleep this late."

"Sure, we do—sometimes. Besides, we're on vacation. And I knew you were extra tired from that long trip to Denver." He stared out the window as he spoke. "I want you to enjoy yourself, and if you're so tired that you need to sleep in, you should sleep in. Doesn't matter to me."

"Well, I'm not used to wasting the morning like this. We did this a couple of times recently at home. That's not like us."

"We're getting older."

"And we can't let that happen. *You* certainly don't act

older most of the time. I swear, I'm the one who will have to keep up with you instead of the other way around."

Randy threw off her covers and rose. "You must be hungry. I know I am. At least I washed up later last night, so all I have to do is get dressed and pin up my hair and put on a little lip rouge. You'll have to give me a few minutes. I didn't plan on sleeping in."

"I can wait." Jake grinned. "I *did* kind of wear you out last night."

Randy waved him off. "I thought it was the other way around."

Jake laughed. "You have to go a long way to wear *me* out, Mrs. Harkner." He watched her remove her nightgown, enjoying the sight of her nakedness as she pulled on clean underwear and a camisole. "You need help with that camisole?"

Randy cast him a frown. "No! You'll end up taking it *off* again and we'll spend another hour in bed, and then I'll have to wash up and get dressed all over again. I'm famished and intend to eat. And, I'm anxious to visit the dining car. I just wish I knew what to wear. Lord knows I don't have anything fancy enough for Chicago once we get there."

"You brought along a couple of perfectly beautiful dresses and hats. For now, wear an every-day dress. We'll be on this train another couple of nights. I'm dressing the way I always dress at the ranch—boots and all."

"You're a man and a cattle rancher. People forgive men for not dressing fancy."

"You'll be doing plenty of shopping in Chicago. Buy whatever a woman needs to wear in society. By the time you're done, we'll probably have to get an extra trunk to haul everything back home, because you'll buy for Evie and Katie, too—and the grandkids, knowing you."

"Don't forget you told me to buy some fancy

underwear and sleep wear," Randy told him as she pulled on her slips. "I believe the word you used was *risqué*."

Jake watched her lovingly. "The more *risqué*, the better. As far as dresses, you could wear a potato sack, and people would only see that beautiful face and hair and complexion. Come to think of it, you hardly *weigh* more than a sack of potatoes."

"And at my age, that could change any time." Randy pulled on a soft green dress that buttoned down the front. "Poor Katie frets about gaining weight. I wish she wouldn't worry about it."

"So do I. Lloyd loves every inch and pound of her. She's a gorgeous woman. Besides, she always loses weight after her babies are born. It's just too bad what happened this last time. She loves giving Lloyd babies. Meeting Katie after losing Beth was a godsend for Lloyd, and he knows it."

"I just hope they've agreed on a way to keep her from getting pregnant again too soon."

"They'll figure it out. We never had to worry about it." He cussed under his breath. "Jesus, Randy, I'm sorry. I didn't mean—"

"I know. I came to terms with not having more children a long, long time ago. And maybe it was best. The way we had to live, it was best we only had the two." Randy started twisting her hair up on top of her head and pinning it there with combs. "And we have wonderful children, Jake, and lots of grandchildren, so we've still been blessed."

Jake looked out the window. "We sure have. But I should have been with you when you had Evie and went through that surgery alone."

"Jake, we promised not to talk about those things." Randy worked on her hair then put cream on her face.

"Life is what it is. We can't change the past. We can just enjoy what we have now."

Jake rubbed at his eyes. "We stopped in Cheyenne really early, and I couldn't see who got on the train because we're so far back in the chain of cars. I think there are nine in all. They might have added one during the night. I felt the train jerk back and forth a couple times." He stood and stretched. "Anyway, we're well beyond Cheyenne and headed straight east. It'll be flat like this all the way to Chicago. I'll miss the mountains, but we should get to Chicago on time."

Randy saw he wore his single-holster gun belt. He took one of his .44's from the bench where it lay and holstered it. Then, to her surprise, he stuck a second .44 in his belt.

"Why are you wearing guns?"

"You know I'm not about to take chances with you. I'll wear my suede jacket. It's long enough to cover my gun belt, so people don't get all nervous at the sight. Besides, we're still in outlaw country, and there's freshly-minted money on this train."

"There is?"

"One of the porters told me yesterday."

"And you chose not to tell me?"

"We were safely locked into this Pullman. But now we're going to the dining car to eat." He walked closer and grasped her arms. "Don't worry about it. You know how I am."

"That's the problem. And remember, you're no longer a lawman."

"No, but *outlaws* haven't retired, and they never will. Until we make it Chicago, I'm taking nothing for granted."

Randy leaned up for a kiss. "You've lived not trusting people for far too long." She walked past him to the washroom. "I'll take care of personals and clean my teeth.

After that I'll put my hat on and be ready to go. It will be nice seeing who else is on this train."

"Let's hope so." Jake donned his black Stetson and pulled on a tan suede jacket.

Randy came out from the washroom, pinned on a small, green velvet pillbox hat, then wrapped a matching knitted shawl around her shoulders that matched the green in her dress. "Let's go eat."

"I'm all for that, ma'am. And, by the way, you look beautiful."

"Thank you, Mr. Harkner."

Jake grinned as he followed her to the door at the front of the car.

"We need to tell Frank or Lou to send us clean sheets, and fresh food for snacking," Randy said as they walked onto the platform at the front of the car.

The train was rolling along at full speed, and Jake kept hold of her arm. "Be careful," he told her. "From here we have to go through two passenger cars to get to the dining car. Watch out for these walkways." They stepped across the narrow steel bridge over the hitch and into the next car.

Jake reached around her to open the door to the passenger car ahead of them.

It was not until they stepped inside and closed the door that they both noticed the passengers, terror in their eyes, looking in their direction. At the far end of the car a gun-wielding man stood over Frank the porter, who lay in the aisle bleeding profusely. Another man, who had apparently been sitting in the last seat, stuck a gun in Jake's back.

"I saw guns on you, Mister," he said in a soft growl. "Drop them. *Now*! Or that woman standing in front of you will die when I put a bullet through your back and into her."

# CHAPTER 23

Randy stood frozen in place. She felt Jake's grasp on her arm tighten.

"I said get rid of those guns," the man behind Jake repeated. "I've never shot a woman, but if I pull this trigger at this close range, you know damn well what will happen."

"Shoot him, Cal!" the man at the front of the passenger car shouted. "He came from the Pullman car. They told us Jake Harkner was back there. That must be him! *Kill* the sonofabitch!"

Cal shoved his gun harder against Jake's back. "I just want to enjoy a few seconds of having Jake Harkner himself at my mercy," he yelled in return.

Everything happened in a matter of seconds then. Jake shoved Randy hard into an empty seat to her right, and as she fell, the passenger car exploded with gunfire. Women and children screamed, and men yelled at their wives to stay down. Randy's head hit the side of the train car, and she landed between the seats. At the same time, she saw Jake falling, heard the familiar *boom* of his guns.

Chaos ensued.

"Jake!" Randy shouted, sure he'd been shot.

He got to his knees, pointing a gun at each end of the car. "Stay down!"

"He's dead!" someone at the far end of the car yelled.

Randy tried to crawl to Jake, but he was already on his feet and hurrying to the front of the car. The man called Cal lay in the aisle right in front of her, groaning and bleeding. Dizzy from hitting her head, Randy still managed to reach out and take his gun out of his hand. Her own hands shaking, she held it on him as she managed to get to her knees.

"Take his gun," Jake was shouting to someone at the other end of the car. "Make sure he's really dead. And somebody help Frank!" He hurried back to Randy, took the gun from her and handed it to a man across the aisle. "Hang on to that and shoot any sonofabitch who comes through these doors waving a gun!" he ordered. He looked at Randy with terror-filled eyes. "Tell me you weren't shot!"

His words sounded muffled. Randy's ears still rang from the gunfire inside the confinement of the train car, and she felt woozy from the blow to her head. "I . . . don't think so. I just . . . hit my head."

Jake holstered one gun and reached to grasp her arm. "Jesus Christ, your head's bleeding. You stay right here, understand? Stay right here—no matter what!"

Randy saw blood on his shirt where his jacket flapped open. "Jake, you're hurt!"

"It's superficial. I know when there is a bullet in me."

"I see a *lot* of blood!"

"Don't worry about it. I'm sorry I shoved you like that, but I had to get you out of the way."

"Please just stay here."

"You stay still, understand? I'll be back for you."

"Jake!"

He was already on his feet. He kicked Cal onto his back and planted a foot onto a bleeding belly wound. Cal let out a horrifying cry, begging Jake to stop, but Jake pointed a .44 straight at the man's middle.

"Mister, you picked the wrong fucking train to rob! And you risked my wife's life doing it. How many of your gang are on this train?"

"Fuck you, Harkner!" the man screamed.

Women and children were still crying, and the train continued to roll, the engineers far in front unaware of what was going on in the last passenger car.

"I asked you a question!" Jake pointed his gun at Cal's gut and thumbed the hammer back. "One belly wound is bad enough. Do you want another one?"

"No! No! No! Please! Stop!" Cal screamed.

"Tell me how many more of your gang are on this train. And where they are!"

Just then a man appeared outside the far door. The dead shooter had been pulled between two seats, but Frank still lay on the floor. The third man looked through the glass.

"What the goddamn hell?" he shouted as he managed to shove the door against Frank's feet. "Cal! Sid!"

Jake's gun boomed again, shattering the glass and hitting the robber while he was halfway through the door. He cried out and fell, then disappeared. No one could mistake the odd thump under the train car then.

"Oh, dear God," a woman moaned. "I'm going to be sick."

"I asked you how many!" Jake roared to Cal. "I just shot one. That makes three! Where are the rest of them?"

"Oh, God," Cal groaned. "One in . . . other dining car . . . two in the . . . mail car."

"Who's ahead of us?" Leaning closer, Jake put his gun to Cal's forehead. "You've got to have men somewhere ahead to get the money off this train. Tell me what's ahead, or I'll blow your brains out!"

Cal was turning white. "Three . . . more . . . with horses . . . wagon."

"*Where?*" Jake shouted.

"Couple more . . . miles . . . east."

Jake rose. "Somebody pull this sonofabitch out of the aisle. Put him on the floor in front of that last seat." He looked toward the other end of the car. "Somebody down there, help Frank into a seat." He stumbled a little.

"Jake, my God, you're still bleeding," Randy cried. "Don't go any farther with this!"

Rage flamed in Jake's dark eyes. "Just stay right where you are. Don't get up. I'll be back." He headed toward the front of the train, re-loading as he went. He stopped and turned.

"You down there!" he shouted to the passenger holding Cal's gun. "Anybody who isn't me or a lawman comes through that door, shoot him! If something happens to my wife because you're too much of a coward to pull that trigger, you'll fucking deal with me!" He turned to a man at the front of the car. "Take the dead man's gun and do the same. Don't let anybody into this car unless it's the law or me."

Jake walked out and crossed the platform and into the next car as Randy moved into the seat so she could see out the window as she waited in terror. Two men sitting in front of her got up to move Cal out of the aisle. He let out a sickening cry of pain and started crying like a child.

"Fucking . . . ruthless . . . sonofabitch!" he yelled in agony. "I hope you *die,* Harkner! You . . . goddamn, murdering . . . outlaw!"

"Was that really Jake Harkner?" the man across the aisle, still holding Cal's gun in shaking hands, asked Randy.

"Yes."

"You're *married* to him?"

"Thirty-three years." Randy put a hand to the throbbing wound at the right side of her forehead. "He's a good man."

"There ain't *nothin'* good . . . about that man!" Cal wept.

"It appears to me like you were stupid to threaten him," said one of the men who'd moved Cal. "Could have been he's more angry that you threatened his wife."

The passengers had quieted, but women still sobbed quietly, and children sniffled as they hugged their mothers. The train whistle blew as the train began to slow down for a right-bending curve, which gave passengers on the car's right side a chance to see up ahead.

"There's some kind of barrier up there," a man exclaimed.

Randy jumped slightly when she heard several shots fired somewhere up ahead. *Boom! Boom! Boom! Boom!* She knew the sound of Jake's guns, but his shots were mixed with others.

*The mail car!* She grasped her stomach in fear he'd been shot again.

"We're all going to die," a woman wailed.

"Harkner's probably dead," one man lamented. "He was already wounded and can't handle that many men."

The train slowed more but couldn't stop before hitting the pile of rocks on the tracks. The jolt made people scream causing several to slide forward off their seats. Then came more gunfire. Too many shots to count.

Randy could see three mounted men waiting by the rock pile, a wagon with them. One tried to ride off but was shot from his horse. Although the air was filled with the sound of gunfire, she again recognized Jake's weapons. Another man waiting outside went down, and the third man threw down his gun and raised his hands, then jumped off his horse and laid down on the ground.

The gunfire finally ended. People's screams and frightened talk quieted. Everyone waited.

"There he is," a woman exclaimed from the other side of the car.

Randy hurried across the blood-stained aisle to the back door and out onto the platform to see Jake stumbling toward her. He looked a little confused.

"Jake! I'm here."

He holstered the gun in his hand and held the other in his left hand, but that arm hung limply. Randy guessed the gun was still too hot to shove it into his belt. He grabbed the railing with his right hand, wincing as he climbed up onto the platform.

"My God, Jake, how bad are you hurt?"

Jake pulled her into his good arm. "Doesn't matter. You come first. Your head is bleeding. My God, Randy, I shoved you so hard. It was the only way I could think of to get you out of the way before that man's gun went off."

"It's all right. Come into our car and lie down. Let me see where you're bleeding."

People opened windows, shouted back and forth. Porters and engineers ran up and down the tracks asking after the injured.

"Mister Harkner!" Lou, their personal porter, climbed onto the platform where Jake and Randy stood. "You two are hurt! Come on into your private car. I'll get some help."

"Hang on to my wife. I don't want her to fall." Jake's voice had weakened some.

"Yessir!" Lou took Randy's arm. "Man, that was somethin'. I saw it all from the kitchen car. Ma'am, your husband shot an outlaw in the dining car, then came plowin' through our kitchen car and into the mail car—

bullets flyin'! He saved a mail guard's life. The other was already dead. Man, I sure have a story to tell my kids when I get home."

The three of them made it into the Pullman, where Jake collapsed onto the bed.

## CHAPTER 24

*July 15 . . .*

Peter picked up the base of his black candlestick telephone and unhooked the receiver to listen. "This is Peter Brown."

"Peter! Are you sitting down?"

"Who is this?"

"It's Jeff."

"Well, hello, Jeff! I'm at my home office today. I didn't know you had my number here."

"Sure, I do. And it's a good thing. I have some news that will knock you out of your chair."

Peter glanced at a grandfather clock in the corner of his office. Three o'clock in the afternoon. "Well, since the Harkners are on their way here, I've a feeling the news is about them. No one is a better newsmaker than Jake Harkner."

"You've got that right."

"Good God, don't tell me Jake shot somebody on the train."

The reply was laughter. "Well, actually, yes. He shot and killed six men and wounded two more. Another one threw himself on the ground and gave himself up."

"What!" Peter set the tube of the phone back on the desk and leaned into it as he spoke. "What in God's name are you talking about?"

"A train robbery! Can you believe it? Somebody tried to rob the train Jake and Randy were on. Word is, one put a gun in Jake's back and told him to give up his .44s or he'd fire. Randy was right in front of Jake, and the bullet could have gone through him and into her. You can imagine how Jake reacted to someone threatening Randy."

Peter gripped the phone's mouthpiece and kept it close as he leaned back in his chair. "Jeff, please start over. I'm envisioning all kinds of things. Is Randy okay?"

Jeff laughed more. "I figured you'd ask about Randy before you asked about Jake."

"Okay. Okay. You know I'm concerned about him, too."

"Well, all kinds of stories are coming through the wire here at the Journal. It all happened about ten this morning, and news is spreading fast, thanks to telephones and the telegraph. All I know is that a total of nine men set out to rob the train they were on. And, by the way, Randy is fine. A bump on the head. I guess Jake had to throw her aside to keep her from getting shot. He took a bullet across an upper rib from behind, I guess, but he's okay, too. He'll probably have some stitches. Anyway, they say Jake had two guns on him when he started shooting."

"What else is new?"

More laughter. Jeff went on to describe what details he knew about the robbery and Jake's part in stopping it. "Those men planned to unload some freshly minted money on its way from Denver to Chicago. Boy, did they get a surprise! Instead of being greeted by their fellow outlaw friends, they were greeted by an outlaw, all right, but it was Jake Harkner. Can you just picture it? I've seen the man in action back in Oklahoma, and it's something to watch. I sure wish I had been there!"

Peter grinned and shook his head. "I wouldn't have minded seeing that myself. Are you sure Randy is all right?"

"We'll find out when they get here, but they might be a day late. Bodies need to be counted, lawmen and reporters want to interview Jake. The train will probably be held up longer at every stop it makes. And hey, both the U.P. and the Denver Mint are considering giving Jake a reward. I bet the Federal government or the bank in Chicago will, too.

What a great way for Jake to arrive here. It was big enough news that he was coming at all, but to stop a big train robbery on the way . . . half of Chicago will probably be at Grand Central to greet him."

"Okay, Jeff, slow down. When you get started on Jake, you don't know when to quit. Give me a minute to absorb all of this. Do you think Jake will need my services as his lawyer when he gets here?"

"Who knows? Maybe to approve another book deal. He's arriving a hero."

"And he hates that kind of attention. Things like that make him ornery as hell. You'd better get word to Lloyd and Evie. They might hear about this without details, and they would be worried to death. They should know their parents are all right. I'll make arrangements to have a doctor ready here as soon as they arrive in case they need one."

"I already sent the family a telegram explaining the whole story, but considering how remote the J&L is, it will take a few days for them to get the news."

"Thanks. I'm glad you got word to them. Lloyd will be beside himself. You know how he is about his father."

"I hate to rejoice over someone else's mishaps, but this

sure gives me something new to write about in those columns about Jake."

"Yes, it certainly does." Peter sat up straight. "As soon as you know when Jake will actually arrive at Grand Central, let me know and I'll meet you there. Thanks for letting me know about this before I read it in the newspapers. I'm sure the headlines will be bold."

"They'll probably be a third of a page high. Come to my office first, Peter. We'll go to Grand Central together, so we don't have trouble finding each other later. Maybe we can get into the Pullman before Jake and Randy get off and check on them before they're attacked by reporters."

"That sounds like a good idea. 'Bye, Jeff." Peter hung up the receiver and put it back on his desk, then leaned farther back in his rich, leather chair and rubbed at his eyes. "Jesus, Jake."

He worried about how all of this might have affected Randy. What a nightmare for her. He could hear those guns booming inside the train car. It must have been deafening for everyone involved. He had no doubt that the first gunman's threat to Randy is what lit Jake's fuse. Once he exploded, Jake Harkner didn't hesitate or worry about bullets or his own life. Jeff had once described him as nitroglycerine. Peter could not think of a better comparison.

# CHAPTER 25

*July 18 . . .*

"Jake, let me look at that bandage."

"Leave it! God knows I've had worse wounds."

Randy set her hairbrush on the dressing table. She was already in her nightgown. This was their third night on the train, after numerous stops where they were pulled to a sidetrack so reporters could interview Jake, and authorities could interview him and thank him. Once they had had to get off the train completely to be taken to a detective's office for questioning. They had to stay in a hotel that night and now would arrive in Chicago a day late. The regular passengers had been put on a different train so they could be on their way without the long stops.

Two million dollars. That was the total of the payload Jake had saved—a mixture of gold and silver coins, and bars of pure gold—all being shipped to the Philadelphia mint because Denver's facilities were not yet complete. Investigators were working on finding out how outlaws knew about the shipment, and promises for a big reward had already been made to Jake.

Randy's heart ached over Jake's pain. When he threw

her aside and ducked, the bullet meant for his back went through his upper left side, cracking a top rib and creating a gouge big enough to require fifteen stitches. Thank God the bullet had skimmed across the outer rib and not harmed his lung.

There was no laudanum available for the stitches, and Jake refused to down enough whiskey to dull the pain. Randy's stomach still hurt at the thought of how much he'd perspired and how hard he'd bitten into a piece of leather as the doctor, whom they luckily had found on the train, stitched the wound closed.

"I really should check and be sure there isn't blood on that bandage, Jake."

He sat in the loveseat watching the scenery fly past the window as dusk dimmed the view. He wore only an unbuttoned shirt and denim pants. No shoes and no guns.

"I already looked in the mirror in the washroom. There are only a couple spots of dried blood. Nothing fresh."

"Jake Harkner, you were passed out for hours after the doctor got done with you. Ever since then you've paced and smoked and have hardly talked to me. I've let it go because I knew you didn't *want* to talk about it, and you were disgusted with having to answer so many questions from reporters and lawmen every time we stopped somewhere. But you need to remember that tomorrow we'll be in Chicago, and there will be more publicity and interviews. You have to get out of the mood you're in and decide to grin and bear it. We can have peace and quiet when we get to Peter's."

"Peace and quiet—and time for that bruise on your forehead and cheek to fade a little?"

Randy marched over to the window and closed the heavy drapes so he couldn't see outside. Arms folded, she faced him. "That's what's eating at you the most, isn't it?

That I hit my head, hurt my shoulder, and I have a bruise on my forehead."

Jake met her gaze, and she saw disgust in his eyes that he'd caused her injuries. Kneeling in front of him, she pushed a piece of his dark, wavy hair behind his ear.

"Jake, if I didn't have these bruises, I would probably be *dead*. So, you tell me what you did wrong."

He sighed, studying the slight swell on her right cheek. He pushed her hair back from her right forehead and temple and scowled at the dark bruise there. "Seeing these bruises and knowing it's because I shoved you so hard just brings to mind things I'd rather forget. My father literally threw my mother across the room more than once."

Randy grasped his hand and kissed his palm, then put his hand to the side of her face. "These hands could kill me in one blow, but never once have I feared you would *ever* use them on me for anything but love and gentleness. You never have and you never will. The fact that you regret hurting me just shows how *not* like your father you are."

Jake swallowed back the tears Randy saw glistening in his eyes and ran a thumb over a small bruise under her eye. "It wouldn't be so bad if it wasn't for the fact that that bastard wanted to kill me because of who I am, and who I am keeps hurting you without me even trying. Don't you see? Now you're all bruised because of that. And I saw the pain in your eyes when that doctor re-set your shoulder."

Randy leaned forward and kissed him, but his lips remained rigid. "And now, it doesn't even hurt." She stroked his hair. "You couldn't help that robbery, and you can't help being the kind of man who'd step in and take care of things. So, I don't want to hear any more about it." She kissed him again, with no response. "Come to bed. Get some sleep. Tomorrow we arrive in Chicago, and it's going to be a big, big day. There's sure to be a crowd at Grand Central Station waiting for the hero of the day, and—"

He put fingers to her lips. "Don't call me that," he said sternly.

"*They* will call you that, whether you like it or not. Let them see you as famous and brave and heroic, because you are, Jake. You saved a two-million-dollar payload, and you went through nine men to do it. To others, that is phenomenal and exciting."

Jake shook his head. "You're impossible."

Randy rose, pulling at his hand. "Come on. Come to bed and get some sleep. You'll need your strength tomorrow, and with all the picture-taking, I want my Jake to look fully as tall and strong and handsome as he normally is."

Jake scoffed as he rose. "I wanted a quiet, low-key vacation that would be all about *you*, not me."

"And I fully intend to have a wonderful time," Randy answered with a smile. "If you insist on being punished for having to shove me out of the way, then rest assured, I will bring you a different kind of pain when I go shopping at the most expensive stores in Chicago. I will punish you by giving your *wallet* a hard punch."

That finally got a smile out of him. "You can hit my wallet all you want."

She put her arms around him and rested her head against his chest. "You keep smiling like you did just now. You know how that smile melts me. And you smile for whoever is there to greet us tomorrow morning."

Jake moved his right arm around her.

"It will take me a couple of days to be able to hug you fully. It hurts to stretch out my left arm. And in a few more days I'll do more than hug you."

"All I've ever needed is you beside me. The rest can wait. I just don't like it when you get in these dark moods." Randy pulled away and started pulling his shirt down over his shoulders. "Let me help you out of this and out of your pants. I want you to sleep tonight instead of pace and fret and smoke and grumble. That wound will heal better when you get some rest."

"Yes, Ma'am."

Randy looked up to see he was still smiling.

"You can be like a damn mother hen sometimes," Jake told her.

"And *you* can be a lot like that rooster you hate back home. Believe me, when you behave like that ornery beast, this hen won't be letting you fertilize her eggs, if you know what I mean."

Jake laughed as he grabbed the back of a chair and stepped out of his pants. "Don't you know those hens probably love the way that rooster struts? That's how the male bird attracts the females. The male is always bigger and more colorful."

Randy just shook her head. "Get into bed. You might be bigger and more colorful, sometimes in all the wrong ways, but this little hen is giving you an order." Randy gave him a little shove. "Go to bed and get some sleep. And stop blaming yourself for what happened with those train robbers."

Jake winced with pain as he crawled under the covers. Randy turned out the lamp and joined him. "I'll keep trying not to touch you so you can get comfortable," she told him.

"No. I miss you lying close," he answered. "Come and lie against my right side."

"Are you sure?"

"Of course I am."

Randy nestled into his shoulder, and he moved his right arm around her. "I'd better hold you close before you are introduced to lawyer Peter's world of mansions and theaters and filthy rich shopping and dining with the elite.

You are about to become the most pampered woman in Chicago, Mrs. Harkner."

"*You* have pampered me for thirty-three years, Mr. Harkner."

Jake snickered. "Tomorrow you will find out you don't know the real meaning of the word."

Randy turned her face to him and scooted up a little. "Jake, what do you always ask me when you are making love to me?"

He sighed and pulled her closer. "Who do you belong to?"

"And what do I always say?"

A train roared past them on another track. "Jake Harkner."

"And that's all that matters." Randy leaned in and kissed him, a kiss that turned passionate with unspoken words. Randy settled in against him again. "Now, go to sleep," she ordered. She listened to the clickety-clack of the train wheels as they rhythmically hit seems in the rails beneath them, and moments later she heard Jake's deep breathing as he fell into a much-needed sleep.

July 19 . . .

Morning came all too soon.

Jake started awake when the train's whistle echoed loudly, and he realized the Pullman was moving very slowly. It jerked to a stop before he could even rise. He winced with pain when in his sleepy state he forgot about the stitches under his left arm.

"Damn," he muttered.

He ran a hand through is hair and walked over to peek through the curtains into the huge terminal of Grand Central Station. He was astounded at its size and realized then why the train whistle had sounded so much louder a moment ago. Several trains sat waiting to either unload or to take on more passengers.

He gazed upward at the immense glass and steel ceiling of the train shed, amazed at the building's architecture. Another train pulled in, steam hissing and billowing from its release valves as it slowed to a stop. Every sound was magnified inside the immense terminal.

He looked down again and noticed a crowd gathering outside the Pullman, some of the men carrying big box cameras. More and more people joined them and talked excitedly, some pointing toward his and Randy's car. Someone noticed him looking out the window and pointed. "There! Is that him?"

Jake quickly jerked the curtains closed. "Shit," he muttered, suspecting the worst. He dreaded leaving the Pullman.

Grumbling, he shook the bed to nudge Randy awake. "Time to get ready, baby. The circus has begun."

She stretched and sat up. "We're here?"

"Yes. We are in the biggest terminal I've ever seen, so this must be Grand Central. I'll go clean up. It won't take me long. Ring for some fresh coffee, will you? I'll have a cigarette and drink some while you get ready." He walked around the bed and knelt in front of her as she sat up. "How's your head?"

Randy shook back her hair and touched her forehead. "Better than yesterday. What about those stitches?"

"I half forgot about them until I rolled over on my left side when I got up." He kissed her lightly. "I'm more worried about what's outside this car. There's a damned crowd gathering out there. I suspect there are more standing on the other side of our Pullman, and probably more behind us. I can't tell how many because I can't see straight out the back. I wish we could send them away. I don't like you being in the middle of all this."

Randy kissed him back. "Those people out there are going to wait as long as it takes to get a glimpse of you, so there is no sense in wishing them away."

Jake rose and grabbed clean underwear and a shirt from one of their bags. "This is ridiculous."

He reached for his denim pants and headed for the washroom. "I'll wear my black suede fringed jacket. I really liked the one I wore coming here, but you can't get blood stains out of suede, so now it's ruined." He went into the washroom and Randy walked to a window on the opposite side of the car to peek outside.

"Oh, dear." She saw a big crowd, some of whom pointed the minute she parted the curtains. She closed them quickly. Realizing Peter and Jeff could show up any time, she hurried to the forward door to ring the service bell, then pulled off her night gown and put on her camisole, quickly hooking it closed. She hurried to put on the rest of her underwear, slips and all.

Everything went fast after that.

"We need coffee," she yelled through the back door when the porter came. She threw on her robe and went into the washroom after Jake came out.

Wash. Dress. Brush hair. Drink coffee. Pull hair up and pin with combs. Jake smoked and ate a sweet roll, neither of them saying much.

Randy adjusted a deep blue velvet hat and pinned it into her hair, which she wore swept up at the sides and held with combs.

"Remember what I told you last night, Jake. Those people out there are excited about seeing you. After all the bad things you've been through in your life, putting up with a little attention won't hurt you. Be kind."

"*Kind*? I killed six men four days ago. And I'm

supposed to go out there and smile and say *Howdy, folks?* They don't know the *real* me. If they did, they would all run for their lives."

"Well, I think the *real* you is pretty wonderful." Randy rose from her dressing table. "And, you don't have to be all smiles. Just answer their questions and don't be rude."

"Yes, Ma'am. Any more orders?"

Randy smiled. "Sorry. I know how much you hate this. If not for that robbery, we would have arrived with far less attention. I'm sure Peter and Jeff aren't happy about this either."

"Are you kidding? Jeff is probably popping his buttons over this – lots of food for more stories and articles. He probably wishes he'd been there for the robbery. He's like a little kid with things like this."

Randy chuckled as she smoothed the skirt of her baby-blue dress, trimmed in the same deep blue velvet as her hat. The fitted bodice accented her figure. She adjusted her bangs and the hat's netting to help hide the bruise on her forehead.

"You look beautiful," Jake told her. "I'm sure Lawyer Peter Brown is far more excited about seeing you than seeing me. He will be properly taken with you in that dress."

Randy put her hands on her hips. "You know I always want to look beautiful just for *you*. And Peter and Jeff should be here any minute. Help me get our baggage in order. Look in the washroom for anything left behind. All we need to do is throw these last-minute things into the carpetbag sitting on the bed."

They hurriedly finished packing, and Jake took the carpetbag into the sitting area and plopped it atop their several other bags. He turned, and Randy looked him over. Denim pants over black Western boots, white shirt, black string tie, black suede jacket. He wore a black Stetson and looked every bit the picture of power.

"You look really nice. How do those stitches feel?"

"Like stitches. Painful and irritating. My whole left side is sore, and my leg hurts, too." He walked around the partition to the buffet and poured himself more coffee from a silver serving pot. "I forgot to tell you that a reporter at one of my interviews said Jeff sent a wire to Brighton to be delivered to the family," he told Randy in a raised voice. He came back into the sitting room. "I'm glad he thought of it. Lloyd and Evie would be worried to death if they heard about that robbery some other way."

Randy drank a little coffee out of his cup. "Jeff is always on top of things."

Someone knocked on the rear door.

"Jake! It's Peter and Jeff." Peter called. "You two dressed and ready?"

"Yes!" Randy called back.

Jake leaned down and kissed her, lightly at first, then more deeply. He followed by kissing her eyes, then the right side of her face. "You did a good job hiding that bruise. You okay? No headache or anything like that?"

Randy adjusted the silver concho that kept Jake's string tie clasped. "No headache. You have to stop asking me."

"I can't help it." Jake set his cup aside and grasped her hands. "You look like you just stepped out of a fashion magazine."

Randy smiled. "Thank you. I got this dress in Brighton."

"Listen, when we go out that door, you remember to stay close to me."

"I will."

"I don't want to lose track of you for one minute in such a busy place."

"Yes, Sir."

He sighed and kissed her yet again.

"Randy – "

"If you say you're sorry one more time, Jake Harkner, I will slap you."

He grinned. "Is that supposed to scare me?"

She laughed lightly. "I'd be better off telling you that if you keep apologizing, I'll refuse to go to bed with you for two weeks."

"Now *that* scares me."

"I thought it would."

Peter knocked on the door again. "Jake! Are you two ready?"

"He's probably hoping to find you half dressed," Jake grumbled.

"Oh, stop it! Go open the door."

Jake sighed and adjusted his hat. "Let's get this over with."

## CHAPTER 26

Jake lit a cigarette before going to the door to greet Peter and Jeff. As soon as he opened the door, cheers and claps filled the air, along with, "There he is!" "That's him!"

Jake stepped back, scowling. "Get the hell in here so I can shut this door."

"Well, it's good to see you, too, Jake," Peter said as he and Jeff came inside.

Jake closed the door and surprised Jeff with a big hug, lifting him right off his feet. "Jeff! My favorite sidekick! How the hell are you?"

"Good! Good! It's always good to see you, Jake." Jake let go of him, and Jeff stepped back, looking like a twelve-year-old next to the much taller, broader Jake. They shook hands vigorously.

"You still writing all those lies about me?" Jake asked.

"Of course, I am. I love exaggerating all of it. Dime novel stuff, you know. Makes both of us richer."

They both laughed as Peter removed his hat and stepped closer to Randy.

"Randy," he said with a smile, "you look awfully calm

for having gone through that wild robbery. I have to say, that dress and that color look lovely on you."

Randy smiled and embraced him. "It's always good to see you and Jeff again," she said excitedly. Peter kissed her cheek as they hugged. "And thank you for the compliment," Randy said as she stepped back, "but I'm not as calm as I look." She noticed Jake cast them a sidelong look.

The handsome, dapper Peter Brown, who wore an obviously expensive silk suit, tie and vest, a gold watch chain hanging from the vest pocket, kept hold of Randy's arms as he stepped back with a look of true concern in his brown eyes. "I heard you hit your head pretty bad. Are you going to be all right?"

"Of course! Don't I *look* all right? Jake is the one who's hurting this morning, so he's a bit ornery. His gunshot wound from the robbery had to be stitched up – fifteen stitches with no medication for the pain. And his leg is bothering him, too."

"That's too bad. We have so many things planned for both of you." Peter turned to Jake and put out his hand when Jake loomed up beside him.

"Peter, it's good to get together for enjoyment and not because I need a lawyer," Jake told him.

Randy felt relief at Jake's cordial attitude. Although both men respected each other completely, there was always an unspoken tension between them.

They shook hands before Jake moved to Randy's side and put an arm around her.

"We will go right to my place from here," Peter told them. "You two can take as much time as you need to relax and heal." He turned his attention to Jake. "Randy says you're still in pain, Jake. I intend to have a really good doctor come out to the house tomorrow and take a look at that wound and check Randy out also. And he told me he has something new to talk to you about – something that might help that pain in your leg. As long as you two are here, you might as well take advantage of a top-notch physician. I know Brian is a damn good doctor, but living so far from the closest means of communication, it's hard for him to keep up with the latest medical advancements. Doctor Beemer will give you some literature to take back to him, as well as some new pills for pain and for infections."

"I did promise Brian I would see a doctor while I'm here, so he will appreciate the information. Thanks for thinking of it."

Randy left Jake's side to give Jeff a big hug. "Jeff, how are your wife and children?"

"Good. They're good. We'll all go out to eat while you're here. My wife is dying to meet you two. She had a lot of trouble with both her pregnancies, which is why she's never been able to join me when I come out to the J&L. But she's fine now."

"Oh, I'm glad! We always look forward to your visits, and Jake loves getting together with true friends. You know him. His true friends can be counted on one hand, and you are certainly one of them —you and Cole and Peter."

Jeff squeezed her arms, his deep brown eyes magnified by round, thick spectacles. He wore a tidy suit not nearly as fitted as Peter's, and his thick light-brown hair was parted in the middle and slicked back neatly.

"I sure never expected to get involved in something like that robbery," Jake was telling Peter. "We were headed for the dining car when that first man stuck a gun in my back. I don't exactly take kindly to someone threatening to spoil my breakfast."

Jeff and Peter both laughed.

"Guess I won't be interrupting you when you're eating

at *my* house," Peter joked. He shook his head. "Jeff and I imagined all kinds of scenarios for what happened during that robbery. And I want to apologize for all of it, Jake. If I had known about gold being on your train, I would have picked a different schedule." He glanced at Randy again, and Jake did not miss the adoring look in the man's eyes before he looked back up at Jake. "Be that as it may, Jake, you'll have to face those people waiting outside this Pullman and answer a few questions to appease them. And let the reporters get some pictures. We have a police escort ready, so we can get the two of you out of here quickly once you have satisfied that crowd out there."

Jake sobered. "You know I hate exposing Randy to rude questions and prying eyes." He put an arm around her again. "These last few days haven't been any easier on her than on me."

"Of course not." *Ever protective,* Peter thought as Jake pulled his wife closer. Jake Harkner had not changed one whit from the man he had met and known back in Oklahoma. Randy always came first, and right now he hovered over her like a stallion protecting its mares. "The police and I will make sure she's well protected from that bunch out there," he assured Jake. "Just answer some questions, and we'll be on our way."

"How is the family?" Jeff asked Randy.

"Katie lost a baby just a couple of weeks ago," Randy answered. "But she's doing well now."

Jeff shook his head. "Oh, that's too bad about the baby. Lloyd must have taken that hard."

"Yeah," Jake stated. "He had a little run-in with Jack Daniels over it. You know his problems with whiskey. To add to his troubles, we are having problems with nesters and the government over free grazing land being opened up for settlement. Right now, I'm concerned with keeping the settler issue from turning into a range war. I'll have to keep you informed on how that goes. I'd like you to print the truth back here about what's going on so people know it's not always the cattlemen who are the bad guys. I already have a couple of situations to tell you about."

"Hmmm," Peter mused, "I don't like the sound of that. Jake, you remember that's something the *law* has to deal with. I know you all too well, and I want my next trip to the J&L with Treena to be for enjoyment, not to defend you again."

"I'll do my best to be good, but trouble rides a fast horse, Peter, and my horse is pretty fast." He kept his arm around Randy. "Speaking of Treena, Randy and I were disappointed she isn't here."

Peter smiled. "Believe me, she very much wanted to be —mainly to see her Magnificent Jake, as she still calls you. But she'll be in France for a while nursing her mother."

"I'm so sorry for Treena and her mother," Randy said.

"Thank you." Peter gestured to the door of the Pullman. "We're riding to my place in an enclosed coach, so once we're on our way you two won't need to put up with more public exposure."

"Let's get going then," Jake said. "Have the porter load our baggage so we can make a dash for that coach after I answer a couple questions." He put out his cigarette in a nearby ashtray, then opened the carpetbag to take out one of his guns. He slipped it into his belt under his black jacket.

Peter frowned. "I hope you don't plan to use that on someone in the crowd."

"Only if they insult Randy," Jake joked. "Hell, you know I never go anywhere unarmed, especially when I'm among strangers. Some men want the reputation of killing me, remember?"

Jeff and Peter glanced at each other.

"Those are mostly reporters out there," Jeff reminded

him. "*I'm* the one who might get shot because we're friends, and I'm the one who gets all the good stories about you."

"Let's just hope that train robbery is the only exciting thing about this trip," Jake told him. "I'm all for lying low at Peter's place for a few days."

"That's fine with me," Peter told him. "Let's go answer some questions then get you two out of the limelight."

Jake kept an arm around Randy. "I don't want Randy away from my side between here and that carriage," he told both men. "Peter, keep her between you and me. Jeff will be busy taking notes and you are the only other man I'd trust with her if we get separated."

Peter's eyebrows rose in surprise. "Coming from you, I take that as a compliment."

"It is." Jake gave him a wry smile. "Just don't get *too* confident."

Peter grinned. "Jake, when it comes to you, I am never confident of *anything.* You are far too unpredictable."

Jeff spoke to someone just outside the door, and moments later several porters came in to get Jake and Randy's baggage. Jeff and Peter followed them out, waiting on either side of the platform while everything was loaded into the back of the waiting coach.

Jake kept Randy close as they finally exited the Pullman and stood between Peter and Jeff. Cheers, whistles, and applause echoed loudly against the train station's high ceiling.

"Jake Harkner, stand still there and let us get some pictures!"

"I don't believe this," Jake muttered to Randy. He took off his hat, gave them a nod, then put his hat back on.

"Were you hurt?" another asked.

"A bullet nicked a rib. I'll live."

"Where are those famous guns, Jake?"

"In a safe place."

"Yeah, on your person," another man yelled.

The whole crowd laughed.

"I see an ivory-handled gun in your belt," the reporter added. "Let's see the whole set—gun belt and all."

Jake shook his head. "I'm in civilized country now. I can't go walking around with guns on my hips."

That brought more laughter.

"As far as we're concerned, you can!" someone yelled.

Several in the crowd wrote frantically while flash powder exploded from several different locations.

"Did you feel like a marshal again during that robbery?" another asked.

"I was only thinking about keeping my wife and others from getting hurt," Jake stated.

"They might have been hurt from your own stray bullets."

"Not from *my* guns. I don't miss."

More cheers and laughter. More applause.

"We sure would like to see you in action. What will you do with the reward money?"

"No one's told me about any reward."

"You're sure to get a big reward, maybe two or three different ones. It should run in the thousands!" A tall man at the front of the crowd shouted the words.

"We'll see."

"Is everything Jeff Truebridge wrote about you really true? All those gunfights? That big one in California? The shootout in Guthrie?" a man in the middle of the crowd yelled.

"Jeff's a good writer—a trusted friend and a good reporter. It's true."

"Then you really did shoot your own father?" The question came from the tall man in front.

"Oh, shit," Jeff muttered.

The crowd quieted.

Randy could feel Jake's left arm around her tighten, even though it was his left arm and must be giving him pain. "Jake, let it go. Please," she said softly.

"Keep your questions respectable!" Peter shouted. "That's too personal!" He turned to a policeman standing nearby. "Get that man out of here before Jake makes him regret that question. Another one like that, and someone will end up bloody!"

"We'd like to see Jake Harkner in a damn good fist fight," another man yelled. "I heard he put a man's eye out once with a busted beer mug."

Two policemen dragged away the reporter who had asked about Jake's father.

"Hey!" he protested. "I had a right to ask that. What about Dune Hollow? How many men did you and your son kill there, Harkner? You think wearing a badge gave you the right to kill that many? How'd you handle things with your daughter? Are you really just a murderer? You killed six men two days ago!"

"Get him out of here!" Peter yelled again.

Jake clung to the platform rail with his right hand.

"Leave it be, Jake." Jeff put a firm hand on his arm. "This isn't the high plains on a ranch in the middle of nowhere. You do what you're thinking, and you will end up in jail. Your way won't work here in Chicago."

Jake glanced at Jeff's hand on his arm. "Jeffrey Truebridge, do you really think you could stop me?"

Jeff grinned nervously at the teasing look in Jake's eyes. "Hell no."

"That man wanted pictures plastered all over the front pages of tomorrow's newspapers of you slugging someone," Peter told Jake.

"And I would love to oblige him," Jake answered.

"Don't listen to that man, Harkner," someone else

shouted from the crowd. "You did a good thing, stopping that robbery. Gave us all something to talk about for a long time to come."

More flashes went off.

"You're a brave man!"

"We understand about a man regretting his past," another shouted.

"Hell, you're a *legend*!"

"How'd you get such a beautiful wife, Harkner?"

"He forced her at gunpoint," someone joked.

"Does he look to you like a man who has to force a woman to do *anything*?" The question came from a woman.

Rousing laughter followed.

"Sounds like something Gretta would say," Jake said aside to Randy.

Randy felt Jake's tension. He was struggling to deal with the situation.

"I'll bet you knew how to handle those robbers because you used to be just like them," someone shouted.

"That's why a judge in Denver appointed me as a marshal in the worst outlaw territory in the country," Jake answered. "I didn't ask to be a lawman. It was a punishment."

"Why did you go after those other robbers in the mail car, Harkner? You could have stayed where you were and let them rob the mail car."

"They would have found out I'd already killed three of their men and they would have come looking for me. It's a lot easier the other way around – stamp out trouble before it comes looking for you. Besides, my wife was with me, and I didn't want her involved."

More pictures.

"How did you meet her?" someone else asked. "And why does she put up with you?"

"Neither one is any of your business." Jake urged Randy toward Peter. "Get her out of here."

"Do you consider men like yourself a dying breed, Mr. Harkner?"

Things quieted again. "I reckon I am," Jake finally answered. He turned to Jeff. "Let's go." He hurried to catch up with Peter and Randy before anyone in the crowd could move behind them and perhaps grab Randy for a picture or say something rude to her. Jeff scurried to keep up. Someone tried to ask Peter a question.

"That's all the time we have," Peter stated in a loud, firm voice. "These two people are wounded from that robbery and very tired from a long trip. You will get other chances to talk to Jake."

Suddenly surrounded by Chicago policemen, Peter, Randy, Jake and Jeff all hurried to the waiting coach. They climbed inside as more flash powder exploded and reporters kept shouting questions.

They closed the doors and shuttered the windows.

"Take us home, Bennett," Peter yelled to the driver before turning to Jake. "I'll make sure only the most respected reporters attend the next interview," he told Jake. "This was a crowd I couldn't do anything about, but it won't be that way next time. No more questions about private things, and nothing off-the-cuff. Jeff and I will scan the questions before any interviews take place."

With his right arm, Jake pulled Randy close against his shoulder and kissed her hair. "You all right?"

"I am, now that we're away from those awful reporters."

The coach clattered away, the sound of the horse's hooves mixing with the *clop, clop* of other horses, the clanging bell of a nearby streetcar, chugging automobiles —horns honking—the bang of a nearby vehicle backfiring.

"Jake, I'm sorry about those couple of rude remarks,

but this is exciting as hell for city folks," Jeff told him. "You'll be all over the papers in the morning."

"Well, I guess the *reason* for it is better than my mug on a Wanted poster."

Randy hugged him across his middle, snuggling closer.

"After dinner at my place, the two of you can go sit on the terrace and enjoy the view of Lake Michigan—maybe walk on the beach," Peter offered. "I guarantee you will love that. This will all blow over, and you'll see the best parts of Chicago. The meals and the shopping and the museums—all of it."

Jake cast Peter a wry smile. "I should *be* in a museum – a statue of me as part of the past."

"It wouldn't surprise me one bit if that happens someday," Jeff answered.

Outside a policeman blew a whistle. Another streetcar passed them. Horses whinnied, and more automobiles honked and backfired. All the noise and commotion reminded Jake that he *was* indeed becoming a part of the past.

That last reporter had been right. He was a dying breed.

## CHAPTER 27

*July 20 . . .*

Vance came charging down the rise that led to the homestead, whistling and yipping to draw attention. He dragged a pack horse behind him, the horse's head stretched forward to keep up with the fast pace of the lead horse. Vance waved a newspaper in the air.

"Listen up, everybody! Gather around!"

"What on earth?" Katie picked up little Donavan and stepped outside, followed by Stephen and Lloyd, who'd just come home from mending a corral fence. Ben had been eating lunch with them. He came outside holding young Jeffrey.

"Why do I have a feeling this has something to do with my father?" Lloyd told Katie. "You'd better go get Brian and Evie. They are probably having lunch, too. At least from the look on Vance's face, it looks like the news might be good."

"Evie is already running over here," Katie noted. "You know your sister. If she thinks this has something to do with your father, she'll start to panic."

Ranch hands came walking and riding in from the barn

and closer fields as Vance drew up his horse in front of Lloyd's house. He was grinning from ear to ear. "Get the rest of the kids out here," he told Lloyd, "And Katie's parents."

"What the hell are you hollering about?" Lloyd asked.

"I'll tell you as soon as everybody gets here. I hate having to repeat a story," Vance answered. "By the way, some of the things you wanted me to pick up in Brighton are on the pack horse there. I hope I didn't break or lose anything from riding too hard. Charlie is bringing everything else by wagon."

"I thought you would get back from taking my folks to Denver sooner than this. Everybody else is already back, except for you and Charlie."

Vance dismounted and tied his horse. "And it's a good thing. We had to wait for flour that got delivered late, but that was just long enough to get a telegram sent to Brighton to be delivered to you. It's from Jeff Truebridge."

Lloyd lit a cigarette as Evie reached them, Brian right behind her carrying little Esther. Sadie Mae and Tricia, who'd been playing with dolls just inside the door at Evie's house, bounded out onto the porch holding the dolls, then ran to join the others. Young Jake followed, carrying baby brother Cole in his arms. Katie's parents joined them all, as did Gretta, who'd been feeding the chickens. She walked up beside Cole.

"I hope this is good news," Gretta said aside to Cole.

"You ain't the only one. Look at Lloyd. He's about to bust with worry."

"Lloyd, what's happened?" Evie walked up and grabbed hold of her brother's arm.

"God only knows," Lloyd told her. "But Vance is grinning, so calm down."

Vance waved the newspaper again. "I got this here copy of the *Denver Journal* when I was picking up supplies in Brighton. It's got a story in it from five days ago. Soon as I saw the headlines, I headed straight back here, since I already had the supplies." He took a piece of yellow paper from his pants pocket. "And I picked up this telegram, too. The messenger in Brighton was going to bring it out, but he saw me and told me to bring it. All this is already old news, but not to us!" He handed the newspaper to Lloyd, who opened it to see the bold headline.

JAKE HARKNER SPOILS TWO MILLION DOLLAR TRAIN ROBBERY!

"What!"

Evie gasped and pulled the paper out of his hands. "Is this real?"

"Sure is!" Vance stated. "Everybody in Brighton is talkin' about it." He looked at the men standing nearby. "Ole' Jake foiled a train robbery! The train he and Randy were on was carryin' gold and silver coins and solid gold bars from the Denver Mint to a mint in Philadelphia. The damn payload was worth two million dollars!"

The men whooped and whistled, joking about the robbers picking the wrong train.

"The shipment was supposed to be a secret," Vance added, "but somebody by-God knew about it. Nine men! Jake killed *six* of them single-handedly. Wounded two more and only one was left unscathed."

Gretta shook her head and grinned.

"Sonofabitch," Tommy said under his breath.

Evie continued reading the article.

"I'll bet some of them robbers just about wet their pants when they realized it was Jake Harkner they were comin' up against," Cole added.

Evie handed the paper to Lloyd. "Lloyd, daddy was shot, but it says he's okay. I hope that's right."

Lloyd quickly scanned the article, then handed it to Katie.

"Boy, I wish I was there to see pa in action," Ben exclaimed.

"Me, too," Young Jake added. "Pow! Pow! Pow!" He used his hands and fingers as pretend guns. "Grampa still knows how to go after the bad guys!"

"I can see it now," Stephen said. "I bet he fired those guns so fast that those men never got a shot off."

"Well, *somebody* got a shot off because your grampa was hurt," Evie told them. "It's just too bad so many men died. I'm sure daddy didn't want to kill so many, but in a situation like that, him against all of them, I suppose he couldn't help some of it. At least three of them lived."

"And I'll bet pa isn't happy about the extra attention this must be giving him in Chicago."

"Lloyd, read that telegram from Jeff," Katie asked him. "He'll be more honest about how bad Jake is hurt. And the article says your mother was slightly hurt in a fall, whatever that means."

Lloyd unfolded the yellow paper while the newspaper was passed around to others. "It's dated the sixteenth," Lloyd told everyone. "Jake stopped a train robbery," he read. "Wounded across upper left rib. My direct sources say he is hurting, but it was a clean wound. No damage to lung. Randy bruised from a fall, but nothing dangerous. Upon their arrival, both will be taken to Peter's home to rest and will see a good doctor. Do not worry. They will be fine and are in good care. Will keep you informed." Lloyd handed the telegram to Evie and rubbed at his eyes. "Jesus," he muttered. "This could only happen to my father."

"Whad'ya wanna' bet somebody threatened Randy?" Gretta said loudly. "That telegram says she was bruised. Nothing gets Jake's haunches up like his wife being threatened or hurt! I'll bet that's why he shot practically every one of those no-goods. He didn't foil that robbery to save all that money. That's not Jake. He did it to protect Randy and the people on that train."

"I agree," Cole added. "Lloyd, does that newspaper article say anything about a reward?"

"It says that the Federal Government is considering a hefty reward," Evie told them. "It doesn't say how much."

"Pa won't take it," Lloyd told all of them. "You know how he hates that kind of attention."

"He might not take it for himself, but I'll bet you and Evie will find your bank accounts suddenly get a hell of a lot bigger," Cole put in. "Ain't that what he did with that reward money they tried to give him for stoppin' that robbery in Boulder a few years back?"

Lloyd smiled with fond thoughts of his father. "He did."

"Hell, I'll bet he never figured bein' such a mean sonofabitch the first thirty years of his life would end up makin' him rich," Vance joked. "Between all those rewards and that book Jeff wrote, he will be as rich as that lawyer, Peter Brown. Or at least you and your sister will be."

Lloyd grinned and shook his head. "We'll see." He rubbed at the back of his neck, feeling a headache coming on. "You men had better get back to work. He turned to Stephen and young Jake. "You two help Vance unload those supplies. Charlie will be coming in tonight or tomorrow morning with more."

The joking and laughing continued as everyone returned to their daily chores. Lloyd took a cigarette and match from his shirt pocket and turned to Evie. "Can you believe it?"

"Knowing our father? I most certainly can. I just hope his injury really is something simple."

Lloyd watched the men walking away, Gretta walking with them.

"Poor Jake," her heard Cole comment. "Trouble follows him like a calf follows its ma's tits."

More laughter and whistles.

Lloyd shook his head as he sat down on a bench against the front of the house and took a deep drag on the fresh cigarette. He knew damn well that Jake hadn't taken the robbery lightly at all. He was probably pretty upset about it, especially since Randy had apparently been involved.

The rest of the family sat or stood around.

"Is Grampa okay?" Sadie Mae asked, looking ready to cry.

"Sure," Lloyd assured her. "He and Grandma are both fine. You know Jake is good with his guns, Sadie Mae. You always talk about how loud they are."

"Yeah, they are," Tricia said, covering her ears.

Katie handed the newspaper to Brian. "Why did I expect something like this?" Brian commented.

"Because you know my father all too well," Lloyd answered.

Evie sat down beside Lloyd and put a hand on his arm. "Thank God things turned out well, as far as we know."

Lloyd put a hand over hers. "Don't they always with Pa? The man is like a hickory branch," Lloyd assured her. "He doesn't break. He doesn't even bend. He just comes right back and whacks the daylights out of whoever hurts him or hurts any of the rest of us."

"Well, there is only so much a man can take, my dear brother, including you. You be careful around those nesters you've been keeping an eye on."

Lloyd leaned back, smoking quietly for a moment. "So far they are all legal, and have good intentions," Lloyd told her. "That doesn't mean I'm happy about what's going on, or the loss of grazing land. We will just have to be extra smart about our own grazing land and save certain areas for winter grass. At least we haven't seen any sign of Brady Fillmore or that Grizzly Smith." He pulled his arm away. "And before you know it, the folks will be home again. God knows everybody feels better when Jake is around, but there is usually more trouble when he is." He looked over at Katie, who sat in a rocker nearby. "You okay?"

"Yes." Katie stood. "I just get scared at first when I hear of big news coming. After what happened to you in Denver, and Jake in Mexico, my nerves are a little rattled when it comes to headlines and telegrams."

Lloyd rose and walked over to her, leaning down and kissing her cheek. "Go on back inside, honey. I'm not real hungry anymore, so I am going over behind the barn with Ben to finish that fencing we were working on. " He put a hand to her back and led her to the door, then turned to Ben, who looked ready to cry. Katie went inside, and Lloyd reached out and tousled Ben's thick, blond hair. The kid seldom wore a hat, and his hair was always a mess and looked like he'd just been through a windstorm. His fair skin was always ruddy from the sun. "Come help me with that fencing, Ben, and stop worrying. Jake is okay."

"I miss him. Every time he goes away, I think about Mexico," the young man told Lloyd. "He's all I've got, Lloyd."

"Not true." Lloyd wrapped an arm around Ben's neck in a mock choke hold, then urged him to walk with him back to the barns. "You've got *all* of us, kid. Remember that. You're special to Jake. He adopted you because he wanted you to have the kind of father *he* never had. He sees himself in you, and for all his ruthless bravado, Pa has a soft spot for kids and women."

"He does, doesn't he?"

"Yes, and keep in mind that this whole family is *your* whole family. We'll talk about it more when we have time.

Right now, we have to finish fixing that fence behind the barn."

Evie watched them walk away, then turned to Brian. "Leave it to Daddy to walk right into big trouble, even on a pleasure trip to civilized places."

Brian grinned. "You should be used to it by now," he reminded her before giving her a kiss. Then another kiss. Then another.

"Brian, Katie and the girls are watching. And there are men over there by the watering trough who can see us."

"And since when can anybody stand outside on the J&L without a bunch of men being around?"

"Mommy and Daddy are kissing," Sadie Mae said, pursing her lips at Tricia, who did the same. Both girls giggled.

"You girls come back to the house with us," Brian told them with a smile. "We have to finish lunch, and all of you need to take your naps." He picked up Cole from where Young Jake had set him in a chair, and they walked back home behind the girls. "Do you have that newspaper?" Brian asked Evie.

"Right here." Evie held it up, then laid it on the kitchen table.

"We'll read that article more thoroughly after we put the kids down for their naps." He chuckled. "Two million dollars. Two *million* dollars!"

Evie couldn't help laughing with him. "I'll bet Daddy had no idea how much money he saved for the Federal Government. If he had known at a younger age how much that train was carrying, he might have robbed it himself." They both laughed harder.

"Trouble is, they didn't *have* trains out west when Jake was younger," Brian reminded her.

"Well, they did in the South, and that's where daddy got his reputation."

Brian sobered a little and shook his head. "The world is changing fast, Evie—maybe *too* fast for somebody like Jake. There are probably a few people who don't like the fact that he decided to take the law into his own hands."

Evie set a loaf of bread on the table as the little ones sat down. Brian set Cole into a wooden highchair, then noticed his wife's equal concern.

"I thought of that. But Daddy was doing what comes as naturally to him as breathing. And I suspect his days as a marshal in Oklahoma kind of kicked in without him even being aware."

Brian walked around the table and drew her into his arms. "All that matters is that he and your mother are okay, and so is everyone else on that train." He kissed her again. "Now, sit down. I'll slice the bread."

"Can you believe it?" Brady Fillmore shoved a newspaper in front of Kyle Pendergrass and Grizzly Smith. "What did I tell you? The man doesn't have just *nine* lives. He's got about *fifteen* lives!" He looked at Kyle. "You won't ever bring Harkner down, Pendergrass."

All three men sat in a saloon in Brighton. Pendergrass studied the headline while Grizzly Smith grumbled, "He's done it again. I got this voice from that sonofabitch all them years ago, and now the bastard is *still* stoppin' men who are just like *he* was! He's a goddamn sinner turned saint. It ain't fair! He should still be sittin' in prison, not sendin' *other* men there."

"*Lots* of things aren't fair," Pendergrass shoved the newspaper aside. "But Harkner is going to meet his match when he gets home. With what I have planned, he'll have *no* lives left! I'll make sure of it, and it won't matter if I'm faster than him or not."

"That makes no sense," Grizzly complained. "You keep sayin' that, but you've never explained what you mean."

"That's because plans work out better when you don't tell too many people about them." Kyle leaned forward. "Look, we conned those folks who settled near the J&L into hiring us as help, right? They are even building a bunk house for us, and soon we will be living there full time as hired hands. Our whole plan is to get close to the Harkner ranch in a way that's not much noticed, and we have found a way to do it. Lloyd Harkner won't be able to do a thing about it because we will be working out there, *legitimately*. We have a right to work, and with so many of those settlers needing help, nobody can stop us from working for them."

"We know all that, but *then* what?" Brady grumbled.

Kyle's dark eyes glittered with excitement. "Okay, listen, and keep this to yourselves. Once we get a handle on activity along the border with the J&L, and stay peaceful so's they quit being so watchful, we strike. Somebody gets shot – sniper style. A range war starts, and amid all the chaos, somebody real important to Harkner gets hurt . . . maybe worse . . . and big Jake himself comes roaring back home madder than a horny bull that's being kept from a cow in heat. I'll have that fucker charging through anything that gets in his way, just to get revenge. He'll be after *me* . . . and I'll be waiting for him . . . with you two and maybe even more hired guns backing me up."

Brady grinned. "Sounds like it just might work, and with so many new people moving onto land all around the J&L, nobody can prove who started it all."

"I like it," Grizzly added. He raised a shot of whiskey. "To the downfall of Jake Harkner." All three men slugged down a drink, then poured themselves another.

"You make it sound too simple," Brady told them.

"It *is* simple." Kyle poured all three of them another shot.

"Not when Jake Harkner is involved." Brady shoved his shot glass aside. "We need more men than just the three of us. Jake has handled a whole gang of men more than once. I'm going to take a quick train trip over to Wyoming and the closest town there. I'll spread the word that anybody who wants to be in on helping bring down Jake Harkner is welcome to join us. Besides, we need extra men if we are going to do some rustling and kill a few of the settlers' cattle and tear up fences and crops. If we're going to get to Harkner and make it look legal, we need to start trouble that looks like it's the fault of the cattlemen."

Grizzly fingered his beard. "Makes sense. We already talked about getting' help."

"Well, you'd better make a fast trip while Jake is gone," Kyle offered. "Get back here in time for us to get something going – maybe get Lloyd Harkner and some of the cattlemen stirred up. If we can create the beginnings of a range war, it will be even harder for the law to pin a shooting on any one person. We just have to make sure that whoever gets shot, it's somebody that will set Jake Harkner out for blood and bring him right to us."

Grizzly nodded. "Shouldn't be too hard. J&L men are always prowling around the northern end of the ranch on account of that's where most new people are settin' in."

Kyle slugged down another drink. "Like I said – I have a plan. And now both of you understand what we have to do." He shoved Brady Fillmore's drink back in front of the man. "Drink up, Fillmore. You'd best leave right away tomorrow for outlaw country."

Brady fingered the shot glass, feeling uneasy about going up against Lloyd or Jake. But they owed him, didn't they? He picked up the shot glass and downed the whiskey.

# CHAPTER 28

*July 27 . . .*

    *My dear family,*

    *This will probably be my only letter other than the first one I sent just to assure you your father and I were not seriously injured in the train robbery. We have been here over a week and will probably stay at least two more, but we miss all of you and the J&L, so we might return a little sooner.*

    Randy paused her writing to look out at Lake Michigan. She sat at a white wrought-iron table and chair beneath a vine-covered canopy over a huge terrace partway down a bluff between Peter's home and the lake.

    *Peter's fifteen-room home is, indeed, extravagant – a mansion made of stone and featuring a turret-style great room overlooking a private beach,* she continued writing. *And those fifteen rooms do not include a ballroom on the third floor, where he entertains some of the mayor and top councilmen of Chicago, as well as lawyers and doctors and business owners. The terrace where I sit now is several steps below the kitchen, which has all the most modern equipment - every convenience known to man, or I should say woman, and a cook to do all the work. Expensive furnishings and lamps, huge plants, carpets and paintings* decorate every room and hallway, and maids keep things spotless and make the beds every day. Peter even has a personal butler, but he seems completely unaffected by all the wealth and glamor that surrounds him. He has been the same friendly, down-to-earth man all of you knew back in Guthrie, the same man who comes to visit the J&L and always fits right in.

The bedroom she and Jake shared held a huge, incredibly soft four-poster bed, with silk sheets and gloriously soft, puffy quilts and pillows. Randy smiled at the thought of how much Jake liked that bed and how much they had already made use of it.

*Your father is already healed,* she wrote, *although his rib is still a little sore. Peter and Jeff have taken us on tours all over the city, and every place we go, people want to meet Jake. Jeff's wife, Elly, often accompanies us. You would like her. She is young and very pretty. She dresses plain and wears her beautiful dark hair in a long, thick braid down her back. She is so shy around Jake, and I'm sure she has trouble believing Jeff actually rode with Jake back in Guthrie.*

*Jake has been interviewed to the point that I am not sure how much more he will put up with. You know how he hates attention. He still cannot quite fathom his fame, and doesn't understand why people would care about an "old outlaw," as he puts it.*

*We have seen the Field Museum, with a collection of artifacts from the 1893 World's Columbian Exposition. We have seen live theater and an opera and will be going to more. Your father, of course, doesn't care for opera, but, as you well know, he has trouble letting me out of his sight. I'm sure he'd rather be at the stockyards, where he feels more at home. He has been there and said to tell you he has never seen more cattle in one place in his life, not even on the J&L or in Denver. I obviously would not be fond of the smells, so I haven't gone there. And although Jake grumbled about going to the opera, I could tell he was quite mesmerized by the incredibly moving singing and orchestration,* and the grand, colorful costuming. I think a couple of nights ago he temporarily fell in love with one of the female singers, whose voice cannot even be described. We were allowed to meet her backstage, and she practically drooled over Jake. He in turn couldn't give her enough compliments. What a gentleman he can be. When we left, I poked at him and reminded him he had a wife. It was all in good fun, and I think it was good for Jake to see all that artful beauty. He's seen so much ugly in his life.

 I hope Katie and Evie can come here sometime in the future and see all this. These grand theaters are something to behold, and Jake and I have been treated like a king and queen visiting from some other country. When I think about how far away the J&L is, it sometimes seems like we truly are in another country. I visited a garden conservatory that stole my heart. I have never seen so many plants and flowers in one place, and now I have ideas for more landscaping around home. I have shopped in the grandest stores, and have been pampered at a spa Peter says Treena goes to every week. My, what a life she leads, but she is in France, so her friend Rebecca has taken on the duty of showing me all the finest stores, hair salons, restaurants, women's clubs and all the other places wealthy women go. I can see by the worried look I sometimes catch in Jake's eyes that he wonders if I will ever want to come home, but of course I will. My love and my life belong in Colorado with the man I have loved all these many years and with our beautiful family. I miss all of you.

 Lake Michigan is spectacular. Other than the oceans, it is hard to believe so much water can exist as one body. I imagine the Great Lakes very much resemble what oceans probably look like. Jake has, of course, seen the Gulf of Mexico, but I have never seen a large body of water, although we were not that far from the Pacific when we lived in southern California . . . so many years ago. Jake compares the lake to the wide, high, endless plains of eastern Colorado, because you can see so far. The way he described it told me he misses home. He says the rhythmic waves of Lake Michigan remind him of the bend and wave and flow of prairie grass on windy days. Your father can be surprisingly poetic..

Jake visited an indoor shooting range a few days ago and was, of course, the center of attention. One of Peter's friends brought a fancy handgun along to show it off to Jake and the others. The silly man challenged Jake to a shooting contest. Yes, that's how foolish he was. I can see all of you smiling. According to Peter, the fancy gun jammed before this man could get off two shots, and by then Jake had fired all six shots from his .44, all dead center of the target. Apparently, the other man cussed a blue streak and promptly left the shooting range, thoroughly embarrassed. So far all of Peter's other friends have been truly kind and accommodating, and respectful with their questions and interviews.

Tell Brian that Jake finally agreed to see a doctor Peter recommended, Doctor Ronald Beemer, a tall, older man with very white hair and contrasting dark mustache and beard. He was very thorough, and he called Jake an enigma, something he's been called before. Beemer thinks he is unusually healthy for all he's been through and all his past wounds and scars. You should know that Dr. Beemer also examined me and said I am in good health, thank the Lord. Best of all, he gave us a new kind of pain medicine for Jake's leg that is not addictive. It's called aspirin, and it's made by a company in Germany called Bayer. It's a pill, not a powder, but it can be hard on the stomach, so Jake has to eat when he takes it. But he's pleased with the results and said to tell Brian aspirin will be available to all doctors very soon, so Brian should go to Denver and find out about it. Jake is bringing some home with him.

"You writing a book?"

Randy turned. "Jake!" She set a plate over the letter so it couldn't blow away, then rose to greet him by wrapping her arms around his middle. "I might as well be writing one. I've been scribbling away for nearly two hours, but I have so much to tell, and it's such a beautiful day for sitting outside." She stood on her tiptoes for a kiss. " With Peter at work and you and Jeff running around the city all day, I decided I'd send one long letter home to the family and tell them what we've been doing."

Jake tucked a piece of her hair behind her ear. "That *would* take a book."

"I also intend to keep adding to the journal I started. I never want to forget one thing about this wonderful trip."

Randy stepped back and looked him over. "You look extra good today. This trip has been so good for you. What did you and Jeff do today?"

"Believe it or not, I went with Jeff on a murder investigation. Some days his job is pretty darn exciting. The bigger the city, the more crime to take care of."

"Well, that's certainly something that shouldn't shock a man like you."

Jake grinned. "The only difference is the criminals are brought to jail by policemen in uniforms and motorized paddy wagons instead of draped over the backs of horses, like I used to haul them in back in Oklahoma."

Randy noticed he'd already changed his clothes and wore only a half-buttoned shirt and denim pants. He had a blanket draped over his shoulder, and she looked down to see he was barefoot. "You aren't wearing any shoes!"

"I thought we'd go for a walk on the beach. Sit down, and I'll peel off your stockings and shoes. And take those combs out of your hair."

"Jake Harkner, what do you have in mind?" She sat down, and he reached under her dress to grasp the elastic tops of her stockings, the back of his hand touching private places teasingly as he did so. He pulled the stocking off, taking her slip-on shoe with it.

"Remember talking about all the places we've made love for the first time?"

Randy began pulling the combs from her hair. "The

beach?" She glanced at the house. "There are maids and a butler and a cook up there, Jake, and sometimes people walk on the beach."

He reached under her dress to remove the other stocking and shoe. "And we have never made love on the shores of Lake Michigan. It's time for another first. This is our very, very, very belated honeymoon, remember? Let's make the most of it."

Randy shook out her hair. "Jake, if someone sees us—"

"They won't. I walked this beach alone the other day when you were napping, and I found a little cove where you can lie in the sand under a big rock that hides you from above." He removed the second stocking and shoe, then kissed her foot, her ankle, and up along her leg to her knee. Randy took pleasure in the fact that he seemed totally relaxed and happy, a rare mood he'd been in most of the time since they arrived. She treasured the handsome and genuine smile on his face, moments when he showed no sign of being haunted by his past or even worried about the future.

"Stand up, and let's get those slips off," he told her. "I'm glad you're wearing that plain gingham dress. It will make the walk easier for you. Did you get some rest earlier?"

"Yes. I slept. I ate. I slept some more. I ate again. I came out here to write a letter, and then you came home. It's been a perfect day."

She stepped out of her slips, and Jake hung them over her chair, then grabbed her hand and half ran with her down the sandy slope to the beach.

"Jake—your leg. You don't usually run like this."

"I'm all right. The soft sand makes it easier."

He pulled her to where the waves lapped up onto the beach, and Randy screamed when he got her part way into the water, and the bottom of her dress got wet.

"Jake, I'll be a mess when I get back!"

"Who cares?" He put the blanket around her shoulders, then pulled her close and kissed her deeply, running one hand into her undone hair and grasping it tight.

A gentle breeze blew soft tendrils of his hair around his face, and Randy drank in his dark perfection. He picked her up and carried her several yards north to the little cove then took the blanket from her shoulders and spread it over the sand and sat down, reaching up for her. Randy took his hand and let him pull her down beside him. He laid her back and moved on top of her, kissing her over and over.

"You've enjoyed this trip so far, haven't you?" He ran a hand along her leg and up under her dress.

"Yes. Thank you for this, Jake."

"Tell me you haven't decided to stay here and live like the most beautiful woman in the world deserves to live."

Randy grinned. "Don't be silly. It's just a vacation, Jake, not a lifestyle for a woman like me."

She studied his eyes and saw the sudden need there—the need to be loved and to be assured he wouldn't lose her. She leaned up and kissed his full lips, ran her hands over the hard muscle of his arms and shoulders. "Don't ask me who I belong to, Jake, because you *know* I belong to you."

He traced a finger over her lips and along her chin. "I was upstairs changing, and I saw you sitting down here. You looked so alone, and I remembered how you looked that same way back in Kansas, when I rode out of your life."

"Right here in your arms is the only place where I feel loved and safe. You've been the most wonderful husband a woman could ask for."

"I try, but I wouldn't say I'm the most wonderful." He ravished her mouth—an invasion of body and soul.

"Oh, you most certainly are," Randy answered. She raised her hips, and Jake pulled off her bloomers while keeping up his searching, branding kisses. He unbuttoned his jeans with one hand and pulled himself free, then entered her, working his already firm penis over her swollen need in that way he had of bringing her to a deep climax.

This was Jake. This was a quiet cove on a beach, just the two of them. This man always made her feel beautiful, and she responded with a keen desire to please him in return, to soothe, to tell him with lips and touches and by taking him deep inside that he was all she wanted or needed. She felt his life throb into her, and she arched her hips in response. He groaned with his release, then kissed her several times over.

"I don't know what got into me," he said. More kisses. "I didn't even touch you first." More kisses. "I didn't make this as good for you as it should have been. Are you all right?"

She put a hand to his lips. "I'm fine. You didn't need to touch me first. Just lying here with you and seeing the want in your eyes is all I need."

He gently ran his fingers inside her. "I was too quick. You need more."

"I'm fine."

He grinned. "Admit it. You still want something in there."

She laughed and pulled him down to her, burying her face in his neck. She loved the power that hovered over her, power that could be incredibly gentle. "Truth? Yes, I wasn't quite finished with you."

He entered her again, filling her, keeping up a gentle rhythm until another demanding climax welcomed every inch of him. She whimpered with every thrust, their intercourse lasting several minutes this time.

They lay quietly together then, listening to the soft splash of waves on the beach and the call of seagulls. Jake rolled to his side and pulled her close. Randy felt a change in his mood, and she leaned in to kiss his cheek.

"What's wrong? You seemed so relaxed and happy when you came to get me, but something is different."

He sighed deeply. "It's nothing I can name—just something that's nudging at me, a gut feeling about what could be going on at home."

"Lloyd knows what he's doing, and he has plenty of help. The neighboring ranchers are adjusting to more settlers, and Hal Kraemer is keeping an eye on everything." Randy raised up on one elbow to meet his gaze. "We've talked about this before, Jake, and you've been fine with it. Let yourself enjoy what's left of our time here. We've seen and done some wonderful things and have stories to tell. This is the best gift you've ever given me, Jake, other than your love. Everything will be okay."

He reached up and stroked her hair. "I see you in that house up there, and shopping with those fancy women, and I see how you fit right in. It just makes me love you even more for choosing life with a man who had nothing to offer you but heartache when you married him."

She grasped his hand and kissed his fingers. "You offered me more love than most women ever get to enjoy, all packaged into a big, tall, handsome man who would die for me. No woman could want more than that." She sucked in her breath then and sat straight up. "Jake, Peter will be home any time, and I'm a mess! I need to wash or something."

Jake grinned and sat up. "Take off that dress and your camisole. You can wash in the lake."

"*Naked*? Jake, people walk on this beach!"

"I've watched. No one walks along here that often. Strip down, woman. I'll wrap the blanket around you and carry you to the water. You can wade your sweet little butt out far enough to wash what needs washing. Come right back to me, and I'll wrap the blanket back around you and bring you back here to dress. The rest of you will still be a beautiful mess, but you'll be a *clean* beautiful mess."

"Do we dare?"

"My pants will get wet, but that doesn't matter. I'll wash and change when we get back to our room. And the water is plenty warm. I've waded in it more than once."

Randy put her hands to her cheeks. "Jake, I left my letter up there."

"It's fine. I saw you set something on it, so it won't blow away."

"Jake Harkner, this is crazy!" She turned so he could unbutton her dress, then pulled it off. Jake helped her unlace her camisole, then leaned down to kiss each breast before walking a bit away to shake out the blanket. He wrapped it around her and picked her up, carrying her to the water.

"Why do I always let you talk me into these wicked things?" Randy laughed.

"You love it." Jake tossed her into a wave and Randy screamed as the cool water hit her. She took a quick dip, laughing at herself. "No woman my age should be doing this." She quickly splashed herself clean and hurried back to let him wrap her in the blanket and carry her back to the cove.

"Oh, dear Lord, I hope no one saw."

Jake chuckled. "This gives you something exciting to enter into that journal."

Randy gave him a shove. "Go away and let me get dressed before someone *does* come along."

"Well, hurry up. Don't forget that we left half your clothes up on the terrace."

"Oh, my goodness, I forgot! Peter might come home and see!"

"I thought that by now I would have taught you not to be so bashful about everything."

"You're thinking about the kind of women you grew up with, Jake Harkner. I'll never be that bold!"

Jake grinned and helped her pull the laces on her camisole. "You are when you're with me," he teased.

"That's different. You have a way of banishing all my inhibitions and making me behave in some very wicked ways."

"My pleasure, Mrs. Harkner."

Randy laughed and kissed his chest where his shirt was still open. "I'll always remember things like this, Jake. Always. It reminds me that this all started with just the two of us. I love these silly moments."

Jake shook his head and picked up the blanket. He walked a little bit away, watching up and down the beach while she dressed. It dawned on Randy that he hadn't brought a gun along, which meant he truly was relaxed and happy. She prayed life could stay this way from now on.

## CHAPTER 29

*July 28 . . .*

"They look like ordinary folks, Lloyd." Cole rested a forearm on his saddle horn and squinted to study the homestead below, located on a piece of land a couple of miles north of Echo Ridge, adjacent to J&L's northern border. A barn was still under construction. The cabin, and what looked like a bunk house, were both new.

Lloyd, Cole, and Ben remained on their horses, watching the movement below. "Are you sure that's not *J&L* land, Lloyd?" Ben asked.

"No, little brother. See that funny-looking ridge of pink rock to your right?"

"Yup."

"That's the northern marker. Run your gaze straight across to that gully far to the left. That's the line. When we get the chance, you and I will ride the entire border of the J&L so you can learn what's ours and what isn't. It will take a few days to cover it all."

"We're really close to somebody else's property then," Ben pondered.

"Yes, we are, but we have a right to check things out.

When I rode with pa back in Oklahoma, I learned to always act on a gut feeling, and my gut tells me something isn't quite right about those three men building that fence down there. I can't make them out, so we're going down there and pay those folks a little visit." He turned to Cole. "And when we get back to the homestead, send men out here to round up the cattle that have strayed into the north pasture. I count only about twenty head, but there might be more over that rise to the west. I'm not taking the chance that somebody down there will decide they want some fresh steaks, or a few good head of cattle to start their own herd."

Cole nodded. "I'll make sure of it."

"And anybody caught rustling gets hanged this time," Lloyd added.

"Couldn't agree with you more," Cole told him.

Lloyd urged Cinnamon forward, and Cole and Ben followed, all three riding casually so as not to stir up trouble where it didn't need to exist. They crossed the border of the J&L to see that all three men building a fence wore guns. Two of them simply had a handgun shoved into their belts, but the third man, who had his shirt off because of the heat, wore a full gun belt low on his hip. All three paused and stepped back a little when Lloyd rode closer. He halted Cinnamon and whirled the horse sideways, glaring down at none other than Brady Fillmore. "What the fuck are *you* doing here?"

Brady stepped back a little more, but grinned. "Just doing a hard day's work for some fine homesteaders who need the help, Lloyd."

"Damned if it ain't Lloyd Harkner!" The words came from Grizzly Smith, who stood nearby, resting his arms on a shovel. He turned to the third man. "There he is, Kyle. Jake Harkner's son, a regular chip off the old block."

Lloyd studied the third man. He glanced at his silver-handled .45 and took note of the way he wore it. "You're no goddamned farm hand, mister. No settler I ever met wore a gun at all, let alone low on his hip. What the hell are you doing here with these two no-goods?"

"Nice to meet you, too," Kyle answered, resting his hand on the butt of the gun.

"You'll get a real *painful* greeting if you try pulling that .45," Lloyd told him.

Cole and Ben rode up to flank Lloyd.

Keeping his attention on Kyle, Cole pulled his rifle from its boot and rested it across his lap. "Mister, if you've a mind to use that-there gun, you'd better think twice. A chip off the old block is right. Lloyd is as good as his pa, and there ain't nobody faster than Jake Harkner, so if you're workin' out here as some way of gettin' to Jake, you might as well go back where you came from."

Kyle eyed Lloyd, then snickered. "A gunman stays alive by knowing when to draw and when *not* to draw. And it's not Jake Harkner's son I want the reputation of killing."

A shot rang out, and Kyle's hat went flying while Ben had to ride his horse in a circle to calm it. It took him a moment to realize the shot came from Lloyd's gun, drawn and fired so fast he never realized Lloyd had made the move at all.

"What the hell!" Kyle swore.

"A gunman worth his shit would have been ready for that," Lloyd told him. "And my pa's even faster than I am. But you make one more remark about killing him, and you won't *need* to worry about how fast he is, because I'll kill you *myself*! Now, unload that .45 and toss it aside. Something tells me you're a back-shooter!"

"You've got no right, you fucking bastard!" Brady Fillmore swore. "And you probably *are* a bastard. According to Grizzly here, your pa spent half his time up at that gold mine while your ma was alone down in Virginia City. Who's your *real* pa, Lloyd?"

Lloyd, still holding his smoking gun, fired at Brady's foot. The man screamed and fell, grabbing at his boot. Kyle Pendergrass tossed his gun aside and backed up more. The air was filled with Brady's curses as two more men and a woman came running from the distant cabin.

"We'll report you for this!" Grizzly shouted at Lloyd.

"Go ahead." Lloyd holstered his gun. "I can't help it if my gun mis-fired. It tends to do that when someone insults my mother." He turned his attention to Brady. "You never learn, do you, Fillmore? I know you and that bearded piece of shit with you are up to no good. You really think I believe you're just helping out?" He turned his attention to Kyle then. "What's your full name?"

Kyle raised his chin. "Kyle Pendergrass. You ever hear of me?"

"No. *Should* I have?"

"I've killed a couple of men who thought they were faster than me."

"Just a couple?" Lloyd goaded. "My father ran out of room to notch his guns for every man *he's* killed. You planning to be another notch?"

"No, you arrogant son of the devil! I'm planning to—"

"Shut up, Pendergrass!" Grizzly interrupted.

Lloyd studied all three men closely. "Maybe I should have lowered my aim a little and shot him through the forehead instead of just shooting his hat off," he told Grizzly. "What's going on here?"

Brady still lay on the ground crying and holding his foot. Blood poured out of his boot and through his fingers.

"All we're doin' is helpin' these settlers," Grizzly told Lloyd, "against bullying cattlemen like you. You had no right shootin' Kyle's hat off—and shootin' Brady in the foot!"

"I had *every* right! Nobody insults my mother and threatens to kill my father." Lloyd turned his attention to Pendergrass again. "You called me the son of a devil, and Mister, you're right. You'd better hope the devil himself doesn't come looking for you, in the form of Jake Harkner! You're alive right now. If you want to *stay* alive, you'd be best to leave Colorado all together." He looked back at Grizzly. "And be goddamn careful where you put up that fence. Make sure it's not on *J&L* land, or I'll tear it down!"

By then the woman and the other two men had reached the scene. One man was a burly six feet tall with a big belly and balding head. The dishwater-blond woman looked tired, and the second man was tall and solidly built, but not a man at all. He looked fifteen or sixteen years old, and all three looked confused.

"What's going on here?" the balding man asked.

"What's going on is you've hired the wrong men to help work this place," Lloyd answered. "They have a lot more in mind than building fences and guarding against wolves. What's your name, Mister?"

"Stuart Mitchel. This here is my wife, Alexandra, and my son, Barney. We're legitimately settled here, and we aim to be good neighbors. Why the hell are you shooting at these men?"

"They're no-goods, and you should fire them. I'm Lloyd Harkner, owner of the *J&L*." He indicated Ben. "This is my brother, Ben. And beside him is our best hand, Cole Decker. Do you have papers proving you can settle here?"

"I sure do." Stuart put his hands on his hips. "You Jake Harkner's son? I wouldn't mind meeting Jake, since we'll be neighbors. We don't want any trouble."

"My father is away right now," Lloyd explained. "He doesn't want trouble, either, but we've had run-ins before with Fillmore and Smith here. I've just met Pendergrass, but he's no damned farm hand, Mitchel. He's a gunman, and he' up to no-good. I *guarantee* it."

"We're just earnin' an honest livin'," Grizzly told Lloyd.

"You probably haven't done an honest thing in your life," Lloyd answered. "Tell Mitchel here how you got that scar on your throat, and that scratchy voice." Lloyd addressed Stuart again. "My father did that to him. Years ago, when Smith tried to rob a gold shipment from the Yellowjacket Mine in Nevada. Smith still carries a grudge, Mr. Mitchel. And Fillmore there hates my family, which is why he set fire to one of our best grass valleys. He's also a cattle thief, and if I find one head of cattle missing in the next few days, you'll have to answer for it, even if it's one of these no-goods who took it."

Mitchel backed up a little. "I've got no intentions of rustling cattle."

"Then you'd better get rid of these three."

"We're going to report this to Hal Kraemer," Brady hollered. He screamed when young Barney pulled off his boot. "My toe! I lost my big toe!"

"And that's twice I've let you off with your life, Fillmore," Lloyd reminded him. "Something like this happens a third time, you won't be around to complain to Hal Kraemer. Just be glad *Jake* isn't with us! If he heard that insult to my mother, you'd be missing more than a big toe."

"I, uh, I'll get rid of them, Mr. Harkner," Stuart Mitchel told Lloyd. "But I need the help."

Lloyd glanced at Cole. "What do you think?"

"I think Ben and I should stay here and make sure these three leave quietly. We can help 'til Mitchel hires a couple other men. Might as well be good neighbors. You can't stop this, Lloyd, and it's more likely we can share grazing if we get along with those who put up fences on free range."

Things quieted a moment while Lloyd lit a cigarette and Mrs. Mitchel wrapped her apron around Brady Fillmore's foot. Lloyd took a deep drag on the cigarette and held Cole's gaze. "Do you think that's what Pa would do? Leave a couple of men here to help?"

"I do. 'Course I ain't so sure he'd let Fillmore go, but then you and Jake have talked about changin' your ways, on account of new laws. Might as well be good neighbors as long as the Mitchels here settled legally."

Lloyd kept his cigarette between his lips as he spoke. "I'll send Tommy Tyler and Win Lee out here to help out 'til Mitchel can find someone else. You and Ben can stay here until they relieve you." Lloyd addressed Stuart Mitchel. "I have to get back to the homestead, but I'll leave my brother and Cole here for a couple of days to make sure these three troublemakers leave without harm. They can keep an eye on things and help with that barn while you go into town and find more hands. You might find help closer if you ride over to the Twisted Tree. Henry Till might have a couple of men to spare. Meantime, I'm sending a couple of other men here to help out. Does that suit you?"

"Suits me just fine. I appreciate the help – and the advice."

Lloyd glanced over at Kyle Pendergrass, who was helping Brady to his feet. "I don't trust Pendergrass," he told Cole as he watched the man help Fillmore hop back toward the bunkhouse. "Keep an eye on him, especially 'til all three of them are good and gone. You have a better instinct for men like that than Ben does. Meantime, I'll send Tommy and Win Lee out here soon as I can."

"Sure thing." Cole turned his horse and motioned for Ben to follow him around the unfinished end of the fence.

Lloyd watched them slowly walk their horses behind Kyle and Brady. Grizzly picked up Kyle's gun and Brady's boot, then turned to Lloyd.

"You think you can keep takin' the law into your own hands," he snarled, "just like your pa. But some day, boy, you'll *pay* for it."

"Maybe, but not today. Get out of my sight before I heard you back to the *J&L*. If I do that, you just might not be seen again. Hand that gun to Mitchel there. I don't want it still in your hand while I'm riding away with my back to you."

Scowling, Grizzly handed Kyle's gun to the farmer. He stormed away, and Stuart Mitchel looked at Lloyd.

"Thanks for sending help. This is all new to us. A man doesn't know who to trust out here."

"You got that right, Mitchel. But you can trust me and J&L men as long as you stick to your own property. There's nothing we can do about new settlers taking up free range, but the law is the law, and we have to change with it, I guess. Just be careful who you hire. This country is still full of outlaws and renegades and men ready to take advantage of people. If that bunch comes back, let me know. My men and I will take care of them."

Mitchel nodded. "I'll keep that in mind. I look forward to meeting your father."

"Jake is a better man than you might think. Stay on his good side, and you will have some friendly neighbors. This is hard country, Mister Mitchel. Like I said, watch who you hire." Lloyd tipped his hat, then turned his horse for home. He was worried sick about how bad things might get before his parents got back. The last thing they needed after a vacation from all of this was to come home to a range war.

## CHAPTER 30

*August 6 . . .*

Peter handed his suit coat and hat to his butler. "Things go okay here today, Dennis?"

The butler smiled. "Yes, Sir. Mr. and Mrs. Harkner had quite a relaxing time. I believe they slept in. They were in the bedroom all morning and—uh—well, later in the morning I heard quite a bit of laughter."

*Leave it to the maids and butler to know every little thing that's going on in the house,* Peter thought. "That's a little more information than I needed, Dennis."

"Yes, well, Mrs. Harkner is upstairs now helping Matilda change the bed and do some cleaning."

"Why on earth is Mrs. Harkner helping the maids?"

"Sir, Matilda told her she needn't lift a finger, but Mrs. Harkner insisted. I suppose the pioneer woman in her has trouble letting others do the work."

Peter grinned and sat down in a nearby chair to pull off his shoes. "Knowing Randy as well as I do, I guess I'm not surprised."

"Yes, well, in the meantime, Mr. Harkner is in the kitchen having coffee that Sarah made for him at his request. She made a second pot so there would be plenty in case you came home early. Our old cook would have been surer of herself, but Sarah spilled some of the coffee grounds in the first pot and had to remake it. I believe Mr. Harkner makes her a bit nervous. It must be his reputation, but he has been kind to the help, a real gentleman."

"Oh, he is *always* quite the gentleman around women – at least the proper ones," Peter replied. "Actually, even around the *im*proper ones. He was raised by that kind." He shook his head as he reached for some slippers beside the chair. "But then Jake is Jake. He can make *anybody* nervous just by his persona. I've *been* in that position, but once you get to know him, he can be a hell of a friend."

Dennis grinned. "The man shows quite a bold presence wherever he goes, doesn't he?"

"To say the least."

"Is there anything you need, Sir?"

Peter stepped into his slippers and rose. "Just put my shoes away. I'm going to join Jake in the kitchen."

"You should know, Sir, that the man has his guns laid out on the kitchen table to clean them. I hope it's all right that I told him he could use the oil and tools from your antique gun collection. You did say to let both Jake and his wife have full access to anything they need. I laid an old towel over the kitchen table to protect it."

"Of course, it's all right. I told Jake when he was looking at my collection that he could use whatever he needed. And damned if he didn't know how all those guns worked, in spite of how old some of them are. The man knows guns like the back of his hand."

"Yes, sir."

The butler walked off with Peter's shoes, and Peter headed for the kitchen, where Jake's .44's lay on the table, one in several pieces. At the counter, Jake was pouring himself a cup of coffee. He wore denim pants, no socks, and a sleeveless undershirt. Old scars from his father's beatings and from the horror he'd suffered in Mexico showed a little at his shoulders, and his dark, wavy hair looked wet. A still-lit cigarette sat in an ashtray on the table.

"Good morning," Peter said. "Or I guess I should say good afternoon."

Jake took a sip of coffee as he turned. "Morning, Peter."

"Dennis tells me you and Randy had a relaxing morning." Peter walked over to pour his own cup of coffee.

"You might say that." Jake grinned. He set his cup on the table and sat down, picking up the disassembled revolver. "Sorry I'm half dressed. It's hot as hell already, and I didn't think you'd be back so soon. I'm sure Randy will bring me a shirt and scold me for not putting one on."

"Mmmm-hmmm. It *is* hot." Peter removed his tie and loosened the top buttons of his shirt. "Is your hair wet from romping naked in the lake, or in the shower?"

Jake chuckled in a low, rich tone. "Shower. Randy loves that thing. I had to promise to find a way to put one in at the house when we get back. That's something you don't find in cattle country. People there would consider it a waste of water."

Peter poured himself some coffee and set the cup on the table. "Well, I can have my builder draw up a diagram of how to install a shower if you want. You could take it back with you to help whoever might put one in for you. Showers are kind of a new idea. And of course, here we don't have a water problem."

Jake took yet another piece off the disassembled gun and began cleaning it with a soft cloth. "I haven't cleaned these things since the train robbery. I don't usually let it go that long, but I figured I shouldn't need these while I'm here."

"I certainly hope not."

Jake stopped and picked up his cigarette. "You've been a very gracious host, Peter. Don't think I haven't noticed you go out of your way to give Randy and me a lot of private time. Randy has loved every minute of this, and, of course, the shopping." He drew on the cigarette, exhaling with his words. "My pocket money and bank account have taken quite a blow, but it's worth it to see her so happy. That's what it's all about." Jake put the cigarette down and sipped some coffee. "I can't help seeing how well my wife fits into this lifestyle. I'm sure you haven't missed that either."

Peter realized he'd better be careful with his words. "Randy can fit into *any* lifestyle. She's that kind of woman, gracious and caring and unselfish, no matter who she's dealing with. And she lives a pretty damn good life out there on the J&L, don't forget. She wouldn't have it any other way if it meant being without you. I resigned myself to that fact years ago. I think you and I have a fairly good understanding about that."

Jake quieted as he picked up a gun part. Peter waited, not sure what to say. "We do," Jake finally answered, keeping his eyes on the gun part as he fitted it against another. "Speaking of which, I want you to take Randy to those art galleries on your own tomorrow. Things like that don't mean much to me. I think I'll stay here and sit and watch that beautiful lake and try to figure out how in hell we could ship some of that fresh lake water out West."

Peter scoffed. "We will never let that water go anywhere. It's too precious."

"You don't need to tell a Western cattleman how precious water is." Jake whirled the chamber of the .44. "Or how precious a good woman is."

Peter tried to gauge his mood. "You sure you want me to escort Randy tomorrow? I'm surprised you would let her out of your sight."

Jake shrugged as he paused and glanced at Peter. "The kind of places you go aren't exactly places where someone has to worry about crime, and you always have your driver along. Randy will be fine, and you and she are good friends. God knows I've had women friends few wives would ever put up with." He whirled the chamber again and made an adjustment. "Why don't you just say it, Peter?" he added. "You would love a day alone with my wife. And I think she would enjoy the same. She just doesn't talk about it, but I know that woman inside and out. And I know true friendship." He set the part down and picked up another to clean it. "Besides, you are one of the most honorable men I've ever met. You have never flaunted your wealth in an arrogant way, and you're pretty damn down to earth – nothing like some of the other men I've met who run in your circle."

Peter eyed him closely as he shook his head. "I knew you would see right through some of their bullshit, as I'm sure you would call it. But they are still glad to meet the infamous Jake Harkner. And I take what you just said about me as quite a compliment, although you aren't always easy to figure. You're sitting there with those famous, intimidating guns, and telling me to spend a day alone with your wife. I'm not real sure how I should take that."

Jake smiled slyly. "Hell, you've loved Randy for years. I've known that since we lived in Oklahoma. She's *easy* to love. She is beautiful, intelligent, gracious, and devoted. Half the men on the ranch would marry her in a heartbeat if they could have her. Even *I* fell in love with her just about the first time I set eyes on her, and she *shot* me! I looked down at that damn little gun in her hand, and my first thought was *'What a woman! I want her.'*

Both men couldn't help laughing, but Peter's was a rather nervous laugh. Things remained quiet for a few seconds as

Peter drank more coffee and Jake held the gun up to the light of a window to look through the barrel.

"You, uh, never fail to come right out and say it like it is, do you, Jake?"

"Might as well be honest with each other." Jake set the gun back down and met Peter's gaze. "When I first met you, I didn't like you. That's no news. I read men pretty damn good, and I knew you had feelings for Randy, and you were rich and successful and educated and all the things I wasn't. I also know that rich men usually get what they want." He started polishing another part. "Working for you back in Guthrie kept Randy busy and kept her mind off wondering if I'd make it back every time I had to leave. I finally figured out how much your friendship helped her through some bad times, and I'm grateful for it.

You were there for her when she needed surgery and I *couldn't* be there. You saved my neck from a rope back in Denver, and your friendship with men in high places is the reason I was released early from that hellish job as a lawman. I sure didn't *choose* living like that, and I hated being away from Randy so much." He met Peter's gaze again. "You and I have a connection few men can boast, even though there have been plenty of times I wished you weren't a part of our lives at all."

Peter cleared his throat and drank more coffee. "Well, Jake, all I knew about you when you first came to Guthrie was that you were one rough, mean sonofabitch who I couldn't believe could actually be good to a woman. I was picturing you being gruff and ornery to Randy, maybe even hitting her at times, but I came to know the real you through her and the way she talked about you. When you asked me to go with her for that surgery and told me I was the only one you would trust to make medical decisions for her, I felt a whole *new* respect for you." He stared at his coffee cup as he spoke. "I would never press Randy into some kind of choice, because I know damn well what that choice would be, and wealth and lifestyle have nothing to do with it."

Jake picked up his cigarette and drew deeply on it again, then exhaled smoke as he pressed it out in the ash tray. "I've had plenty of women friends, Peter, most of them the kind most men don't think of as just friends. Randy understands those friendships have always been platonic, and she understands why. And if the day comes we can't be husband and wife in every way, we will still be together because we need to breathe, and we *can't* breathe without that closeness. All the times I rode out of that woman's life, I never failed to come back, because I had to get my oxygen. "

Sarah entered the kitchen, and Peter noticed she wore a nicer dress than normal, and a clean, starched apron.

"Oh!" she said, blinking big brown eyes at him. "I didn't know you were home, Mr. Brown. Is there anything you need? Shall I make you men something to eat?"

"No," Peter rose to pour himself more coffee. "You can leave, Sarah. And pull those French doors closed."

"Yes, Sir." Sarah smiled at Jake, who nodded back. "Can I get you anything, Mr. Harkner?"

"Thanks, Sarah, but I'm good at raiding an ice box. I had a sandwich earlier. I suppose my wife is still up there helping Matilda clean."

"Yes, Sir. We keep telling her she doesn't need to do any of that, but she says she's not used to being waited on, and that she's not about to start now. She even made Matilda sit down because she looked tired."

Jake chuckled. "That sounds like Randy. She's good at giving orders, even to me. My little granddaughter teases me about grandma being the boss of me."

Sarah giggled and left, closing the kitchen doors.

Peter leaned against the counter and grinned. "I hear Sarah spilled coffee grounds earlier when she was making coffee for you."

Jake tightened a screw on his gun. "I told her to quit being so nervous around me. I promised not to shoot her, and she giggled like a six-year-old. She's a sweet young lady." Jake turned the gun over and tightened another screw. "She's dark and pretty – reminds me of my mother and about the same age. My mother was still young when . . . " Jake cleared his throat. " . . . when she died."

Peter drank more coffee as he watched him warily and decided it might be wise to change the subject. "Do you mind telling me the *real* reason you want me to take Randy to the art galleries alone tomorrow?"

Jake set the gun aside and stood up, walking to the French doors to look out at the lake, his back to Peter. "I just want you to reassure Randy you will always be there for her. When the day comes that I *can't* be there, and that day is coming, I like knowing that besides family, she'll have a solid friend who will never fail her. In situations like that, sometimes just family isn't enough. Besides, when something happens to me, Randy and the rest of the family will need some honest legal help, and you know everything about us and drew up the papers about royalties on that book Jeff wrote, and you're the executor of what I guess you could call our estate." Jake turned. "I'm ten years older than Randy, older than you, for that matter. Someday, because of that, or because some sonofabitch decides to make a name for himself, my wife will be widowed. Going out of this life in a blaze of glory is a real possibility for a man like me. I hope it never happens, but it's a shadow that hangs over Randy and me all the time." He sighed deeply and ran a hand through his hair. "Randy holds you in high regard. She loves you in a special way."

Peter scowled. "Like a *brother*?"

"I don't know. Maybe. But I think it's more than that. She takes comfort in knowing you're someone who would always be there for her if I can't be. I think she would draw strength from you as an outsider who doesn't *need* to love her, but loves her anyway."

Peter frowned in surprise. "I hardly know what to say, Jake. You can be pretty moody. I'm not sure what you want of me."

"Sure, you know. If all my wife does is hold on to you when something happens to me, and all you do is hang on to keep her from going to her knees, that's all I care about. She's the kind of woman who *needs* holding. And believe me, if you think it's easy for a man like me to tell another man to be there for my wife, think again. Randy cares about you, and I appreciate the fact that you've been constantly respectful of our marriage."

Smiling sadly, Peter set his cup on the counter. "Jake, I think the reason your wife and family love you so much, despite your past, is because they see that little boy down inside who is so damn happy to be loved that he steals everybody's hearts. You don't take your family's love for granted, and that love is your weakness. If you go out in a blaze of glory, as you put it, it will be because of that one weakness. It's the one thing that could bring you down, tough and able as you are. Nearly every dangerous encounter from your past has been from you protecting someone you loved, and you got hurt in just about every one of those incidents. One of these days you will be killed, or sent to prison if you aren't careful with new laws. Your love for your family and your determination to protect has become your nemesis. It all started from not being able to protect your mother from your father. I understand that, and so does Randy. It's why I always defend your actions. If I thought for one minute you were just a blood-thirsty killer with a black heart, things would be different. But in spite of your intimidating presence on the outside, I know what a big heart lies on the inside. You don't know any other way to defend but by violence because every time you get into a fist fight or a gun fight, you're fighting you *father*. You're landing into *him* for what he did to your mother – making up for that eight-year-old boy who was helpless. I understand that better than you think."

Jake rubbed at his eyes. "Maybe so."

"And yes, I'll be there for Randy," Peter told him, "in whatever way I *need* to be there for her. Treena understands that. She always has. She's a strong woman with common sense, and she is very wealthy in her own right. We have an understanding I don't think I need to explain to you, and she would get along fine without me, if it ever came to that."

Jake ran a hand through his hair and began pacing. "I figured that. Some people marry for convenience. Some marry out of desperate love, even though they damn well know they don't belong together. Randy and I married for that reason."

"And that kind of love really threw you, didn't it?" Peter told him. "I know the fine line you walk between light and darkness, Jake, because Randy and I talked about it more than once. And I honestly hope I *never* have to be there for Randy, because seeing her happy with you is *worth* it. *That's* how much I love her. No other man will ever take your place in her heart.. Your father beat it into you that you're no good, but don't you kid yourself. You are *better* than most men. I think what throws people off is the way you look – tall and dark and intimidating, the way they picture an outlaw would look, so they still see you as one. Jeff said that once. He said you have the hard look of a man just released from prison."

Jake snickered. "It's the hard look of a man who's had the shit beat out of him too many times and returned the favor just as many. I'm a scarred-up mess. I quit counting the bullet holes a long time ago." He paced again. "As far as the look of an outlaw, outlaws come in all shapes and sizes, and sometimes they wear expensive suits and are smooth talkers. You can't judge by a man's size or how he dresses. I can usually pick out the no-goods. I've met a few right here in Chicago, including lawyers and councilmen. They don't fool me. I've been around too long. You don't have to carry a gun and rob banks to be an outlaw. There are a lot of other ways to rob people of their money, and some of the men I'm talking about are your friends."

Peter smiled. "Are you saying I'm one?"

Jake walked to the French doors. "Hell, no. If I thought you were that type, we wouldn't be friends." He faced Peter. "But I'm betting you can name some of them. You're no fool either."

Peter chuckled. "Sure I can. I've even defended a few." He folded his arms. "Please stop pacing, Jake, because you are making me nervous. I'm worried I'll say the wrong thing and end up on the other side of this kitchen."

Jake stopped and faced him. "Jesus, Peter, I would never do that. I appreciate your honesty, and I have to say I'm surprised by your remark about me being better than most men. Coming from you, that's a real compliment. I've never known a man who could make me like him when I shouldn't."

Peter smiled softly. "Then let's just realize that we admire and respect each other for quite different reasons. All I know is you are a man who acts on his emotions instead of reason, and those emotions are often ***explosive***. Don't let them get you into trouble again, or get you killed. Either way, I'll be there for Randy if necessary, but only in whatever way she'd *want* me to be there. You just remember how much she loves you and needs you. I don't know how many times she has referred to you as '*my Jake,*' as though you were the most precious thing in her life."

The doors opened, and Randy stepped inside. Peter turned away and Jake walked back to the table.

"Well, now," Randy said. "What's going on in here? I could cut the tension in the air with a knife."

Peter looked at Jake again, and there it was. The man's mood could turn on a dime when his wife came into the picture. It was almost astonishing how the darkness in his eyes vanished the minute Randy showed up.

"We were just talking." Jake looked Randy over. "And you look beautiful, as always. I hear you've been doing the maid's work while the maid sits and watches."

Randy put her hands on her hips. "I certainly have. She looked tired, and besides that, I'm used to doing for myself." Randy looked at Peter. "Thank you for all the wonderful pampering, Peter, but I just can't get used to being waited on."

Peter shrugged. "This is supposed to be a relaxing vacation for you. I didn't have you come here to do more than the *maids* do."

"Well, then, you don't know me so well at all. I've been doing my own cooking and cleaning for too many years to sit back and give orders to others."

Jake grinned. "I already told Sarah that you don't have any trouble giving *me* orders. I already understand from Sadie Mae that you're the boss of me."

"And don't you forget it. God knows you're the kind of man who *needs* to be bossed around." Randy walked up and threw a shirt at him.

"We are in civilized places, so put that on, Mister Harkner." She leaned up for a quick kiss. "I don't know what you two have been talking about, but I hope you haven't been rude to Peter, Jake. No host could be more gracious and generous—"

"We were just talking about guns and laws, and how Jake is going to have to be a little more careful about both," Peter interrupted.

"Well, I certainly have to agree." Randy gazed intently at Jake. "I caught your expression when I first opened those doors, Jake, so don't pretend you two were having a jovial conversation. What's wrong?"

Jake leaned down to kiss her once more. "Absolutely nothing." He put on the shirt. "In fact, I was just telling Peter that I'd like him to take you to the art galleries tomorrow. That's something you two would like, but not me. I'll stay here and enjoy a day of not answering reporters, and not being stared at, and not being asked questions about my outlaw days and what a sonofabitch I used to be, and why I killed my fuck—" He caught himself. "My father."

Randy frowned. "Jake?"

He took another cigarette from a tin on the table and lit it with a match he took from his pants pocket. "I was just telling Peter you two haven't had one minute to talk alone since we got here. You're good friends. If I could let you dance with that wife-stealing Vance Kelly at that cookout, I can let you and Peter spend a day together."

"Jake. What's really going on here? *Talk* to me."

Jake took her hand and leaned closer. "I *am* talking to you. Spend tomorrow with Peter. That enclosed carriage is like riding in a safe, and considering the people Peter runs with, I won't have to worry about you being in the wrong parts of town." He glanced at Peter, then back to Randy.

"Besides, I know Peter carries a gun inside his vest, and he'll damn well use it if he has to."

"Of course, I would," Peter agreed. "As long as it's not *ten* men I have to go up against," he joked, holding Randy's gaze. "In that case, you *would* need Jake."

Randy folded her arms. "I *always* need my Jake. I also know when he's been talking about something that tears at him emotionally. But I can tell neither one of you is going to give me an honest answer about that." She looked up at Jake. "I am surprised you are willing to let me go to the galleries tomorrow alone."

"You and Peter are good friends. It's okay." Jake began gathering the gun parts. "Do you think I'd let you go off in this city without me, if I didn't feel you'd be safe, or if I didn't trust Peter?"

Randy closed her eyes and sighed. "I suppose not." She looked at Peter. "What about Treena?"

Peter frowned. "What *about* Treena? She adores you."

"Well, I'm not so sure she'd care to hear you're running around Chicago with another woman while she's clear over in France."

Peter chuckled. "Treena would understand. And I'm not 'running around' with another woman. I am taking a friend to see art galleries, and probably to lunch. If that husband of yours thought for one minute it could turn into something more than that, he wouldn't tell me to take you. Besides, Jeff will want to come with us to take more of his endless notes."

Jake leaned closer and kissed Randy's forehead. "Go have fun tomorrow. You and Peter deserve some time to visit without me around."

Randy frowned, arms still folded. She met Peter's gaze again. "Did I hear him right?"

"You heard." Peter sighed. "Just accept that your husband is in a generous mood. In the meantime, since the pioneer woman in you insists on helping around here, I could stand some of that wonderful bread you bake. Is it too late in the day to make it in time to rise and bake for supper?"

"If I set the dough in the sun to rise faster, and if we eat a little late, there's time. Have Sarah show me where things are. And what about a late lunch? Are you two hungry?"

"I already ate a sandwich," Jake answered. "Maybe *you* are the one who should have something to eat. You're still too damn skinny, and you need something to build up your strength, after all those chores you've been doing upstairs."

Randy waved him off and turned away. "I'm fine. And if I'm going to make bread, then hurry up and get those guns off the table. You know I hate the smell of gun oil. You should have worked on those outside."

"Yes, Ma'am."

"And button that shirt and tuck it in."

"Yes, Ma'am."

"And go downtown this afternoon and find a suit for the ball Peter is planning for us. You should probably wear a tuxedo."

"Yes, Ma'am."

Jake placed some cartridges into the chamber of the gun he had just cleaned, then whirled the chamber and snapped it into place.

He shoved the gun into its holster, then threw the holster over his shoulder and picked up a small screwdriver and the several pieces of the other .44. "I'll put this back together on the deck below." He leaned down and kissed Randy once again. "I love you."

"Hold up," Peter called out. "I haven't told you two what I was doing at the office this morning."

Jake and Randy both faced him.

"Well?" Jake asked.

"I was wiring your reward money to Lloyd and Evie's accounts in Denver. I'm sure they'll give Ben his share, but you should set up an account for him when you get home."

"How much was the reward?" Jake asked.

"Thirty thousand from the Federal government, and a combined twenty thousand from the Philadelphia and Denver Mints."

"Oh, my gosh!" Randy gasped. She put her hand to her mouth and faced Jake. "That's fifty thousand dollars!"

Jake just shook his head. "Well, guess I'm good for *something*."

"You told me if there was a reward I should send it to Denver," Peter told Jake. "But since you have some time left here, and since your wife is having fun spending your money, I kept aside four thousand in cash in case you need it before you go home. If you think you need more than that, I can float it to you, and you can make arrangements with the bank in Denver to pay me back."

"It's enough." He winked at Randy. "Once we get home we'll use some of it to put that shower in at home."

Randy gave him a light shove. "Go finish cleaning those guns."

Jake grinned and walked out through the French doors. Randy faced Peter.

"Fifty thousand dollars! Peter, I think he's a little embarrassed. He is always uncomfortable taking reward money."

Peter chuckled. "I wish he would recognize his own worth, Randy, but he never does."

"Well, I hope you two weren't arguing earlier."

Peter scoffed. "Not at all. We simply had a bit of a heart-to-heart."

Randy studied the gentleness in his blue eyes. "He truly values your friendship, Peter."

"And I value his, but I also know there are moments when he'd like to deck me. I never let myself underestimate that man, and I try to do my part to keep him 'in the light,' as you so often put it. But no more talk about that. I am going to take you to those art galleries tomorrow. And in a few days I am holding a grand ball for you and Jake. All the big names in Chicago will be there. Treena's friend Rebecca told me you have purchased the perfect dress."

"Yes! Peter, Rebecca has been wonderful to me, taking me shopping and to lunch at some very fancy restaurants – introducing me to all the ladies of Chicago's high society. You wouldn't believe some of the things they ask me about being married to Jake. I find it really amusing, but really, they can ask some of the most personal questions. *What's it like being married to a real outlaw?* That's the most common question. Honestly, these women have no shame. They want *details*. I don't think I need to tell you what kind. " She started looking through cupboards for bread pans. "And Rebecca is one of the worst! She goes on and on about Jake right in front of me, as though it should mean nothing to me. I swear, she would steal Jake in a minute if she could, even though she's *married*, let alone the fact that *Jake* is married, too! That woman can be so blatant about such things."

Peter laughed. "Oh, believe me, I know what Rebecca is like. She is quite the partier. Her husband is much older. I think he just puts up with her so he can bring a beautiful woman to grand occasions. She married him for his money, and he damn well knows it. Just don't judge me by the kind of people in my circle, Randy. It's just the life I lead, mostly because it's the life *Treena* leads, and because a lot of my clients are those same people. I'm not much affected by any of it."

"Of course you aren't. You are so much better than some of the rather shallow people I have met, but they have all been kind and accommodating. I don't pretend to understand the way they live. I just accept it and am having a wonderful time."

Peter caught her staring out the French doors at Jake. "And you don't have one worry that Jake would take some other woman's offer, do you?" he asked her.

Randy shook her head. "Not one doubt."

Peter sighed as she continued watching Jake. "Don't worry about him, Randy. We had a good talk."

"About me, I suppose?"

"That – and other things. You know him better than anyone, honey. Sometimes he just needs to spill out the bad so he doesn't explode. Kind of like releasing the steam in a pressure cooker. One of those damn things exploded for real once, right here in this kitchen. The lid went clear to the ceiling. Thank God the cook wasn't leaning over it, or she'd be dead."

Randy quickly wiped at a tear. "You're trying to change the subject, but that's okay." She took a deep breath and smiled. "Peter, I did buy the most wonderful dress! It's black. And the design is that new snug fit instead of a big, full dress, but it does have a long train. Jake will love it!"

*And that's all that matters to you, isn't it?* Peter shook his head and smiled. "Oh, I'm sure he will. He is very, very proud of his beautiful wife, and he loves you beyond measure."

Randy sobered. "Yes, well, that's what sometimes worries me. Some men can love *too* much, and Jake is one of them."

Peter nodded. "I agree. And yes, some men *can* love *too* much." He turned and opened a bottom cupboard, deciding not to allow Randy to see the love in his *own* eyes. He leaned down and pulled out three bread pans. "Is this what you were looking for?"

Randy brightened. "Yes! Go get the cook to help me find all the ingredients I need."

Peter bowed to her. "Yes, Ma'am." He gave her a smile and left, and Randy walked to the French doors that led outside. She looked down at the deck where Jake sat staring out at the lake.

*What is going through that head of yours, Jake? You aren't sending me off with Peter tomorrow just to be nice. What were you two talking about?*

It was as though he was trying to push them together, and that very definitely was not Jake. Watching him now, she saw that "aloneness" about him that she had never been able to reach. *Pa is the loneliest man in the world, in spite of all the love around him.* Lloyd told her that once. It broke her heart to realize her son was right.

# CHAPTER 31

*August 7...*

"Do you think the Mitchels will sell their place to us?" Brady Fillmore stirred the small campfire over which a freshly-killed rabbit hung roasting on a spit.

"They will, but why give them any money at all?" The words were spoken by Buck Potter, a gunman with a mouth full of bad teeth. Buck scratched at three-day-old stubble on his face. "I think we should just do them in and bury them. Otherwise, they might decide to tell their neighbors they think we are up to no good."

Brady shivered with disgust at the suggestion. Out of the two men who had come to join in the downfall of Jake and Lloyd Harkner, Brady figured Buck to be the most dangerous of the two. And also the vilest. "You're talking about killing innocent people," he told the man.

"Might have to," Buck answered, as though it meant no more to him than shooting a turkey. "Me and Lenny robbed a bank up in Wyoming before we came here, and I ain't anxious to part with the money if we don't have to."

"That bother you?" Buck's partner, Lenny McCarthy

asked Brady. McCarthy was a kid of only twenty-two, and he was incredibly fast with a gun - fast enough to be cocky about it. He made Brady nervous, always drawing and twirling his gun, as though anxious to kill someone with it. Kyle Pendergrass rounded out their little five-man gang that included Grizzly Smith.

"I just don't know that we need to go so far as to hurt a woman and a family," Brady told Buck. "It's not them we're after."

"I'll go as far as I need to go, if it means getting a chance at Jake Harkner," Buck answered. "The Mitchel spread is the perfect location. It's right on the border of the J&L and is mostly in the open. So, if Jake comes charging at us, he'll be easy to see." Potter grinned. "And easy to bring down. That man's death will make the news in no time."

"It's the *son* I have a beef with," Brady reminded him. "I know Jake has the bigger name, but Lloyd is a real chip off the old block. He wanted to hang me a few years ago for that fire on the J&L, and now I'm limping around like a damn one-legged coyote because of that bastard. He shot me in the foot not long ago. So just make sure you get father and son *both*, not just Jake. It's a bet one won't come charging after us without the other."

"With what we have planned, they will be chargin' at us, all right," Grizzly answered. "And both are rich cattlemen. It'll be easy to claim they came to our little settlement and tried to bully us out. We can even shoot some of our own livestock and say the Harkners did it. I tell you, this is something we can get away with, if we're smart and careful."

"Fact is, we could kill the Mitchels and bury them, then claim we found them murdered and claim the Harkners likely did it because they came along and tried to bully us off the property," Buck suggested. "We could even shoot one or two other of the new settlers – sniper-like, and shoot some of their livestock. We could claim Harkner men did that, too. Anything we do to make J&L men look guilty gives us more reason to shoot Jake himself down if they come onto Mitchel land, which will soon be *our* land."

"Nobody around here would believe the Harkners would kill a woman and a teenage boy," Brady argued. "They are good neighbors to most folks around here. We have to do this the right way, or we'll end up with our heads in nooses."

"You worry too much," Buck grumbled.

"Buck is right about the Mitchels," Lenny said. "We can't just let them go free to talk to others."

"I don't want any part of something like that!" Brady told him.

Buck whacked him across his left cheek with the back of his hand. "You'll do what we *tell* you to do! Don't get any ideas of quitting this thing, Fillmore! Not this late in the game! I'll *kill* you before I let you go running off to wag your tongue to the law or to neighbors! You got that? Don't be a fucking *coward*!"

Brady blinked and rubbed at his cheek. He regretted the trip he took to Brown's Park, a haven for outlaws in the mountains. That was where he'd found Buck and Lenny, who were both very interested in gaining the reputation of killing Jake Harkner.

Kyle Pendergrass lit a cigarette. "After the way Harkner's son humiliated me when he ran me off at the Mitchel place, I want him just as much as I want his father." He drank some whiskey from a flask he'd set nearby. "He's as bad as his pa. If we take care of *both* of them and make it look legitimate, the *J&L* will fold. It can't be run without those two."

Buck slugged down more whiskey of his own. "We need to keep harassing the neighbors like we've been doing. A little cattle rustling – shoot some of their livestock here and there – trample newly-planted crops. This time of year most folks let their cattle wander and fatten up for winter, so it should be easy pickings for us. We won't steal any cattle that belong to the bigger cattlemen because we want the newer settlers that it's them doin' the dirty work."

"I think Lloyd has been sending men to the Mitchels to help them finish their barn," Grizzly reminded Buck. "If he catches us there and not the Mitchels, he'll suspect we've done our *own* dirty work."

"Then we will leave the Mitchels alone for a while yet," Lenny answered. "It's all a matter of timing. We can still do some rustling and knock off a few head of cattle – anything that stirs up the newer settlers and sets them against the cattlemen. Everything we do has to give us a reason to shoot down the Harkners. Once we get the rumors flying, we can convince neighbors that the Mitchels pulled up and left because of all the trouble, and they sold us their land. That's the story we will tell. And soon after, somebody from the J&L is going to get shot, and me and Buck and Kyle will do the shooting! The cattlemen will think it was new settlers that did it, and when they figure out the direction the trouble came from, they will come riding right into the sites of our guns. And you can bet the Harkner men will be right out front."

"I'm pretty sure I convinced three other men to join us," Kyle told them. "I talked to them back in Denver. They should be along any day. And once we make more trouble and convince other nesters that it's the cattlemen doing it, I'm thinking we could maybe even start charging some of the settlers for our protection – make some extra bucks while we wait for the big day. That Marshal

Kraemer can't be everywhere at once and they know it. They'll gladly pay us to help stop the cattlemen."

Grizzly's eyes lit up. "I never thought of that! A couple of men at the settlers' meetings would gladly join us in a coalition of sorts. We make it known we're here to stay, and we can have the newer settlers eatin' out of our hands."

"I can't wait to face Harkner." Lenny drew and whirled his gun again. "Bam! Bam! Bam!" he said childishly. "That old man is going to meet his Maker, and *I'm* the one who will bring him down. My name will be in all the headlines."

Brady shook his head. "Kid, Jake Harkner doesn't look or behave like an old man. Don't kid yourself that age means anything with him, because it doesn't. Grizzly and I both learned that the hard way." He rubbed at a cut on the side of his face and scowled at Buck. "You'd better remember that Jake Harkner can be more ruthless than you ever *thought* of being. You make him mad enough, and you might regret it."

"He's the one who will regret coming after us," Buck sneered.

They all jumped when Lenny suddenly fired his .45. A small bird fell from a tree behind Brady.

"Goddamn it, Lenny, quit showing off!" Buck told him.

"Shooting a bird is a whole lot different from standing up to Jake Harkner," Brady told the kid.

Lenny aimed his gun at Brady. "Don't be telling me I can't beat a man in his sixties to the draw. I ought to make you eat those words."

Brady swallowed and moved back a little. Lenny burst out laughing and holstered his gun.

"Fuck you," Brady grumped.

"Go right ahead, Fillmore. I'll pull my pants down."

"Shut up, Lenny!" Buck ordered. "And keep in mind

we aren't all that far from J&L land. One of their men might have heard that gunshot, so quit being careless."

He took the rabbit off the spit and shoved it onto a tin plate. "Everybody eat. We have some riding to do."

"The *real* trouble will start when I bring down a couple of J&L men in a few days ," Lenny said, "and it just might be one of Jake's kin. I've heard he goes a little crazy when one of his own gets hurt, like what he did in Denver when that man shot his son point blank. He almost got himself hung for that one."

"That's how you intend to get Jake to come running?" Grizzly asked him. "Shoot somebody in the family?"

"Can you think of a *better* way to get him to come to us?"

Grizzly looked at Brady and knew by the look in his eyes that Brady was thinking the same thing he was . . . that maybe they'd bit off more than they could chew by bringing Buck and Lenny in on their scheme. He moved his gaze to Lenny. "I don't like shootin' kids. If you're gonna' shoot somebody, start with Lloyd. At least he's a grown man. Brady wants him dead anyway. Or start with one of the Harkner ranch hands."

"I'll shoot whoever is in my sites," Lenny shot back. "Man or boy. It doesn't matter. My high-powered rifle has a scope on it, so they don't even have to be close. And when you sniper-shoot somebody, you don't stop them first and ask them their name. Quit fretting about maybe hitting a kid!"

They all ripped off pieces of the rabbit and started eating.

"Rest easy," Buck told them between bites and licking his fingers. "When this is over, we'll be famous, plus we'll all maybe own the Mitchel place. And you just might get back some of the land you lost to the Harkners, Fillmore," he told Brady. "You could even send for your wife and family back in Louisiana. That's what you want, isn't it?"

Brady swallowed a piece of meat. He was caught in his own web of plans now, and there was no changing it. If he tried to get out of this, he was a dead man, no doubt about it. "Sure," he answered.

# CHAPTER 32

August 7 . . .

"Hmmm. Nice picture, Mrs. Harkner."

Jake sat on the bed in his underwear, reading the paper that had come early that morning after Peter had left for his office.

Randy stretched beside him and rubbed her eyes. "What picture?"

Jake handed her the newspaper. "Society page."

By a streak of morning sunlight Randy looked at the front page of the *Society* section. There, right in the center, was a picture of Peter and her sitting together and smiling at each other.

NOTED ATTORNEY PETER BROWN SEEN LUNCHING ALONE WITH THE WIFE OF NOTORIOUS GUNMAN, JAKE HARKNER, the caption read. *Attorney Brown's wife is currently vacationing with family in France. Could there be more to this story? Will Peter Brown be next on Jake Harkner's hit list? There just might be more exciting news here before Harkner heads back to his ranch in Colorado. Will he take his wife with him? Or will he be going home alone?*

Randy gasped as she sat up straighter and put a hand

to her chest. "How *dare* they print something like this!" She looked at Jake. "That reporter sprang out of nowhere and took this picture without permission. I didn't think it would be used because it was just a casual lunch the day Peter took me to those art galleries." She read the caption again. "What will Treena think?"

"How about what *I* think?" Jake turned to press out his cigarette in an ashtray beside the bed.

Randy looked at him wide-eyed. Her eyes started to tear. "Why would you think *anything* of it? You know me better than this. We were just eating lunch."

Jake took the paper from her, tossing it to the floor. He put an arm around her and laid her back on the bed, moving on top of her. "You look awfully happy in that picture, Mrs. Harkner. Fact is, you were laughing together when you came back that day."

Randy studied his eyes. "Please don't tell me you think there's anything to that picture, or the caption. Surely you aren't *jealous*!"

"I could be."

"You could also be out of your mind! If you believe one word of that garbage, Jake Harkner, then I'm disappointed in you. And don't forget that my going alone with Peter to those galleries was *your* idea."

Jake kissed her softly, then grinned. "I'm sure Peter will have some explaining to do with Treena. Rebecca and some of Treena's other friends will likely send her that article and drop some gossip along with it."

Randy covered her mouth. "Oh, no! That's terrible! I'll have to write Treena myself. She's such a lovely woman. I wouldn't want - "

Jake kissed her neck. "Don't bother. I suspect Treena and Peter have an understanding about you. Let him take care of whatever he needs to. And I'm betting Jeff will have his own version of that lunch and will print something right away that will stop the nonsense. He was there with you, right?"

"Of course, he was. We were never truly alone together, Jake. Jeff was with us the whole time."

"Then don't worry about that picture and article. Jeff will fix it."

"How can I *not* worry? I don't' want that kind of gossip. It's mean to make something out of Peter's and my friendship."

Jake kissed her lips, deeper this time.

Randy held his gaze. "Jake, tell me you were joking about that bothering you. You said Jeff would stop such nonsense. You *do* believe it's nonsense, don't' you?"

"Yes." Jake grinned. "I'm teasing you. But I know how easily it could be true because you'd fit so well into this life, far better than you ever fit into mine."

Randy wrapped her arms around his neck, clinging a bit desperately. "You know I could never, ever love another man. You're my Jake. There is no one else like you. Please don't be upset—"

Jake stopped her with another kiss, then raised up on one elbow and looked down at her. "Hold on a minute. Jesus, Randy, you looked like you were *scared* of me. You still do. You've **never** looked at me that way. Do you really think I'm **upset** with you?"

"I don't know. That awful picture and those awful words . . . And we've never been faced with a picture of me cozying up to another man on the front page of a newspaper."

"Well, you weren't exactly sneaking around behind my back. Like you said, I'm the one who told you to spend the day with Peter." Jake kissed her again.

"Were you *afraid* of me just now?"

"No! Well . . . a little. Some men get really angry if they think —"

"You can't really think I was going to *hit* you or accuse you of cheating. You know me *better* than that! In the thirty-three years we've been together, have I ever laid a hand on you?"

"No."

"Then where is this coming from?"

Randy brushed at a tear. "Well, back in Guthrie, you were pretty angry when you first confronted Peter with how he felt about me—"

"And did I turn that on *you?*"

"No."

"Of *course* I didn't. That was between me and Peter. Randy Harkner, don't you *ever* be afraid of me. *Ever!* How can you think I'd harm one hair on your head, after what we've been through together? You know how I feel about that, and God knows I've given you reason enough not to trust *me*. That's probably the best thing about us – how much we trust each other."

Randy traced a finger along the scar at the side of his face. "I guess it's just . . . no man likes to see a picture of his wife with another man plastered on the front page of a newspaper, especially when he already knows that man has feelings for his wife. It's so unfair to you, and to how much we love each other."

"And as long as *we* know that, nothing else matters. The only thing wrong with that article is that it made me realize what it would be like if I really *did* go back to Colorado without you." He kissed her again. "It's unthinkable." Another kiss. "How many times have I told you I can hardly breathe without you?" He ran his hand under her night gown.

"I know. I just—when you asked if I had considered what *you* think—and then you threw the newspaper onto the floor like you were angry."

He kissed her neck. "I *was* angry, but not at you. I'm

angry at the reporter who wrote that. He'd better not show up at that ball Peter is having for us. Things might get ugly."

"Oh, Jake, I'm so sorry."

Jake kissed her again. "You didn't ask for any of that. Fact is, you look pretty damn good in that picture. A woman worth gossiping about."

"I don't *want* to be gossiped about. I love my husband."

"Well, I was counting on that when I told you to spend the day with Peter." Jake kissed her again, deeper this time. "And you being upset about those lies is one of the things I love about you."

He moved an arm under her waist and lifted her against him. "Randy, even if everything in that article was true, I would never lay a hand on you. You know that, don't you? After what I saw my father do to my mother, I could never hurt a woman. You've known that these thirty-some years."

"Jake, I would never betray your trust."

"Of course you wouldn't." He kissed her again. "Look at me," he told her.

Randy met his gaze, those dark eyes she'd learned to never fear. "There isn't one thing you could do that would make me hurt you or even *want* to hurt you. God knows that if you *did* leave me, I would damn well deserve it. But it would by-God shatter my heart into a million pieces, and I wouldn't want to go on living. I *couldn't* go on living. So don't you dare ever give thought to me laying one finger on you the wrong way. Understand? Never in our married life have I seen that little bit of fear in your eyes – not even in that wagon the first night I took you and wasn't very nice about it. Remember that?"

Randy smiled through tears. "Of course I remember. How could I forget that passion?"

"You glared right back at me without an ounce of fear and said the one thing that hit me in the gut like a fist. You said, Go ahead. *Just don't take me like your father would take a woman.* That woke me up. I didn't hurt you then and I've never hurt you in all these years. When I saw that little spark of fear in your eyes, I saw how my mother used to look at my father, and I don't *ever* want to see that in your eyes. Not ever. Understand?"

"Yes."

Randy smiled softly and ran one hand into his hair, studying the few gray and white streaks in his otherwise thick, nearly black mane. "And as long as I'm in these arms, I know that the bad out there can't reach me, not even lies in a newspaper."

Jake leaned down and kissed her cleavage. "Lady, *I'm* the 'bad.'"

"Oh, but your kind of bad is so very good."

"And who do you belong to?"

There it was – the question he always asked. She studied those eyes. No anger. Just adoration. "Jake Harkner. Always and forever."

"You bet."

Somehow her bloomers came off. Their kisses grew deeper, as did their desperate groans of need for each other. Randy suspected there was a secret part of him that did want to make sure she knew who she belonged to. Her nightgown came off, as did the bloomers she wore under it. Jake

tossed them to the floor and removed his long johns, then kissed and licked his way down her body, her ankles, her knees, the inside of her thighs, that most womanly part of her that belonged only to Jake, her belly, her breasts, her throat, her mouth, making her groan with want and whisper his name.

"I need you," he said softly in her ear. "You're my whiskey. Did I ever tell you that?"

"Jake, I'm right here and I'll always be right here." He moved between her legs and pushed his hardness inside her. The way he made love to her always emboldened her to the point she had no inhibitions, no objections to anything he wanted to do with her.

He knew every move that she loved, every place on her body that responded to his touch and his kisses - kisses that grew deeper and hotter as she became lost beneath him. She felt buried under his power, completely at his mercy, and that was fine with her, because this man who could be so brutal against an enemy was never anything but utterly adoring when he was with her. She sucked in her breath with each hard push. In these moments he never demanded anything, but at the same time he had a way of gently commanding she let him do whatever he wanted with her. She never gave thought to saying "no." Why would any woman say no to this?

"Yo te amo, mi quiero."

Randy cried out his name as she climaxed, and her insides pulsed with a need to pull him deeper. Always there was that desperate need to prove to each other that they were right here together. They were okay. They were happy and well, and none of the bad outside their bed had been able to take away from this ability to melt into each other and become one.

His life spilled into her, but he kept up the rhythm so that within a minute or two he was invading her all over again, rubbing her sweet nest in a way he knew would bring on her own second climax.

"Mi querida esposa, lo nuestro sera eterno," he groaned close to her ear. "Tu y yo estaremos unidos eternamente." He invaded her mouth with more hot kisses, and she felt his life surge into her again. He relaxed then and kissed her neck before moving to her side. "I have something to show you," he told her. He rolled onto his back, bringing her with him so that she lay across his chest. He pointed to the nightstand. "Open that drawer. There's something in there for you."

Randy kissed him. "What have you gone and done?"

Jake ran a hand over her back. "See for yourself."

She reached over and opened the drawer, then smiled at seeing a long, black velvet box inside. She smiled as she took it out of the drawer. "Jake, you already bought me a gorgeous, and too-expensive, wedding ring in Denver."

"That was a few years ago, and you needed something better than that plain gold band I put on your finger when we married at Fort Laramie. And now you need something to complement that dress you bought for Saturday night. I haven't seen it yet, but what's in that box should be perfect for any dress."

Randy felt like crying at realizing he'd thought to buy her something for the up-coming ball. She sat up more, holding the box in her hands. "I'm so sorry about that article, Jake."

"Quit apologizing. It wasn't your fault. Peter's either. The person I'd like to lay into is the man who took the picture and made it look like something more than it was. Let's just agree not to talk about it anymore."

Randy sighed with love and anticipation for what might be in the box. She faced Jake. "You know you don't need to buy me things, don't you?"

"I *love* buying you things. It's just that out at the ranch, a woman doesn't need much when it comes to fancy. Then again, you're so beautiful that you can make a plain cotton dress with no slips look good enough for wearing to meet the queen." He sat up behind her. "And who knows when or if we'll go to anything quite so fancy again as the ball

Peter has planned for us a couple of days before we go home?"

Randy opened the box and breathed deeply in surprise. "Jake! You shouldn't have. This must have cost a *fortune*!"

"Who cares? We're rich from that reward."

Inside the box was a diamond necklace. Designed to look like a rose, each little petal of the pendant was a separate diamond. The delicate chain was white gold. Randy put her fingers to her lips and started crying. "Jake, it's *beautiful*! When did you get this?"

"While you were out flirting with Peter at that restaurant," he teased. "I figured whatever happened between you two, I'd better be ready with something to entice you back to me."

Randy picked up a pillow and hit him with it. "Stop talking like that, or I'll—"

"You'll do what?"

"I don't' know, but I'll think of something." She got off the bed to find a handkerchief and wipe at tears of joy and gratefulness at the beautiful gift. "Jake, come put it on me."

"You're still naked."

"I don't care." She walked over to the bed and sat down on the edge of it. "Put it on me. Let's see how I look wearing nothing but a diamond necklace."

"Hell, I won't argue that one."

Randy took the necklace out of the box and held it out to him.

Jake scooched up behind her. "It's pretty delicate. I don't know if these big, rough, rancher fingers can finagle the clasp." He took the necklace from her and managed to open the clasp. He put the necklace around her neck and secured it. "There."

Randy stood and walked back to the dressing table mirror. "Oh, Jake! It will look so beautiful with my dress.

And with the diamond earrings we bought years ago in California. Remember that?"

He smiled sadly. "There are things about California I'd rather *not* remember." He looked her over. "You make a hell of a model, Mrs. Harkner. Maybe you should pose for those painters who like to paint naked ladies."

"Oh, stop it! Besides, you'd have a fit. You'd sit there beside me with a gun pointed at every one of the painters, warning them they can look but don't touch."

Jake laughed. "You really like the necklace?"

"How could any woman *not* like it? I can't believe you thought of this." Randy faced him. "For a man who knows mostly horses and cattle and guns, you certainly have good taste in jewelry."

Jake kissed her and laid her back again, moving on top of her. He kissed the necklace. "I'm glad you like it."

"I love anything and everything you give me, but mostly I love *you*. And don't be thinking we should make love again, Mr. Harkner." Randy gave him a light shove. "I have to clean up and get dressed. I'm supposed to meet some women later at a public library."

Jake frowned and kissed her cleavage. "You mean I have to wait until tonight to make love again?"

Randy smiled and scooted out from under him. "That's exactly what I mean. And I'm looking forward to today. I've never seen a library the size of what's here in Chicago. We are going to a big book store afterward. I intend to buy some books for Evie and Katie, and some children's books. Heaven knows we don't have much access to those things out at the ranch." She turned to the mirror and looked at her necklace again, fingering it lightly. "I'm going to wear this when I go. Some of those rich, fancy women will be insanely jealous, not just of the necklace, but of the fact I am married to Jake Harkner."

"I'm not so sure that's something anyone else should be jealous of." He sat up and lit a cigarette.

Randy caught a hint of sadness in his last remark.

"You're as wonderful as you are handsome, and just as smart and successful as their husbands, and those women know it. They would give anything to be married to a man as exciting and brave and able as you are." She picked up a robe and held it in front of her as she walked over to lean down and kiss him. "The necklace is beautiful, Jake, and so thoughtful. I am never taking it off. I'm even going to wear it in the shower. How did you manage to pick out something so perfect?"

He shrugged.

"All I have to think about is how beautiful you are, and how tiny you are. And you love roses. Put that together, and it's easy to find a piece of jewelry that fits you."

Randy knelt in front of him. "Tell me again that you're all right about that article. I'm so sorry you saw that on the same day you were going to give me this gift."

He grinned and set his cigarette in an ash tray, then smoothed some of her hair behind her ear. "Randy, it's *me*. Jake. The man who loves and trusts you beyond measure. But I intend to make Peter feel *extremely uncomfortable* when I go downstairs later. He's probably thinking I might have a few words for him."

"Oh, Jake, don't you dare!"

Jake chuckled. "This could be fun."

"And I know your sense of humor. Have some mercy."

"And spoil the fun?"

Randy pushed at him. "Don't be mean. And put out that cigarette for now. We need to take a shower."

"Together again?"

Randy smiled mischievously. "Yes."

Jake quickly put out his cigarette. "I'm all for that."

Randy laughed as he walked over and picked her up in

his arms to carry her to the washroom. "And when we go to that ball Peter has planned for us, let's dance so close that we give those jealous women something more to gossip about."

"We'll damn well do that." Randy put her arms around his neck and kissed him.

"Do you still have some of that good-smelling soap we used last time?" Jake asked.

Randy laughed. "Yes."

"Then let's go get all slippery."

"I have a feeling we will be in there a while," Randy said, resting her head on his shoulder.

"Yeah, well, we definitely need to install a shower at home," Jake told her. "Water might be in short supply where we live, but we'll damn well figure something out. A shower is nice for a lot more than just washing."

Randy laughed. "Keep using your imagination, Mr. Harkner." She loved him this way, so relaxed and happy.

## CHAPTER 33

*August 18 . . .*

"We have to let Hal Kraemer handle the matter of all these new people moving onto range land, Lloyd," ranch owner Bert Cromwell, the *J&L's* southern neighbor, stated.

At Lloyd's request, eight ranch owners had met in the *J&L's* newest barn to discuss an outbreak of cattle rustling.

"Kraemer needs more deputies," Lloyd told them. "The only thing range detectives can do is report what they see. They can't stop any of it. It's too dangerous for one or two men to go up against a bunch of rustlers."

"Bet you and your pa could have back in the day," Henry Till said.

"Thanks, but everything's changed now," Lloyd answered. "Used to be men could handle things the way we always did, but we were also lawman then. Nowadays, any one of us could be jailed or hanged just as easily as the rustlers. It's a shame things are that way, but taking the law into our own hands can lead to more trouble than losing a few cattle is worth."

Most of these men had met at Henry Till's cookout, but signs of more active rustling had warranted another meeting. This time, they met to determine what they could legally do if they caught the rustlers.

"I think whoever's doing the rustling is taking the cattle south and then directly west," Lloyd suggested, "avoiding towns and the railroad. They could be taking them into outlaw country in Utah."

"That's country you and your pa know, isn't it?" Bert asked.

Lloyd shrugged. "It's been years since either of us spent any time there." Lloyd paused to light a cigarette then threw his match into a water-filled bucket nearby. "We should probably send a delegation to Denver and demand that the governor provide more marshals and deputies. And more range detectives, to make sure newcomers abide by the rules. And Colorado needs to give us some solid rules for handling rustlers. My pa was offered the job of range detective a few months back, but he knew taking it would upset my mother."

"Meantime, we shouldn't have to lose livestock just because there aren't enough lawmen around to handle this," Bert spoke up. "We shouldn't be expected to just sit back and let this happen."

"Next thing you know, these nesters will be squatting on land that doesn't belong to them and cooking steaks that came off the butts of our beef," Henry Till added. "This is getting too costly."

"The state should not only provide us with some protection but give us clear instructions on what we can and can't do," Lloyd insisted. "My pa will be back in a week or so. I'm worried about his reaction when he finds out what's been going on. You all know how he can be. I don't want him getting into trouble again."

"Jake knows the rules," Edgar Pratt stated.

Lloyd scoffed. "Knowing the rules and obeying them are two different things when it comes to Jake Harkner."

They all looked toward the barn door when they heard several horses thunder up.

"Somebody get Brian!" Cole yelled from outside. "Ben and young Jake have been shot!"

"Jesus!" Lloyd raced from the barn, followed by the other ranchers.

Cole had gone with Stephen, Ben and Young Jake to the Mitchel place early that morning to help Stuart Mitchel work on a new barn. It was nearly five in the afternoon now. What had happened? The four incoming riders rode directly to Brian and Evie's house, where Brian was already on the porch.

"My God. Jake!" Brian helped his son down from his horse.

Despite a bandana tied tightly above the wound, Young Jake's right thigh was bleeding heavily, and he looked pale.

Cole dismounted and eased Ben down from his own horse. "Need some help here! This kid's too big for me to handle alone."

Gretta came running, yelling Cole's name.

"I'm all right!" Cole told her, even though dried blood was stuck to his hair and down his face. Others helped him carry Ben into the house, with Brian right behind them, carrying his son.

"Stevie! Stevie!" Lloyd yelled before going inside.

"I'm here, pa." Stephen ran to Lloyd from where he'd tied his horse close to a watering trough. The boy flew into his father's arms and broke into tears. "Pa, it was awful! Blood everywhere!"

Lloyd grabbed his arms and held him out in front of him. "Tell me you aren't hurt!"

"No. I'm okay."

"Thank God!" Lloyd kept an arm around his son's shoulders and led him into Evie's house.

"Put them in separate bedrooms," Evie was telling the others. "Second door on the right and first door on the left down the hall." She suddenly jerked in a sob. "Oh, dear God, help them!"

Lloyd hurried up to her and put an arm around her, hugging his sister and his son both. "Hang on, Sis. Wait till we know how bad this is."

Cole came out of the bedroom on the right. "Ben's arm is as bad as can be, Lloyd," he said. "The bullet shattered his elbow. Looks like it came from a big caliber rifle. I did the best I could to stop the bleeding, but I'm afraid he could lose his arm."

The next few minutes were bedlam as both injured boys were put on beds, their wounds temporarily wrapped to stave off the bleeding until Brian could tend to each one.. Young Jake groaned and started crying, while Ben screamed. "My arm! Don't touch it! Don't touch it!"

"Somebody clean off the kitchen table," Brian ordered. "I'll need bright light over it, towels and hot water. Take all the little kids to Clara and Patrick's place, and make sure the girls are out of here. Don't let them see this!"

"The girls are at my house." Lloyd told him. He gave Stephen another hug. "See what you can do to help."

"Sure, pa." Stephen wiped at more tears. Lloyd kissed his forehead. "It's going to be okay, Stephen."

"I put my belt around Jake's leg and pulled it real tight," the boy told his father.

"Good. That was a smart thing to do. Go ask Brian what you can help with." Lloyd walked out the door to address the men waiting on the porch for orders. "Take all the little ones in here over to my place. Tell Katie what happened, but tell her to stay there with the kids for now. And go tell the Donavans to go over there."

Three of the hands ran to gather the toddlers from Evie's place, while two others hurried to Lloyd's.

"The horses are lathered really bad." Vance saw the terror in Lloyd's eyes. "We're all here for you, Lloyd. I don't know all that happened, but stay calm. We'll find a way to get word to Hal Kraemer . . . and to Jake. I'll have a man take the horses to the barn and get the gear off them."

"Send a rider to Brighton right away to wire Kraemer and – " He paused. "Shit," he muttered. "I don't want to tell pa about this, but we don't have much choice. This will really devastate him, and he and my mother will have to get back here right away. God only knows how pa will react when he gets here. "

"Don't I know it? Either way, it's going to take a couple days to get word to them," Vance pointed out. "It's over a day's ride just to Brighton."

"Just make sure you get the law out here *before* my father shows up. And have whoever goes avoid the Mitchel place. I have an idea somebody there is involved."

"But the Mitchels – "

"Just do it, Vance."

Vance nodded and rushed to see to the horses and send out messages.

"Jesus Christ, who shoots at *boys*?" Cole's angry remark could be heard outside. "We were riding to the Mitchel place to check on how things are going there, and as soon as we came over that last rise, we got shot. No reason. No *fuckin'* reason at all!"

Lloyd stepped back inside his sister's house. "Tell me the rest of it," he asked Cole. He could hear Brian and Evie trying to calm young Jake, while Gretta did the same for Ben.

"A shot rang out, and bone and blood flew from Ben's arm," Cole told Lloyd. "He screamed and fell off his horse. Another shot knocked my hat off and creased my scalp. Then another shot, and Young Jake screamed my name, turned his horse and started ridin' off. I told

Stephen to get the hell out of there and catch up to Jake. I pulled my rifle, but I didn't have a goddamn thing to shoot at. I helped Ben to his mount, took his reins so's he could hang on to his pommel. I got back on my horse fast as I could and led his. We rode off and I got us over that rise so whoever shot at us couldn't see us anymore. Then I tied off Ben's arm the best I could. We caught up with young Jake and Stephen and Stephen wrapped his belt around Jake's leg and we headed back here. I can't believe both wounded boys stayed alert enough to keep ridin'."

Lloyd turned away, feeling sick at what this news would do to his parents. He struggled with his own fury at his brother and nephew both being shot. The same could have happened to Stephen. "This was fucking *deliberate!*" he growled. "And I have a pretty good idea who was behind it! I'll gladly hang the sonofabitch myself!"

Evie hurried into another room to grab some towels, and Gretta hurried into the kitchen to grab a kettle of hot water and a wash pan. She put another kettle on, then cleared off the kitchen table.

"Lloyd, go get Teresa DeJesus to help me," Gretta told him. "And we'll need you and Cole to help Brian. You need to bring Ben in here. Much as it's hard for Brian not to work on his own son first, Ben is the worst right now. Brian has to do something quick about that arm."

Evie hurried into young Jake's room with towels, then came out with Brian, devastation in her eyes. Brian walked closer to Lloyd and talked quietly. "I've got to get some laudanum into both of them, maybe even some whiskey into Ben. I poured some alcohol into Jake's leg wound and wrapped it tight for now. I've got to operate on Ben's arm right away. It's just hanging there by a couple of tendons from the elbow down."

"Mom, it hurts bad!" young Jake yelled from his room.

"I know, Jake." Evie struggled against tears, and Brian kissed her forehead.

"Stay strong, honey," he told her. "Our son is young and healthy, and I think once I get the bullet out, he'll make it. Give him some more laudanum for his pain." He looked back at Lloyd as Evie rushed back to her son. "There are two of them and only one of me, so I have to make some choices here." He quickly wiped at tears in his eyes. "I just need to figure out how to stay calm."

"I understand," Lloyd told him. "Thank God we have a doctor among us. I'll help the men bring Ben out here."

He and Cole hurried to where Ben lay, and fury rose in Lloyd's soul at the sight of Ben's arm.

The boy looked up at him with terror-filled eyes. "They . . . shot my arm off!" He wept, trembling violently.

Lloyd leaned over to grasp Ben's face in his hands. "You don't know that. Brian's a good doctor. He'll do all he can. You drink some Laudanum now. It'll help the pain. Brian will take care of the rest. Just trust him, Ben."

"I . . . want Jake . . . " Ben sobbed. "I want my pa."

"We'll get him here fast as we can, Ben. Right now, we have to get you out to the kitchen table so Brian can fix that arm. All right?"

"Y – y – yes," Ben answered between sobs.

Lloyd felt crazy with helplessness. He called Vance and Rodriguez into the room to help carry Ben to the kitchen table, and just then Rodriguez's wife Teresa came inside, rushing over ask Gretta what to do.

The men carried a screaming Ben to the table just as Katie made it to the house. She glanced at a screaming Ben, then turned to Lloyd, wide-eyed with horror. "Stephen!"

Lloyd rushed over and pulled her close. "He's okay. I think he's in the bedroom to the left, helping with young Jake."

"Lloyd, what happened?"

"I don't know for sure, but I have my suspicions, and this could turn into a range war. All I know is somebody shot at the boys when they got close to the Mitchel place, and there is no way the Mitchels would do something like that. Cole says whoever it was, they used a high-powered rifle. I figure it had a scope on it. Young Jake was shot in the thigh, and Ben took a hit in his left elbow." He leaned closer so Ben couldn't hear his words. "Brian is afraid Ben will lose his arm."

Katie sucked in her breath and her eyes teared. "Oh, Lloyd, how awful!"

"There's likely gonna' be a range war now," Cole told Gretta as they both put towels under Ben's arm.

The boy screamed again.

"Lloyd, I need you and Cole to help me hold down Ben," Brian told Lloyd and Cole. "Who did this and what we should do about it can wait."

Lloyd walked over to take hold of Ben's left ankle. He looked at Cole, and Cole saw the devastation in his eyes. "Lloyd, you have to let the law handle things this time."

"*Do* I?" Lloyd shook with a need to hit something. "Just keep me away from whiskey."

"Whiskey only makes things worse and gives you stupid ideas," Cole reminded him. "Jake would never want you to touch that stuff, regardless of what's going on. Wait for him to get here."

A darkness moved into Lloyd's eyes as Vance and Rodriguez joined them at the kitchen table to help hold down Ben, who trembled with terror.

Brian ripped away what was left of Ben's shirt. "Jesus Christ," he muttered. The man never swore, especially not to use the Lord's name in vain. Lloyd knew then just how bad this was.

# CHAPTER 34

*August 19 . . .*

Jake leaned against the frame of the bedroom door and watched Randy walk down the hallway toward him. Because one of Treena's personal hairdressers had helped her with her hair, dress, and makeup for tonight's ball, she'd dressed in another room.

Randy's eyes widened when she came closer. "Jake! You look so handsome in that tuxedo! I've never seen you look more like – I don't know. You look like you would fit right in with all those councilmen and millionaires upstairs!"

Jake just grinned and shook his head. "And I already can't wait to get *out* of this thing. Besides, it doesn't matter how I look. That dress makes me want to take you back inside the bedroom and forget the damn ball."

Randy held out her arms and turned. "You like it?"

Jake shook his head in wonder. "I can't begin to find the right words. You've never been more beautiful."

Randy's hair was pulled back into blond curls that spilled from the crown of her head down over her shoulders, held in place by glittering combs. Her dress was made of a soft, shimmery material that hugged her tiny, hourglass figure, a new style and refreshing change from mounds of petticoats, ruffles and bustles. A sheer black chiffon wrap wound around her still-slender waist and was tied at the side with a glittering butterfly pin. The heart-shaped neckline revealed just enough tempting cleavage to make Jake want to kiss her there, and the shoulder straps were glittering stones instead of cloth. She wore elbow-length black gloves and carried a shawl in one hand.

"The straps are Swarovski crystals," she told him. "It's something new, and expensive, but look how they sparkle! And wearing my hair pulled back shows off the diamond necklace you got me. Jake, it sparkles so beautifully!"

Jake smiled. "That neckline shows off a lot more than the necklace. My God, Randy, you'll have the women gossiping behind their fans and men salivating." He walked closer, running the back of his fingers over the swell of her breasts. "I'm not so sure I should take you up there at all. I'm going to have to keep a close eye on you."

"I got this dress for you, Jake, not for anyone else." She turned again. "Is the back too low?"

"For *me*? Hell, no."

Randy faced him again. "Be honest. Do you want me to wear the shawl? It's lace, with a chiffon overlay that goes with the dress. If you think the bodice or the back are too revealing, I can wear shawl."

"Baby, you look perfect." He leaned down and kissed her cheek. "I want to kiss your lips, but I don't want to spoil the perfect way they are painted. You have never looked more beautiful, Mrs. Harkner."

Randy smiled, her lips lightly colored in soft pink, a hint of rouge on her cheeks, a tiny bit of light-gray powder on her eyelids—like one would see on a wealthy, perfectly pampered woman. She stood back and looked Jake over, studying his black evening dress coat with a plain collar and silk-covered revers. The tails reached to just above the backs of his knees. A white shirt and black bow tie set off his gray and black brocade waistcoat, and the black braided stripes down each gray pant leg matched the waistcoat.

Jake held out his arms. "Do I pass inspection?"

"Well, speaking of salivating, the wives of those men up in that ballroom will need their handkerchief to keep dabbing at the saliva at the corners of their mouths."

Jake couldn't help laughing. "They should see me after herding a few thousand cattle to the railroad stations. Several days riding behind a bunch of cows with no ability to bathe or shave would change their minds."

Randy walked closer and adjusted his bow tie. "I think you're handsome even when you are in *that* condition."

"That's just because you don't love just the good side of me. You love the bad, too."

"Well, all I know is that my utterly handsome husband certainly cleans up good." On a sigh, she added, "You make me as anxious to get back to our room later as you are."

Jake bowed to her. "Then let's get this over with." Jake held out his arm. "May I escort you, Mrs. Harkner?"

"Thank you, Mr. Harkner." Randy took his arm. "I love you."

"Love you, too."

"Shall we make our grand entrance, Mr. Harkner?"

"I suppose. I can hear the music coming from the ballroom, and it sounds like people are already dancing, so most guests are probably here by now." The headed down the hall toward a wide stairway that led to the ballroom.

"By the way, I rented this damn tuxedo. No sense buying one. I sure won't need it once we get home. And I hate these shiny black shoes I'm wearing. I'd rather be wearing my dusty old boots."

"Considering the things you have been through in life, Jake, you'll survive a few hours in a pair of fancy shoes." They both chuckled as they ascended the stairs. "Peter said Chicago's mayor is here, and several councilmen and other leaders, as well as lawyers and doctors," Randy said.

"God help us."

Randy kept hold of the shawl in case she needed it, then walked with Jake up the marble stairway to the third-floor ballroom. Peter stood waiting on the upper landing, wearing a tuxedo with a purple satin vest and tie. His eyes lit up when he saw Randy.

"So, you two finally made it. I wanted you to make a grand entrance, and you certainly will, since everyone else is already here."

Randy smiled and turned. "Was I right about the dress?"

Peter glanced at Jake before answering. "I don't think I need to ask what *you* think of that dress."

"You sure don't," Jake replied with a grin. "Go ahead, Peter. Be honest."

Peter chuckled and bowed to Randy. "My lovely Mrs. Harkner, it is cruel of you to ask me that question in front of your husband, but I've never known a woman who could so absolutely innocently drive a man crazy. And I must say that Rebecca knew exactly what she was doing when she helped you pick out that dress. She told me it was perfect for you, and it most certainly is." He turned to Jake again. "Are you ready for what's inside these doors?"

"Ready as I'll ever be."

"Well, you look . . . I don't know."

"Like an old cowboy wearing a tux?"

Peter laughed. "Jake, you are like a chameleon, a cowboy one day and a fancy gentleman the next."

"Your butler had to help me get into this damn tux," Jake answered. "I've never worn something like this in my life."

"Well, you're dressed like a lot of those men in there, but you still look like an outlaw, as far as I'm concerned."

Jake took Randy's arm. "Then I'll fit right in with all those other outlaws in there."

Both men laughed, and

Peter opened the doors to the ballroom. People brightened and welcomed them, and in seconds they were completely surrounded and answering a barrage of questions.

Rebecca sashayed up to kiss Peter's cheek. "Eat your heart out, Peter Brown."

Peter turned. "What?"

Rebecca laughed. "My dear friend, your self-control is phenomenal. I caught the way you were looking at Randy Harkner from behind."

"Yeah, well, if you knew Jake like I do, you'd understand why I didn't let *him* see it."

"Yes. I saw that newspaper picture. The way you were looking at Randy in that picture, you might as well have shouted 'I love you!'"

"I *do* love her, but not in the salacious way you picture such things. Randy Harkner is one of a kind."

Rebecca glanced at Jake and leaned closer to Peter. "I will grant you that Randy is beautiful, but that husband of hers is just as tempting for a woman. I'm having trouble with my *own* self-control."

"Well, my dear Rebecca, you can do all the tempting you want, but that man has eyes only for his wife. He knows damn well he could never find another woman who would put up with him. Randy is his rock."

Rebecca frowned. "Too bad. I'd leave Duncan for Jake Harkner in a minute."

Peter shook his head. "You would leave Duncan for *any* man younger and more handsome."

"Oh, Duncan knows it. We just have an understanding. He gets to have a pretty wife on his arm, and I get to spend his money." Rebecca chuckled. "I daresay, you and Treena have a similar understanding." She kissed Peter's cheek. "But at least she has a handsome husband of her own and not a wrinkled up old man like Duncan." She kissed Peter again, this time on the lips. "You *do* you realize how handsome you are, don't you?"

Peter stepped back a little but kept hold of her hand. "Rebecca, you have absolutely no shame." He looked her over. Rebecca was a tall, shapely, dark-haired woman in her thirties, with ravishing green eyes that could enchant any man. "And you look lovely tonight. Please behave yourself around Jake and Randy. Randy is already aware of your blatant sexual desires, so don't think you are fooling her. She's just too nice to say anything. Just accept that Jake Harkner belongs to that woman, and I suspect she has very long claws for any woman who would try to do something about that."

Rebecca waved him off. "I'm going to prove you wrong. Jake Harkner can be had, and tonight I intend to have him."

Peter chuckled. "My dear, you will be greatly disappointed – and probably embarrassed. Jake will turn you down so fast you'll be in tears."

"Well, you have to admit it's worth a try. That is the most provocative hunk of man I have ever laid eyes on."

Peter shook his head as he patted her hand. "Go flirt with the other men here," he told her.

"And what are *you* doing later, love? Treena is clear on the other side of the ocean, I might remind you."

"Honey, tonight I need to give full attention to Jake and Randy. This is my party, remember? I have to make sure someone doesn't say the wrong thing to Jake. That could end up with half this room destroyed and a few split lips. Go flaunt yourself around somebody else." Peter left Rebecca and moved in to stay close to Jake and Randy. Jeff and his wife had already joined them, and Jeff, as always, was scribbling notes for his newspaper.

"Mrs. Harkner, you are supposed to be gray and wrinkled from stress and the western sun," Hilda Cummings was telling her. Hilda was a stout, graying woman herself, the wife of a councilman. "However do you do it?"

"I have a lot of help at home. And the love of a good husband and a big family brings joy. I believe joy is what helps keep us young, don't you?"

"*Joy?*" Hilda frowned. "But you're living with – well – Jake Harkner. And you are out there in the wilds of Colorado living a pioneer life."

"And loving every minute of it," Randy answered with a smile. She squeezed Jake's arm tighter. "We have lots of grandchildren, and our homestead is at the base of the Rocky Mountains. You should come and visit, Mrs. Cummings, and see how beautiful it is. It's not a hard life at all."

More comments and questions flowed, most of them directed at Jake, and a good share of them about the train robbery. One man asked what it was like to kill six men in a matter of minutes, with their bullets flying back at him. Another said Jake should put on a marshal's badge again.

"My name is Mark Howell," the man told Jake. "I'm a lawyer for the city." He shook Jake's hand. "From what I hear, the West is still pretty wild, Jake. Men like you are still needed."

"Men like me usually end up stretching the law a little too far," Jake joked. "And then they get their *necks* stretched in return."

Several men laughed.

Peter stayed close by to make sure things went smoothly, but he needn't have bothered. Randy handled some of the questions and comments with the social grace of the most experienced woman of wealth and influence, even sometimes answering questions put to Jake before he could answer them himself. The woman damn well knew which questions were just plain rude, which ones were too painful, and which ones could push Jake too far and send some man flying across the room.

For nearly an hour, various guests posed for pictures with Jake and Randy. Then the reporters insisted on more pictures of just the two of them.

Peter could tell that Jake hated every minute of it. He would probably rather be riding the fence back at the *J&L*, or sitting by a campfire or sleeping out under the stars. Instead, he kept a tight arm around Randy, refusing to leave her side.

"Peter, you're so lost in watching Randy that you hardly know where you are."

Peter turned to see Jeff had joined him. Peter chuckled. "It shows?"

"It does, and you'd better start mingling more before Jake realizes you're salivating over his wife."

Peter gave him a shove. "Did you get enough pictures?"

"I did. This is a nice event. Jake and Randy are handling it well, don't you think?"

"Yes, but don't tell me you aren't as nervous as I am.

The longer this goes on, the more dangerous things become."

"Jake will be pure gentleman for your sake, Peter. He knows you mean well by holding this event, and that to you it's a sign of respect. And Randy is having fun. He'll stay as long as Randy wants, and he won't do anything that would spoil this for her."

A waiter walked by carrying a tray of glasses of champagne. Peter and Jeff each took one just as more dancing started. Randy hung her shawl over a chair and joined Jake in a waltz, dancing close enough to create gossip.

Peter smiled. "They are doing that on purpose, aren't they?"

"Sure, they are," Jeff answered. "You know Jake's sense of humor."

It wasn't long before Randy and Jake separated to dance with others who insisted on getting a turn.

Peter waited until a councilman whirled Randy in his direction, then stepped in. "I believe I deserve a dance," he told Randy.

The councilman thanked Randy for the dance and turned her over to Peter. Randy smiled as she and Peter turned to the lovely violin music. "Are you happy?" Peter asked.

"Deliriously happy! Everyone has been so kind, even the ones who asked rude questions. I know most of those questions were out of excitement over meeting someone like Jake – and out of a bit of ignorance for life on a cattle ranch, or their vision of what an outlaw is like. Poor Jake. People still see him that way, and he hasn't lived like that for years."

"Some might say the way he handled that marshal's job wasn't much different."

"I guess you're right." Randy glanced at Jake, who was

talking with the mayor and smoking a thin cigar. She caught his occasional glances. "This whole trip has been so nice, Peter. Jake and I have seen so many sights, and he loves the lake. That's the one thing I think he'll miss most when we leave, but he misses the J&L more, and we both miss the family."

*The conversation always turns to Jake, doesn't it?* Peter thought. "I'm glad you two have had a good time," he said, and meant it. "Let's just hope things will stay this good for you from now on after you go home."

Randy sighed deeply. "That would be wonderful. All we need now is to get back home without another train robbery."

Peter laughed and whirled her around more, as aware as Randy that Jake was watching their every move. "He never takes his eyes off of you, does he?"

"Not usually, especially away from home and around other people." Randy glanced Jake's way again. "Hmmm. I see Rebecca is approaching my husband for a dance. Heaven knows she would love to get his eyes on *her*. This should be interesting."

Peter chuckled. "I already warned Rebecca that you have long claws."

Randy scoffed. "I haven't had to use them much, but remember that hussy of a waitress at that coffee shop back in Guthrie?"

"The one who made more money doing something else?"

"Peter Brown!"

They both laughed.

"Yes, *that* one," Randy told him. "Anyway, she served Jake some coffee once when were there together, and she bent over much too close to him. The bodice of her dress was – well, you know. Revealing, shall we say?"

Peter grinned. "And the claws came out?"

Randy grinned slyly. "She practically shoved her breasts into Jake's face. I told her that maybe she should put the coffee server in her cleavage. That would give her an excuse to lean over far enough to advertise her wares while she pours the coffee. Jake just about spit his coffee out laughing, and that girl stormed off in a huff."

Peter laughed harder. "That's what I love about you, Randy Harkner. You can be so subtly possessive. Sometimes dangerous things can come in small packages, and you're the small package."

Randy laughed as Jake put out the cigar he'd been smoking and began dancing with Rebecca. "That woman has met her match," Randy told Peter. They continued into another dance as Jake whirled Rebecca to the same waltz. Rebecca deliberately pressed herself against Jake.

"You're being a little brash for a married woman, aren't you?" Jake asked.

"I've been waiting for this since I first laid eyes on you, Jake Harkner." She leaned her head back and looked up at him. "And being close to you is just as moving as I thought it would be."

Jake stepped back, putting some space between them. "I only dance that way with my wife."

"Oh, come now. Men like you aren't true to their wives."

"This one is."

"Really? Well, I have a proposition for you, and I dare you to turn it down."

Jake grinned. "Fire away. It's a free country."

Rebecca laughed in a flirtatious, almost musical way. "My husband sleeps like a bear in winter, and he's not much of a partner anymore, if you know what I mean." She batted her eyes. "I can leave our bed any time, and Peter has more than one spare bedroom. I can find out where yours is and get a room right next to it – maybe one with a door between rooms so you could walk right in without going out into the hallway. That makes it less likely anyone would see. How hard does your wife sleep?"

"Pretty hard, as long as my arms are around her. But if I let go, she's awake within a few minutes, wondering where I am."

Rebecca leaned up and talked more softly into his ear. "A man and woman can get a lot done in a few minutes."

Jake grinned wryly. "I prefer to take a lot longer than a few minutes."

Rebecca closed her eyes and sighed. "Oh, dear Lord. Do you have to make this even harder on me?"

"You started this."

Rebecca shook her head in wonder. "A man like you. Wild and lawless. A man who counts whores among some of his friends. Don't tell me you've never cheated on your wife, Jake Harkner, especially after being with the same woman for over thirty years."

"No, Ma'am, I haven't. You would have to know me a lot better to know the reasons."

"What about *her*? Peter loves her, you know, and he is not above cheating on Treena."

"I can't judge Peter's situation. He's his own man, and I'm sure he and Treena have an understanding."

"Because of Randy."

"I know that, too. But I also know Peter respects a true lady, and my wife is a true lady. Peter highly respects her. If I didn't believe that, I wouldn't consider him a friend, and I wouldn't be staying here at his home."

"There is a fine line between respect and fear," Rebecca joked. "I doubt *any* man would boldly go after the wife of Jake Harkner. But I, handsome man, have no qualms about going after Jake Harkner *himself*. I want you, and I usually get what I want. I *am* filthy rich, I might remind you. I can pay you any amount you ask."

Jake grinned. "You know, Rebecca, you've spent a lot of time with my wife, helping her, showing her around, being a friend to her in Treena's place. I appreciate that, but here you are, trying to get me to cheat on my wife. And, by the way, I'm not a poor man by any means. It's not the grand wealth you or Peter have, but it's decent, and I'm rich in a lot more ways than money, so why don't we just dance and enjoy each other's company in other ways?"

Rebecca scowled. "What about the whores you call friends?"

Jake whirled her toward a third-floor terrace and stopped dancing. "Friends is the word, and that is something else you wouldn't understand. Honey, there are whores who are ladies, and ladies who are secretly whores. I'm not real sure yet which one *you* are."

Rebecca drew a deep breath. "By God you *are* a sonofabitch! Peter told me I'd never get you into my bed."

Jake grinned "Peter knows me all too well, and how I feel about Randy."

"He loves her, too, you know."

"I damn well do know."

Rebecca looked him over. "He could be with Randy tonight, and I could be with you."

Jake lit a cigarette. "Maybe in your world. Not in mine, and not in Randy's. And when it comes to her, not in Peter's world either. He respects her too much."

"Are you saying you don't think I deserve some respect?"

Jake smiled sadly. "Rebecca, I am the last person on earth who has a right to judge somebody else. I'm just telling you like it is . . . for me and my wife. It's that simple. We love each other in a way you could never understand because you haven't gone through some of things we have." Jake looked past her. "Here comes your husband. You'd better dance with the poor man. You married him for his money, I'm sure, so he deserves a dance."

Rebecca's husband walked closer, smiling. His face was flushed from too much drink. "Jake, is my wife flirting with you?"

Jake shook the man's hand. "You might say that, but it's all in fun. And it's been an honor to meet you. In fact, I've enjoyed meeting everyone here. Peter's friends have been –" He glanced at Rebecca. "Very generous. And your wife has been a big help and a good friend to *my* wife."

"Oh, of course! Rebecca is quite the social butterfly." Raines took Rebecca's arm and led her onto the dance floor. Rebecca looked back at Jake as though she was almost ready to cry.

Jake walked back into the main room and talked with a few more businessmen while he waited for Randy to finish her dance with Peter. Both approached Jake, and Peter bowed slightly. "You may have your wife back," he told Jake.

"Thank you for not running off with her," Jake answered, moving an arm around Randy's shoulders.

"And I think Randy should thank *you* for not running off with Rebecca," Peter joked.

Jake snickered. "I suspect you know all about that woman," he told Peter.

"Oh, yes, I know her well," Peter answered. "But she is a devoted friend to Treena, so I try to overlook her faults."

The mayor walked up to them and interrupted their conversation, which led to more questions for Jake. To Peter's relief, there were no incidents as the night wore on. Caviar and all kinds of hors d'oeuvres and drinks were served until people gradually left, most of them drunk and clamoring for one more handshake with Jake. One man hugged Randy a little too forcefully, and Jake pulled him off and asked one of Peter's security men escort him out – "Before I do," he added. "And I might not use the stairs. There is always the terrace."

The man needed no escort. He hurried off on his own.

"Peter, this was wonderful!" Randy told him when nearly everyone but Jeff and his wife had left. She took his hand. "Thank you so much. You've been such a marvelous host. We'll never forget this trip, and I hope Evie and Brian and Katie and Lloyd can make the same trip some time."

Peter squeezed her hand. "They are all welcome any time."

Jake gently pulled Randy to his side again. "Peter, you went over and above. I had to hold my temper at a few of those questions, but after all your work planning this, I didn't want to spoil the evening."

"I heard some of those questions, and I wouldn't have blamed you if you landed a fist into some of those reporters. I appreciate your patience."

"Well, this trip was for Randy. I didn't want to spoil things for her, either." Jake turned to Jeff and his wife, grabbing Jeff's hand. "Jeff, my very loyal and very brilliant reporter friend, it's always good seeing you. Next time you come to the *J&L*, bring the whole family. Your kids are getting big enough for Ben and my grandsons to teach them to ride."

"I can't wait to bring them out, Jake. But the wife here worries that your daughter will try to convert us to Christianity."

Jake laughed. "I'll make her promise not to, but I know she'd love to talk to you both about Judaism. She knows the Old Testament like the back of her hand. Of course, she's still working on me and religion, but we all know that's a lost cause."

"Knowing Evie, I wouldn't bet on that," Jeff told him.

"Your family sounds so lovely," Jeff's wife, Elly, told

Jake. "I can't wait to meet them, especially Evie. I'm sure we'll have a good conversation about religion. From what Jeff has told me about her, it sounds like you two raised a wonderful daughter."

"Thank you, Elly," Randy replied. "We like to think so." She turned to Peter. "It's been a wonderful evening, but I'm so tired, I'm about to fall over."

Jake gave her a squeeze. "Let's get going then." He shook Peter's hand once more.

"Jake, I've never seen you more relaxed," Peter told him. "That makes it all worth it. Even the mayor commented about what a true gentleman you are."

"Yeah, well, this is as good as it gets. Tomorrow I'll be my old mean and ornery self again."

All three men laughed.

"Oh, that reminds me," Jeff said. "I made a bet with Peter that you had one of your .44's with you, Jake. He said you wouldn't bring one to such a fancy occasion."

"Then you know me best, Jeff." Jake patted his left side in the area of his ribs. "I never go anywhere without it."

Peter shook his head. "I should have known."

"You owe me twenty-five dollars, Peter," Jeff joked. "That will hardly break your bank account." Jeff turned to Jake. "Maybe you won't need those guns anymore, Jake."

"I make no predictions," Jake answered. "It depends on the situation with all the free range arguments going on when we get home. Meantime, I'm getting Randy down to our room before she falls asleep on her feet."

Everyone said their "good-nights," and Jake and Randy took their leave.

"We have to get back home ourselves and relieve the woman who is watching the kids," Jeff told Peter.

"I can't wait to visit the J&L," Elly added.

"It's beautiful," Peter told her. "You will love it." He watched them leave, wondering how many years it had been now since he and Jeff met Jake back in Guthrie. What memories. Randy went through so much hell back then, always waiting to find out if her husband and son were dead or alive.

He turned and noticed Randy's shawl draped over a chair at a nearby table. He walked over and picked it up, holding it to his face and smelling her perfume.

# CHAPTER 35

"Jake, you're going to have to help me out of this dress." Randy sat at her dressing table and removed her shoes, then began pulling combs from her hair.

"That's a request I've never turned down," Jake answered.

Randy smiled. "All these fancy, cloth-covered buttons are harder to undo than regular ones, let alone being in back. This dress was made for rich women with maids to help them dress." She laid a glittering comb on the dresser. "All these combs belong to Treena. I certainly don't have need back home for combs with diamonds and rubies in them."

Jake pulled off his shoes and removed his jacket, tie, vest, and side holster, setting everything aside. Randy stood up and turned when he walked over to unbutton the back of her dress while she removed more combs.

"I had an offer tonight from a woman who wanted me to remove *her* dress," Jake said.

"Should I be surprised? You were certainly the center of attention, and don't think I didn't notice Rebecca and how close she tried to dance with you. I'm sure she's the one who made the offer, and she hinted to me more than once – kind of feeling me out to see just how close we really are if you've ever cheated on me."

Jake chuckled. "I've been around saloon girls who were easier to fend off than she was. Something tells me Peter has his own problems with that one whenever Treena is away."

"Oh, Jake!"

"He's just a man, Randy, not a saint. Treena's gone a lot, and Rebecca is no doting, devoted wife, that's sure."

"No more such talk. Let's be sure Jeff gives us some of the pictures from tonight so we can show the family we actually looked like royalty. And by the way, I got a lot of compliments on my diamond necklace. Rich people know quality, and I could tell they were impressed."

Because of the low cut of the bodice, the buttons of Randy's dress started half-way down her back. In seconds Jake reached her waist and moved his hands under the material, pulling her back against him and reaching around to fondle her breasts under the dress.

"I wanted to do this when you modeled this dress for me."

"Don't get any ideas for the moment. I ache everywhere." Randy leaned her head back against his chest. "But that does feel good. I just need you to massage my feet and legs and back, too, not my breasts."

"This is a lot more fun." He ran his hands under the glittering crystal straps of the dress and carefully pulled them down over her shoulders. "Step out of this thing, and I'll massage those other places you mentioned."

Randy let the dress fall and stepped out of it. She wore only ruffled panties under it.

"Sit down so I can take off your stockings," Jake told her.

Randy sat as Jake picked up the dress and hung it on a

clothes rack beside the dressing table. He knelt in front of her to remove her stockings.

"One woman asked what kind of girdle I was wearing in order to fit into that dress," Randy told him. "When I told her it had its own front support and I wasn't wearing anything under it, I thought she'd faint. She looked at me like I was a saloon woman."

Jake snickered as he pulled off her stockings and ran his hands over her feet, her calves, her thighs, along the edge of her panties. "Hell, no saloon woman I ever knew looked anything like you." He leaned forward and kissed her nipples, moving his thumbs inside her panties as he kissed his way up her neck to her lips.

Randy grasped his face and returned his kisses hungrily. "What happened to that massage?" she asked between kisses.

Jake picked her up in his arms and carried her to the bed, laying her on it. "Just let me get the rest of my clothes off."

Wearing only her bloomers, Randy snuggled under silk sheets and a puffy quilt and watched him undress, drinking in the sight of his solid physique as he stripped. He climbed into bed naked, and Randy turned her back to him.

"Rub my back, will you?"

Jake kissed the back of her neck and gently massaged her lower back. Randy closed her eyes. "Oh, that feels good." She breathed deeply. "Oh, my gosh, what about your leg? I should be putting some liniment on it instead you rubbing my back."

"I'll live." He moved his hands to her shoulders and neck. "What do you think about Jeff's wife?"

"Elly reminds me of a quiet little bunny rabbit." Randy smiled. "She's younger than Evie and so quiet, and she is pretty in such a simple way – no frills of any kind. And I think she's a little bit afraid of you."

"Well, look at Jeff and look at me. He's the only man she's close to, and she's always lived in the city. Then I walk into the picture and she probably wonders how on earth Jeff and a man like me ended up good friends. Coming out to the J&L will be quite an experience for her. Did I ever tell you about taking Jeff to Dixie's place that first time he rode with me and Lloyd?"

"Oh, Lord. I don't think I want to hear it."

Jake chuckled. "I told Jeff he'd better learn something about women before he took a wife."

"And I'm sure he learned plenty."

"He did. I think her name was Rose. Jeff had a little trouble getting out of bed to ride with us the next morning."

"Oh, Jake, you shouldn't have done that."

"Jeff wasn't complaining. Of course, that was before he even met Elly."

"How about *you*? Did *you* have any trouble getting out of bed?"

"Hell, no. You know me better than that. I slept with Lloyd. He tossed and turned so much I spent half the night sleeping in a chair." Jake snickered. "Lloyd and I had a good time teasing the hell out of Jeff though. For a few days Jeff lived a life he'd never lived before and never will again. We actually had some wild times with him . . . until that thing happened with Evie. Things got damn serious then."

Randy could feel the change in his demeanor. "Don't go there, Jake. Think about what a wonderful time we've had on this trip, and think about how nice it will be to see the family again. How much longer do you think we should stay?"

Jake kept rubbing her shoulders and back. "I don't

know. Two or three more days at the most. I'm anxious to get back to the J&L and those little granddaughters of mine. They are probably driving Evie and Katie crazy with constant questions about when grandpa is coming home."

Randy was so tired she barely heard his last words. Exhaustion from the long night and the soothing massage caused her to drift off.

"Jake, I'm sorry," she said sleepily. "I just can't stay awake."

He pulled her close, his arms around her in her favorite sleeping position . . . safe in those strong arms.

She fell asleep, but somewhere deeper into the night, or maybe the dark just before dawn, she became aware of the smell of peppermint. Morning peppermint was Jake's way of keeping their kisses sweet when he didn't want to get up and wash first. He was meticulous about scrubbing his teeth with baking soda, sometimes two or three times a day, just because she loved his smile. She turned sleepily and sucked one end of a short peppermint stick while Jake sucked the other end . . . until their lips met in a deep kiss. She loved his touch when she was in this relaxed state.

She realized she was naked. She must have slept so hard she didn't even know Jake had removed her bloomers. They made intimate love without even talking.

The room was dimly lit with a lamp Jake had left on . . . just for this . . . just so he could see and touch and taste every naked inch of her. She grasped his hair and whispered his name, offering herself in heated ecstasy as his lips caressed secret places until a throbbing climax enveloped her. She loved early morning sex, when they were both warm and relaxed.

Jake trailed his lips to her breasts and gently gasped the calf of her leg, urging her to put it over his shoulder as he buried himself deep inside the woman he loved. He met her mouth again, and she could taste her own juices on his lips. He kept hold of her leg as he moved in a gentle rhythm. She was lost beneath his broad chest, and she kissed the solid muscle there, kissed his powerful arms. Something about how he was so incredibly gentle with her stirred her desire to let him use her body however he pleased.

He climaxed inside of her, then lifted her hips and surged into her all over again, his shaft already hard and hot.

"I love being inside you," he groaned. "It comforts me."

He rocked her gently, supporting her hips with his own strength so that all she had to do was lie there and enjoy his thrusts. His breath left him as he released his life into her again, then settled on top of her, resting on his elbows.

"I couldn't stop thinking how beautiful you were in that dress last night."

"Thank you." Randy traced a finger over his dark brows. "I was just as anxious to get to our room as you were. You looked so incredibly handsome last night, Jake. I'm not surprised Rebecca made that offer."

Jake grinned. "You are the only woman I have wanted since I saw you in that supply store."

"Tell me you're happy, Jake."

"Of course I am." Jake rolled off of her and glanced at the bedroom window. "I think I see a little bit of pink sky. Let's just lie here and sleep in. We have three more days to do nothing but make love and eat and walk on the beach. And make love. Did I say that?"

Randy leaned over and kissed his cheek. "You can be such a devil. And you didn't have to tell me about Rebecca, you know."

"Oh, yes I did. You saw me talking with her, and you knew damn well what was going on. You would have been upset if I *didn't* mention it."

Randy kissed his chest. "Oh, I would have just let it go."

"Like hell. I might be good with guns, but you're damn formidable with words when some woman throws herself at me. And I have to say, she's more forward than most of the women I've ever known."

Both laughed, and Jake rolled on top of her again, kissing her throat.

"Part of what I love about you is that you *did* say something," Randy said softly.

"Yeah? Well, I remember when I used to come back from chasing outlaws back in Oklahoma that you always knew if I had stopped at Dixie's place to eat and sleep."

"I know the smell of cheap perfume."

Jake chuckled.

"I actually miss Dixie sometimes," Randy told him. "She was a nice woman, and good to both of us. I'm glad she was able to come to that big picnic celebration we had when you returned from Mexico." Randy ran a hand over his muscled arm. "My God, Jake, I will never forget that awful time, or hearing your whistle when you came back from the dead." She turned and threw her arms around his neck. "Don't ever go that far away again."

"I have no plans to do any such thing."

They kissed again, and Jake moved between her legs. "I want to be inside you again."

Randy opened herself to him. "We can do this all morning if you want," she said softly. They both froze in place then when someone knocked softly on their door.

"Jake, it's Peter!"

Jake looked at Randy and moved off of her. "Jesus, Peter, what the hell do you want this time of morning?" he yelled.

"I'm sorry, Jake, but you both need to come downstairs."

"Hold on." Jake rose and hurried to the washroom, quickly washing himself with a damp rag. He pulled on the bottom half of a clean pair of long johns, then ran wet fingers through his hair and toweled off. Randy pulled the covers over herself as he hurried to open the door just enough to see Peter standing in the hallway in pajamas and a robe.

"What's going on?" Jake asked.

"Just throw on a pair of pants or something and have Randy put on a robe. Come downstairs as soon as you can. Jeff's waiting in the kitchen."

"*Jeff?*" Jake felt alarm building. "What the hell is wrong, Peter?"

Peter sighed and turned away. "Please don't ask me anything more until you two come downstairs. Just hurry."

Jake closed the door and turned to see Randy sitting up and watching him. "My God, Jake, something has happened! Peter sounded really worried."

"From the look on his face, Jeff has something to tell us that we don't want to hear." Jake moved quickly to his suitcase, yanked out a clean pair of denim pants and began pulling them on. "Go wash up the best you can in a hurry. Put on a flannel gown and your housecoat. Jeff and Peter are waiting for us down in the kitchen." His heart pounded with dread.

"Please don't go down there without me, Jake."

"I won't." Jake pulled on a shirt, leaving it unbuttoned. He grabbed a cigarette from the nightstand and shoved a couple more into the pocket of his shirt along with a couple of matches. He lit the cigarette and walked to window to look down at a taxi carriage that had brought Jeff to the house. Coming here at this hour could only mean bad news.

Randy came out of the washroom wearing her night

gown and a robe. She hurried over to the dressing table to brush out her tangled hair, then pulled it back at the sides with combs.

Jake glanced at the diamond necklace that still graced her neck.

He set the cigarette in an ashtray. "Come here," he told her.

Randy hurried over and threw her arms around his waist. Jake held her close. He kissed her hair.

"Look up here, baby."

Randy met his gaze.

"Leave that necklace on, and you remember how much I love you, no matter what has happened." He leaned down and kissed her, a deep, desperate kiss that seemed to say that what they had just shared could soon be lost.

"Jake, whatever this is, please stay strong."

He hugged her close, and they clung to each other a moment before Jake picked up the cigarette and they headed downstairs and into the kitchen. Peter and Jeff sat at the table with coffee.

"Good God," Jake muttered when he saw the look on Jeff's face. He started to let go of Randy's hand, but she wouldn't let him.

Jake took the cigarette from his lips and tossed it into the kitchen sink. "Let's have it, Jeff."

Jeff closed his eyes and ran a hand through his hair. Randy looked at Peter, who shook his head.

"There's been a shooting—more of an ambush," Jeff told Jake. "No one even knows for sure who it was. The telegram didn't give details – just that the boys were headed north to help some new neighbor build a barn." He paused, looking like he might be sick. "Someone shot at them."

Randy sucked in her breath, and Jake tightened his hold on her hand.

"How bad?" he asked.

"Nobody's dead, Jake. Cole got sliced across the top of the head. He's okay. Little Jake took a bullet in his thigh. Stephen is okay. The worst was . . . Ben."

Jake closed his eyes. "What happened to Ben?"

"It was a big caliber cartridge - shattered his left elbow. He's already lost the lower half of his arm."

Jake let go of Randy's hand and turned away. "Jesus Christ Almighty," he said in a low groan.

"Jake—" Randy touched his arm.

"Don't," he told her. "You don't want to feel what's going through me right now!" He stood there, his back to her. "What else?" he asked Peter. "What about Lloyd? Evie? The rest of the family."

"All fine, as far as I know." Jeff walked around the other side of the table, as though to shield himself from whatever kind of explosion might arise from Jake. He still remembered the powerfully enraged Jake he'd known when Evie was abducted. "I'm so damn sorry, Jake."

Jake turned, and there it was . . . the darkness. It was as though thunder rumbled right inside the house.

"Jake, stay calm," Randy warned.

He met her gaze, a look in his eyes that reminded her of the dark horizon and distant rumble of stampeding cattle. He closed his eyes. "I'm sorry. I didn't mean to bite at you about not touching me." He looked at Jeff. "What else?" he asked.

Jeff swallowed again. "That's it, other than saying you need to get home as fast as you can. Brian is trying to save what is left of Ben's arm but isn't sure he can. The telegram said Ben won't let him do anything more until you get there. I already booked tickets for the next train west, which leaves at ten this morning, so there isn't much time. Pack just what you need. Peter's staff will pack and send the rest on another train. J&L men will be waiting for you in Denver. I already wired back to get the information to them of when you will get there."

Peter folded his arms and also stood a few feet away. "Jeff and I are going with you, Jake. Lord knows what kind of help you will need. I already contacted Doctor Beemer. He has agreed to also come with us. Brian might need his help, not just with Ben and young Jake, but God only knows how many J&L men—or you or Lloyd, for that matter—will end up hurt before this is over." He literally shivered at the look in Jake's eyes. "I feel your thunder clear over here, Jake. Don't forget what we talked about a few days ago. Remember the law, and remember you have a lot of men and most likely other ranchers who will help you find and punish whoever did this. And that marshal out there will probably also help. This might even be settled by the time you get there."

Jake gently pushed Randy away.

"Settled?" He turned away and walked toward the French doors that led outside, then faced Peter again. "*Settled?* What kind of men shoot *boys*?" he roared. "*Boys!*" His voice broke. "Jesus Christ, whoever did this wants *me!* And probably *Lloyd!* I have no doubt in my mind who is behind this! Do you really think dancing over there and arresting them and putting them in jail is the *answer*, Peter? I have a hell of a lot *better* answer!"

"If you go charging over to wherever this happened, Jake, you'll be *killed*, because that's probably exactly what they *want!* Let your men and the other ranchers *help* you! " Peter told him. "This isn't the old days, and you aren't even sure who is responsible."

"But apparently the old days are still with us! You can bet it was Brady Fillmore and that bearded fucking bastard he hangs around with who started this! And they've *hired* someone—maybe several men—to help them. If they think they can bring down Jake Harkner by harming *boys*, they will be the sorriest men who ever *walked*!"

Jake headed for the French doors that led out to the patio and the beach.

"Jake, wait!" Randy called to him.

He paused.

"Come back upstairs for now. We have to pack. And I *need* you! Don't leave me behind this time! We're talking about *my* grandson, too, Jake. And *my* son! I love Ben like our own. Right now, you have to stay level-headed, and we have to get ourselves to Colorado! Wait until we get home and talk to Lloyd and the others before you start planning your own personal revenge! You know Peter is right! This is *not* the old days!"

Jake stood there a moment, rubbing at his eyes and visibly trembling. He took a deep breath and faced Randy. "You know damn well it's me they want, no matter how we handle this. And it's *me* they will get – something they will regret to their dying day, which might come a lot sooner than they think!" He walked past her and headed upstairs.

Randy looked helplessly at Peter.

"You won't get home right away, Randy," Peter reminded her. "Three or four days will give Jake time to calm down and think." He shook his head. "I'm so sorry to bring you such bad news."

Randy blinked back tears. "Thank you for thinking about bringing Doctor Beemer." She moved her gaze to Jeff. "And thank you for making arrangements for a train leaving yet this morning." She turned away. "I'd better go help Jake pack."

"Will you be okay up there?" Peter asked.

"Of course. Times like this are when we need each other most."

Randy went upstairs, and Jeff turned to Peter. "This is

going to be bad, Peter. *Real* bad. You weren't with Jake when he went after his daughter back at Dune Hollow. Yes, he had help then, too, but it was all Jake. All Jake. He just about killed himself going after her. He didn't eat or sleep. I know exactly what he is thinking right now. He's just forcing himself to stay calm for Randy's sake. It's not going to last."

Peter shook his head. "I'd better get dressed and packed, too."

"My things are already packed. I told my wife I would go straight to the train station from here. She understands."

Peter heard Randy break down into sobs at the top of the stairs. "Damn it!" he muttered. "The other day Jake told me he'd likely die by going down in a blaze of glory. You know what he meant by that. Randy isn't crying just for those boys. She knows this could be her husband's last days."

Jeff actually felt like crying. "Maybe. But, Peter, if you think Jake can't hold his own in whatever is coming, you don't know Jake Harkner. Back in Guthrie you only saw the aftermath of what he can do, when he would ride back into town with the scum of the earth in tow. You've not seen him in action when he's after men like that. I *have*! I've seen it in Lloyd, too, and it's not something you soon forget. Whoever planned this made a real, real bad choice."

# PART III

*He unleashed against them his hot anger, his wrath, indignation, and hostility . . . a band of destroying angels ...*

*Psalm 78:49*

# CHAPTER 36

*August 20 . . .*

The train whistle wailed into the night. Jake sat in the Pullman with both .44's and his spare .45 lying on a coffee table in front of the richly-upholstered chair in which he'd slept off and on. He had no idea what time it was, and he didn't care, as long as the train did not stop too often. Getting home as fast as possible was all that mattered. It hardly seemed possible it was only early this morning that they received the news. Now they were well on their way to Denver.

Someone knocked on the door at the front of the car. He knew it had to be Jeff and Peter, who were in a sleeper car just ahead of the Pullman. Doctor Beemer also shared the sleeper car.

Jake kept a cigarette between his lips and walked to the front of the car, opening the door for them. "It's late."

"We couldn't sleep, and it's obvious you can't either," Peter told him.

He and Jeff wore pajamas and robes. Jake wore a pair of denim pants but was barefoot and shirtless.

"Come on in," Jake said quietly. "Just don't talk too

loudly. Randy's sleeping on the other side of this wall. I gave her a little of that sedative Beemer offered. He led them past the bedroom area and out into the bigger visiting area, where all three men sat down in plush chairI want her to sleep as long as possible."

"You need *your* sleep, too, Jake," Jeff reminded him. "I remember another time you reacted this way, and you just about killed yourself. That was almost eight years ago, and you aren't getting any younger."

"I *can't* sleep, and my age doesn't mean shit when I'm this angry. Too much on my mind, and too much planning to do. I'm not about to take a sedative that might dull my senses either." In one of the rare times Jake allowed anyone to see his back, he turned and led them past the bedroom area and out into the bigger visiting area. The hard-toned, handsome man Jake was otherwise belied the scars that told of a very harsh life as a boy. Peter supposed he was so preoccupied with what lay ahead that he wasn't even thinking about being shirtless.

All three men sat down in plush chairs. Jake picked up one of the .44's.

"Not sleeping can also dull your senses," Peter reminded Jake.

"Not for me. I've been through this before."

Everyone quieted for a moment.

"I saw the light on through the little windows at the front of your car and figured you might still be up," Jeff said. "I might as well write about this. I've written about everything else, with full respect for your feelings and preferences, like always."

Jake leaned back in the chair and rubbed at his eyes. "I expected as much. If you were some fly-by-night reporter, I'd throw you back out that door." Jake leaned back in the chair and rubbed at his eyes. "And I ought to throw you out anyway for reminding me I'm getting old."

Jeff grinned nervously. "You know I meant that only out of concern. This kind of stress can be bad for the health. You know that from other times like this."

"Yeah, hell, I know you meant well." Jake opened the cylinder on one of his .44's and dumped out bullets before loosening a screw on the cylinder. "The site on this gun is off by a hair," he said rather absently.

Jeff took a pencil from a pocket on his robe. He started writing on a tablet he'd brought with him.

*When Jake Harkner reverts to his outlaw mood, he is most intimidating, even to his best friends,* he wrote. *Right now, the Pullman car he is taking to Colorado feels like a big, dark thundercloud, full of lightning and rumbling.*

Peter remained quiet and just listened. He dearly wanted to ask about Randy, but the mood Jake was in, he worried the man might take his concern the wrong way.

"How do you know the site is off?" Jeff asked.

"I can't explain it. You shoot these things enough over the years, you just know." Jake kept the cigarette between his lips and raised the gun, aiming it at the flickering flame of a candle on a side table across from his chair. "There's a groove across the top of the barrel that's supposed to line up with the site at the end. This one doesn't, but only by about a hair's width." He lowered the gun and looked it over thoughtfully. "You fire a gun point blank like I have this one, and the kick-back from the bullet going right into something can mess up a gun. All that powder and explosive force so close to the barrel. This one has never been all that bad, but I need to know which way it's off." He glanced at Peter. "It's the gun I used in Denver."

*Point blank to a man's head,* Peter thought.

Everything remained quiet for several more seconds.

"Jake, I've never asked you this. Don't take offense," Jeff said.

Jake met his gaze. "What would I do? Throw one of my best friends off the train?"

All three men snickered nervously.

Jeff shrugged. "I just wondered – in your worst days before you met Randy – did you – uh – did you ever kill a man for money?"

The train whistle blew again, and for a few minutes they sat listening to the clickety-clack of the train's wheels as they crossed each rail connection. Jake rubbed a thumb over the gun. "Never. You know me better, Jeff, but considering my past, it's a legitimate question. I'm the type who would most likely go *after* any man who would kill for money. Hell, I was *chased* by men who would kill for money. I killed a man like that right in front of Randy in that supply store when we first met. She didn't know which one of us was the good and which one was bad, so she shot me." He smiled sadly. "Fact is, he was a bounty hunter, the dirty, underhanded kind, so we were *both* bad." He shook his head. "And there Randy stood, all wide-eyed and confused and terrified. I hate for a woman to look at me like that . . . like my mother used to look at my father." He quickly ran his forearm over his eyes, then picked up the cartridge cylinder and carefully screwed it back onto the gun. He snapped it into place and aimed the gun again, pulled back the hammer, checked the firing pin, pulled the trigger.

*Click.*

He pulled back the hammer again.

*Click.*

"The last thing you want in a gunfight is for your gun to misfire or seize up on you. I can't afford for either one to happen."

"Don't forget you have a wife and family who all need you," Peter reminded him. "We talked about that – about doing this the lawful way."

Jake pulled back the hammer again.

*Click.*

"Jeff, did I ever tell you I've thought of making a living as a gunsmith?" he asked, very obviously changing the subject. "I still might, once this mess is over with."

The air hung quiet yet again as Jeff scribbled more notes. "You're different, Jake."

Jake glanced sidelong at him. "Different?"

"You're different from the man at Peter's ball just a couple of nights ago. You even *look* different."

Jake picked up a can of gun oil and squeezed small amounts onto different moving parts of the gun. "A couple of nights ago, I didn't know some fucker blew my son's arm off and tried to kill my grandsons and Cole." He picked up a rag and began wiping at the gun oil, using it to polish the outside parts once he'd oiled the insides.

More silence. Jake finished his cigarette and lit another one.

*He's chain smoking,* Jeff wrote. *He always chain smokes when he's deeply upset.*

Jake slammed the cylinder closed on the second gun, held it up and aimed at the candle.

*Click.*

"I appreciate you bringing the doctor along, Peter. Brian must have his hands full, and more men could end up getting hurt. I don't know *anything* yet as far as what I'm going to do. By the time this is over, I might need a lawyer *and* a doctor, or the worst could happen, and then Randy would need *you*. I'll try to handle this the right way, but when you are going up against men who would kill kids and who aim to make a name for themselves, you never know what to expect."

He took his gun belt from where it lay on the floor and began pushing out the bullets. They clattered onto the table in front of him. There was an edging around the table that kept them from rolling off. Jake picked up each bullet then and used a pocketknife to cut slits in the tops.

"Why are you doing that?" Jeff asked.

"A bullet does a lot more damage when it's hollowed out a little. If you cut slits in the tops and pry them apart a bit, the bullet stays in a man's body and spreads out, doing more damage and preventing it from going through him into someone else, maybe someone innocent." He sighed, an odd bitterness to the sound. "I wish I'd known that when I shot my father. The bullet went through him and into Santana. She was only twelve, but I loved her. I was fifteen and didn't know what the hell I was doing. All I knew was that bastard was on top of that sweet girl. I was going to wait till she was older. I guess he decided she was old enough and figured he'd take her before I could. He was like that. He'd think something like that was funny. He knew damn well I would be home any minute and I'd find them. He liked to torture me that way, so I ended it for good. He could beat me all he wanted, but he wasn't going to do that to the girl I loved." He set a bullet and the knife down. "Excuse me. I need some air." He picked up his cigarette and walked past them and out the back door to the train platform, closing the door.

"I'm really worried," Peter said quietly to Jeff.

Jeff nodded. "His thoughts are running ninety miles an hour. He almost never talks about his father, but when something like this happens he goes right back to that."

"Yeah." Peter rubbed at the back of his neck. "When you hear him tell it in person, it just makes you kind of sick. You can feel his devastation over that girl, and the deep hatred for his father. I told him not long ago that every time he goes after someone, in his mind it's really his father all over again. If it isn't the thing with that girl, it's because of what his father did to his mother. He is constantly defending or protecting."

"Jake!" Randy called from the other side of the partition.

Peter got up and opened the back door. "Jake, Randy is awake and asking for you."

Jake hurriedly tossed his cigarette and came back inside, rushing around the partition to the bedroom area. "I'm right here," Jeff and Peter heard him telling Randy.

"I woke up and you were gone."

"I couldn't sleep. I'm right on the other side of the partition. Jeff and Peter are here, and we're talking. That's all."

"Jake *please* come to bed. I know it's hard for you to sleep, but you need your rest."

Jake reappeared. "Sorry, but you two had better leave."

"Sure," Jeff said. He finished scribbling something while Jake picked up the bullets he'd hollowed out so far and tucked them back into his gun belt. "I'll have to finish hollowing the rest later." Jake spoke the words absently, as though simply voicing a thought.

"You really should get as much sleep as you can, Jake, like Randy just told you," Peter told him. "I wish to hell I could change what's happened, especially after the great time you two had in Chicago. We're all here for you." He turned to leave with Jeff. "Just don't forget there's a judge in Denver who will be furious if you go using those guns again for your own form of justice. You will make my job that much harder."

"I know I have some decisions to make. It's why I can't sleep, but Randy gets scared when she wakes up and I'm gone, so I'd better see to her."

Jeff and Peter left, and Jake locked the door. He turned and leaned against it for a moment. Before this was over, his guns would be smoking hot, and a lot of men were going to get hurt or die. He'd have to do his best to make sure he wasn't one of them—for Randy's sake. If it was up to him, he would let all this end once and for all. If he was dead, men wouldn't be looking for him anymore.

The train whistle echoed into the night sky again. He headed to the bed. Randy needed holding.

Randy had no idea what time it was. It was getting light, so at least it was morning, and they were that much closer to home. For now, she could lie there a while. That's all she wanted to do. She felt weary and depressed. What a terrible way to end their wonderful trip.

She turned over to see Jake beside her, watching her. She vaguely remembered he'd finally come to bed late in the night. "Did you ever get any sleep?"

"Some." He handed her a piece of peppermint. "I've already been up and washed, and scrubbed my teeth. You were sleeping so hard, I just left you here."

She took the peppermint warily, watching his dark eyes—dark not just in color, but dark with suppressed rage. She'd seen the look too many times—violent revenge, sparked by a wrong against someone he cared about—a look of desperate loneliness at thinking his past had again visited them . . .

"What time is it, Jake?"

"Around seven a.m. We'll be on this train another night – should reach Denver mid-morning tomorrow."

He was shirtless. She studied his powerful torso, the scars from all the wounds. There was an aura of danger about him she hadn't felt in a long time. So many times he'd left, almost always riding to what could be his death. "What did you talk about last night with Jeff and Peter?"

He reached out and tucked some of her hair behind her ear. "It doesn't matter."

He moved on top of her. In times like this he made love

to her in a desperate need to assure himself she was still here, still his . . . and with the realization that this could be their last time. It was how he'd made love to her every time he'd left to go after thieves and killers in No Man's Land.

"Randy – "

"Make love to me," she whispered. "We don't know what lies ahead, or when we will get to do this again. And I'm so scared for you."

"Don't be. Things will all work out."

"But I know you. I know how you think."

"Stop talking." His kisses grew deep and hot.

Randy threw her arms around his neck and opened herself to him, taking him inside almost desperately. She whimpered with a need to remember the moment, the feel of him inside of her, his familiar scent, his gentle touches, the way he literally adored her physically. They mated with a clinging need to find ways to comfort each other against tragedy. They rocked together in sweet rhythm, until Jake's life surged into her depths. He moved his kisses to her neck.

"You didn't climax," he whispered.

"I didn't need to. I just needed to feel you making love to me – feel you close to me – inside me. That's all that matters." Randy studied his eyes. "Don't do anything that means I have to live without you, Jake. I know what this is doing to you."

"I've been through these things enough times to know what I'm doing. You should know that by now."

"Please keep a clear head. Let Lloyd and the other men help you, and remember the law . . . and that judge in Denver."

He gave her a sad but reassuring smile. "I'll remember." He leaned down and kissed the rose-petal diamond she still wore around her neck.

"I'll never take it off, Jake. I can't believe you gave it to me just a few days ago. You looked so grand in that tuxedo, and we were so happy." She fought tears as she ran her fingers over his full lips. "Don't let the darkness overtake you. Stay in the light. Tell me again that you will do this the right way."

"As right as I can. Let's just get ourselves home first and help those boys." He settled beside her. "And we'd better try to sleep."

*Thank God he wants to sleep,* Randy thought. He'd been fighting it ever since they left Chicago. She closed her eyes as Jake moved an arm around her and pulled her close. "Keep your arm around me. You know how much I love it right here, where I'm always safe."

Jake gave her an extra-tight hug and closed his eyes. This was what kept him sane – her need for him and his for her. He studied a small ray of sunlight that beamed through the edge of a window shade.

*Stay in the light, Jake. Stay in the light.* That's what Randy was always telling him.

# CHAPTER 37

*August 21 . . .*

"Where in hell are they?" Buck Potter threw in his hand and lit a cigarette. "This waiting is driving me crazy."

"I'll tell you where they are," Brady Fillmore told him. He guzzled some whiskey straight from the bottle. "They are waiting for big, bad Jake Harkner to get home."

"I thought the law would come here and question us real quick," Lenny McCarthy said. "We were gonna' claim we had no idea what they were talkin' about. They have no proof we had anything to do with that shooting. The Mitchels are buried deep, and we've got the papers they signed saying they sold us this place."

"Yeah, and they signed those papers because you said you'd let them go if they did," Brady reminded him. *You murdering bastard.*

"Simple-minded people like that are too trusting," Lenny answered. "And once the law comes and sees we are on the up and up and they can't prove a damn thing, they'll leave. But Harkner won't give up. He's not a law-abiding man. He'll come back, and when he does, we will have a right to shoot him down. There is a judge in Denver who would love an excuse to put Jake away, so that judge won't be upset if he hears Jake Harkner has been shot for bullying and harassing innocent settlers."

"Well, the way some of you are dressed, you look like the goddamned gunmen you are," Brady told them. "You need to look more like farmers."

They sat around the kitchen table at the Mitchel house. The sound of panting and wild lovemaking came from the bedroom, where Chet Ainsley and Stella Flynn writhed together.

"Shut the fuck up in there," Buck yelled. "You two keep it up, Ainsley, and every damn one of us will come in there and have at your whore!"

Stella just laughed. "Come on in, boys. Variety is the spice of life."

"We'd oblige you," Kyle Pendergrass called back, "but fucking a woman is too distracting when you're waiting for Jake Harkner to come bursting through your door."

"If he comes bursting through that door, send him in here," Stella answered, laughing again. "You won't have to shoot him. I'll just fuck him to death! Hell, he's a damn handsome man, and he likes whores. I wonder if age has affected his ability to please a woman."

Grizzly Smith dealt another round of cards. "Bitch," he mumbled. "We never shoulda' let them two in on this. Ainsley ain't no gunman. They only joined us to settle a grudge with Harkner. Stella told me ole' Jake shot Ainsley's holster right off his hip at a cookout not long ago. He's just here to watch the man get his guts blowed out."

"Well, then, he'll get his wish," Buck answered.

"Doesn't matter," Grizzly grumbled. "The fact remains, we need the law to come here now so we can give them the papers showing we own this place legally, and that we're workin' this land like any other settler."

"And what if they find out about the Mitchels?" Brady asked. "What you and Lenny did makes me sick to my stomach. This isn't what I planned."

Buck threw down his cards and rose. "*I'm* sick, too! Sick and tired of your whinin', Fillmore. You're the one who came to outlaw country to find men who'd help you take down Jake Harkner, and now we're *here!* Me and Lenny even robbed a bank first in Brown's Park, so's we'd have money to buy this place and to pay these extra men who came along to back us up if need be." He grinned. "'Course it turns out we didn't need to buy the place after all. Sometimes you just *take* what you want."

"Yeah, well, this whole thing has gotten too big," Brady complained. "And now too many men know about it, and innocent people have been killed. On top of that, Kyle told us the paper in Denver says it was Jake Harkner's grandson and that adopted son of his that you shot. The son might have lost an arm. It's all the gossip in Denver. Killing a whole family like the Mitchels, and shooting kids wasn't in me and Grizzly's plans." He got up from the table and paced.

"And nobody can prove a damn thing," Buck reminded him. "And I'm thinkin' it might be best to shoot *you* dead, too, 'cuz I'm thinkin' you just might chicken out and talk too much when all this is over, just to save your sorry ass! You wanted Harkner dead, and things is workin' out just like they should. All the neighbors and the law will think is that the Mitchels didn't like the rustlin' and other trouble goin' on, so they sold out and left. Who's to know? If they had family back east, they'll figure everybody is just fine out here. It will take weeks, maybe months, for any of them to realize their kin is missin'."

Brady backed away a little as a grinning Lenny moved

beside Buck. "Let me kill him, Buck," the younger man asked. "I need another notch in my gun. Ole' Brady here is another one nobody would miss if he disappeared."

"Now, wait a minute!" Brady protested.

Buck drew his gun and cocked it, pointing it at Brady. "Here's how it sets, Fillmore. Me and Lenny came here for the reputation of bein' the ones to shoot down Jake Harkner. You wanted us. You *got* us. Grizzly there wants Harkner dead, too, bad enough not to bitch about us killin' the Mitchels and maybe killin' a kid. We're here, now, and we brung extra men with us, just like you wanted, and I'm thinkin' we can find a way to bring down Lloyd Harkner later. *Jake* is the one who will make us famous, but we ain't fool enough to think this is gonna' be easy. The only way to make it easy and be able to lay all the blame on Jake Harkner is if he comes here *alone!* So, you tell us how we can make that happen! No posse has come here yet, so they're likely waitin' for Jake to join them. That's my theory. But we don't want him comin' with twenty or so men to back him up. We wouldn't be able to just shoot him down then. He's got to come *alone!*"

Brady swallowed. "You don't know Jake Harkner. Even alone, he'll think of a way to get the better of us."

"Not if he's so ragin' mad that he gets careless," Buck reminded him. "If we did wound or kill one of his sons or grandsons, that should be all it takes. But he'll still come with a posse. You know the man, and you've read that book about him. You tell me what it will take to make him come for us *by himself!* You said the man is crazy protective of his family. Who's the most important to him?"

Brady felt himself breaking into a sweat. He'd been around Buck and Lenny long enough to know that if he didn't cooperate, he was a dead man. "His wife is pretty much the most important, but you'd play hell ever getting close to her. Jake hardly ever leaves her side, and if it's not him, it's his son or some of the men. They all watch out for her. I think something went wrong once – something happened to her to make Jake extra protective, but nobody talks about it. I'm not sure what it is. Either way, I'm thinking what might upset him even more is . . ."

Buck jerked his gun in a way that made Brady jump.

"Is *what?*" Buck demanded.

Brady glanced at Grizzly.

"I'm out of this, Brady," Grizzly told him. "We want Jake dead, and these men can do the job. Tell him what you think."

Brady sighed and ran a hand through his hair. "That last run-in I had with Jake – he was real, real upset because he had his little granddaughters with him that day – two little girls maybe six or seven years old and real pretty. I think if you threatened those little girls, you might get Jake here alone."

Buck grinned. "Well, now, you finally understand what I'm after."

"I have to tell you once more, Buck, that you don't know what a real, real angry Jake can be like. He's no ordinary man when it comes to something like that. The law means *nothing* to him. He's old-school."

"That's exactly what we're counting on," Lenny spoke up.

"And you're gonna' sit down to that table and write a note," Buck told Brady. He turned to Grizzly. "Look through the drawers here in the house. The Mitchels must have some paper and pencil here someplace. Find somethin' and give it to Brady there.

We're gonna' write a note, and one of us will ride to the Aspen Saloon in Denver and pay some unsuspectin' kid to get the note to Jake when his train gets in from Chicago."

"There's no time, Buck," Kyle told him.

"Sure there is, if one of us leaves real quick-like and

rides hard. I figure Jake won't get in till sometime late tomorrow. A man could make it from here to Denver by then. I'm thinkin' it should be you, Kyle. People have seen you around before, so nobody will suspect anything. And you've got a damn fast horse."

"Why have a *kid* give him a note?" Lenny asked.

"Because I figure Harkner has a soft spot for women and kids, and a kid is more unsuspectin'. Harkner would never figure a kid is up to no good. And kids can run fast. You could pay a street urchin to deliver the note to Jake and then take off runnin' before Harkner could grab him."

"What kind of note are you talking about?" Brady asked.

"One that threatens those little girls – tells Jake to come alone or the men who want him will find a way to get to them and sell them to child sex traders. That ought to set Harkner's fuse real fast."

"And boy, when that man explodes, it's a humdinger," Grizzly chuckled.

"Nobody can get to *any* of his family," Brady warned. "Jake keeps them guarded as if the J&L was a prison. Threatening those little girls might not work."

"His kid and grandson got shot, didn't they?" Buck reminded him. "*Everybody* is vulnerable in one way or another. Ainsley in there told us as how Jake's whole family was at that cattlemen's picnic, some of the little ones playin' apart from the others, with only women watchin' them." He kept his gaze on Brady. "And you said sometimes the whole family goes to Brighton to shop. Little girls have a way of wanderin' off sometimes, especially if you offer them candy. You just write the note. Jake will be worried enough to come for us alone. You tell him if he does that, no harm will ever come to those girls."

"Yeah," Grizzly added. "That newspaper article I read a while back says Harkner went clear down to Mexico and nearly died helpin' some young girl he didn't even know escape a whore house down there. If he'd do that for somebody that wasn't even his, he'd sure as hell come runnin' for those little granddaughters of his."

Brady sat down, shaking his head. "I don't go for things like this – not little girls!"

"Well, I *do*," Buck told him. "Little girls are worth a fortune to some men." He sniffed and wiped his nose on his shirtsleeve. "I'm not sayin' *anything* would really happen. All we have to do is make Harkner *think* it could happen – tell him either he comes alone, or one day he'll find his granddaughters *missin'*. All that matters is that he *believes* it. And don't mention or sign any names. We don't want anybody able to prove who wrote the note."

Brady shook his head. "You've never met Jake," he told Buck. "If you had, you wouldn't be threatening his granddaughters."

"Just start writing!" Buck told him. "Pretty soon you'll find out that Jake Harkner ain't God Himself! He's as vulnerable as any other man, and when this is over, he'll be layin' in a pool of blood!"

The men snickered as Brady reluctantly took pencil to paper, scowling as he wrote what Buck told him to write. When he finished, he tossed the pencil aside and stood up. "I need some air."

"Don't get any ideas about ridin' off on account of you don't want any part of this," Buck warned. "I see you ridin' off, I'll shoot you in the *back!*"

Brady stormed outside and stood on the front stoop looking out at the wide swath of land between the Mitchel property and the J&L.

He sighed deeply, worried he had made a grave mistake planning any of this.

He wasn't worried about Marshal Kraemer or the cattle ranchers or anyone else who might come snooping around. The only man who worried him was Jake Harkner. Those men inside had no idea of the wrath they would unleash once Jake read that note. *It won't be Jake Harkner coming for you, Buck Potter. It will be Satan Himself, and it won't matter how many men are waiting for him! We'll all be slop for hogs by the time he's done.*

# CHAPTER 38

*Mid-day, August 22 . . .*

Jake lifted Randy down from the train platform and pulled her into his arms. "The next few days are going to be a real strain on both of us," he told her.

"Then let's not lose track of each other." Randy held his gaze. "Stay with me, and I'm not talking about physically. You know what I mean, Jake. If you and the men think you need to go after someone, make sure you know the whole story about what happened. Don't go riding off with guns blazing until you know you are after the right men. There might be innocent people involved."

Jake touched her cheek with the back of his hand, ignoring a few stares from others inside Denver's Union Station who knew who he was. "I still think I'm right in thinking Brady Fillmore and that Grizzly Smith are behind this whole thing, but I know I have to be careful. Don't worry about that now." He leaned down and kissed her forehead. "First we have to get home to those boys."

"Jake!"

Cole hurried over to them, his loud call echoing inside

the white stone walls of the grand railroad station. More heads turned.

"That's Jake Harkner," some woman said to her husband.

"Goddamn, it's good to see you." Cole grabbed Jake's hand. "Everybody's gonna' feel better havin' you back. I've got several men with me. They're all waitin' outside."

Jake squeezed his hand warmly. "I hear you got a new part in your hair."

Cole removed his hat to reveal a scabbed crease across the left side of his scalp. "Half an inch lower, and I wouldn't be standin' here talkin' to you. Leastways, I'd be missin' my left eye. And it would have been worth it if it meant Ben wouldn't have got shot. Come on! Let's get going."

Peter, Jeff and Doctor Beemer joined them, and Jake introduced the doctor to Cole. "You take Randy and these three outside," he told Cole. "I see our porter coming with a luggage cart. Doctor Beemer and Peter and Jeff have their own luggage with them, but Randy and I managed to pack a few more things than we thought we'd have time for. You know women. They leave on a trip with one suitcase and come back with ten because of all the shopping. I'll go down to the luggage car with the porter and help him find the right things."

"It's not all *that* much," Randy told Cole. "But we do have a lot more coming. Peter is having the rest of our things sent separately."

"One of the men will have to stay here and rent a wagon to bring it all back when it gets here," Jake added. "It shouldn't be more than another day or so."

"Sure." Cole took Randy's arm. She looked back at Jake as though she was afraid to leave his side. He gave her a nod and a sad smile, then turned to walk with the porter to the baggage car. Before he could climb inside, a young boy ran up beside him.

"Are you Jake Harkner? I heard that man call you Jake."

Jake stopped and looked down at the boy while the porter walked on to the next car with the luggage cart. He quickly scanned the people around them to make sure this wasn't some kind of setup to get him shot, but he saw no one suspicious. He turned his attention back to the boy, guessing him to be perhaps eight or ten years old. He had a scrawny look to him, more like a kid who ran wild in the streets.

"I'm Harkner," he told the boy. "What do you want?"

"I'm s'posed to give you this," the boy told him.

Jake frowned and took the piece of paper the boy handed him. "What's your name? And who is this from?"

"I ain't s'posed to tell you." Without another word, the boy ran off, jumping over the coupling between two cars of a train parked beside Jake's and disappearing into a crowd of people on the other side.

Another huge train engine rumbled and steamed into the train station, making it impossible for Jake to tell which way the boy went. He looked down at the folded note, feeling an ominous dread of what was in it. He frowned as he opened it.

*You alone. Nobody else. One of us knows how to get to your granddaughters. If you come with a posse, we will see them coming and disappear, and we will find a way to get to those little girls, just like we got to your son and grandson, and like men once got to your daughter. You will never see those girls again. They are worth a lot of money to the right people. You know what we mean. Don't show this to Hal Kraemer or your son or anybody else. Just you, Harkner. Come to the Mitchel place north of the J&L, and come alone, or risk your granddaughter's lives.*

Jake's blood ran cold. He wadded up the note and shoved it into his pants pocket. He looked around again, again hoping to see someone suspicious watching, but people milled about in a normal fashion. Suddenly, everything went black, so black that he had to grab onto a rail at the side of the car beside him, feeling like he might pass out. "Randy," he said gruffly. He'd promised her to do this the right way, but the thought of little Sadie Mae and Tricia in the hands of men so vile as to threaten little girls made him want to vomit.

"Sir? Are you going to help me pick out your luggage?" someone asked.

Jake blinked and faced the porter.

"Sir? Are you okay? You don't look good. Should I go and get your wife?"

"No!" Jake answered, almost too quickly. The last thing he needed right now was for Randy to see him this way. She would see right through it. He had to get control of himself. He had to find a way to hide this. Someone wanted him to come alone, and he damn well would if it meant protecting those little girls. "I . . . I just am worried about my son and grandson," he told the porter. "Let's go get the luggage." He struggled just to walk, taking deep breaths and telling himself he still had some time. First came home and young Jake and Ben. He had to figure out how to hide this from Hal Kraemer and the men. Hardest of all would be Lloyd . . . and Randy . . . especially Randy. *Act normal*, he warned himself. *Stay in the light. Concentrate on just getting home and being there for Jake and Ben.* He helped the porter load the luggage and followed the man outside, literally struggling not to fall down.

*We will find a way to get to those little girls.*

How? Did it have something to do with the picnic? Ainsley! The man who'd challenged him there. The man who'd once worked for Henry Till. Did this have something to do with him? He stopped between two train cars and vomited. This was so much like when Evie was taken. He didn't eat for days, nor did he sleep. He'd vomited then, too, just at the thought of his beautiful daughter being abused just because men wanted him dead.

"Sir? Do you need a doctor?" the porter asked.

Jake clung to a rail on the car where he stood. He took a handkerchief from his jacket pocket and wiped his mouth. "No. But can you go to the kitchen car on this train and get me some water?"

"Certainly." The porter hurried down to the next car and climbed inside.

*Come alone,* the note read.

*I'll damn well come alone! And whoever is waiting will wish I had come with a posse! Me coming alone will be worse!*

The porter returned with a glass of water and Jake used it to rinse his mouth and spit. Then he swallowed some of the water and thanked the porter, handing back the glass.

"Are you *sure* you don't need a doctor, Mr. Harkner?"

Jake nodded. "I'm sure." He took some peppermint from his shirt pocket. Peppermint. Usually he used it for fun, sharing it with Randy before they made love. This time he needed it to hide any residue from vomiting. It helped get the taste out of his mouth. He ate the whole thing. He had to hide this from Randy.

"Don't say anything to anyone about me being sick," he told the porter. "It's just over something that's my business and no one else's."

"Yes, Sir."

They walked out of the station together and into the bright Colorado sunlight. After all the smog of the city the last few weeks, Jake had almost forgotten how clear the air was here in the mountains. *Good. The fresh air will help me think.*

Randy stood on the other side of a pair of outdoor train tracks. There was a narrow brick road between them, and a few horses trotted by, a couple of carriages. Jake felt like he was in another world, a strange, silent vacuum where things took place all around him, but he wasn't part of it. Cole and Vance and some of the other men stood or sat on horses around Randy, as though to make sure she was safe.

*Good. I don't have to worry about Randy. She will always be safe with J&L men around. And Peter is here.* Damned if he wasn't glad about that.

He breathed deeply again and walked with the porter and luggage cart over to the little welcoming committee from the J&L. Men began unloading the luggage onto a small wagon, putting smaller, more personal pieces behind the seat of an enclosed buggy they had also brought with them. Jake forced himself to concentrate on what Cole was saying when the man approached him on horseback, leading Thunder with him.

"I brought your horse and both your rifles," Cole told him. "We figured it wouldn't hurt to be prepared for anything on the way back. If the wrong men find out you're here and on the way home – well – we just ain't sure what the hell to expect. We just figured we ought to be ready for anything. We figured we'll avoid the Mitchel place on the way home, since the shootin' seemed to come from that area."

"Good idea," Jake answered, trying his best not to face anyone squarely. The darkness that was welling up inside would find its way to his eyes. Randy would see it. He walked up to Thunder and petted the horse's nose, then took his gun belt from the pommel of the saddle and buckled it on. He tied the holsters at his thighs, then took his .44's from where they were tucked into his belt and put them into the holsters. His spare .45 was still packed. He mounted Thunder.

"We brought the buggy for you," Vance told Randy. He started to assist her into the enclosed carriage, but she refused.

"I wore a riding skirt so I could ride with Jake and the men," she told Vance. "They will make it home faster than the carriage will, and I intend to get to my children and grandchildren as fast as possible."

"I don't want you riding out in the open," Jake objected. "It's too dangerous."

"You aren't going to stop me, Jake Harkner." Randy looked at Vance. "Please tell me you brought enough horses."

Vance glanced at Jake, not sure what to do, but Jake just looked away.

"Bring me a horse, Vance, or I'll take yours," Randy insisted. "I'm not letting my husband ride off without me. He'll need me when we get there, and I don't trust him not to take a sharp turn and go charging into dangerous territory on his own."

"Randy, I'm not going anywhere but home," Jake told her, forcing himself to speak calmly and not angrily. This was no time to argue, or he might explode. Then she'd know. She'd know. "It's going to be a hard ride," he added, "with an overnight stay sleeping on the ground, depending on how fast we ride."

"We've ridden together a thousand times, Jake. And I've slept on the ground plenty. Stop pampering me. We don't have time to argue about this."

Jake adjusted his hat. *That's for damn sure.* "You picked a fine time to be your bossy self," he told her, trying to show a touch of humor.

"And right now, I don't trust your mood," she answered. "So, like it or not, I'm going with *you*."

Scowling, Jake turned a restless Thunder in a circle. "The woman has spoken," he grumped to Vance. "Get her a horse." He looked over at the three spare horses the men brought with them, all of them saddled. "The gray mare over there. She's easy to handle, and she's fast." Randy was right not to trust his mood, and that made him even more upset. He turned his attention to Peter. "Peter, you and Jeff take the buggy," he added. "Charlie can drive the luggage wagon along with you. It will take the three of you a little longer to reach the homestead, but we can't help that." He eyed Doctor Beemer. "You much of a rider, Doc? It would help if you could ride ahead with us. You need to get there as fast as possible, too."

"I own several horses and ride often at the stables where they're boarded, north of the city," Beemer answered.

"It's not the same as riding a horse with a Western saddle in rugged country," Jake pointed out. "But we don't have much choice. You might have a sore rear-end by the time we get there."

Beemer grinned. "Those boys need me. I'll manage."

Jake nodded. "I appreciate that." He yelled at Vance to bring along a spare horse for the riders. The men finished loading luggage and everyone climbed onto horses and into the buggy and the baggage wagon.

He buckled it on and tied the holsters at his thighs, then tucked his spare .45 into the belt behind his back. He greeted Thunder by rubbing the horse's nose, then took an ammo belt from around Thunder's neck and put it on, crosswise.

"Jake, you don't look good," Cole told him, "kind of like you looked when we left for Mexico – loaded up for trouble."

"I'm loaded up for trouble, all right." *I have two little girls to protect.* Jake lit a cigarette and took a deep drag.

Cigarettes calmed him. "First things first. We have to get to those boys, and then we have to determine if you and those kids were really bushwhacked, or if some nervous settler thought you were rustlers and shot at them without thinking." Good. *That will make it look like I don't already know what's really going on.* "Either way, whoever did this must have known that the men they shot were on J&L land, which means they might be afraid to admit they did the shooting."

Cole nodded, but the look in his eyes told Jake he had his own theory, and it was probably the same thing Jake already knew.

"Let's ride," Jake said. The whole bunch of them headed down the street away from the train station.

"Jake is in his element now," Jeff told Peter. "He's loaded for bear, and not just with weapons. He's loaded on the *inside*. The only person who dares argue with him right now is Randy, and I'm not so sure even *she* can get away with any harsh words." He watched Randy ride up beside Jake on the mare.

"You sure you want to do this?" Jake asked her.

"Of course."

"It's already getting late. We'll ride 'til dark. You stay right beside me, understand? And if anything goes awry, you do exactly what I tell you."

"I will." Randy reached over and squeezed his arm. "I love you, Jake. Remember all the things we talked about."

Jake felt sick again. He would have to lie to her, something he never did. The note said to come alone, and whoever sent it would damn well regret threatening his granddaughters. "I'll remember," he told Randy.

He turned to Vance, who rode to his left. "Once we get out into cattle country, you stay on Randy's other side."

"Sure."

"Cole, you ride in front of Randy once we get out of

town," Jake yelled to his friend. "Terrel, ride behind her. If anybody thinks they're going to bushwhack us, I don't want my wife taking a bullet."

Horses' hooves clopped against the brick streets. Bystanders watched, talking among themselves.

"We read it in the paper, Jake!" a complete stranger shouted. "I hope you get the sonsofbitches who did it."

Jake ignored the remark. Soon the sound of the horses' hooves turned to the softer rhythm of hooves against dirt and gravel as they moved out of the city.

"Let's speed it up for a ways," Jake told them. "I'm anxious to get home to those boys, and we have some decent daylight left."

The soft pounding turned to something more like thunder as those on horseback took off at a gallop.

Randy stirred awake in her sleeping bag and reached out for Jake, who lay next to her using just his saddle and blankets.

He wasn't there.

She sat up and, still fully clothed. She quickly pulled on her boots and stood up.

"Ma'am, where are you going?" Terrel asked from nearby.

"Jake isn't here," she said, panic in her voice.

"You thinkin' he rode off?"

"I never know *what* to think when something like this happens."

"He told me he was just walkin' off to think, Ma'am. I really think he just wants to be alone."

Randy faced Terrel over the light of a campfire. "I don't trust him not to be missing come morning." She stepped around sleeping men and into the darkness.

"Ma'am, don't do that!" Terrel told her.

Randy paid no attention, but she didn't get ten feet before Terrel, Cole and Vance were right behind her—Cole and Vance standing there in their long johns holding guns. Hearing them, she turned, then put her hands on her hips. "Well, now, aren't you a fine-looking bunch of drinking, womanizing, half-dressed, ex-outlaws? I'm fine. Go back to sleep."

"Randy, we have our orders," Vance told her. "We can't let you go walking off alone. We'd have to answer to Jake for it, and the mood he's in, we ain't about to have to answer to him about a missing wife."

"What's going on here?" Jake loomed out of the darkness.

Randy turned. "I was worried about you."

Jake told the men to go back to sleep, then walked Randy farther into the darkness.

"I just needed to think, Randy. You don't really believe I'd go riding off before seeing Young Jake and Ben first, do you?"

"I don't know what to think about *anything* anymore." Randy stepped in front of him and moved her arms around him. "Jake, those men were right there the minute I walked out of the firelight."

"That's what they were *supposed* to do. Those men are not about to let anything bad happen to you again."

"I know. I'm so grateful." Randy broke into quiet tears, then pulled away and took a handkerchief from a pocket on her riding pants, using it to wipe her eyes and nose. "I'm sorry. Right now, I think I just . . . I have to cry or scream."

"I don't blame you." Jake pulled her back into his arms, glad it was too dark for her to see his eyes. "I feel the same way. I did my own crying over the boys back there on the train, but I can't now. I have to stay hard. I think better that way." He kissed her hair. "I learned how to harden up and let hatred keep away the hurt when I was little and getting beat by my father. And right now, until I know the damn truth, I have to let the *hatred* keep me strong." He sighed and gently pushed her away. "Go back to sleep if you can."

"Not until you come with me."

"I *can't* sleep."

"It isn't good for you not to. Tired men make mistakes. Please, please try. You haven't slept more than four or five hours since we left Chicago. Even when we were in bed I could tell you weren't sleeping. You'll make yourself sick."

*I've already been sick.* Jake sighed and put an arm around her shoulders. They headed back to the campfire and Randy crawled into her sleeping bag. She scooched it closer to Jake and covered him with part of the sleeping bag, then snuggled against him. He turned to his side and pulled her into his arms. She touched one arm and it was hard as a rock. His whole body felt hard.

"Jake, tell me you will listen to Lloyd and Hal Kraemer and the others. Whatever happens, let them help you."

"I will." *I'm so sorry, Randy.*

He was so tense it frightened her.

"I love you," she said softly.

"And we all love you," Vance spoke up out of the darkness.

"Shut the hell up, you no-good, wife-stealing sonofabitch," Jake ordered.

They all broke into light laughter, a wonderful release from the gravity of the situation. Randy felt Jake's arm relax a little.

# CHAPTER 39

*August 24 ... mid-morning ...*

"Grampa! Grampa! Grampa!"

Sadie Mae and Tricia reached them before they could even dismount. Jake climbed down, and both girls grabbed him around the legs.

"Whoa, wait up there! Don't jump on Grampa when he has his guns on." He pulled his revolvers from their holsters and handed them to Cole, then knelt down and pulled both girls into his arms. They smothered him in kisses.

"We were scared you wouldn't come home," Sadie Mae told him. "Ben and my brother got hurt!"

"I know that. And you girls remember that grandpa *always* comes home." He hugged them close and stood, holding one in each arm. *And I'll always protect you.* "I missed you two so much, but remember that grandpa needs to help Jake and Ben right now, so if you want to be really good for me, you need to go back to Katie's house and stay there so you don't get in the way. Okay?"

"We will, grampa," Sadie Mae told him. "And we've

been practicing making our dimples deeper." Both girls gave him silly-big smiles.

"Good. When all this is over, I'll take a real close look." Jake waited while Randy hugged him and the girls all together. She gave the girls kisses before Jake carried them over to Terrel. "Take these two back to Katie's. And you have a couple of men start watching them, even if it means having to sit outside the house day and night, at least until this mess gets settled."

"Sure Jake, but – "

"Don't ask questions. I have my reasons. Just keep it to yourself and do what I ask." Jake gave each one of them a kiss on the cheek. "You two stay together and you wait to come over when Katie says it's okay. Will you do that?"

Both girls nodded eagerly and, one by one, gave Jake a hug around the neck. Sadie Mae started crying. "Will my brother be okay?"

"I'm sure he will. We brought a real fancy doctor from Chicago with us. He'll help your daddy fix your brother all better. Ben, too."

"Are you going to go after some bad guys, grampa?" the girl asked.

"I don't know, Sadie Mae. Just don't you worry about that" He set both girls on their feet. "Go on, now. Grandpa has a lot to do. Peter and Jeff will be coming along later in the buggy. You be sure to give them hugs, too, when you see them."

"Come on, girls. Uncle Terrel will walk you back to Katie's," Terrel told them, taking their hands.

Again, Jake felt the black thunder of anyone even suggesting harming such innocence. He shook away his rage as best he could and turned to see Randy hugging Evie.

More family members greeted them, everyone talking

and hugging at once. Evie exclaimed over Randy's rose-petal necklace.

"Jake got it for me in Chicago, for a grand ball Peter held for us. Oh, Evie, I have so much to tell you. The night of the ball was one of the happiest of our lives, and now this."

Jake walked over and let Evie hug him and Randy together. "I'm so sorry you had to come home to all this tragedy," she told them, wiping at tears. Randy introduced Doctor Beemer to Brian and Evie, and Jake noticed Lloyd hurrying over from his house. Jake saw the deep worry in his son's eyes. He let Evie and Randy talk with Brian and Doctor Beemer as he greeted Lloyd with a quick hug.

"Goddamn, it's good to have you back, Pa," Lloyd told him. "Ben and Jake both need you, and so do I."

"It's good to *be* back," Jake told him as he pulled away. "Jeff and Peter came, too. They should be coming along later with the buggy and a wagon with baggage." Jake studied his son intently. "How's Katie holding up?"

"Good."

"And what about you? I hope you're staying away from that little brown bottle."

"I'm okay. I have to stay clear-headed. This has been so hard on Katie and Evie both, having to help nurse Ben and Jake and watch them in so much pain. Thank God for Katie's parents. They have managed to watch the little ones and keep Sadie Mae and Tricia calm and away from all this. Katie's at the house resting right now. She wanted to come over, too, but she knew you'd be pulled in sixteen different directions. I know you want to go see Jake and Ben right away. Katie has coffee and food at the house whenever you and mom need anything." Lloyd looked off into the distance. "This is such a mess. I'm sorry, Pa."

"Sorry for what? You haven't done anything."

"I should have seen this coming. There has been some rustling going on, settlers complaining that cattlemen are killing their stock and destroying their farm fields. That's not true, pa. And after you left, I had to chase that damn Grizzly Smith and Brady Fillmore and some damn gunslinger named Kyle Pendergrass off a new settlement on the northern border – same area where you had that run-in with Fillmore. The day of the shooting, Stephen and Ben and young Jake were headed there to help the new owners with whatever they needed – kind of a good neighbor thing, you know? But all hell broke loose. Hal Kraemer and his deputies got here earlier. They are at the bunk house with some of our men and men from other ranches. We're all going to meet later, after you tend to the boys. They come first."

Brian and Doctor Beemer joined them, and Jake couldn't help noticing how bone-tired Brian looked. He was thinner and had dark circles under his bloodshot eyes. Jake shook his son-in-law's hand. "Brian, my one consolation when I heard about this was that we have a damn good doctor in the family, but I know this must be really hard on you."

Brian squeezed his hand in return. "I'm just grateful to Peter for thinking to bring along another doctor. And thank God the man brought more chloroform. I was almost out." He shook his head, still gripping Jake's hand. "I'm going to have to cut off more of Ben's arm, Jake. It's already gone at the elbow, but infection has set in. You know what that means. We hoped you'd make it home today, because we can't put off the inevitable any longer."

They all headed to Brian and Evie's house, where Gretta waited on the front porch. She wore a blood-stained apron.

"Welcome back, big guy," Gretta told Jake, her smile sad. "Ben and young Jake have been asking for you."

Jake leaned down and kissed her hair. "Thanks for the help." He let the others go inside and turned to Cole, who waited below the steps. "Keep everybody else out of here for now, but stick around. We might need you to help with Ben."

"Sure, Jake. Your guns are in your saddle bags. I'll take them over to your place and come right back."

Jake thought about the note in his pocket. He had to keep up a front, especially later around Lloyd and the other men. He turned and went inside.

"Ben is half out of it from Laudanum," Lloyd told Jake. "The pain has been awful, but we're afraid to give him too much Laudanum, or whiskey. He throws up all the time."

Jake sighed and wiped at his eyes, an attempt to actually wipe away the dark need to avenge the awful pain Ben and Jake were suffering. *Don't let it show. Don't let it show, especially to Lloyd or Randy.* He noticed that the kitchen table was already cleared and covered with a sheet. Heated water sat waiting on the stove. Doctor's tools were laid out on a smaller table nearby.

Jake removed his hat and hung it on a hook near the door.

"Pa!" The word was spoken in a groan and came from a nearby bedroom. "Pa—"

"Grampa," Little Jake yelled from another room. "Grampa, Gretta said you're home!"

Jake unbuckled his still-empty gun belt and tossed it onto a love seat, then turned to Gretta. "Do you have the stomach for what is about to happen? I hate for Evie or Randy to have to do too much."

"I've seen it all, Jake. I've been helping all along. Poor Ben has suffered long enough. Brian is right. More of that arm needs to come off. I know that's devasting for a kid that age, but getting rid of the infection is going to help his pain."

Jake nodded. "Introduce yourself to Doctor Beemer and help him with more boiled water and such. Show him where he can clean up a little while I talk to the boys."

"Grampa, I want to stay, too," Stephen spoke up. "Let me help."

It was the first time Jake even realized his oldest grandson was standing nearby. He looked forlorn and ready to cry.

"Stephen!" Jake pulled him close. "Thank God you're okay. Cole said you were along, too."

"It was real bad, grandpa," Stephen said, his eyes tearing.

"I know that. And now Ben and young Jake will need your help. Right now that help means just sitting someplace quiet and once this is over, helping Gretta and Evie with caring for those boys."

Stephen nodded. "I know."

"Grampa!" Young Jake called out again.

"I have to get in there." Jake patted Stephen's arm and hurried into the bedroom where young Jake lay with his leg elevated. Randy stood near him, bathing his forehead with a wet cloth. She met Jake's gaze and drew in her breath.

"Jake, what is it? I don't like the look in your eyes."

*Damn!* He closed his eyes. "It's just – " He looked down at young Jake, then glanced at the bloody gauze wrapped around his left thigh. "Just this whole situation. I'll be all right." He leaned over his grandson and grasped his shoulders.

Young Jake broke into tears. "I feel better now you're home," he sobbed to Jake.

"Brian says you will be okay," he lied for the moment. He hadn't even had a chance to talk to Brian in detail about young Jake. "It's just going to take time."

The boy sniffed and wiped at is eyes. "It's just like when you got shot in the leg back in Guthrie, isn't it?" he asked. "Mom said you were protecting me. She said you put me into a potato crate so those men's bullets couldn't get me. She said you were wounded the same way as me."

"And I got better and was fine after that. You will be, too." Jake leaned down and kissed the boy's forehead, glad to notice he didn't seem to have a fever. "Right now, I need to go see Ben. You understand, don't you?"

Jake nodded. "'Course I do. He's hurtin' bad, grampa. I'm just glad you're here. I feel better just knowing that. Ben will, too. We both missed you a lot."

Jake took hold of the boy's hand and squeezed it. "You do everything Brian and your mother tell you to do, understand? They know what's best for you. Right now, you get some rest while I go see to Ben. Both of you will be fine. I'm sure of it."

"Grampa, we never saw 'em. We never saw nothin'. I thought they'd killed Ben and Cole."

"I know all about it. Don't you worry about any of it. Lloyd and I and the others will find out what happened, and if it was on purpose, we'll make sure whoever did this goes to prison." *Unless I get to them first.* Jake couldn't shake the vision of his granddaughters in the hands of such men, let alone what they had already done to Ben and Jake. "You rest, Jake. I'll come see you again once I help the doctors with Ben." He kissed the boy again and left the room.

Randy headed for the door to see about getting a clean wash rag. She ran into Evie, and their gazes held, both women very aware of what this was doing to Jake. Randy fought tears.

"Pray for your father, Evie. I saw something in his eyes just now, something I didn't like."

"Mother, I started praying for him the minute this happened." Evie took hold of the delicate rose pendant her mother wore. "This necklace is a symbol of how much daddy loves you. It's so beautiful, just like his love for you. You remember that and stay strong." Evie hugged her. "Trust God."

# CHAPTER 40

Ben shook as he grabbed Jake's hand and begged him to stay by his side. "I'm scared, Pa," he wept. "It hurts so bad, and now it's gonna' hurt more."

Randy knelt on the other side of the bed, her heart aching for both Ben and Jake. Jake sat on the edge the bed and smoothed back Ben's white-blond hair with his free hand.

"Ben, what hurts is the infected part," Jake explained. "I've had infections, and when they're gone, you feel one hell of a lot better." He looked at Evie and asked her to hand him a fresh, cool rag. He sponged Ben's face and forehead. "We brought a big-time doctor from Chicago with us to help, son. Brian is doing all he can, but he's tired, and sometimes when a man is deeply worried about somebody he loves, it's hard for him to do what needs doing all by himself. He's real glad Doctor Beemer is here. You can trust him to get rid of your pain. Between him and Brian, you are in good hands. And this doctor brought some chloroform with him, so you won't feel anything at all, and you don't need to drink any more of that awful Laudanum or whiskey."

"Pa." Ben's whole body jerked in a sob. "I won't never be a real man if they cut off my arm. I won't be able to go hunting with you like we were gonna' do with my new rifle, or wrestle down calves for branding, and no girl is gonna' want me."

"Whoa! Hold up there." Jake raised his voice slightly and straightened, an authoritative look on his face. "I need you to pay attention to what I'm going to tell you."

The boy sniffed and nodded.

"This might be embarrassing to any women listening," Jake warned, winking at Ben.

"So if some woman present wants to leave, she's welcome to it."

"I am used to your wild stories, Jake Harkner," Randy answered, trying to keep up the good humor.

"God knows nothing embarrasses or offends *me*," Gretta added with a chuckle.

"Dear Lord," Evie said softly. "I've just learned to put up with daddy's stories. As long as the little ones aren't here, I think I can handle this."

"All right, but I warned all of you," Jake told them. He folded his arms, keeping his gaze on Ben. "Ben, of all my faults, lying isn't one of them. I've never lied to you, and I never will. Your grandma can attest to that fact."

Randy cleared her throat. "We will discuss that later, but I *will* attest to the fact that your father never lies to his *children*," Randy told Ben.

Jake glanced at her with a fake scowl, then looked back at Ben. "Your grandmother is mixing lying with just saying nice words to keep somebody from getting mad. Sometimes I have to do that with her."

Some of the others snickered.

"In the meantime, I have something to tell you," Jake told Ben, "and it's the damn truth. When I was not a whole lot older than you and running with some bad, wild men, one of those men had one arm – just his right one. I never knew his real name, but they called him Honky-Tonk because he loved dancing with the saloon girls."

"Why did I know this would involve saloon women?" Evie muttered.

"Good God, pa, are you really going to tell *that* story?" Lloyd asked.

"I promise to clean it up," Jake said with a grin.

Brian and Doctor Beemer came to the doorway.

"I'm telling you true, Ben," Jake continued. "Honky-Tonk had only his right arm. He never told us how he lost the other one, but it didn't' matter. He did *everything any* man can do. He rode, robbed, hunted, drank, raised hell, rustled cattle, saddled and unsaddled his own horse, and played cards like any other man. He danced. He could run. He could draw and shoot a gun. And he even packed a punch that knocked a man clear across the room so bad that the other guy never even fought back." He leaned a little closer. "And best of all, the whores loved him, if you know what I mean, and I think you do. They practically fought over him."

Gretta broke out in laughter, and Evie covered her face and turned away.

"That's really true?" Ben asked. "I think you're . . . " He winced with pain. "Pullin' my leg."

Jake shook his head. "May God strike me dead if I'm lying. Missing an arm won't stop you from *anything*, son. When you're better, we'll go elk hunting, just like I promised. We'll practice until you can use a rifle with one hand, and until you're just as able to handle yourself in every other way as Honky-Tonk could."

"Do you really think I can do all those things?"

"I *know* so."

"What happened to Honky-Tonk?" Ben asked.

Jake shrugged. "I'm not sure. Outlaws move around a

lot. Here today and gone tomorrow. He moved on, and I expect he kept raising hell for a long time. Like I said, that arm didn't keep him from doing everything any other man can do, and it will be like that for you. All the men on this ranch, and Lloyd, and me—we'll all help you re-learn how to do things you've always done. You're a big, strong, good-looking young man. You sure as hell won't have any problems getting women, if *that's* what you're worried about. Of course, that's something none of us can help you with. All I can say is that Doctor Beemer is cutting off your arm, not something a lot more important."

Stephen giggled. Even Ben managed light laughter while Randy just shook her head and Gretta gave out her signature laugh. "Jake, you are the most honest man I've ever met. Just say it like it is, I always believed."

Evie just kept her hands over her face.

Jake ruffled Ben's hair. "Women won't give a damn about that arm, Ben. You still have your other arm to put around a woman and hold her close, and women love that. Just ask your grandma. The rest of what needs doing will come naturally when some pretty girl falls in love with you. And believe me, the two of you will have a whole lot of fun figuring it all out."

"Good Lord!" Evie exclaimed.

Gretta just laughed again, and in spite of the crude story, Randy had to smile at how Jake managed a snicker out of Ben, a moment of humor to take his mind off of what was coming. Doctor Beemer walked over and put a hand on Jake's shoulder. "Your father is right, Ben. Plenty of men have learned to get by just fine with one arm. I was eighteen or so myself during the Civil War, and a lot of men lost limbs in that war. I've known a lot of men who managed fine with one arm or one leg, some missing *both* legs. Most of them were already married or got married after that and had lots of children. Let's get you fixed up so you can start re-learning a few things and getting back to real life. I can see you have a whole great big family to help you, and a father who understands just about anything life throws at someone."

Ben gripped Jake's hand with surprising strength. "Don't let go of me, Pa."

"Not for a minute."

"Even while they're cutting my arm off?"

"Even then. But Doctor Beemer's going to have you breathe in some chloroform, so you'll sleep through most of it. That stuff really knocks you out, so don't be afraid." Jake leaned in and kissed Ben's forehead. "You ready? The sooner we do this, the sooner you and I can go hunting."

"Okay."

Randy leaned in and kissed Ben's cheek. "We all love you, Ben." She saw the terror in the boy's eyes, then almost gasped when she caught the temporary dark fury in Jake's as he glanced at her when he got up. Before she could say anything, Jake, Lloyd and Doctor Beemer carried Ben to the kitchen table. Gretta hurried to the front door and called Cole to come inside and help.

"You wouldn't believe the story Jake just told Ben about a one-armed man," Gretta told Cole.

"Oh, hell, I've heard that one. If he told it with women present, I can guarantee it's a lot seedier when only men are around."

Gretta laughed again. She hurried back to the kitchen and leaned down to pat Ben's cheek. "Kid, when you're better, you ask your grandpa to give you more details about Honky-Tonk. Cole says he left a few things out, and Laughter is good for the soul, Ben. It will help you heal."

Ben managed another grin through tears. Cole held one of his legs then while Lloyd held the other. Jake kept hold of his hand as Beemer unwrapped bloody gauze from the wasting, dying stump of the boy's left arm. He turned to Gretta.

"Pour plenty of alcohol on the wound." Gretta hurriedly obeyed, and Randy stood behind Jake with her hand on his back. Beemer turned Brian. "Start applying the chloroform."

Brian poured chloroform onto a piece of gauze and put it over Ben's mouth and nose.

"Be careful," Beemer told him. "I know he's close to a man in size, but he's still a child."

In seconds, the boy passed out.

"Hand me the saw," Beemer told Gretta.

With a shaking hand, Gretta did as he asked.

"I want all of you to know that this instrument is specially made for this," Beemer told them. "It's extremely sharp, so this will be quick." He took a deep breath. "Brian, Ben seems in a deep enough sleep. Hold the top of his arm away from his body as far as you can. Let's get this over with."

Randy turned away, and Jake pressed an arm across Ben's chest and kept a tight hold of his good arm.

Everyone winced at the sound of sawing, but just as Beemer promised, it was over quickly. He had Gretta use a thick pad to take hold of a hot iron they'd kept on a stove burner, then put a hand over Gretta's and helped her hold the hot iron to the end of Ben's arm to cauterize the open would.

Everyone grimaced at the hissing sound and the smell of burning flesh. Ben jerked, and Brian gave him more chloroform while Jake held the boy tighter, remembering the pain when Brian had to cauterize his leg wound back in Guthrie. *Someone needs to die for this!* He kept the words to himself, but he damn well meant them.

"I know this is hard for everyone," Beemer told them, "but cauterizing the wound will sterilize the end of Ben's arm and will seal veins and blood vessels." Gretta set the hot iron back on the stove, and Brian wrapped Ben's arm tightly with clean gauze. Everyone shivered a little and took a deep breath of relief.

"You can carry him back to bed," Beemer told Jake and Lloyd. "He'll be unconscious for a while." He looked at Gretta. "This young lady and I will watch over him. Brian, you need some rest, and Jake, you and your wife have had a long trip and you've been through a lot today. Once you get Ben back to bed you should go lie down and get some sleep. You, too – Evie, is it?"

"Yes."

"You need to rest, too. And Lloyd, go home to your wife. I'm told she's still a little weak from losing a baby. You can all take turns helping watch both boys once you've had some rest."

"Thank you, Doctor Beemer," Randy told him, wiping at tears. "You've been a blessing."

"Thanks for calling me a lady," Gretta murmured to Beemer. "You don't know the half, Doc."

"Oh, I'm beginning to understand a lot of things," he replied, smiling. He patted Gretta's shoulder. "You are a strong, caring woman, Gretta."

Taking hold of Ben on either side, Jake and Lloyd carried the boy back to the bedroom, where Evie had put a clean sheet on the bed.

"I'd like to get some rest like Beemer told us, Pa," Lloyd told Jake as the women tucked Ben in, "but we need to go out there and talk to the rest of the men and to Marshal Kraemer."

"I know." Jake straightened and took a deep breath. "I'll go through our luggage and get my guns and pack the right gear after the meeting. One thing is sure. We all need to leave in the morning and see what's going on at the northern border. I'm going to see young Jake once more. I'll be at the bunk house after that."

Randy stepped aside and let Jake and Lloyd leave the room, then thanked Gretta for all she'd done.

"Hell, I've dealt with beat-up whores and miscarriages and wounded cowboys—everything from cuts from broken bottles to bullet wounds," Gretta told her. "This is just more of the same." She held Randy's gaze. "You go take care of that man in young Jake's room and keep him from turning to his wild side. He's really struggling. I can see it."

"I see it, too."

Gretta glanced at her necklace. "That sure is some necklace. I remember when Jake had me help him find the best jewelry store in Denver so he could buy you that beautiful wedding ring you're wearing. He loves you so much, and I'm sure he wants to do the right thing here, but Jake is Jake, and he's on fire inside."

"Oh, believe me, I am well aware of what this is doing to him." Randy ached everywhere from tension. She hurried into young Jake's bedroom to see Jake hugging the boy and assuring him he'd be all right.

"You and Ben help each other get better and we'll *all* go hunting sooner than later."

"Okay, Grampa. I'm real glad you're home."

"So am I. You let Doctor Beemer look at that leg, and you do whatever he tells you to do, all right? Don't be afraid if he says he needs to operate on it a little more. You can trust him, and Brian says he's seen no infection, so that's a real good sign."

"I'm going to talk to the men, pa – let them know how things went," Lloyd told Jake. "We'll be at the bunkhouse waiting for you." He turned and hugged his mother, then left.

Jake rose and faced Randy, opening his arms to her. "You okay?"

She wrapped her arms around his waist and rested her head against his chest.

"I'm not sure." She leaned back to meet his gaze. "It all depends on how *you* are."

"I don't know yet. Lloyd and I have to talk to Hal Kraemer and the men. Go home and get some rest. I'll be along."

"*Will* you? Promise me, Jake. And don't forget that you promised Ben you would take him hunting when this is over. I saw the look in your eyes a few minutes ago after you told that story to Ben. Don't you dare do something to get yourself killed."

"Just trust that I know what I'm doing." *They threatened the girls!*

"Jake – "

"*Trust* me, Randy. Have I ever failed to come back to you?"

"What does that mean?"

*It means I have to leave you. I'm so sorry, but I have to do this alone. It's what they want.* Jake checked his words. "It only means that when I ride out in the morning with Lloyd and the others, I'll be fine . . . and I'll be back." God, how he hated lying to her. He *never* lied to her.

"Keep it legal, Jake."

"I will. You go to the house and clean up now. I'll be along after I talk to the men."

"Make that a promise," Randy again demanded.

Jake looked her over and sighed. "I already told you I'd be there. Besides, back in Guthrie, didn't I always hold you at night just before I had to leave for something like this?"

"And right now, you're full of a hundred different emotions because this is personal. I know what you're like when that's the case. You make sure you come to the house later. And tomorrow – just remember how these boys were bushwhacked. You have no idea what's waiting for you out there. God knows the foothills offer a hundred ways for a man to shoot someone without being seen at all."

"Randy!" Jake pressed her arms and leaned down to kiss her forehead. "After three years in No Man's Land, I think I know what to watch for. Now, go home and wait for me." He left her and walked out, taking his gun belt from where he'd left it lying on the loveseat.

Randy walked to the door to watch him walk away, her heart aching for how he'd had to hang on to Ben while Doctor Beemer sawed off the boy's arm. She knew that must have had a deep affect on him, but she couldn't quite read his emotions, and that worried her. Besides that, he had to be bone tired, not a good combination for a man determined to find who had done this.

She turned to Evie, who stood near the kitchen table she'd just scrubbed vigorously. "I'm going home for a while and wait for your father."

"Wait," Doctor Beemer told her. He came around the table and up to Randy, handing her a small bottle. "Take this with you and put a couple of drops into some tea or coffee before you go to bed. It will relax you."

Randy took the bottle. "Thank you."

"Daddy will be all right," Evie told her, coming around the table to give her a hug. "So will the boys. I know it's so because I am going to pray real hard for all of them. Just remember that daddy has a lot of help. This isn't like when he sometimes rode off alone after thieves and murderers back in Oklahoma. Things have changed, mother."

*But Jake hasn't.* Randy couldn't explain the heavy feeling in her chest. "I'll remember." She left, and Brian sighed and walked closer to his wife, putting an arm around her waist. "Your mother is really worried."

"She's afraid Daddy will do something truly crazy this time," Evie answered.

"Well, love, I don't know what you mean by *truly* crazy. We've seen him in action, and I don't think you can compare any one thing Jake has done to any other. Jake is just Jake, and crazy is crazy. The list is long."

Evie closed her eyes. "And that is exactly why I'm worried."

# CHAPTER 41

Jake came home after dark to see Peter sitting near the fireplace in a velvet chair. A small lamp was on, and he was reading. He looked up and set the book aside.

"I'm glad you and Jeff made it," Jake commented. "But you're lucky you didn't have to watch Beemer cut off Ben's arm. It was horrific."

"I have no doubt. I'm really sorry you had to go through that, Jake."

"Blood messes like that don't usually bother me, but when it's your own kid, that's another story." Jake plopped his hat on a hook near the door. "Thank you again for thinking to bring Beemer along. This has been a nightmare for Brian." Jake headed for the kitchen table. "Jeff has been at the bunkhouse taking notes on what we talked about. I figured I'd find you here."

"Per your instructions, I might remind you." Peter felt uneasy at the darkness in Jake's eyes. "You told me to be here for Randy when I arrived, so here I am. Besides, Evie told me to come over here and sit with her, too, but Randy wasn't much for talking. I just stayed to reassure her she wasn't alone in the house, and I promised I would go and get you if you weren't back by nine. She was afraid you would stay out with the men all night – said you get that way when you're worked up about something."

Jake scoffed. "I'm worked up, all right. Where is Randy?"

"Upstairs. She went up about an hour ago to take a bath and go to bed. She put something in her coffee that she said Doctor Beemer told her to take to help her rest." Peter stood up. "We both had coffee, and all she talked about was you, of course. I'm tired myself, so now that you're back, I'm going to the Donavans' to get some sleep. I'm told that's where I am to stay. Lord knows I won't lack for something to eat over there. I might have to kidnap Katie's mother and take her back to Chicago with me so she can be my cook."

Jake managed a smile. "I wouldn't blame you." He placed his spare gun and a rifle onto the kitchen table, along with his loaded gun belt.

"Well, I will let you take over here," Peter told Jake. He could feel Jake's thundering mood as he walked past him to the front door.

"Peter," Jake said.

Peter waited.

"Thanks for staying. In case you are wondering, the boys seem to be resting peacefully. I looked in on them again before I came over here. Beemer says everything went better than he expected and there isn't a lot of bleeding."

"I'm glad of that." Peter looked him over. "Did you and the men come to an understanding over what to do tomorrow?"

Jake nodded. "We're heading to the Mitchel place in the morning. It's obviously the best place to start. We just have to hope we get that far without being sniper shot."

Peter noticed Jake wore a badge on his vest. "So, you're

riding as a Deputy Marshal again?"

"I am. I'll try to keep you from having to defend me at a trial, but no guarantees." Jake glanced at the stairway, then back to Peter. "There are times when I'm almost afraid to face that woman."

Peter grinned. "You know her better than anyone, so it's up to you if you want to face her. She told me she ordered you to keep things legal this time, and to come here before you leave out in the morning, so don't worry. She would only beat you up later if you *didn't* show." Peter turned but hesitated once more, facing Jake. "Jake, just remember that the badge you're wearing gives you permission to arrest certain men so the law can take care of things. It's not a license to kill."

Jake turned away. "Just be here for Randy if things go wrong, Peter."

"I'd rather not have to, and you know what I mean by that."

Peter left, and Jake closed and locked the front door then removed his boots and vest and unbuttoned his shirt. He glanced at the grandfather clock by the door.

Nine p.m. It had been a long day and he was bone tired, but there wouldn't be time to sleep. Somehow he had to leave in the night and do what needed doing. He headed upstairs and into the bedroom, where Randy always kept a small lamp lit in one corner. She was sitting up against some pillows but looked half asleep.

"You're all heading to the Mitchel place in the morning, aren't you?" she asked.

"Yes," Jake answered, hoping he sounded sincere. He removed his denim pants and sat down on the edge of the bed to remove his shirt and undershirt. Aching with a need to rest, he crawled into bed beside his wife and studied the beautiful, gray-green eyes he loved so much. The glowed beautiful by the dim lamp. "There will be enough of us that we shouldn't have a problem," he assured her. "Kraemer deputized Lloyd and me and most of the others. About ten of us are going, but we have no idea what to expect." *I'm so sorry to lie to you, but this is the only way, Randy.*

"They'll be waiting, Jake, and they want *you*. I'm sure of it. That's why they did this awful thing."

"Randy, it's not like I haven't been in situations like this before. This is no different from all the times I rode out after killers and thieves back in Oklahoma."

"I know." Randy reached out and stroked his hair. "Did you eat something?"

"Yes. At the bunk house. I'm okay."

"But you must be so tired."

"I'm too anxious to get moving on this to be all that tired."

Randy leaned in to kiss his lips. "You used to always make love to me before you rode out after the bad guys. Are you too tired for that?"

He smiled sadly. "I am *never* too tired for that."

Randy smiled softly.

"Jake, I . . . I took a little of that sleeping medicine Doctor Beemer gave me. I'm sorry. I should be . . . more awake."

"It's okay." *God, I'm so sorry, Randy. I have to go alone . . . tonight. I'll do everything in my power to come back to you.* Jake wasn't so sure he would survive this time. He had no idea how many men were waiting for him, but he was determined to figure out a way to get to them. *The girls. I have to think of those sweet baby girls.* He leaned in and kissed Randy deeply, in a way he hoped she would always remember, then removed her night gown and kissed his way down her throat, over her breasts, her belly, then secret places as he pulled off her panties. She was sleepy and warm. That was good. She wouldn't catch on to his real mood like she usually did. She wouldn't see the look of desperation in his eyes.

"I have to . . . help with tending to the boys . . . tomorrow," she said rather absently, as though she was hardly aware of his touch at first.

"Let's just think about this for now," he told her

Randy breathed deeply as she responded to his touch. "Jake," she said softly. She wrapped her arms around his shoulders and kissed him passionately as he explored her depths until he felt her climax. By then they were lost in each other, their lovemaking as desperate as it always was when the future was uncertain. And this time, she had no idea just how uncertain it really was.

He pushed himself inside her, groaning with emotion, wondering if this was the last time he would invade this woman who loved him in spite of all his faults. He moved rhythmically, smothering her with kisses as she cried out and arched against him, as though to take in as much of him as possible. He moved his hands under her bottom to support her response to his thrusts.

"Who do you belong to?" he whispered.

"Jake Harkner," she groaned, always and forever."

"*Siempre requerdes cuanto te amo,*" Jake said softly as he invaded her soul. "*Tu eres mi vida.*"

Afterward, Randy settled into his arms. "I'm sorry I'm not more awake, Jake."

"Don't worry about it. You need your sleep." *Sleep hard, so you won't know I'm leaving.* Thank God the medicine had dulled her senses. The woman usually read him well. Right now, she would normally demand to know what he was really thinking. He could seldom fool her or keep something from her. He watched her a while, kissed her lovely mouth, kissed the rose-petal diamond necklace she still wore. "We've had a hell of a life, haven't we?" he said in a near whisper. He moved off the bed. She was so loved by so many. *They will all take care of you. And much as I hate the thought of it, Peter will make sure you never want for anything.*

He felt his heart shatter at the thought of any other man touching what belonged to Jake Harkner. *Who do you belong to?* How many times had he asked her that when he was claiming her as his own? She looked so beautiful now, lying there with her hair spread out on the pillow, her perfect body still something he took pleasure in touching, tasting, invading. She trusted him so devotedly. *And now I'm breaking that trust. Please forgive me.*

He fought tears at the thought that he might never see her again. He told himself it was time to turn to the outlaw deep inside, or maybe the lawman. Was there much difference? He covered her with a quilt, then quickly washed and dressed. He went to the top drawer of his dresser and lifted some undershirts to remove his mother's Crucifix, the beautiful cross he'd taken for himself and hidden from his father after his mother's murder. He'd managed to sneak the cross from around her neck before his father threw her and his little brother into that horrible dirt grave and forced him to help bury her. The Crucifix was all he had left of his mother, and it had always brought him good luck in times of danger.

He put the cross around his neck and under his shirt. *Don't look back,* he told himself as he walked out and down the stairs. He pulled on his boots, then strapped on his .44's and tucked his .45 into his gun belt behind his back. He pulled on a leather vest onto which he'd pinned the deputy's star Kraemer had given him. He put on his hat.

There was no fighting this, not with two innocent little girls involved. It was time to be the old Jake. For the last couple of years he'd done a pretty good job of adhering to the new rules of life and love and revenge, but something had snapped – something he wished he could control but had never been fully able to master. Men were going to die later today, and he might be one of them.

The wind picked up. Jake figured that was good, as it shrouded the sound of footsteps and a horse's hooves. He checked the gear he'd packed earlier onto Thunder. Everything was ready so he could get out of here quickly. He knew the lay of the land beyond the homestead, and the moon was bright tonight. Normally Lloyd had men posted all over the J&L as guards, but tonight nearly all the men were at the bunkhouse, having come in for the meeting, so he didn't have to worry about one of the men seeing or hearing him once he got away from the homestead.

Every man had his instructions, but they wouldn't need them. He would take care of what needed to be done before Lloyd or Kraemer or any of the others reached the Mitchel place. Not only was he protecting his precious granddaughters, but if this worked out right, he just might save his son from the risk of being shot. Lloyd was the important one from now on. This place and everyone on it needed him. He and Evie and all the grandkids were part of a future men like himself didn't belong to.

*A dying breed.* How many times had he heard that phrase?

He led Thunder out of the stall, then started to mount up when he heard the *click* of a gun.

"Where do you think you're going, Jake?"

Jake turned to see Cole standing in the next stall. He let out a deep sigh and mounted Thunder in spite of the fact that Cole held a gun on him. "Cole, you aren't going to use that gun on me, and you damn well know it." He guided Thunder out of the stall.

"Jake, what the hell do you think you're doing?" Cole repeated.

"You no doubt know *exactly* what I'm doing."

"You're makin' a big mistake."

Jake paused to light a cigarette. "I've always banked on the element of surprise, Cole. You know that. Whoever is at the Mitchel place is going to get the surprise of their lives. I promise to ask questions first and make sure nobody innocent dies, but you by-God know there isn't one innocent man there. Arriving in the dark hours of early morning is the best way to get onto that property without them knowing it."

"Goddamn it, Jake, don't do this! You promised your wife. And what about Lloyd?"

"I'm doing this *for* Lloyd. My son is a fine man who is needed right here. I'm not taking the chance of him getting hurt again. We almost lost him up in outlaw country and again in Denver. I'm not letting anything else happen to him. Just tell him and . . . " *Randy!* She lay upstairs in that bed they had shared too many times to count, loved him when he didn't deserve that love . . . "And Randy that I'll do all in my power to make it back here."

"It took you almost a whole year to get back from Mexico."

"Well, I'm not in Mexico, am I? I'll be half a day's ride away from here. If something goes wrong, all of you will find me easily enough, but I know what I'm doing, Cole, and I need you to help me by giving me a couple of hours start."

Cole lowered his gun. "Shit, Jake, Lloyd about beat the

hell out of me when I came back from Mexico without you. What do you think he'll do when he finds this out, and me knowin' you left? I could fire this gun right now, and every *J&L* man would come runnin' to stop you. Besides, you don't even know this has somethin' to do with the Mitchel place, and if it does, you ain't got no idea how many men you might be facin'."

"I *do* know the answer is at the Mitchel place. How many men are involved doesn't matter." Jake reached into his pocket and pulled out the note. "Some street kid handed this to me when I first arrived back at the train station in Denver. He ran off before I could catch him and find out who gave it to him."

Cole frowned and took the note.

"That right there tells me the Mitchel place *is* the place we have to go. It tells me a lot more than that, and it's the reason I have to do this alone."

Cole shoved his gun into its holster and walked over to the dim light of an oil lamp to read the note. Jake headed to the barn door as he read it. "Give me a couple of hours head start," Jake reminded Cole. "That's all I ask."

Cole finished reading the note. "Jesus," he muttered. He looked up to see Jake move through the door. "Jake! Wait!" He ran to the barn door, but Jake had already disappeared into the shadows beyond the oil lamps that hung outside.

"God help you, you crazy sonofabitch," he muttered. *Damn you, Jake! You made me leave you behind in Mexico. Now this.* He couldn't help the lump that formed in his throat as he shoved the note into his own pocket. He didn't need any explanations. Someone had threatened those two precious baby girls. He knew Jake Harkner real good, and that threat was all it took. The man had asked for a couple of hours head start, and when a determined Jake Harkner had a plan, it was more dangerous to mess up those plans than to just let him go. He'd seen the driven, out-for-blood Jake down in Mexico, and come hell or high water, the man was bent on protecting those little girls. When it came to something like that, common sense and self-protection flew right out the window. So did law and order, which in Jake's mind was entirely different from plain old justice.

# CHAPTER 42

Lloyd awoke to pounding on the front door. He hurriedly pulled on denim pants and rushed downstairs, grabbing a handgun on the way. "Who is it?"

"Gretta! Lloyd, you'd better come out to the barn. Your mother is in hysterics."

Lloyd opened the door.

"I brought Cole a cup of coffee, and the next thing I know, your mother's running into the barn looking for Jake. Cole says Jake rode out of here a good two hours ago!"

"*What*? What time is it now?"

"Four a.m. Randy is beside herself. She landed into Cole and socked him for letting Jake go. You'd better get out there."

Lloyd took off running.

"I already woke up the men at the bunkhouse," Gretta yelled. "I'll go get Evie!" Gretta headed for Evie's house, gripping her stomach. "Oh, my God, Jake," she muttered. "*Why*?"

Shirtless, Lloyd shoved his gun into the waist of his pants as he ran. Several ranch hands and Marshal Kraemer were already in the barn, looking amazed and not sure what to do.

"How could you let this happen?" he heard his mother scream at Cole as she stood there in a robe and bare feet, her hair down and a mess. "They'll *kill* him this time!" Cole reached out for her, but she pounded her fists against his chest and shoved at him, telling him not to touch her. "Why didn't you *stop* him?"

Lloyd handed his gun to Terrel and hurried over to grab his mother from behind, wrapping both arms around her.

"Mom, stop it!"

Randy tried to wiggle out of Lloyd's grasp. "He knew! He *knew*! He let your father ride off alone!" She kicked and fought. "You know what that means! He won't come back this time!"

Lloyd tightened his grip. "Calm down, damn it! If I hold you any tighter, I'll break a rib." He dragged her away from Cole, who bled from a split lip. "What the hell? Did my mother do that to you?" he asked Cole.

"She socked me a good one. I sure hope you don't intend to add to the bruises, Lloyd. You did enough damage to me when I came back from Mexico without your pa. I'm a little tired of gettin' beat up on by a Harkner."

Evie and Gretta rushed in, joined shortly by Jeff, pad and pencil in hand. Peter rushed in behind all of them, followed by Katie, who was still tying her robe and looked confused.

"Cole!" Gretta rushed over to her husband, while Evie and Katie hurried to help Lloyd with Randy.

"Mother, what's going on?" Evie asked.

"He left!" Panting, Randy burst into tears. "Your father left by himself." She struggled for breath. "Nobody knows who's out there waiting for him! He's *alone*! He's always been so alone!"

Lloyd kept a firm hold on her as he faced Cole. "What the hell did Jake tell you?"

Cole pressed his lip against his shirtsleeve. "It's like she said. Your pa came out here a couple of hours ago loaded up to kill fifty men. He gave me this note – said some street kid ran over and handed it to him back at the train station when he first arrived in Denver." Cole held out the piece of paper.

"Read it!" Lloyd asked, still hanging on to Randy.

Cole sighed and read the note loud enough for everybody to hear.

Randy seemed to wilt in Lloyd's arms like a dying flower. "Oh, my God," she lamented. She turned slightly and wept against his arm. "The girls! You know your father. That's all it took to get him to go there alone."

"Now I know why Jake was so concerned about those girls when he first got back," Terrel spoke up. "He told me to keep watch on them. I didn't quite understand why he brought that up, but now I know he already had that note."

"They want him bad," Cole said. "And they figured out how to get him."

Lloyd embraced his mother. "Mom, go back to the house with Evie and Katie. Let me and these men do what needs doing."

"It will be too late," Randy sobbed.

"Maybe not. Pa always does everything he can to come back – for you. You know that. He's never done something like this without a plan, and he's had a good three days to think about this."

Peter walked over to Lloyd and touched Randy's shoulder. "Come on, Randy. Let's get you back to the house. You know Jake. He's a smart man when it comes to situations like this. He'll think of something that gives him half a chance."

"Come on, mother," Evie told her. "We're wasting time. Lloyd and Marshal Kraemer have to go after daddy. I'll go back to the house with you, and we'll pray together."

Randy turned to her with a desperate wildness in her eyes Evie had never seen before. "He promised he wouldn't do something like this. How did he keep this from me? I always know what he's thinking."

"He fooled *all* of us," Lloyd told her, hanging on to her arm. "He knew how we would react."

Evie glanced at her brother, sharing a look with Lloyd that said, *We've lost our father.* She ran a hand over her mother's hair. "I'm sure daddy is so sorry he had to keep this from you," she told her, "but you know how stubborn he can be."

"I never should have taken that sleeping medicine," Randy sobbed. "I would have read his eyes, felt his distress. I might have been able to stop him."

"You ain't gonna' ever stop Jake Harkner once his mind is made up on somethin' like this," Cole told her. He looked at Lloyd. "I tried, but I would have had to shoot him to make him stay, Lloyd. He told me to give him a couple hours head start. That means he had at least some kind of plan that we might have messed up if we went out after him right away. One good thing is, we know exactly where we have to go, and God knows Jake has gone up against more than one man before and survived."

"But he has no idea how many men are there! There is only so much even a man like Jake can do." Randy looked up at Lloyd. "He took his mother's Crucifix. You know what that means."

Lloyd's heart fell a little more. Taking that cross was a sign Jake knew he just might be *meeting* the woman in another life before this was over. He always wore it for the most dangerous situations. Lloyd gave Randy a last, reassuring hug. "And he believes that Crucifix keeps him safe, mom, so don't look at this in such a bad light. Go on with Peter and the girls now."

Randy pressed a hand against the scar on Lloyd's chest, left from the bullet that had almost killed him back in Denver. "I can't lose both of you. I couldn't bear it. So don't be careless, Lloyd. Come home, and bring your father with you."

"I'll be fine. I have all these men behind me. Go on with you now."

Peter took hold of her arm. "Jake gave me orders once to take care of you when he couldn't," he said, "so lean on me and let's get you back to the house." *If all you do is keep her from going to her knees, that's all I ask.* Peter remembered Jake's remark. It was as though the man knew this was coming. "Come on, Randy." He kept a tight hold on her as they left with Evie.

Katie looked pleadingly at Lloyd. "Let Marshal Kraemer and the rest of the men do this with you, Lloyd. Jake wouldn't want you doing anything foolish because of him."

Lloyd struggled against the devastation he felt inside at knowing he might not see his father alive again. He put a hand to the side of her face. "I have plenty of help, and I have a great big family depending on me, so don't be worrying. Just go help my mother."

Katie grasped his wrist and kissed his palm. "I love you," she said softly before walking out. Lloyd faced the men. "Get loaded up. I'll go get a shirt on and get my things fast as I can. Pa is over half-way to the Mitchel place by now if nothing went wrong. By the time we get there, he'll damn well be needing our help." *If he isn't already dead by then.* He didn't need to say the words. He knew that same thought was on all their minds as they disbursed without comment. Terrel handed Lloyd's gun back to him before heading out the door.

"We'll be ready in less than ten minutes," he told Lloyd.

"Sure. Thanks." Lloyd called to Hal Kraemer as he, too, started to walk out.

Kraemer faced him, frowning. "I know what you're going to say, Lloyd."

"I'll say it anyway. Don't hold this against my father, Hal. It's bad enough that those men nearly killed Ben and young Jake, but to threaten little six and seven-year-old girls? You know what just the thought of that does to a man like Jake. And at the moment, I'm right with him in a desire to permanently remove any sonofabitch who would even *consider* harming such innocence, especially when one of those girls is my own daughter, let alone my *sister's* little girl!"

Kraemer rubbed at tired eyes. "I don't know if that judge back in Denver will understand, but I'll do my best to *make* him understand. The bad part is, it might not matter, because Jake might not live through this one." Kraemer turned away and headed for the bunkhouse.

"I already have my horse and gear ready," Cole told Lloyd. "I'll saddle Cinnamon for you."

"Thanks."

"I'm damned sorry, Lloyd. I was just about to come for you when your mother came chargin' out here lit like a stick of dynamite. I just let her pound on me. How in hell could I stop her without hurtin' her?"

Lloyd grinned sadly. "It's probably my pa she'd like to beat on right now. I'm sure she's sorry for hitting you, and if my father survives this, he'll have one angry wife to deal with." He turned away, his heart heavy.

Note pad still in hand, Jeff walked over to Cole as soon

as Lloyd left. "Cole, what's your gut feeling about Jake making it through this?"

Cole ran a hand through his hair. "I'm tryin' to think good thoughts, Jeff, but I'm feelin' kind of sick – know what I mean? I love that man. After what we went through in Mexico, I was hopin' nothin' like this would ever happen again."

Jeff's eyes teared, and he turned away. "I enjoy writing about Jake, but I sure didn't bank on something like this." He took a deep breath and quickly wiped at his eyes. "If we find him dead, I don't even like to *think* about what that will do to Randy and the rest of the family."

Cole walked to the stall where Lloyd's horse was kept. "Jake's family ain't the only ones who would grieve that man's death, as you well know, Jeff. I've already been through thinkin' he was dead when he didn't make it back from Mexico for so long. I felt guilty for that, and now I feel guilty again."

"You did what Jake asked you to do. There is nothing wrong in that .God knows I know what that man is like once his mind is made up. I remember that from when I rode with him back in Oklahoma. You just have to mount up and hang on and hope you can keep up with him."

Cole wiped at his eyes. "That's a fact. I just wish Brian or that Doctor Beemer could go with us. I have a gut feelin' Jake will be needin' both of them."

Jeff sighed. "Ben isn't out of the woods yet. Beemer needs to stay here, and you know Brian wouldn't want to leave his son. Young Jake could take a turn for the worse, too. Jake would want Brian to be here for the boy, and for Evie. We just have to hope that whatever happens, Jake can get back here for help. Maybe he won't get hurt at all."

Cole snickered and shook his head. "You know that's not likely. You might end up writing the boldest headline you ever had to write, Jeff, and you know what I mean."

Jeff walked to the stall that held the horse he'd been told he could ride. "Yeah," he said quietly. He shoved his notebook and pencil into his supply pack. He wouldn't be carrying a gun. It wasn't necessary, what with the rest of the men armed. Even that probably wouldn't matter. Once Jake was done with the men he was after, *nobody* would need a gun.

# CHAPTER 43

Jake made his way east for several miles before turning north. He figured that whoever was at the Mitchel place expected him to come barreling in from the south, a suicide approach. This way would take a little longer, but surprise was better than speed, and the landscape here was familiar to him. The east side of the Mitchel place sloped outward from the mountains, thrusting into the high plains like toes from a foot. The area was wild, still unsettled land—the kind of country no one wanted to claim because it was too dry and rocky, far from the best grazing land and not much good for farming. Last spring he and Vance had tracked stray J&L cattle into this area.

He was surprised when Thunder's hooves made a light splashing sound. The narrow arroyo through here should be dry this time of year, but he remembered one of the men mentioning a pretty severe thunderstorm had hit the J&L just a few days ago. It must have been enough to temporarily feed a mountain runoff. Such things were unpredictable in these foothills.

He'd ridden hard off and on, preserving Thunder's long-distance ability as best he could without losing too much time. He'd already made it to the eastern entrance to the Mitchel property and headed into a continuing wind that swept down off the mountains and into his face with a slight groaning sound to it. He felt blessed by the wind. It was blowing away from his target, which meant that the horses there wouldn't smell him or Thunder approaching, and the sound of Thunder's hooves wouldn't likely be heard.

The sun wasn't fully up yet when he came upon a wooden fence he guessed had to belong to the Mitchel homestead. The eastern sky was now pink, with just a hint of light from a sun that would soon light up the mountains.

He slowed Thunder and dismounted, walking the horse past an empty corral and to a second line of fences from where he could see the dim outline of a house in the distance, and some out-buildings between the house and the corral. Men could be anywhere now, and he needed to make sure those inside the buildings were the right target.

*The girls. Think about those girls.* That part of him that had learned the lesson of patience and doing things the legal way over these many years struggled in his heart and head against that part of him that could not abide an innocent child being abused, or even threatened. It was the reason he'd nearly beat Ben's father to death, the reason he'd risked his life to save Evie and his beloved Randy, the reason he'd gone to Mexico . . . and the reason he'd killed his own father for raping Santana. These men had bushwhacked young boys, then threatened two sweet, trusting, innocent little girls who depended on their grandpa to keep them safe. That was his job, wasn't it? It was his fault they were threatened, so it was up to him to do something about it.

He tied Thunder to the fence, then slung his extra ammo belt across his chest and pulled a shotgun from his saddle. He grabbed four extra shotgun shells from his saddlebags and shoved them into his pants pocket, then hooked his hat around his saddle horn. Its wide brim might show up too well. He leaned over and climbed through the fence, then headed on foot toward a distant, dim light, carefully making his way amid some grazing cattle in yet another holding area. *Probably stolen,* he thought. He quietly patted their rumps and moved slowly so as not to startle them.

When the sun rose a bit higher, he hid behind a big steer that paid no attention to him when he leaned on its back and took a moment to scan the scene before him.

One man sat on a fence rail several yards ahead, his back to the east. Looking around, Jake realized the corral held only steers—no bulls or cows. Apparently, they'd just been moved here for grazing because the grass was still thick and high. That was good. The grass muffled his footsteps.

He moved with stealth among the steers, which paid him no attention and kept grazing. He could hear the man on the fence humming a tune, and as he snuck even closer, he smelled whiskey.

*Whiskey in the morning. Good.* Jake wondered how many men would have lived longer if they'd just laid off the damn whiskey that dulled their brains and made them careless. Laying down his shotgun, he pulled a Bowie knife from its sheath at his side and leapt forward, grabbing the fence-sitter from behind and clamping a hand over his mouth. He yanked the surprised drunk to the ground, throwing him onto his back and putting a knee into his chest. He held the knife under the man's nose and leaned close, keeping his voice down. "If you yell, I'll carve you up like a fucking pig to slaughter, understand?"

The man nodded vigorously. Jake pressed the knife against the man's upper lip as he reached down with his other hand and yanked the man's gun from its holster. He threw it aside, then ripped off the man's hat and tossed it into the darkness. "Get up! Walk to the far side of this corral. One wrong move and I'll sink this knife into your liver!"

He moved off the man and quickly picked up his shotgun, using it to give the man a shove. The man stumbled among the cattle to the darker side of the corral. Jake returned his knife to its sheath and hit the man's left arm with his shotgun. "Turn around!"

The man turned, swallowing as he faced Jake, who was much taller than he. Jake couldn't see his face clearly, but he was brawny, and the dim morning light lit him up enough to show a head of messy hair that hung to the man's shoulders. Jake shoved him hard against the fence rail and held him there with the shotgun.

"I don't think I need to tell you what this shotgun would do to you at close range, mister, but I don't want to kill you, understand?" Jake spoke in a near whisper. "I just want some questions answered. And keep it *quiet!* Who are you?"

The man looked down wide-eyed at the barrel of the shotgun resting against the middle of his chest. "Name's Larry Banks. I'm just a drifter . . . came here to work."

"And you're a *liar!*" Jake shoved the shotgun harder. "You came here to get a chance at killing Jake Harkner. Right?"

Banks swallowed. "Y . . . you . . . you're him, ain't you?"

"You bet your ass I am! Tell me who shot my son and grandson—and who else is on this property!"

"Please don't kill me, Harkner. I know you reputation, but I don't wanna' die. I came along after the fact – just lookin' for work. That's the God's truth. I *swear!* I stayed on just to see what would happen if you did come along. I ain't got nothin' against you personal. And I didn't have *nothin'* to do with hurtin' those boys. May God strike me dead!"

"I want names," Jake growled, "and *numbers*. How many men am I up against?" He pulled back the hammers on the shotgun.

"Eleven, if I'm thinkin' straight – twelve countin' me," Banks quickly whimpered. "One's a true gunman, name of Buck Potter. So's his friend, a trigger-happy kid named Lenny. He's the one who shot at your boy and your grandson. That's how they tell it. As God is my witness, mister, I wasn't even here then. I wouldn't have agreed to somethin' like that. Buck figured it was the best way to bring you here. Him and Lenny are the ones you *really* want."

"I want *all* of the men lying in wait for me! Who else is over there?"

"Bearded guy called Grizzly. And some man who hates you and your son Lloyd, name of Brady Fillmore. They ain't much good with guns, but Buck is. He's from outlaw country. So is Lenny. I think they are both in the house. There's some fancy guy from New Orleans in there with them, too, name of Kyle Pendergrass. The other gunman's named Frosty James. I – I think he's in the bunkhouse. Fillmore might be there, too."

"That's seven, counting you. Tell me all of it!" Jake shoved the shotgun hard again.

"Please don't," Banks begged. "I've got a wife and kid in Greely. I work . . . all over . . . take money to the family when I can."

"Working for men who will shoot kids doesn't say much about you, Mister." Their conversation continued in a hoarse whisper.

"I didn't know! I didn't know they would do that! It was all Buck's idea to shoot those boys! I *swear*!"

"My son lost an *arm*!"

"Oh, Jesus, I'm sorry! I'm sorry!" Banks told him, starting to cry. "Damn it, Harkner, I didn't know what I was gettin' into!"

"Name the rest of them!"

"An Indian called Hawk. Couple of Mexicans—Julio and Benito—just cowboys. A little short guy they call Stumpy. I think two or three of 'em are in the bunkhouse – maybe a couple keepin' watch closer to the house. The rest are in the house."

"Any women?"

"Yeah. A whore from Denver. Stella Flynn."

*Why am I not surprised?* "Anybody else?"

"A—Ainsley. Chet Ainsley . . . from the *Double T*."

*Ainsley!* That little bastard would regret this.

"What happened to the Mitchels?"

"I – I just noticed you're wearin' a badge. You a lawman again?" Banks grunted when Jake rammed the shotgun hard against his breastbone.

"Answer my question!"

Banks swallowed and actually started crying. "I didn't have nothin' to do with that either!" he sobbed. "I swear!"

"What happened to them?"

"Buck and Lenny . . . they killed 'em . . .buried them out behind the barn."

"The whole *family*?"

Banks cringed. "Please, mister! *Please* don't kill me! I've gave you lots of information. When I found out what really happened – " He sniffed and jerked in another sob. "I wanted to leave. So did that there Brady Fillmore. But Buck and Lenny, and that there Kyle and the bearded guy – Grizzly – they swore they'd kill anybody who tried to leave. Fillmore – he's the one who hired them – up in outlaw country, but I know he regrets it. You – you – you know what men like that are like. You was one once yourself, weren't ya? You know they mean it when they threaten to kill you."

"I never hurt or killed a *woman!* Or a *kid!* I ought to blow your head off!"

"I *told* you!" Banks wept. "I had nothin' to do with *any* of it. I came along afterward, and they wouldn't let me leave. Please! I've got a *family!*"

Jake backed away and ordered Banks over to where Thunder was tied. Banks obeyed, nearly collapsing from wobbly legs.

"Take the rope off my horse," Jake ordered. "And if you want to live, stay quiet!" He noticed the eastern sky was getting slightly lighter. He had to move fast once he took care of Banks.

With a shaking hand, Banks took a rope off Thunder's saddle. Jake ordered him to sit down against a fence post. "Put your arms around behind you," he told Banks. "Wrap them around the fence post."

Banks did as Jake asked, his nose running and tears still streaming down his face. He hunched his shoulder to wipe his nose on his shirt. Jake eased the shotgun hammers back into place and laid the gun aside. He tied Banks's wrists tightly behind the fence post, then wrapped the rest of the rope around the man's body and to the post. He jerked hard, making the man whimper again. "I can't hardly breathe," Banks complained.

"Be fucking glad you *are* breathing!"

"You mean you're gonna' . . . let me live?" Banks asked. "You ain't gonna' slit my throat or somethin'?"

"It's against my better judgment, but I read a man's eyes pretty good, and I think you got caught up in something you didn't really plan on turning out this way."

"I did! I did! Thank you!"

"Keep your voice down!" Jake jerked hard and finished tying him.

"Y – yes, Sir. And you ought to know that most of the men are sleepin' off a drunk in the cabin. That should give you an edge. Might be one or two out by the barn keepin' watch, but since no cattlemen or the law came right away after those boys was shot, we figured the marshal and some J&L men was makin' some kind of plans—that you would come with a whole posse, by daylight – and from the south."

"Well, you and the rest of them figured *wrong*! That's what I'm banking on."

"Brady figured nobody could prove they had anything to do with shootin' them boys. They'd send the marshal lookin' someplace else, but they'd keep goadin' you 'til you came for them by yourself. If you was the one to come for them, you'd be the guilty one, and they would have the *right* to shoot you down."

Jake knelt beside Banks. "Well, Banks, stupid men make stupid decisions, and you and those men over there just proved that. I'm leaving you for the law to find. You make sure they know I could have killed you, but I didn't. Believe me, there was a time in my life when I *would* have, without even asking questions. J&L men will come along in an hour or two. Your only hope to stay out of prison is to tell the truth about what you know."

Banks nodded vigorously again. "I will! I will!"

"Yeah, well, I need some insurance that for now you won't holler out a warning to those men over there." Jake untied the man's neckerchief and stuffed it into his mouth, then untied his own and tied it around Banks's mouth, pulling tightly and tying the ends around the fence post so Banks was gagged, and his head was held against the post. He stood up. "You were right about that posse riding in from the south, Banks, but by the time they get here, I'll have already done their work for them. For now, count your *blessings*."

He walked over and picked up his shotgun, then untied Thunder. Banks watched as horse and man disappeared into a stand of trees beyond the corral.

Brady Fillmore stretched in his bunk and realized he had to pee. He sat up, rubbing his eyes, then squinted to see a clock on the wall across from his bed. He sensed it was dawn, but when he looked out the window, he saw that only the top rim of the sun was beginning to show. He thought he saw the figure of a man walking toward the bunkhouse and figured it must be Larry Banks coming in. That meant it was his turn to go sit on the east fence. "Shit," he muttered. He wanted to pee and go back to sleep.

He ducked out of his bunk and stood up, stretching again. It was plenty warm out, so he figured he could trot out to the privy in his bare feet. He walked closer to the wall clock to see it was only five-thirty. He ran a hand through his hair, then turned up a lantern in the corner for a better view. He headed for the door then, but it suddenly burst open.

Brady jumped back, wide-eyed. There stood a tall man who was armed to the teeth and holding a shotgun.

"*Jake!*"

## CHAPTER 44

All hell broke loose in the bunkhouse, so newly built that it still smelled of fresh pine. Three more men leapt from their bunks, two of them reaching for guns that hung in belts draped over the bed posts. The gun belonging to the third hung on the wall, and he couldn't get to it in time.

Jake's shotgun boomed, hitting one man who'd grabbed his gun. His body sailed backward, over a table and onto an empty bunk. Jake fired the other barrel at the second man who'd already raised his gun to shoot Jake. That man's gun fired as he went down, winging Jake in the left arm. Jake grunted and stumbled backward from the impact, and at the same time, the second man's bloodied body hit the wall and slid down, leaving a massive blood stain. Brady Fillmore and the fourth man stood frozen and staring, wide-wide with shock and fear.

"Jake, I – "

"Shut the fuck up!" Jake growled at Fillmore. "I already know what went on here and who is responsible! You mess around with men like that Buck and the one called Lenny, you mess with *death*, Fillmore!" Jake struggled to keep his senses as the pain in his arm worsened.

"I didn't want any of this, Jake," Fillmore whined. "I – I'll help you! Let me have a gun and I'll back you up."

"Like *hell* you will!" The words came from the fourth man, who by then had grabbed his gun from a holster that hung on the wall. He fired it at Brady and Brady fell to the floor, screaming about his knee.

"You traitor!" the fourth man yelled. "Buck shoulda' let Lenny kill you!" The shootist turned on Jake, raising his gun. By then Jake had tossed his shotgun and pulled one of his .44's. It was aimed straight at the fourth man's forehead.

"Go ahead!" Jake urged the fourth man. "Try getting off a shot before I can blow your head off!"

"What the fuck?" the fourth muttered. He was a short, stubby man with a graying beard and mustache. "Who the hell are you?" he asked, staring at Jake in disbelief.

"I'm your worst *nightmare!*" Jake growled. He walked up to the man and slammed the .44 across the side of the man's head. He heard a distinct cracking sound when he did so. The man grunted and landed against a top bunk, then fell to the floor, his head bleeding profusely. Brady Fillmore still lay on the floor holding his knee and crying with pain.

"Jake – don't shoot me! Please! Get me some help!"

"Why would I help you, you murdering, baby-raping sonofabitch! You'll answer to a whole posse when they get here! Let *them* help you! In the meantime, you can lay there and *suffer!*" Jake holstered his .44 and hurriedly picked up his shotgun, breaking it open and quickly re-loading. "Who are those other three men?"

"The old one – that's Frosty James," Brady answered, panting. "The man you clobbered was called Stumpy – just an old cowboy. The first man was called Julio."

*Good. Four down and seven to go.* Jake slammed shut the shotgun. "You never learn, do you, Fillmore? I gave you a chance once when I kept my son from *hanging* you! And then you came along and threatened me when I had my little granddaughters along! You *still* haven't learned your lesson! Now you're part of a plan to kill me, which included trying to kill my son and grandson and threatening two innocent little girls!"

"None of that was my doing!"

"You're the one who hired the men who *did* do those things! You're just as guilty!" Jake walked up and held the barrel of the shotgun to Fillmore's head. "Time was, I'd make your head disappear!" he growled. "I'd gladly do it if you were aiming a gun at me!" He grabbed up Frosty's handgun and dropped it next to Brady. "Go ahead. *Use* it! Give me an excuse to blow your fucking brains out!"

Fillmore curled into a fetal position. "N – no. I won't do it!" He began crying like a child.

"You worthless piece of cow shit!" Jake grabbed the extra six gun and threw it across the room. He heard footsteps then, someone running. Two men reached the bunkhouse door and Jake whirled, letting loose with both barrels. The first man flew completely out of the doorway and the second man cried out. "My eye! My eye!" He ran, yelling all the way. "Jesus Christ, I think it's Harkner! He blew Hawk's head off! Stay in the cabin!"

"Shoot him, Ainsley!" another man shouted from farther away.

So, he'd wounded Chet Ainsley, the damn fool.

"*You* shoot him!" Ainsley yelled back. His voice faded as he kept running. "Some of those shotgun pellets hit me in the eye!"

Jake couldn't be sure just where the man had run, but most likely it was to the cabin for protection.

"It *can't* be Harkner out there!" someone else yelled. "How would he get here in the dark, and without us hearing him?"

Jake darted to the doorway and waited a moment, his back against the wall where no one at the house could see him. He glanced down to see someone lying on the ground with most of his face missing. The only thing distinctive was his long, black hair. *The Indian*, Jake figured. *The one called Hawk. Five down, and one gravely wounded.*

"You . . . fucking . . . bastard," Brady wept.

"You brought this on yourself, Fillmore, and I'm not the one who shot you! I'd gladly blow you in half right now, but the thought of you crippled and rotting in prison is just as pleasing." Jake tossed the shotgun aside again. It would be no good for distance, especially not for shooting at men through the cabin windows. From now on he would depend on his .44's. He drew one and darted outside, jumping over the faceless dead man.

Immediately, shots rang out from the cabin. Bullets whizzed past, one skimming across his right cheek. He ducked and rolled, moving behind a nearby privy so he could take a moment to study his surroundings. He winced from the added pain. He figured he might not get out of this alive, but he would do enough damage that no one who came along later would be in any danger.

*How many down? Four in the bunkhouse, the one called Hawk at the bunkhouse door, Larry Banks still tied out in the corral . . .*

That left six at the cabin—plus the woman. He didn't trust Stella Flynn any more than he trusted the men, but he wasn't all that worried about her. And Chet Ainsley was probably squirming in a corner somewhere crying about his wounded eye. He'd be no threat.

"Go get him, Buck!" someone shouted from inside the cabin.

"*Fuck* that," someone else yelled. "I think Harkner is

wounded! You couldn't ask for a better time to take him down! Jake Harkner is *mine!*"

"Have at it, boys," Jake muttered. *Go ahead and argue over who will have the glory of killing me. I might go down, but I'll have a real good time killing every one of you before I hit dirt.* He noticed movement near an unfinished barn behind the cabin.

*The barn those innocent boys were helping build.* Jake's left arm stung like hell, and he could feel blood pouring down over his wrist, as well as more blood running off his cheek and down his neck. He forced himself to concentrate.

"By God, Lloyd, I sure could use you right now." Someone was over by that barn. He'd have to keep an eye open for him.

*I've got your back, pa.*

It was as though Lloyd was right here beside him. How many times, back in Oklahoma, had Lloyd told him he had him covered? Too many to count.

"Let Lenny take him," someone inside the house argued loudly. "He's supposed to be the fastest."

"Not faster than *me!*" someone answered. Jake figured it was either Buck or the one called Kyle. He realized he had a better chance to get out of this alive if he faced the gunmen out in the open, rather than trying to make it to the barn or up to the cabin without getting shot. They were the ones with cover. He had nothing once he left the protection of the privy. The men inside were arguing over who'd be famous from this, so he figured maybe he could work on their egos.

"You men in there want the reputation of killing me? Come on out here and face me like *men,*" he yelled. "Ganging up won't bring you any glory. It only shows what cowards you really are!"

He heard voices but couldn't make out all they were saying.

"Go ahead and kill them all, Jake!" a woman's voice rang out. "Then come on in here, and we'll have a good fuck to celebrate."

Jake heard a slap. "Shut up, bitch!"

"That you, Ainsley?" Jake shouted. "I know you're in there. When I kill the others, you'll be next, and I won't just shoot your holster off or shoot your eye out next time. I'll aim for something more important, and you won't be fucking any more women when I'm done."

"You're a goddamn murderer, Harkner!" Ainsley screamed. "You know I can't fight it out with you! I can hardly see, you bastard! People think you ain't no outlaw anymore, but you've got 'em all fooled! Once an outlaw, *always* an outlaw!"

Just as Jake figured, a man stuck his head out from around a back corner of the cabin again. If Ainsley kept talking, that man would be distracted.

Ainsley obliged.

"I seen you at that cookout, Harkner," he goaded. "Dressed all fancy and dancin' with that woman you call your wife. I'm bettin' you never legally married her. Men like you don't get married. They just fuck women for free. You met her in a saloon, just like all them other whores you ran with, didn't you? I'll bet you'd like to kill all of us and spend the rest of the day with *Stella*, then go home to your supposed wife and fuck her, too."

Jake fired. The man at the corner of the cabin fell.

Now he was down to five.

"Shit!" someone swore. "He got Kyle."

*So, just two of the five left are gunmen,* Jake thought. *Buck and Lenny.* "The two of you who think you can take me, come on out," he yelled. "I already know your names! Buck and Lenny! You're the ones who think you can take me, so come on out and do it!"

"I seen you're bleedin'," one of the men yelled back. "You ain't in no shape to take either one of us, Harkner!"

"Come out here and find out! I'll face you both at the same time. That'll give you an even better advantage." He heard arguing from inside the cabin.

"You're a murderin' sonofabitch," one shouted back, "We don't believe you'll fight fair! You'll shoot us soon as we walk out of here!"

"When it comes to facing a man in the open, I'm *always* fair," Jake yelled in return. He winced with pain and felt himself growing weaker from loss of blood. *Think of the girls,* he told himself again. "I'm giving you a chance to claim you killed Jake Harkner in a gunfight," he shouted. "That's what you want, isn't it?"

Everything quieted for a moment.

"All right, we're comin' out! It's Buck Potter and Lenny McCarthy! Ever hear of us?"

"Hell no! But it's been a long time since I rode in Outlaw Country."

"A long time is right, old man. You're slower and rustier now. And you're *wounded!*"

Jake could tell the voice came from a younger man. *Must be the one called Lenny.* "Come on out and put me to the test!" he dared them. "Keep your hands in the air on the way out. I won't shoot 'til it's a fair fight! I'll put my hands up, too. You have my word."

"We're supposed to trust that?"

"My word based on my reputation," Jake answered.

"That sure as hell don't say much!" the young one shouted. "Your reputation ain't worth a shit!"

"It is when it comes to using guns! I've never double crossed any man who faces me honestly. Do you want the fame you'll get for killing me in a fair gunfight, or not?"

He heard more arguing. Finally, someone yelled out the

window again. "All right! We're comin' out the front door. This is your last day alive, Harkner!"

Jake waited. Finally, two men walked around the corner from the front of the house. They wore only long johns and gun belts. The younger one wore two revolvers. The other, who surely was Buck, wore one gun. He looked middle-aged, and his sandy hair stuck out in all directions, a man who'd obviously been rudely disturbed from a whiskey sleep, Jake figured. The man grinned, his teeth protruding in obvious misalignment. Both men had their hands in the air.

Jake removed his extra gun belt from around his chest and tossed it, then stepped from behind the privy, his own guns holstered. He raised his hands.

Buck grinned. "I'll be goddamned. You're wearin' a badge."

"I asked to be deputized, so I could *legally* shoot you."

"Did you kill the rest of the men?"

"You don't see any of them walking around, do you?"

Buck glanced over at Hawk, whose brains lay in the grass. "You're one murderin' sonofabitch, ain't you? Jesus Christ, don't you ever aim to just *wound* somebody?"

"Occasionally, but not when that somebody deliberately hurts someone in my family. And I might be a murdering sonofabitch, but I don't shoot *boys*! You're the one who shot my son and my grandson, aren't you?"

"You bet I did," Buck sneered. "At least one of 'em. I ain't sure which one. Lenny here shot the man and the other kid – big kid with blond hair. Which one is he, Jake? Son? Or grandson?"

"Makes no difference. They're both mine, and you will regret you ever pulled a trigger on either one of them!"

"You won't live to *say who* did it, Harkner. You're old and your wounded. Me and Lenny here are fast as lightning, and I see from the blood on your arm and streamin' down your face that you've lost enough to be getting' weaker."

"I've been hurt before. It never stopped me. And before I'm done, I'll make sure Lenny there loses an arm, like my *son* did. And just to make sure it's self-defense, I'm going to let you draw first."

Jake had hardly got the words out before both men went for their guns, Lenny drawing both of his at the same time.

Two or three seconds. That's all it took. Jake drew and fired both .44's before either man could get off a shot. The *booms* echoed against the nearby mountains. He kept firing, hitting Buck three times in the gut and chest, but shooting Lenny in the knees. He didn't want him dead yet.

Buck died instantly. Lenny stared wide-eyed and turned to his side, trying to pull himself with his arms to where he'd dropped his guns.

Jake walked straight up to him and kicked both guns away. "Look up here at me, Lenny," he growled.

Lenny rolled onto his back. "You won, Harkner," he groaned. "You have to . . . let me go."

"*Do* I?" Jake stepped on the wrist of Lenny's outstretched right arm and emptied the rest of the bullets from both his .44's, into the man's elbow, separating his lower arm from the upper. Lenny screamed the word "No!" through all of it.

"My God! My God!" he cried when the firing stopped.

"You'll be dead before too long." Jake holstered one .44 and began reloading. "Then the pain will be over."

"Kill me now!" Lenny begged.

Jake grinned. "I'm enjoying the sound of your screams too much." He realized his darkest side had finally taken over, but figured he was slowly dying anyway, so what did it matter?

*Come back to me.* This time it was Randy who spoke to him.

"I'm so fucking sorry, Randy," he muttered.

The sound of a horse galloping off to the south pulled his gaze in that direction. The horse carried one man and a naked woman. Whichever man had chosen to run, Stella had fled with him.

No matter. The law would catch up with them. He started for the house when a shot rang out. A bullet brushed across Jake's right shoulder, just enough for him to feel its power. He whirled and fell. He'd been so bent on making Lenny suffer that he'd ignored the fact that two men were still inside the house. He struggled to remember.

Grizzly Smith! And Ainsley! He rolled to his knees and managed to stand up. Bullets flew as he ran to a broken-down wagon.

"You're *dead*, Harkner," someone yelled from inside. "All you have to do is come through the door."

The voice was hoarse and scratchy.

*Grizzly!*

"I'll come through that door, all right," Jake muttered softly. He pulled the spare .45 he always carried at his back, and with that and his re-loaded .44, he ducked his way around the wagon and charged up the cabin steps. He kicked the door open, barging inside without even knowing where the two men were. Both his guns blazed away, until one man screamed. "You bastard!"

Jake fired in the direction of the man's voice, then heard something fall to the floor. In his pain and loss of blood, Jake couldn't make out the man's face clearly, but he figured it must be Ainsley. He could tell the man's face was a mess, and it was Ainsley he'd wounded in the eye when he shot Hawk.

*That leaves Grizzly Smith*, he thought, hoping he'd

counted right. He waited for the room to clear of gun smoke, his vision scrambled from blood pouring down his cheek and from pain in both his shoulder and his left arm, which was throbbing worse now.

"Come on out of that bedroom, Smith," he demanded. "I know you're in there!"

"Promise you won't shoot," Grizzly begged. "My gun jammed! I'm helpless. Just let them arrest me."

Jake cocked his .45. "Let me see you walk out unarmed."

The cabin hung quiet for a moment.

"You're a fuckin' madman, Jake Harkner! I don't believe you won't shoot me."

"I damn well *will* shoot you if you don't give up your gun and come out of there, *now*! Your chances are better if you do what I tell you."

More silence.

"Ok. I'm comin' out."

"Arms in the air," Jake ordered. "No gun!"

"Ok, Ok!" Grizzly showed his left hand and left leg, then suddenly bolted from the bedroom, firing wildly.

Jake felt a jolt to his chest. It sent him against the wall. Then came another slam to his chest - then a penetrating pain in his lower left side. He fired two shots in return before his own wounds overwhelmed his strength and senses. He saw blood on Grizzly's chest, watched him lurch backward into the bedroom before going down.

Again, all was quiet. An ugly blackness moved through Jake's body, as though fire was in his blood.

"Randy," he whispered. He shoved the .45 into the front of his gun belt and put his .44 into his second holster. He managed to get to his feet, then stumbled outside, knowing all too well how badly he was wounded. He figured he might have enough blood and energy left to get to Thunder. The horse was tied behind the bunkhouse.

He staggered out the door and made his way in that direction, falling twice, getting up twice.

*Randy!* He'd promised he'd come back. His head began to reel, his thoughts a tumble of visions—dead men lying everywhere. Was Lloyd involved in this? No. And now he wouldn't be. His son would be okay, and that's all that mattered.

*Ben!* Poor Ben had lost his arm. And Randy. He had to get back to Randy. But maybe that wasn't possible now. It was then he saw his mother standing near his horse, holding his little brother's hand.

"*Madre! Hermann!*" he mumbled. *She wasn't dead after all. And there was little Tommy! He was only eight years old the last time he saw Tommy. Why hadn't he aged? And his mother, still so young and beautiful.*

But no. They *were* dead, and he'd been forced to help bury them. Jake could hear his father screaming at him to get the shovel. He could feel the sting of the man's belt. He remembered trying to wake up his mother. *Don't leave me!* Maybe now that's why he clung to Randy the way he did. *Don't leave me! You're all I have.*

He tried to reach his mother. He had to help his her . . . help his poor little brother. He tripped and fell, got up again. He had to get to them before his father killed them. He was grown now. He could stop him.

*Go home to your family, son,* his mother told him. *Tommy and I are well and happy.*

No! He had to protect his mother, but there she and Tommy stood, beautiful and smiling. *I can help you now, madre.*

*Esta vez no, mi hijo. Algundia estaremos juntos. Ve ahora en felicidad. Que dios te bendiga.*

*Not this time?* She'd told him. Was he not supposed to die? *Someday we will be together. Go now in happiness. God bless you.*

But . . . he had to help them. He started toward them again, but they faded away. He fought to keep his senses long enough to reach Thunder. His mother had said "not now." But the pain! How was he supposed to live through this? He *wanted* to die. It was time. He put a hand to his chest, where his mother's Crucifix lay close to his heart. Hot. It felt burning hot.

"Randy," he muttered again. He couldn't die without seeing her once more. *Then* he would let go of this life called Hell.

He found Thunder and grabbed the fence rail to steady himself as blackness came over him in waves. Fumbling, he untied the horse. Then, with all the effort he could muster, got his left foot into the stirrup and managed to mount the horse. As soon as he did, he saw his blood on Thunder's mane.

*Thank God, I'm the only one hurt.* Lloyd and the rest of the men would be okay.

Now he just had to get home . . . to Randy . . . to young Jake and Ben.

He was supposed to take Ben hunting. Elk season would be here soon, and those beautiful beasts would be roaming around the ranch like they owned it. The family always stood on the veranda and just watched the elk graze, knowing there wasn't a damn thing humans could do about it. It was time to come down to the grasslands and fatten up for winter. The thought made him smile.

He leaned forward and grabbed the reins. "Go home, boy," he groaned.

All stray horses eventually found their way home, didn't they?

Taking the same pathway Jake had used to come there, Thunder headed east first instead of south. Somewhere in the back of his mind Jake reasoned that Lloyd and the others would be coming in straight from the south.

Thunder was going in the wrong direction, but he didn't have the strength to guide the horse.

Too much blood. He felt it soaking his shirt. His vest. His saddle. Thunder's mane. He thought he saw some drip onto the ground as Thunder kept heading east.

Suddenly, he saw a bright light. He felt warm, and, strangely, he felt no pain. Just warmth. And a flood of love unlike anything he'd ever known before. Was it his mother again? Had she come for him after all? *Is this what it's like, Evie? Is this what Heaven is like?*

*But that couldn't be. God would never accept a man like him into a place like Heaven.* Only Satan would want a man who'd had killed his own father. That was such a long time ago, but it felt like yesterday. He wanted to weep at the thought that he could never make it to Heaven, because that meant he would never see Randy again . . . or Evie . . . or his grandchildren someday.

He touched the Crucifix. It wasn't quite so hot now.

"Randy. *Lo siento, favor perdoname, mi querida esposa.*"

# CHAPTER 45

Cole and Lloyd walked around the small house, its floor covered with bullet shells and tumbled furniture. "That looks like that Ainsley fella' from the cookout," Cole said rather absently as he studied one man lying in a corner.

"Grizzly Smith's here in the bedroom, all shot up," Vance called.

"Jesus Christ, where's my father?" Lloyd studied the wall beside the front door. "Look here! Somebody's been shot by those men over there. It put him against the wall. Look at all the blood, but there's no body. This man somehow killed those other two, even after they shot him." He looked at Cole.

"Sounds like somethin' Jake would do," Cole said sadly.

Lloyd kicked the table over. "*Fuck*!" he roared. "God damn it, pa, where are you?" He studied the wall again, then bloodstains that left a trail out the door. "He made it outside," he told Cole and Vance. "Help me find him!"

All three men traced blood stains through the door and onto the porch, then on down the steps.

Cole shook his head. There was simply too much blood

for whoever this was to survive. Even a man Jake's size couldn't lose that much blood, could he? He watched Lloyd storm away, screaming for the others to find Jake. *They don't need to find Jake,* Cole thought. *I'm watching him right now, Lloyd – the build, the looks, and most of all, that intimidating temper. Jake Harkner ain't never gonna' die as long as you're around.*

Lloyd charged up to two men who were searching what was left of other bodies. "To hell with these murdering bastards!" he shouted. "Find my *father*! I think he's hurt bad! Search the barn and outbuildings!"

"His extra cartridge belt is over here," Charlie yelled from near the privy. "And there's two more dead men over here. Looks like they died in a regular gun fight. Maybe Jake against both of them."

"There's one over here by the bunkhouse," Terrel shouted. "His head's mostly blown off!"

Jeff stumbled out of the bunkhouse and vomited. "There's three bodies in there – and a man who says he's Brady Fillmore! He's still alive – shot in the knee!"

Lloyd ran to the bunkhouse and leapt over Hawk's nearly-headless body as though it didn't bother him in the least. He lunged inside the bunkhouse Seconds later a man started screaming. "No, Lloyd! Don't move me! I can't stand it!"

In the next moment Lloyd was dragging Brady Fillmore out of the bunkhouse. He threw him down on the grass. "Where's my *father*!"

"I don't know! I don't know!" Fillmore answered, his face stained from earlier tears. "He could have killed me, but he didn't. He didn't even shoot me! One of the *other* men did. I offered to *help* Jake. Honest to God! But the old man in there crippled me and I couldn't do a damn thing. Jake shot the others and then shot Hawk and ran out. All I heard after that was a lot of shooting and a lot of yelling and screaming!" Brady groaned and curled up. "Help me! Somebody do something about my knee! I don't know what went on after Jake left the bunkhouse."

"I ought to finally *hang* you!" Lloyd told him. "Maybe by your ankles, so you can suffer for a long time with that knee pain. I wonder how many days it takes a man to die if he's hung upside down!"

"Please, Lloyd! I swear to God I didn't want any part of what those men did! It was two shootists – Buck Potter and Lenny McCarthy. They were from outlaw country! This whole thing blew up way worse than I ever wanted! I would never... hurt kids!" Brady broke into tears again.

Lloyd pointed his six-gun at Brady's head, but Hal Kraemer was there by then and grabbed Lloyd's arm. "Don't do it, Lloyd! It would be murder! This attitude is what got your father where he is right now."

Lloyd hesitated, turning dark eyes to the marshal. His long hair had come loose, and some of it hung over one eye.

"It's a new world, Lloyd. You aren't in Oklahoma backing up your father. This mess here is over, and you have a big family back home who needs you. If Jake is dead, they are going to need you even more, with *them*, not in prison."

Lloyd turned away and holstered his gun. He pulled his hair back behind his shoulders, realizing he'd lost his hat somewhere.

"I found a body at the corner of the house," Kraemer told him. "It was Kyle Pendergrass, that gunfighter from the south. I met him at one of the farmers' meetings."

"Well, now, he won't be getting' in any more gunfights, will he?"

Lloyd stubbornly wiped at tears in his eyes. *Pa, where are you?* He felt five years old. *I'm not ready to go on without you.*

"Keep looking for Jake!" Cole yelled. "Wherever he is, he's bleeding real bad!"

Kraemer left to shout more orders, and Lloyd threw his head back and took a deep breath. He turned to Terrel. "Pa's shotgun is in the bunkhouse. Get it, will you?" He walked over to where Charlie stood over the bodies of the two dead men who lay near the privy. They wore only their underwear and gun belts, their handguns lying in the grass beside them.

"Looks like these two must have drawn on Jake," Charlie said. "Pretty fuckin' stupid, huh? I'm bettin' they challenged him, thinkin' to make a name for themselves. And look here." He pointed. "All them empty shells piled up beside that guy's arm. Somebody deliberately blew it completely off."

"Yeah. And there's no wondering who did it." Lloyd knelt and picked up a spent shell. "These are from Pa's .44's." He groaned. "This guy must be the one who shot the boys, and pa found out. He wouldn't have done this if he wasn't sure. Looks like he had a showdown with both men at the same time. That's no challenge for somebody like Jake Harkner." He rose and faced Charlie. "That mess in the house . . . somebody must have got Jake by surprise. I think he was already hurt and confused. He must have barged into that house without thinking." He turned away, scanning the entire landscape. "Pa, where are you?"

"This is worse than Dune Hollow." Jeff was standing near Charlie and Lloyd. "At least Jake had a lot of men with him then. He wasn't responsible for – " He hesitated. "It's hard to believe one man is responsible for all of this."

"It's easy for *me* to believe," Lloyd answered. "They shot young boys and threatened Tricia and Sadie Mae. That's all it takes."

*If ever anyone had a doubt that Jake Harkner can handle himself against big odds, the aftermath of what I have seen today only proves age hasn't affected the man's abilities in the least. But what we have found is also a good indication this might have been Jake Harkner's last showdown.* "God, please prove me wrong," he muttered.

Fifteen men had ridden to the Mitchel place, including Marshal Hal Kraemer and three of his deputies, and three men from the *Double T*. The rest of the *J&L* men had been left behind to guard the homestead and watch for Jake to show up.

Lloyd walked back to Brady Fillmore. One of the *Double T* men was wrapping the man's knee. "Tell us what you know, you worthless bastard!" he asked Brady.

Fillmore was pale from loss of blood mixed with fear of what Lloyd might do. He explained what happened in the bunkhouse. "I think Stumpy got your pa in the left arm, but it all happened so fast, I can't say for sure. I . . . I didn't draw on Jake or anything. The Indian over there . . . him and that Ainsley guy from the *Double T* . . . they came along, shooting at Jake. Jake was reloaded by then. He opened both barrels on Hawk and wounded Ainsley. Ainsley ran off, and your pa kind of stumbled out of the bunkhouse. After that I didn't see anything, Lloyd, as God as my witness. I just heard a whole lot of shooting."

Lloyd turned away. "My God, Pa—"

"Lloyd, the wall clock in the bunkhouse was shattered, but I noticed the hands stopped at five forty-five," Jeff told him.

Lloyd pulled a pocket watch from his pants and popped it open. "It's ten a.m." He looked at Jeff with tired, bloodshot eyes. "If pa was hurt, he's been lying out there somewhere a good four hours. God only knows how long it will take to find him, and the trip home will take another two to four hours, depending on the condition he's in when we find him . . . *if* we find him." His chest hurt with the very real possibility that Jake was dead.

Vance gave a loud shout from a corral to the east, where he'd ridden in search of Jake. "Hey, everybody! There's another man over here! He's alive!"

Lloyd took off running, followed by Cole, Jeff, and Hal Kraemer, who yelled at the rest of the men to keep searching the premises for Jake's body and to gather identification from the dead bodies. The man Vance found yelled from cramping pains in his legs and arms from being tied so tightly for so long. Vance sliced the ropes with a knife.

"Please don't kill me!" the man begged. "Jake left me alive on purpose. He knew. He could tell I didn't have anything to do with those boys." The man started crying. "Or the Mitchels," he sobbed.

"What's your name?" Marshal Kraemer asked.

The man coughed. "Larry." He spit and threw up. "Larry Banks. Please, I need some water."

Lloyd grabbed a canteen Cole had brought along and bent down to throw water over Banks's face and the front of his shirt. "I'll let you drink some when you tell us where my *father* is!"

Larry lifted his head and just stared at Lloyd for a moment. "Jesus, you look just like him. I hope . . . you ain't gonna' kill me, are you? Your pa . . . he let me live," he repeated.

"Where is he?" Lloyd shouted.

"Give him a minute," Kraemer told Lloyd. "Let Vance finish getting those ropes off him and stand him up. Get his circulation going and let him have some water."

"You ain't gonna' hang me, are you?"

"No," Hal told him, "but you're going to help us understand what went on here and where Jake Harkner might be. The more you tell us, including names, the easier it will go on you, and the less likely I *will* let Lloyd

Harkner hang you." The marshal and Vance helped Larry stand up.

Larry grasped his stomach and bent over, vomiting again. He ran a hand through his hair and wiped at his mouth with his shirtsleeve. "I thought Harkner was . . . gonna' kill me for sure." He looked at Lloyd. "Your father said . . . he figured I got caught up in somethin' I didn't understand, so he let me live." He started crying again. "He was right. I didn't have a damn thing . . . to do with those boys. I swear! I came along afterward."

Lloyd shoved him against the fence railing. "What did you mean about the Mitchels? You said you didn't have anything to do with the Mitchels."

Larry hung his head. "They're . . . dead. That gunman . . . Buck Potter and his friend, Lenny. They did it. You'll find their bodies . . . buried behind the barn."

"Jesus Christ," Lloyd groaned, turning away. "*All* of them?"

"Yes, Sir, but I didn't even know that when I first hired on here. Swear to God. I never even had a chance to meet those folks – didn't know them at all. By the time I started findin' out the truth, I couldn't leave. Buck and Lenny, they swore they would kill anybody who tried to leave. And I'm . . . I'm so sorry about the Mitchels . . . and those boys."

Lloyd whirled and grabbed the man by the throat.

"You'll be even *sorrier* if my father is dead!" he told Banks. He squeezed the man's throat. "Where is he? Where's my *father!*"

"I don't know!" Banks gagged on the words. "I swear!"

"Let go of him, Lloyd," Kraemer told him. "Let him have some more water. I don't think he knows any more than what he's just told us. Apparently your father believed him."

"He did!" Banks told Lloyd. He rubbed at his throat and took some deep breaths. "He's a fair man when he knows the truth. I can tell!" He coughed and choked the words out. "All he wanted from me . . . was how many men there were and their names. I helped him! Honest! I told him everything!" The man sniffed. "Is everybody over there dead?"

"Not all of them," Lloyd told him. "Brady Fillmore is alive. A couple of them might have got away."

"They did if . . . " Banks paused. "Well . . . would your father shoot a woman? Did you find one in the house?"

They all looked at each other.

"Hell, no! Jake would never shoot no woman!" Cole answered.

"Never," Lloyd added. "Who are you talking about?"

"A whore. A man by the name of Ainsley had her with him at the house."

Lloyd closed his eyes and sighed. "Was her name Stella Flynn?"

"Yeah! Yeah, that's it."

Lloyd rubbed at the back of his neck. "We didn't find her over there. She must have gotten away."

Larry looked at Marshal Kraemer. "I'll cooperate any way I can, Marshal," he told the man. "Names and everything I know. I think Harkner meant to be fair at first, but I saw kind of a crazy look in his eyes when I told him about Buck and Lenny killing the Mitchels. And I told him those two are the ones who shot those boys. They bragged about it. And they forced Brady Fillmore to write a note that might make Harkner come out here alone." He shook his head and faced Lloyd. "If I knew what happened to your father, I'd tell you, but I couldn't see anything from here. All I know is, all that shooting . . . it sounded like the end of the world. A couple of times it stopped, then started again. Then it finally stopped for good."

"Come with us and tell us if all the men are accounted

for," Marshal Kraemer told Larry. He ordered Vance and Cole to take the man closer to the house, then turned to Lloyd. "They killed that whole damn family. I see no real loss here, but it's hard to draw a line between law and lawlessness here, Lloyd, "

"They shot a woman and her husband and son!" Lloyd trembled with anger. "The Mitchels were good people. Men who shoot at boys and then do something like that deserve what these men got!"

"Maybe so, but don't fall into your father's old school thinking, Lloyd. You know that doesn't hold anymore."

"And my father came here because of that note, Hal. His little granddaughters were threatened, and knowing what these men already did, you know damn well they would have followed through with those girls if pa hadn't come out here alone. That's why he did this. You have to let this go. He knew he'd likely be killed this time! I have a feeling he is already suffering, maybe not even alive. Most of what happened here had to be self-defense. They *wanted* him, Hal. And they *got* him, even though it cost them their lives."

The marshal rubbed at tired eyes. "They got him, all right. Right or wrong, I have a feeling this might be the end of what was turning into a range war, so that much good might come out of it."

Lloyd nodded. "I think most everybody on both sides will want this to end."

Hal sighed. "I hope so, but you and I both know that the dark side of Jake Harkner also came here for revenge."

"He was ready to do this the right way, Hal. I know him. If not for that note, he would have waited. He *wanted* to do this the right way, but there is a part of pa that is still that little kid protecting the people he loves. Where is the crime? You tell me."

Some of the men began digging graves, and Lloyd could hear Brady Fillmore still crying from pain.

"You have to report this the right way, Hal. Pa is sixty-three years old, and he's prone to pneumonia and already hurts from old wounds. And now he could be hurt so bad he'll never be the same. Please let him and my mother finally have some peace!"

"I've never seen a bigger mess than what Jake left behind there."

"And *he's* a mess—down deep inside." Lloyd's voice broke on the words.

Hal closed his eyes and shook his head. "Damn it!" He watched another man vomit. "The best I can do is report to that judge in Denver that we came in on the tail-end of this and did some of the shooting ourselves." He met Lloyd's gaze again. "You can tell your men that so if they are questioned, they will know what to say."

"I will." Lloyd swallowed.

"It's against my better judgment, but I know Jake better than you think. We happen to be a lot alike in some ways. I would have loved riding with you and him back in Oklahoma."

The two men shook hands.

"I'll still need to conduct a proper investigation," Hal said. "But if Jake is wounded bad, which is obvious, I'll give him and the family some time before I come around asking questions. I just hope you *do* find him alive. No one has found him around here, even in the outer pastures, so you're going to have to get some men together and figure out where in hell Jake went. I have to stay here and finish cleaning up this mess."

"Thanks, Hal."

Lloyd hurried past him and ordered some of the men to mount up and spread out to look for tracks.

"It won't be easy, Lloyd," Charlie told him. "We've

pretty much trampled over any tracks left by somebody leaving."

"If he's wounded as bad as I think he is, he's not in his right mind," Lloyd said sadly. "God only knows where he went."

Men rode in all directions for one last sweep. They whistled and shouted, calling for Jake.

Vance rode up to Lloyd. "Lloyd, if Jake headed for home and was wounded, seems to me he would have ridden directly south, figurin' he'd run into us heading this way, and he'd get some help. We've developed a pretty solid pathway north and south, so seems like he would have used that to be sure we found him."

Lloyd thought for a moment. "But we never met up with him, which means he didn't ride south at all."

"Exactly," Vance answered. "I think he went in a different direction."

"He must have ridden here from a different direction. They would have been watching the southern approach. The mountains rule out the west, and to get to the north side, he'd have to go a good thirty extra miles. That would have taken too much time."

"That leaves east," Vance told him. "Last summer Jake and Cole tracked some stray J&L cattle that wandered northeast from our land and ended up in that rugged, sloping country east of here that nobody wants to settle in. We followed those strays down a little green valley that would have been easy to ride through at night. It leads right up to this place."

Lloyd nodded. "Good thought." He took a pre-rolled cigarette from his shirt pocket and yelled to Cole.

"Go get my horse and come with me and Vance! We're riding east to look for pa!" He lit the cigarette and glanced at a buckboard wagon that sat near the still-unfinished barn. "

If pa is still alive but wounded, we can't throw him over a horse. It would kill him. Have the men hook up a couple of the dead men's horses to that wagon. We can throw a mattress from the house into the back and cover it with one of our own sleeping blankets. We can get him home a lot quicker with a wagon."

Vance rode off, hollering orders to Jeff and Charlie to hitch some horses to the wagon and come with him and Lloyd. Minutes later, men dragged a mattress out of the cabin.

One of Kraemer's deputies rode over to where Lloyd waited. "We'll have two or three of the men head south and spread out a little," he told Lloyd, "just in case Jake did go that way and his horse strayed off the main path."

"Thank you," Lloyd answered, feeling as though he lived in a world removed from reality. He drew deeply on his cigarette, then muttered as he exhaled. "Don't give up, Pa." He sure could use a drink right now, but he could hear Jake chastising him for it. *You don't want to turn into my father, Lloyd. Believe me, the best think you can do in life is stay away from whiskey. It would destroy you.*

Lloyd quickly wiped at his eyes and nose again before Vance returned with Cole and Jeff. Charlie rode beside him and brought Lloyd's horse with him. Cole and Jeff's horses were tied to the back of the hay wagon, and both men rode in the wagon seat.

"We'll find him, Lloyd," Jeff tried to assure him.

"Yeah, sure," Lloyd answered, not sounding very confident as he mounted up.

All five men left, heading east. *You'd better be praying hard, Evie*, Lloyd thought. *I'm counting on you and that faith of yours.*

## CHAPTER 46

Navigating the wagon along the uneven, rocky terrain of the eastern slope the men followed was tricky, especially avoiding larger rocks that could break a wagon wheel. Cole whistled and cooed at the lead horses, keeping to the smoothest path he could follow.

A trickle of water glittered in the noon sun, the little stream the men followed mere mud in most places, deeper pools in others. They had been searching for nearly two hours, and the sun was high and hot. Lloyd feared that by now, if they did find Jake, he had been bleeding far too long. He couldn't begin to imagine his father's body being lifeless. Jake Harkner always seemed *bigger* than life – invincible. He could hear the man's voice, his laughter. He could see him riding across the plains and foothills, as sure on a horse as he was on his own two feet . . . even more sure with those .44's. Those guns were getting old, but not in Jake's care. Jake kept them cleaned and oiled and repaired in like-new condition. Lloyd doubted any gunsmith had a better knowledge of firearms than Jake Harkner did.

The only sound was the occasional soft whinny of one of the horses, the light splashing of their hooves in and out of the stream, and a rhythmic squeak in one of the wagon wheels. Cole slapped the reins to the wagon horses, and the sound reminded Lloyd of the time his mother slapped the back of his hand for reaching toward a stove burner. The only arguments she and Jake ever had was over disciplining him and Evie. Because of how he was raised, Jake couldn't tolerate any kind of spanking or even yelling – a stark contrast to how vicious he could be against anyone who would harm someone he loved.

The thought his father's discipline problem made Lloyd smile. It was a wonder he and Evie hadn't grown up the most spoiled brats of all spoiled brats, but when Jake wasn't around, Randy would gently explain that *Daddy's father was mean to him, but there are gentle ways to discipline that are only because mommy loves you.* Now that he had kids of his own, Lloyd understood how hard it must have been for his mother to find ways to make them behave without upsetting Jake. Of course, there were long periods of time when Jake wasn't there at all, so Randy had full reign to discipline him and Evie however she thought necessary. Even so, Lloyd figured that down inside Jake knew Randy was right in her view of teaching the children right from wrong, because their arguments never amounted to much later on. Jake couldn't stand to discipline his children, but he doubly couldn't stand to argue with Randy.

For the first couple of hours the men barely spoke, all five of them lost in their own thoughts of dread and impending grief.

"It's too fucking quiet," Lloyd finally spoke up.

"Quiet, like *death* quiet," Charlie muttered.

"Hang in there, Lloyd," Vance told him in a louder voice. "Don't ever count Jake out."

"Lloyd!" Cole halted the wagon and pointed. "Buzzards! Up where those big swells from the mountains move into flatter land. That dark dot up there looks like a horse."

"It *does!*" Lloyd kicked his horse into a hard run, feeling sick at the knowledge that buzzards sometimes started picking at a man's eyes before he was even dead.

Vance followed at a hard gallop, followed by Charlie. Cole snapped the reins to the team, speeding up as much as possible around mud and rocks. Jeff hung on to the seat bar for dear life. By the time they were close enough to see that the horse was, indeed, Thunder, Lloyd was already bent over a body that lay half in a pool of water and half out. Vance shouted and waved his arms at the buzzards, shooting at some of them and forcing them away.

"They didn't pick at him, did they?" Cole asked as he handed the reins to Jeff and jumped down from the wagon.

Lloyd was frantically splashing water over Jake's chest. "No, thank God! He's been bleeding, though, really bad. Pa, wake up! Wake up!" He splashed more water. "Maybe the cold water will help stop the bleeding. That could be why he decided to lay down in it. There must be some kind of spring right here. There's more water in this spot than anyplace else in this valley."

"This whole area might be worth more than people think," Vance commented. "I didn't know there was a natural spring here." He knelt beside Jake, noticing he was covered in so much blood that it was hard to tell just how many wounds he'd suffered. His shirt and vest were completely soaked in it, and the right side of his face was covered with dried, scabbed blood. The left sleeve of his shirt was stuck to his arm, and his denim pants were soaked in blood near his left hip bone.

"I think he's alive." Lloyd quickly wiped at tears. "A man stops bleeding when he dies, right? But all this blood was still wet in places that weren't in the water. My God, he's so covered in blood it's hard to tell how many wounds there are."

Cole knelt beside Vance and studied the body. "Are you sure he's alive?"

"No! I mean . . . I think so," Lloyd answered. He let out a little gasp of effort at not breaking into crying. "God damn it, I don't know! I can't wake him up!" He leaned close to Jake's ear. "Pa! Pa, can you hear me? Wake up, you sonofabitch! Don't you fucking die on me!" He couldn't stop the tears then as he kept splashing water over Jake.

"Lloyd, hold up a minute." Cole grabbed his hand. "Just calm down. Let's make sure he *is* alive." He reached over to feel for a pulse at Jake's neck. "Feel his wrist," he told Vance.

Everything was quiet for a moment.

"I feel a faint pulse," Vance told them.

"I do, too." Cole looked at Lloyd. "We can't just keep putting cold water on him. We've got to get him to Brian and Doctor Beemer."

"That's a good two hours, maybe longer." Lloyd wiped at tears with his shirtsleeve. "We can't go very fast, and we've been heading mostly east, so we haven't gotten much closer to the homestead."

Cole unbuckled Jake's gun belt. "Let's get these guns off him, and his vest and boots." He started to unbutton Jake's shirt. "Shit," he muttered. "This shirt's all stuck. If we pull it off, something might start bleeding again."

"Let's get off what we can and get him into the wagon," Vance said. "And we'll have to cover him good. This cold water might be good for stopping the bleeding, but he's probably in shock. I've been told a man in shock needs to be kept warm."

The four of them managed to get Jake's guns and boots and vest off, then loaded him into the wagon bed. "Lloyd, you sit back here with him," Vance said. "We'll wrap him good in blankets and you can keep your arms around him to help keep him warm. Rub him all over real good. That helps."

Lloyd settled into the mattress and against the side of the wagon bed and grasped Jake under the shoulders. The other three men helped scoot Jake farther inside and across Lloyd's legs. They threw four blankets over him. Lloyd put his arms around him and bent his knees a little, holding his father close.

"Pa, can you hear me? We've got to get you home *alive*, understand? Mom is counting on you coming back." He looked at Vance. "Shit, he's starting to tremble."

"He's in shock" Vance rustled up two more blankets and climbed into the wagon to throw them over Jake. "Let's get him home fast as we can."

Cole tied Lloyd's horse to the back of the wagon." "Thunder will need a good scrubbin' when we get home," he commented. His mane and neck are soaked in blood, and I'm thinkin' this saddle is no good now. It's too stained."

Vance threw Jake's clothes, guns and boots into the wagon.

"Charlie, you ride back to the Mitchel place and tell the men there we found my father," Lloyd told the man. "Then get a fresh horse and head south as fast as you can and try to catch up to the men who headed that way. High-tail it to the homestead and tell Brian and Doctor Beemer we're bringing pa in. They should clear off the table at mom and dad's place and be ready with hot water and anything else they might need!"

"Right." Charlie glanced at Jake, then to Lloyd. "God be with you both, Lloyd." He turned his horse and rode away. Cole climbed into the wagon seat beside Jeff and snapped the reins. Vance took Thunder's reins and rode beside them.

"Pa? Can you hear me?" Lloyd repeated. "I'm right here. I'll take care of you, like you took care of me in Denver. I'll stay right with you. I promise."

Lloyd had never seen Jake quite so pale in spite of his dark skin. "Cole, he has a real bad color to him."

"Just keep talkin' to him. He'll know it."

Lloyd leaned close again. "Pa, why didn't you take me with you? We've always had each other's backs." He grabbed Jake tighter when the wagon hit a dip and bounced hard.

Jake let out a grunt but didn't open his eyes.

"Pa? You with me? Talk to me. Show me you're going to fight. Don't you fucking die on me, Pa! Don't you die before Mom can give you a piece of her mind about breaking your promise to her. Don't make this all worse for her by dying before she can tell you she loves you." *Keep talking. Maybe it'll help. Maybe he can hear me.*

Jake groaned and squeezed Lloyd's arm when the cart hit another bump. "Saw my . . . mother," he mumbled. "Needs me."

Hope swelled in Lloyd's heart. "No! *We* need you, Pa. Your mother is in a good place. She's trying to tell you that it's not time for you to go to her yet. She's okay now. She's someplace where nobody can hurt her. Don't go to her yet, Pa. Not yet. She wants you to stay here." Lloyd pulled Jake closer and said softly in his ear, "Stay with me, Pa. I love you more than any man ever loved his father."

"That's . . . why," Jake muttered, eyes remaining closed. "Don't want . . . you . . . hurt again."

Lloyd couldn't help his tears. "Pa, if you love us, you won't give up. Please don't give up! Mother needs you."

"Randy."

"Yes, Pa! You have to go back to her. Randy needs you."

"Need her . . . to breathe."

"Then you keep breathing 'til we get home to Mom. Okay? Keep breathing, and then she'll *help* you breathe."

"Girls. The . . . girls . . . "

"They're fine. They're back home waiting for their grandpa to get back."

"Watch out . . . for them . . . "

"Pa, nobody is left to threaten Tricia or Sadie Mae. And they will be broken-hearted if you die. They need *you* to *protect* them, understand? If you die, who is going to watch over those little girls?"

Jake wilted a little, letting go of Lloyd's arm.

"Pa? Hang on! You hang on!" Lloyd held him close and wept.

Jeff wiped at tears and shoved his small tablet into a jacket pocket. He couldn't write. He closed his eyes, visualizing the entire Harkner family and all the men and neighboring ranchers making the trek up to Echo Ridge to bury Jake Harkner.

He shook away the thought. Life had never been more exciting than since that first day he met Jake back in Guthrie. He'd been so intimidated he almost wet his pants.

*He fills the room when he walks into it, no matter how big that room is.*

Who said that? Jeff couldn't remember. Maybe he'd said it himself, in one of his many columns about Jake. It didn't seem possible now that the ball Peter held for Jake and Randy back in Chicago was just a few days ago – all the primary Chicago dignitaries there – the richest of the rich – Randy so utterly beautiful, Jake looking nothing like an old outlaw – so well groomed – that winning smile that charmed the women who'd hung around him. Jeff could still hear the orchestra music. He could still see Jake and Randy dancing close while people stared.

Jake and Randy were so damn happy that night. Randy glowed in that beautiful dress on her tiny frame, the rose petal diamond necklace sparkling against her throat.

How sad that it had all ended this way.

# CHAPTER 47

Randy's hands shook as she spread a second sheet over the kitchen table. "The table is so hard," she said rather absently. "We should find a way to make it softer. If he's hurt as bad as Charlie said, we can't put him on such a hard table."

Doctor Beemer put a hand on her arm. "Something too soft makes it harder to find wounds and harder to operate, Mrs. Harkner. Why don't you let Gretta and Mrs. DeJesus do this? You go wait with your daughter and with Katie."

"*Si, mi amiga,*" Teresa told Randy. "Go and wait, so you are rested before *Senor* Harkner gets here. He will need you to be strong."

Randy grasped the hand of her long-time helpmate. "You will stay close, right? I mean, sometimes when Jake is hurting or upset, he says things in Spanish, and I don't understand him."

"*Si*, I will be close by." Teresa gently pushed Randy toward Peter, who took her arm.

"Come on, Randy. Come over here with me and Evie and Katie. Katie's folks are watching all the little ones and trying to keep them calm and away from here. The boys are resting over at Evie's, and Katie's mother promised that once we know what's happened with Jake, she'll tell them as gently as possible and try to keep them calm."

Randy met Peter's gaze, his soft blue eyes showing true concern. "What if he doesn't make it home alive?" she asked in a near whisper.

"It's Jake. One thing I've learned from back in Guthrie is that the man will suffer the worst pain there is if it means making it back to you. I'm sure he is sorry he didn't tell you what he was going to do, but that will make him even more determined to make it back here, don't you think? He's probably worried about how much trouble he's going to be in with his wife."

Randy managed a smile and let Peter keep an arm around her as he led her over to Jake's favorite chair, the big, red leather one near the fireplace. Evie sat nearby, her head bowed in prayer, and Katie sat in the love seat, her elbows on her knees and her face buried in her hands. Randy faced Peter again. "Charlie said . . . "

"Don't pay any attention to what Charlie said," Peter told her. "Remember that Jake is with Lloyd, who next to you, loves that man enough that he'll do everything in his power to keep Jake alive. He won't let Jake give up."

Randy sat down in the chair, remembering all the times she and Jake had sat in it together, his arms around her. Those arms. That safety. What was she going to do if he never put his arms around her again? She curled into the chair, and Evie came over to sit on the foot stool in front of it.

"Mother, let me pray with you."

Katie broke into tears. "Pray for Lloyd, too," she sobbed. "He loves his father so much. He has to be in his own hell right now."

Peter moved to sit on the love seat beside Katie and put a hand on her shoulder as Evie prayed aloud. He turned to glance out a front window to see several J&L men standing around, waiting to help haul Jake into the house when he got there. Peter shook his head in wonder. Everyone back in Guthrie knew how ruthless Jake Harkner could be as a lawman, and Peter had no doubt he'd once been equally ruthless as an outlaw in his younger days. Gunfights, fist fights, brothels, prison, a hellish childhood, killed his own father . . . but everyone here waited silently with heavy hearts, all dreading the fact that the man could be dead. Even the men were worried, and probably neighboring ranchers.

Jake Harkner was loved beyond measure when he should be hated. Even Peter wanted to hate the man, but there was a charisma about Jake that could not be denied or ignored. He had a way of stealing people's hearts and loyalty, and a man, or woman, couldn't find a more loyal, devoted friend, or father, or grandfather . . . or husband. Even if Jake died, Peter already knew he wouldn't have even the slightest chance of winning Randy's heart. It would always, always belong to Jake, even in death. All he could do was be there for her in every other way, as he'd promised Jake – a friend, legal counsel – nothing more.

"Here they come!" someone shouted outside.

Randy bolted before anyone could stop her. She was out the door and down the steps and running toward the on-coming wagon, even though it was still only part-way down the hill that led to the homestead. Evie ran out behind her, calling to her.

"Mother, wait! You'll be tired out before daddy even gets here!"

Randy slowed and turned, looking lost and confused. Evie caught up with her, as did Charlie on horseback.

"Ma'am, let them come in. You can't do nothin' till they get Jake to the house. Come on. Get up here behind me." He took his foot from the left stirrup and grasped Randy's arm, helping her up. She rode behind Charlie back to the house, and Tommy Tyler rode out to bring back Evie.

Peter lifted Randy down. "Come inside, honey. They're almost here. We'll all just be in the way until they get Jake inside."

Evie joined them, and Katie waited at the door, looking anxiously toward the approaching wagon. "Lloyd," she whispered. Her husband had such a big, big heart when it came to his parents. He'd abandoned them and turned to drink when Jake went to prison, and he'd never forgiven himself for it.

Jeff and Cole finally reached the house and pulled the wagon to the front steps. Peter kept a tight grip on Randy as the men climbed down. Others gathered to help get Jake out of the wagon. "Be careful!" Lloyd told them. "I couldn't even count all the bullet wounds."

"Oh, my God," Randy exclaimed.

"He still alive?" Charlie asked.

"I think so." Lloyd came up the steps behind the men who carried Jake inside, and the look of devastation on his face made Randy's heart fall.

"Lloyd – "

Lloyd stopped grabbed her close. "I don't know if he'll make it," he said in a strained voice.

Randy stepped back to see his shirt was covered in blood. Lloyd helped her up the steps and into the house, and Randy gripped her stomach as she hurried over to the kitchen table, where men laid Jake out.

Lloyd put an arm around Katie, literally leaning on her for a moment. He wiped at tears. "Stay back, honey, while I help. Pa might wake up and somebody has to hold him down and keep him still."

Katie stared at the blood on Lloyd's shirt. "Oh, Lloyd! Tell me you aren't hurt, too."

"No. It's all pa's blood." Lloyd's voice broke as he said

the words. He kissed Katie's cheek and urged her to go sit down. He turned to see how he could help Jake. Doctor Beemer and Brian were giving orders so fast it was hard to keep up, and Randy leaned over Jake, smoothing back his hair.

"Jake, I'm here. You're home now."

Jake just moaned, opening his eyes for a moment. "Can't . . . breathe . . . "

"Yes, you can!" Randy answered. She leaned close and kissed him, breathing into his mouth. "Do you feel that, Jake? Stay alive. Feel my breath."

"Someone bring an extra lamp over here and hold it up for us," Brian ordered.

Vance was still inside the house. He hurriedly brought over a table lamp and plugged it in, holding it high.

"Evie, open the kitchen curtains so more sunlight can come in," Brian asked.

"Everybody out but family and maybe Cole," Doctor Beemer said. "We might need him and Lloyd to hang on to Jake. Vance, you can stay, too." He gently touched Randy's shoulder. "You have to stay back a little, Mrs. Harkner."

"He needs me."

"He knows you're here. Just move around and stand at his head. Put your hands at his temples and keep talking to him." Beemer turned to Cole. "You and Gretta help get his clothes off. Gretta, you'll have to wet some rags with warm water. I can already see we'll need to soak his shirt good first to get it off. It's stuck to him from dried blood."

Gretta quickly obeyed while Lloyd and Cole got the rest of Jake's clothes off and covered him with another sheet.

"I don't see any leg wounds, Brian," Lloyd told his brother-in-law. "From what I could tell on the way here, all his wounds are from the belly up."

"Looks like this wound across the right side of his face is superficial," Beemer said.

Randy touched the ugly cut on Jake's cheek. "My beautiful Jake," she whispered. She leaned close again and whispered in his ear. "Jake, I'm here. You're home. You made it home."

"I think the one across his right shoulder is superficial, too," Brian told them. "But that left arm doesn't look good."

"The arm is the least of our worries for the moment," Beemer answered. "It's the wounds to his middle that worry me – the possible damage inside. Help me make sure we find all the wounds."

"There is one down here by his left hip," Gretta told them. She wiped at it with a wet cloth, seeing the ugly bullet hole once she got some of the dried blood out of the way."

"Jesus," Lloyd groaned. "I didn't even see that one."

"Okay, everybody stay calm," Beemer told them. "Let's get his shirt unstuck and wash off as much blood as possible. It's the only way to see the bullet holes. We need to roll him over a little and check his back also. If a bullet went in the front but didn't come out the back, that's our biggest worry. I'm already seeing a bruised look to his belly and chest area, which means internal bleeding."

"Oh, God help him!" Evie wept. She started to walk closer, but Peter put a hand to her waist. "Stay back a little, Evie. Your husband and Doctor Beemer need a lot of room. And Jake needs your mother right now. Your best help is your prayers."

Jeff came inside but stayed over by the fireplace, quietly scribbling more notes. *A considerable amount of joy and energy will be drained from my life if Jake Harkner dies*, he wrote, not even sure if or how he would use the words.

For now he wasn't doing much more than putting his feelings into words, as though it might help his grief.

"My God, he's lost so much blood," Beemer said, almost as though to himself. "That's our biggest danger. Even if we can patch him up, his heart and kidneys and liver might not survive so much blood loss."

Teresa put two more kettles of water on the stove to heat as the men rolled Jake onto his side.

"*Damn* it," Brian swore. "Nether bullet in his chest area went through."

"There is an exit wound down here by his hip," Gretta told them.

"Then we know what we have to work on first," Beemer told them. "We have to dig the two bullets out of his chest . . . and *fast*. Brian, start loading him up with chloroform. He might seem unconscious, but we'll find out different when we start probing for those bullets." He started peeling Jake's shirt off. "My God!" he said as he pulled it away from Jake's chest.

"What is it, doc?" Lloyd asked.

Beemer shook his head. "We might have to dig out only one bullet. Look here."

Everyone around the table studied Jake's chest as Beemer threw Jake's ripped, bloodied shirt to the floor. They all stared at something literally embedded at the center of Jake's chest.

Randy drew in her breath. "It's his mother's Crucifix!"

"What's left of it," Lloyd added.

Doctor Beemer started to remove the cross, then looked closer. "It's partially melted into his skin. There's a damn bullet flattened right into the middle of it!" He looked at Randy. "This Crucifix saved his life. That bullet would have gone straight into his heart and killed him."

"Dear God," Evie wept from farther away. "I knew it! I knew God was with him!"

Jake stirred and groaned and tried to sit up.

"Keep him down!" Beemer ordered. "Brian, go ahead with that chloroform. He probably has a collapsed lung, and he needs to stay still. If he comes fully awake the pain will be unbearable."

"I know the pain of a chest wound." Lloyd held down Jake's leg as Jake tried to bend it and get up.

"*Mi madre! Madre!*" Jake struggled again to sit up.

"Pa, stay down. Cole, take this leg, and Vance, hold his other leg! I'll keep him from sitting up." Lloyd moved to hold down Jake's shoulders.

"*Mi madre! Tengo que ayudarla.*"

"He say his mother needs him," Teresa told them, tears in her eyes. She stood in a corner behind Doctor Beemer. "I think maybe he is seeing her."

Lloyd gasped in an effort not to cry. "On the way here, he stirred awake once and told me he'd seen his mother," he told Teresa. "He wanted to go to her."

"Teresa, tell him he must stay here!" Randy asked her good friend. "Tell him he doesn't need to go to his mother. She's fine now. She's happy. Maybe he will think you are his mother speaking to him."

"*Si, Señora.*" Teresa nervously came closer as Jake became more restless and started reaching out for something. Lloyd pinned his arms, while Vance and Cole continued holding his legs and Beemer pressed on Jake's shoulders. Jake continued to rage in Spanish.

"He is saying, *Leave her alone! Stop hitting her!*" Teresa told them.

"He say something about his little brother, too. He say, *I will help you.*"

"Jesus, in his mind he's eight years old." Lloyd groaned.

Teresa spoke soothingly in Jake's ear. He answered

and, although tears ran down the sides of Jake's face, he calmed.

"He say, *I am sorry, my mother.*" Teresa dabbed at her own tears. "I tell him do not be sorry, my son. He was strong and brave, but he was too little. I tell him God saved him and let him live to be a man to help others and that he must live for that reason. He must stay here with his family and protect them. I tell him I am safe and happy, and his brother and I are with God and the bad man who hurt us is dead. I tell him he is forbidden to come to me yet. It is not what God wants."

Jake calmed down.

"Oh, Teresa, I am so glad you are here," Randy told her.

"I keep heating the water now." Teresa dabbed at more tears as Randy took her place near Jake's head again and leaned close.

"Stay with us, Jake."

"Randy?" Jake spoke her name.

"I'm right here."

"Can't . . . breathe," he repeated.

Her mouth close to his, Randy whispered, "Take my breath, Jake. Breathe for me." She blew against his mouth again.

"Randy." He reached up and grasped her hair, his grip tightening as he tried sitting up yet again, then cried out with pain. Brian immediately covered his nose and mouth with a cloth soaked in chloroform.

"Step back, Randy. If you breathe in any of this you'll be on the floor. We don't need you passing out on us."

"Be careful," Beemer told Brian. "I know I told you too much of that can kill a kid, but it's the same for a man Jake's age, even though he's a big, solid man. It could stop his heart, especially after the pressure of that bullet practically pushing that cross into his chest. There could be damage we don't know about – bruising at the least."

Jake's grip on Randy's hair loosened as he breathed in the chloroform, and Randy stepped back to let Doctor Beemer do what needed doing.

"We also need to remember Jake had pneumonia in prison," Brian told Beemer.

"Sometimes pneumonia leaves scar tissue. That and his smoking are another reason to be careful with the chloroform."

"Let alone the fact that the bullet we are looking for is likely lodged in his lung," Beemer added. He picked up his scalpel and looked around the table. "Anyone who thinks they aren't strong enough for this should leave."

No one left.

"You might need every one of us," Vance told the doctor. "And some of us have seen things we never talk about."

"I wouldn't leave Jake's side right now if my *own* life depended on it," Cole added.

"My mother and I sure as hell aren't going anywhere," Lloyd told Beemer.

"This man *is* my life," Randy said with agonizing sorrow.

Beemer sighed. "I'll use this scalpel to shave the cross off his skin first. It's going to be in the way. Brian, once I start digging, keep an eye on his reaction to make sure he's got enough chloroform in him." The man deftly pried off what was left of the Crucifix.

"Lord, it's like he's been branded by God Himself," Gretta muttered.

Beemer started cutting and

Jake groaned Randy's name and reached for her with his right hand.

Randy took his hand and squeezed. "I'm right here, Jake. Hold on to me."

Using a stethoscope, Brian listened to Jake's heart and his breathing while Beemer did the cutting. Off and on, Brian applied more chloroform.

"Mrs. Harkner, when this is over, keep him slightly sitting up," Beemer told her. "He's less likely to develop pneumonia that way. If he coughs a lot, that's okay. His body will need to expel excess fluid for several days—maybe weeks. I'm as worried about pneumonia or infection as I am the wound itself. I just wish I didn't have more cleaning and stitching to do on his other wounds once I'm done. I'll work as fast as I can."

"I'll have some men bring a bed downstairs," Randy answered. "It will be easier for me to take care of him down here. I'll have plenty of help lifting him and such."

"No!" Lloyd told her. "I don't want you doing *any* of it. You've been through enough, and you've nursed him through other wounds too many times. I'll do most of it myself. And God knows you can't *begin* to lift him."

"Lloyd, you have a ranch to run."

"And I have a father who needs me. He nursed me like a two-year-old child when I was shot in Denver. It's my turn now, and the men can take care of whatever chores need doing. I don't want you doing anything but feeding him."

Everyone winced as Beemer probed until he found the bullet. Jake let out a shuddering groan as his whole body shook, and Brian applied a little more chloroform.

Beemer dropped the flattened bullet into a wooden bowl Gretta handed him. "I'll help with is care, too," Gretta told Randy as she set the bowl aside. "And Teresa is here to help with cooking and washing the bed clothes and such. You have all kinds of help, Randy. Take advantage of it."

Everyone quieted as Beemer studied the open wound. "The lung is only partially collapsed," he told Randy. "But I do see a little scar tissue. I'll stitch up the wound and clean up and stitch the others. I think most of the bruising in his chest cavity is a combination of severe bleeding and the trauma of that bullet hitting the crucifix. That must have knocked him backwards. Either way, the bleeding has slowed considerably. His body will absorb the blood that is left inside him. We just have to pray infection doesn't set in. Let's clean up and stitch the rest of his wounds and hope the ones in his arm and down by his hip haven't done any grave damage."

Brian helped Beemer, and Randy kept hold of Jake's hand, shivering at the blood-soaked sheets under him. Both doctors worked for another two hours, washing, cutting, stitching. At times Brian applied more chloroform, and Randy clung to Jake's hand, feeling sick every time he squeezed extra hard because she knew that meant he was feeling pain.

"If this man lives, he is going to be very, very weak for a long time," Beemer commented. "The body takes weeks, maybe even months, to rebuild this much blood loss, and he's a big man, so it's going to take that much longer." He finished stitching Jake's upper arm.

Lloyd ordered Vance and Cole to bring a full-size bed from the guest room into the great room while both doctors worked on wrapping all the wounds. Randy continued talking softly to Jake as Lloyd, Teresa and Gretta washed as much of the dried blood from Jake's skin as they could. Beemer kept checking Jake's heart, declaring it sounded stronger now than when he was first brought in.

"He will experience considerable weakness and dizziness," Beemer told them. "Don't let him try to get up and walk on his own because he will be in danger of falling. I am guessing he'll be stubborn about that, so tie him down if you have to."

"Pa? *Stubborn?*" Lloyd said. "The worst, most obstinate mule in the West can't hold a candle to my father when it comes to stubborn."

"Mother will keep him in line," Evie added. "She'll chain him to the bed before she lets him get up by himself."

Beemer grinned. "Well, make sure a man is here at all times until he's steadier. He'll need to be moved around for obvious reasons, and a hundred-pound woman's not going to be able to do that."

"Well, I volunteer to help with his baths," Gretta joked.

Vance chuckled.

"I'm not so sure that's a good idea," Cole joked. "And I'm betting Randy won't allow it."

Everyone in the room joined in on full-out, though nervous, laughter. Even Beemer smiled.

"Stay ready with plenty of gauze," Beemer told Gretta. "There is likely to be more bleeding. The man has more holes in him than a cooking strainer. You'll need to continue changing his dressings." He turned his attention to Randy, who still held Jake's hand and had drawn his hand closer to kiss it. "Mrs. Harkner, there is something I need you to do several times a day for at least a week, maybe longer."

"Of course," she answered, keeping Jake's hand in hers and reaching out with her other hand to smooth some of his thick, dark hair away from his forehead. "What is it?"

"Well, I read the book."

Randy frowned and met Beemer's gaze. Everyone else quieted, thinking the doctor's statement a bit strange.

"By that I mean . . . Jake's description that you are the air he breathes really touched me. And now, we need to reinflate Jake's lung fully and *keep* it inflated so that in a week or two it will *stay* that way. A partially collapsed lung can be very painful, let alone not good for the healing process. You need to make sure Jake takes a lot of deep breaths, as deeply as possible in spite of the pain it will bring him. He has to understand how important that is. But right now, this first week, he will be too weak to even try, so someone needs to give that lung some exercise and help it reinflate on its own."

Randy frowned. "What can *I* do?"

Beemer sighed. "You can breathe *for* him. You can hold his nose and breathe into his mouth – exhale as hard as you can and push your breath into him. It won't hold much oxygen, but the forced air will make his lung expand. Because of his size you will have to exhale as hard and long as you can, a good ten times every hour or so. I think it will help. Can you do that?"

*She's the air I breathe.* Jeff remembered Jake's description of Miranda the very first time he interviewed him back in Guthrie.

"I'll do anything that will help," Randy told the doctor.

*I always had to come back to her, just to get my oxygen.* Jeff had written that down when Peter told him about his conversation with Jake back in Chicago.

"My mother probably weighs less than half what my father weighs," Lloyd told Beemer. "Spiritually, it will be good for pa to know she's breathing into him, but I'll do some of it just to make sure his lung expands like it should. I don't think my mother can breathe hard enough for a man pa's size."

Beemer nodded. "Probably not," he answered Lloyd, "but Jake needs to know she's here and breathing for him at times. She's the key to him wanting to live. I have a feeling she's the reason he hung on to get back here alive in the first place. By all rights, your father should be dead, but in examining him back in Chicago I could see he has an incredible inner strength and tolerance for pain, so that gives us hope. All kinds of complications could still set in, but deep breathing will help rebuild his blood and damaged lung." Beemer turned his attention to Randy. "Sometimes the spiritual need is just as healing as physical help, so do what you can, and let Lloyd help."

Randy stroked Jake's hair. "I will."

Evie walked over to her brother and mother and took their hands, asking everyone else in the room to reach out to each other. Randy took hold of Brian's hand. He took Beemer's, and on around the room – Katie, Peter, Cole, Vance, Teresa, Gretta, Jeff . . . Evie recited the 23d Psalm . . . "The Lord is my shepherd . . . Yea, though I walk through the valley of the shadow of death, I shall fear no evil, for Thou art with me . . . Surely goodness and mercy shall follow me all the days of my life, and I will dwell in the House of the Lord forever."

Randy thought about the lovely place she'd told Jake she wanted them to be buried . . . on Echo Ridge. *Lord, don't make me have to take Jake up there until I'm ready, too. I could never leave him all alone up there, where we've known so much love and joy and peace.*

"Randy . . ." Jake spoke her name again.

She leaned close. "I'm right here, Jake."

" . . . girls. Where . . . are they?"

"They're fine. They are both at Katie's house right now, playing together."

"Got to . . . protect . . . "

"Pa, the girls are fine," Lloyd told him in a strong voice. "Those men can't hurt them now. You lie still and get well. Don't worry about the girls. We are all watching out for them." He looked at Beemer. "Do you think he even knows where he is?"

"I doubt it," Beemer told him. "He's still in a confused world of chloroform and pain."

Evie walked around the table to take hold of Jake's hand while Lloyd asked Cole and Vance to help him bring a bed into the main room. "Daddy, it's Evie. You'll be okay now."

Jake groaned. "*Madre* . . . "

"No, daddy, it's me – Evie. Your mother is fine. She told you so herself, remember?" Evie squeezed his hand. "She wants you to stay with us for a long time yet."

Jake opened his eyes a moment, and his gaze rested on Randy. "Sorry. So . . . sorry."

"I know you are, and I know why you did this, but you have to fight to live now, Jake."

He passed out again.

# CHAPTER 48

Mid-November, 1899 . . .

*I have never been through such heartache as watching how Jake has suffered,* Randy wrote to Jeff. *Three different times we thought we'd lost him. His heart stopped two of those times, and Lloyd breathed for him while Brian pressed rhythmically against Jake's heart until it started beating again. The third time was a bout of pneumonia. Jake became so congested that he was bent over, unable to draw in a breath. It took me and Evie and Lloyd several minutes of pounding his back and forcing air into his lungs, over and over, until finally he was able to clear his breathing tubes enough to breathe on his own again. Brian was gone that day, helping deliver a baby at the home of a new settler family.*

*Jake finally recovered from the pneumonia and is gaining both weight and strength. This time I think he is truly on the mend and that the worst is over. He washes and dresses himself most of the time now, so I don't need quite so much help as I did at first. Still, he tires easily—but he seems stronger every day and is acting more and more like his old self.*

*As you know, Lloyd faithfully helped him that first month, to the point that Jake ordered him to go tend to his wife and the* ranch, and let the other men take their turns. But Lloyd has still been here more than he's been home, and I feel sorry for Katie. She has been so patient and loving. She knows how close Jake and Lloyd are.

Three weeks after Jake's surgery, Jeff had returned to his family in Chicago. And, certain Brian could take care of Jake and the boys, Doctor Beemer had gone with him, as had Peter. Randy still felt sad and melancholy over Peter's departure, and not just because of the beautiful memories of joy and adventures they shared from her and Jake's wonderful visit to Chicago. She knew Peter left because he was falling more in love with her. He didn't need to speak the words, and out of respect for what she and Jake shared, he'd not said a thing. Treena was finally home, and it was time to face the realities of life, one of which was the fact that Randy's heart and soul belonged to Jake Harkner and always would. Peter Brown would always be her dearest, dearest friend, but never anything more, and Randy took strength in just knowing he would always be there for her in any hour of need. But it was best he lived twelve hundred miles away and only came to visit.

*I don't know what I would have done without the strength I drew from Peter's loving support that first month,* she continued writing, well aware that Peter also read her letters. *Or the constant and loving help from Lloyd, who loves his father beyond measure. And Gretta and Cole and some of the other ranch hands have given so much time and effort into helping. They all think so much of Jake. I allowed Gretta to bathe Jake the first month, when I was just too worn out to do it. I can just hear you laughing about that, but I figured a woman like Gretta has seen and done it all, so – in her words – "what is another naked man to me?" But you know Jake. Weak as he was, he teased Gretta something awful, and once she came to me and declared she was "never going to help that man again." I knew she didn't mean it.*

Gretta is one of the strongest women I know, and I told Lloyd to take the men aside and order them not to tease Cole about her. He knows some of those men were Gretta's customers once, but I told Lloyd that if I ever hear that one of them disrespected her in any way from here on, they would have to answer to me. Gretta is a very caring woman and has become a good friend. I don't know what I would have done without her help, and she did things Evie and Katie couldn't have helped with.

Ben is recovering beautifully, and learning to do things with one arm, including keeping that arm around Gretta's daughter, Annie, who has become such a beautiful young woman. Every time he looks at her, Jake knows what he suffered in Mexico was worth it. Annie came to stay for the winter, and she and Ben have grown close. Jake was right. A man doesn't need two arms to love a woman. The pair of them are so young, but their eyes sparkle with love for each other.

Little Jake is walking without a limp now. And Sadie Mae and Tricia come over every day at noon to serve Jake his lunch, insisting that he let them place their dolls around him first to "love on him." Can you picture it? Big, bad Jake Harkner surrounded by dolls. It is a source of never-ending teasing from the men, especially Lloyd, who loves getting his father riled up. But Jake secretly loves it, and his desire to make sure the girls are just fine still lingers. Can you imagine what it is going to be like when those girls are old enough to take an interest in men? There isn't a boy or man within a hundred miles of here who will be brave enough to ask to date Jake Harkner's granddaughters. Jake will find every excuse in the world to keep them away.

Randy paused to drink some coffee. She glanced over to see Jake was still sleeping in his favorite chair by the fireplace.

Thank you for the wonderful photos you sent. The children and grandchildren were so taken by that picture of Jake and me at Peter's ball. Katie and Evie can't get over the beautiful diamond necklace Jake bought me, and they are thrilled with the books and perfumes and soaps and beautiful material I bought for them and for the children.

We will remember our trip always, the libraries and museums and opera, the theaters and grand music and shopping, the exotic foods and lifestyle, and Peter's castle of a home. But we likely will never go back to a big city. We belong here in Colorado on our beautiful ranch in the Rocky Mountain foothills. Things have been peaceful ever since the awful day they brought Jake home so badly wounded. All the ranchers gathered together to properly re-bury the Mitchels. We offered our lovely family plot right here on the J&L for the burial, and Evie sang and prayed over them. We all wept over such innocent lives lost, and we will put up grave stones in the spring with what information we could find on them.

We had a huge snowstorm a couple of weeks ago, but as usually happens down here in the valleys and foothills, most of the snow dissipated, even though the mountain peaks are so loaded that we often hear the rumble of avalanches. That will get worse as winter rages on, but right now we are having an unusual warm spell for November. Colorado can give you the most unpredictable weather, but I remember Peter telling me once that it's the same in Chicago because of the lake. Here it is because of the mountains. It is warm today, but we could be buried in a blizzard tomorrow and praying the cattle will survive the harsh winds on the plains. Right now, the children are playing outside wearing just light sweaters, and -

Randy paused when someone knocked on the door. She set her pen aside and hurried to open it to see Charlie standing there. "Marshal Kraemer is comin' in," he told her. He glanced over at Jake, who had awakened at the knock. "How you feelin' today, Jake?"

Jake grimaced as he rubbed his eyes and sat up straighter. "I've felt a lot worse, and I've felt better." He started to rise.

"Jake, let someone help you," Randy told him.

Charlie started over to help, but Jake refused. "I can manage." He got to his feet and walked toward Randy, but then stopped and put a hand to his ribs.

Charlie took his arm. "Don't be so damn stubborn," he told Jake.

"I don't like being helped. I'm not used to living like this."

"Then stay out of trouble," Charlie said. "That's what me and the other men are here for." He helped Jake to the kitchen table.

"Thanks, but I've been getting around pretty good."

"Is that your way of tellin' me not to tell the men you needed help just now?"

Jake grinned. "Maybe."

"Then I'll tell them you flipped cartwheels all the way to the table," Charlie joked.

"Charlie McGee from Tennessee, I think you'd better go back where you came from."

"Well, you ain't foolin' any of us, and we ain't expectin' you to walk out of this house with guns on your hips and ready to ride any time soon. Every man out there is glad you're up and around at all."

Jake sat down gingerly and met Charlie's gaze. "You said Hal Kraemer is coming in?"

"He's probably up to the house by now."

Jake glanced at Randy. "He probably just wants to discuss a few things and legally close the investigation." He ran a hand through his hair. "I need some coffee or something." He looked down at himself. "Am I decent?"

"Of course you are," Randy told him. "Gretta and I helped you wash and dress this morning," she reminded him. "You were just taking a short nap. You look fine." She sobered. "Jake, what if Kraemer is here for more than just to talk?" Randy asked.

"I don't think he's here for anything more," Jake

answered. "No matter what the reason, he's not going to haul me off to jail in the shape I'm in right now. Pour me that coffee and get out some extra cups."

Randy breathed deeply against a nagging worry.

Jake told Charlie to go get Lloyd. "He should be here. And tell the men to go on about their business. If they gather around near the house, it will just make Kraemer wary and uneasy. Same with Evie. Tell her to stay away. She gets all worried and protective. Sometimes her behavior makes me look guilty even when I'm not."

Charlie smiled. "Sure, Jake." He left, and Randy re-lit the stove under a kettle that was already plenty hot. She faced Jake with her own concerned look.

"Come here," Jake told her.

Randy walked around the table and stood in front of him, thinking how thin he still was. He still had a long way to go to get back to the Jake she'd married, the Jake she needed to hold her in the night. But right now, just seeing him sitting there, alive and healing, made her want to weep with joy.

Jake reached out and took her hand. "Relax and let me take care of this," Jake told her. "Don't try sticking up for me. Sometimes that's worse than saying nothing at all."

Randy nodded, and Jake squeezed her hand gently.

"Randy, I know we have a lot to talk about. I never lie to you, but I did this time, and I've put you through hell. I wouldn't blame you if you'd gone back to Chicago with Peter."

She slowly shook her head. "Oh, Jake, how can you say that?"

"Because I know what this did to you. Hopefully, I have a few good years left, and I intend to spend them making it up to you. I promise that someday down the road I'll be healed enough to be the husband you need."

"You have *always* been the husband I need. You're my

Jake. I believe part of our marriage vow was *for better or for worse, in sickness and in health, as long as we both shall live.* I've had sickness and dark moments when it was you who had to be there for me, Jake, times when I needed you to rescue me, and there you were, risking life and limb for me. There is nothing to forgive. All I need is your promise you will never keep something like that from me again. I ask for nothing more."

Lloyd came inside the house then, the tall, graying Hal Kraemer right behind him. Randy quickly wiped at tears and put on a smile. "Hello, Hal. Have a chair at the table," she told him.

Hal nodded a thank you and removed his hat, hanging it on the corner of a nearby chair before taking a seat at the head of the table. Jake and Lloyd shared a look of concern as Lloyd sat down across from his father and Hal put his hand out to Jake, two rugged, older men who belonged to a West that no longer existed.

"How are you doing, Jake? You certainly look better than the last time I saw you."

Jake shook the man's hand. "I *feel* a lot better than the last time you saw me. I was still full of holes then, but that Doctor Beemer did a good job of sewing me up."

"I can see that. I've kept tabs on you, Jake – had my deputies come here a couple of times to see how you were doing. I have to say, I am amazed you lived. You certainly have a way of surviving disaster."

Jake shrugged. "Only by God's will, according to my daughter. God and I don't exactly see eye to eye, so I just have to be grateful every time He decides to let me live. I've just never understood why."

"Well, understanding Godly things is beyond most men, especially those who seldom step foot into a church," Hal told him.

Jake didn't miss the hint. "I don't stay out of churches

because I don't believe, Hal. It might surprise you to know I *do* believe. I'm a baptized Catholic. But I stay away from churches out of respect for all things holy that shouldn't be tainted by a man like me."

"Oh, I think you underestimate your – uh – worthiness, Jake. For instance, I know you offered your own family burial plot to give the Mitchels a proper, decent re-burial and funeral. I find that very generous of you and the family."

Jake studied the man's eyes but still couldn't quite read them. "That is thanks to my daughter, Evie. As you know, she is a very Christian, caring woman. If God grants me any favors, it's because of her, not because of any worthiness on my part."

Marshal Kraemer nodded. "Maybe so." He frowned as he studied Jake. "I will say, your color is certainly better, but you sure could stand to put on more weight. It's obvious you have a lot of healing left to do."

Jake glanced lovingly at Randy. "My wife will fatten me up on that bread of hers. Her pies aren't bad either."

Hal chuckled and turned to Randy. "Ma'am, with you for a nurse, I have no doubt Jake realizes he has plenty to live for. How are you doing? I'm sure this has not been easy on you."

Randy set a cup of coffee in front of Kraemer and turned to pour one for Lloyd. "I'm tougher than I look, Marshal," she answered. "And when it comes to my husband, I'll do whatever it takes to help him and protect him, although it's usually the other way around." She set coffee in front of Lloyd. "When you're married to someone like Jake, life is pretty unpredictable. You either accept that, or you don't. I accepted it the day I married him." She poured a cup for Jake and walked around the table to set it in front of him, sharing a look that said *I love you.* "I am going to take care of some knitting over by the fireplace," she told the three men before facing Kraemer again. "I'll let you three talk about whatever it is you came here for, Marshal. I just hope Jake is still sitting here when you leave. He's far too weak - "

"Rest assured, I didn't come here to take your husband away," Kraemer said before she could finish.

"Never? Or for the moment?" Randy asked.

Kraemer met Jake's dark eyes. "Probably never," he answered.

"Randy, it's okay," Jake told her.

She kept her gaze on the marshal. "I hope so." She walked to the fireplace then and sat down in a rocker to take up her knitting. The marshal glanced at Jake's guns that hung high over the door. "Have you cleaned those guns since you used them at the Mitchel place?" he asked.

The two men shared a challenging look. "I haven't touched them." Jake swallowed some coffee. "Lloyd cleaned them for me, and if things go right, I hope I never have to touch them again. But you didn't come here to ask me that, Hal, or even to see how I'm doing. Why don't you get to the point?"

Hal sighed and drank some of his coffee. "My God, Jake, *why*? We were all ready to go over there with you."

"You *know* why. You know about that note. They told me to come alone, so I did."

"But you knew we were all ready to ride with you. You came as close to dying as anything you've experienced."

Jake shook his head. "I came closer down in Mexico. I was left beaten and naked in the desert. If not for an old shaman who found me, we wouldn't be sitting here talking right now. I didn't even know Annie, but when I hear a woman is in that kind of trouble, all I can see is my father beating my mother . . . and doing what he did to a twelve-year-old girl who was special to me." Jake shifted uneasily, the way he always did when talking about his father.

"Pa, don't," Lloyd told him.

"It's okay." Jake eyed Hal intently. "In this case, two sweet little girls were threatened," he continued. "It was bad enough that those men shot and wounded young boys, but when I saw that note – "

"I understand," Hel told him. "But that note was their admission of guilt. We could have used it in court."

"No one signed it. They might not have been able to use it at all. Those men would say that anyone could have written it. And I couldn't take the chance that riding in there at full force wouldn't risk those men scattering and us not finding all of them. Again – we had no names, other than knowing Brady Fillmore and Grizzly Smith had made a little trouble, we had no proof of anything else. If they got away, that could have meant some of them were free to find a way to get to my granddaughters. I have no doubt they meant what they said in that note. I had to go alone. Besides that, I had to think about Lloyd. Those men had already bushwhacked young Jake and Ben and Cole. It's only by the grace of God they didn't wound Stephen. They could have been lying in wait again. Lloyd already nearly died in front of my eyes back in Denver. This ranch and everybody on it depends on him."

"They depend on you, too."

"Not as much as on Lloyd. This is about seventy-five percent his place, Hal. This was his dream, and I don't want that stolen from him by a bunch of thugs. And if those men managed to get their hands on my little granddaughters, I don't need to tell you what men like that are capable of. And don't forget that they killed an entire family, all innocent people. Ben and young Jake cried when they found out about that. They had been helping the Mitchels build their barn."

Hal nodded. "I know all that. I came out here to tell you that we've caught the man who got away, and the woman who was with him. They are talking, so we know the despicable men who did all this. And, of course, we have testimony from the man you so graciously left alive, tied to a fence post. They all verified that Buck Potter and Lenny McCarthy killed the entire Mitchel family in cold blood and shot your son and grandson, as well as threatened your little granddaughters. And we know that Brady Fillmore was shot by one of their own men, not by you. But nine other men died, and truth is truth, Jake. It was you who shot them."

"You're damned right. What I did was no different from going after the scum of the earth back in Oklahoma when I was a marshal there."

Jake began to perspire. "And you *did* give me a badge," he reminded Hal.

"Pa, stay calm," Lloyd told him. "You don't look good."

Jake paid him no attention.

"What kind of men lie in wait for *boys* and shoot them without giving them a chance to fight back, without any kind of warning and without showing their faces?" he asked Hal. "My fifteen-year-old son lost an *arm* because of that shooting. He went through ungodly pain and terror. Do you know what it's like to hold down your own son while a doctor saws off his arm? And it was all because those men wanted *me*! Lloyd was shot in Denver because of *me*!

My *daughter* has suffered because of *me*! My *wife*—" Jake caught himself. "Now a grandson and another son. Because of *me*!"

Randy set her knitting aside and rose. "Jake, don't," she begged as she hurried back to the kitchen to stand behind him. She gently rubbed his shoulders. "Stop blaming yourself."

"Who else is there to blame?" Jake began to tremble. He took a deep breath and ran a shaking hand through his hair. "I went alone because I didn't want my son or any of the J&L men to go riding over to the Mitchel place and risk getting bushwhacked like the boys were," he told Hal. "I didn't even want *you* to get hurt. Those men wanted *me*. I've done a lot of bad in my life, Hal, things I've never even told my wife or children about. But I by-God never hurt a woman or a child, and I can't tolerate that in someone else."

Hal shoved his coffee aside and rested his arms on the table, leaning closer to Jake. "Jake, I understand your every move, and I can't say I wouldn't have done the same thing. I'm not here to judge you or arrest you or any of that. I've talked to Judge Carter, and because of what those men did to the Mitchels and to those boys, and because what you did stopped what could have turned into a range war, he's letting this go. But he . . . and *I*, for that matter . . . need your solemn vow that if anything even remotely close to this situation comes up again, you won't take matters into your own hands. Let the *law* take care of it, or at least use this army of men you have right here at your disposal. Can you promise me that much?"

Visibly shaking, Jake again wiped at perspiration on his forehead. "All I can say is I will try to hold off for the law. If you will remember, I *was* the law once, and I didn't kill every man I went after. I brought in as many alive as I could, but when someone is pointing a gun straight at you, you shoot back."

"And you were damn good at your job. I know you never asked to be a marshal, Jake. It was part of a prison sentence – an outlaw assigned to go after outlaws. A judge decided that you knew about men like that and how to track them and how to bring them in, so because of new evidence of innocence on some of the charges against you, he reduced your prison sentence and sent you to Oklahoma, where you did a damn good job of bringing law to a lawless land. But somewhere along the line, you've gotten law and lawlessness mixed up. Yes, there is evil in this world, and you've seen the worst of it in your father, and in the kind of men you had to deal with back in Oklahoma. Believe me, I understand that. I have to go after men like that all the time, and seeing so much evil leaves a man angry and wanting to just go rid the world of that kind of evil. There was time in the lawless West when a man could do that, but not anymore. It's time to leave those guns hanging right where they are and let the *law* take care of things."

Jake leaned back and reached up behind him to take Randy's hand. "I have to defend those I love."

"Of course you do." Hal rubbed at the back of his neck. "But defending yourself or others and deciding to be judge and jury are two different things, Jake. You know what I'm saying. And don't think I don't understand how you feel. You and I both come from another era, when men *did* have to wield their own justice. But we just can't do that anymore. I think Lloyd understands that, so give the gavel over to him. Let Lloyd take over the helm and enjoy whatever years you have left, Jake." Hal glanced at Lloyd. "Be careful that you don't take up where you father left off, Lloyd," he warned, "especially since you rode with him back in Oklahoma. I know you have a lot of his nature in you, but you grew up different from Jake. Be careful with your own choices. Everything is changing now, and the way we all once lived is considered the *old* west. This is the *new* west, laws and all."

"I am well aware of the changes taking place, Hal," Lloyd agreed. "And I know how hard it is for my father.

This last thing took a lot out of him and my mother both. It took a lot out of the whole family. Pa knows that."

Kraemer scooted back his chair and stood up. Jake followed suit, and the two men who'd known only old west mentality shook hands again.

"It's a different world out there, Jake. You must have seen that when you went to Chicago."

Jake nodded. "I saw plenty." He let go of Kraemer's hand. "I much prefer life out here on the high plains and on the back of a horse."

Hal grinned. "I totally agree. We are headed into a new century in just another month or so. It won't be long before you'll see roads built in places you never thought, and automobiles on those roads. You will have a telephone out here and won't have to wait days for news or to get to a doctor. Men like us and like a lot of those out in that bunkhouse are going to be left behind. Even ranching is changing. Buyers back east want better bookkeeping. Some ranches are being bought up by corporations that want better cattle counting, things like that." He turned to Lloyd. "Your father has had to adapt to changes in lifestyle and in dealing justice, Lloyd, and you will have to adapt to the changes in ranching."

Lloyd stood up and shook Hal's hand. "I'll figure it out. This ranch means a lot to me. I intend to preserve it for the kids and grandkids." He squeezed Hal's hand. "All I want now is for my parents to have some peace."

"Let's hope that happens." Hal picked up his hat and nodded to Randy. "Ma'am, thank you for the coffee. I have come to see you as a woman of strength and courage. Any woman who can put up with a man like Jake has to have both. Most women would have left him years ago. Why didn't you?"

Randy folded her arms. "I love him, flaws and all. He has a way of making a woman feel treasured and adored . .

. and safe. Totally, completely safe. That's how we started out. He rescued me from a trading post where I lay dying from a snake bite, and we haven't been apart since, at least not by choice."

Hal grinned and faced Jake. "You're a lucky man, Jake Harkner."

Jake moved an arm around Randy's shoulders. "And I damn well know it."

The marshal donned his hat, said his good-byes, and left. Lloyd walked around the table and faced his parents. "You okay?" he asked his father.

"I will be when I go sit down in that big chair over there and watch your mother knit." He pulled Randy closer. "I like just looking at her."

Lloyd smiled sadly. "Kraemer is right, you know. Things are changing, and you and I both have to change with them." He put a hand on Jake's shoulder. "I understand all of it, pa, and I don't care what anybody else thinks about the past, or what they believe. I know the truth, and I'm damned proud to be a Harkner."

Lloyd left, and Jake pulled Randy into his arms. "I remember when he was born, up in Virginia City, Nevada. I looked at that baby boy and being a father scared the hell out of me."

"I remember," Randy told him. She leaned up and kissed his chin. "And look how he turned out. You didn't need to be afraid of being a father. You just needed to be yourself and raise Lloyd with the kind of love you never had as a child." She sighed and blinked back tears. "How could that have been thirty-two years ago? Almost thirty-three now. In less than two months we'll be in a new century . . . nineteen hundred. It hardly seems possible."

"We're getting old, Mrs. Harkner."

Randy looked up at him. "You think so?" She smiled. "Something tells me that as you get better you will find a way to stave off old age a little while longer. I can't picture you sitting in a rocking chair and using a cane when you walk. And you are still my handsome Jake."

Jake snickered. "Heat up some bread for me. I have to put on a lot more weight, woman, and one thing you're good at is fattening me up." He kissed her gently. "You're good at other things, too, but it's going to take some time before I'm strong enough for that."

Randy gave him a sly grin. "Then I'd better go fix you some of that bread."

# CHAPTER 49

*February 12, 1900 . . .*

*Jake has improved beyond what I expected.* Randy started another letter to Jeff. *He is closer to my strong, handsome, healthy Jake again, although he still can't overdo some things. However, he's stubbornly determined not to let age or his wounds stop him from doing all the things he's always done. The man's resilience continues to amaze me.*

*Our sixteen and eighteen-year-old lovers, Ben and Annie, are still crazy about each other. I think we might have to let them marry in spite of their ages, or we might end up with a new but – well – slightly illegal addition to the family, if you know what I mean. I think Ben and Annie have figured things out in that department, and Jake was right. A man can love a woman just fine even though he only has one arm. You and Peter just might end up getting an invitation to a big wedding here at the J&L later this summer. It's bound to be a wild celebration, especially if Jake is fully well by then.*

Randy couldn't help a soft chuckle at the thought, which got Jake's attention. He looked at her from where he sat in his leather chair reading a several-day-old newspaper.

"What are you writing over there?"

Randy smiled and put down her ink pen. "Just another letter to Jeff."

"Don't be giving away any personal secrets."

"We *have* no secrets from Jeff." Randy smiled. "I miss him."

"Do you miss Peter, too?"

"Of course, I do. Don't you?"

"Hell, no. I don't need that handsome, filthy rich man who's ten years younger than I am hanging around here. Not when I haven't made love to you in, what? Months? I'm thinking it's time to do something about that."

Randy grinned. "I was beginning to wonder if you'd ever bring it up again, but I wanted you to be strong enough."

Jake smiled, looking her over lovingly. "I'm damn well strong enough. Come sit on my lap and let me put my arms around you. I promise I won't break."

Randy rose and walked over to his chair. "Mr. Harkner, after all you've been through, I'm not worried about you breaking. You're like an oak tree. Remember up on Echo Ridge, when you said you were the tree and I was the vine? That was such a beautiful day, and we were so happy. That seems like such a long time ago now." She carefully sat down on his lap and put her head on his shoulder.

Jake moved his arms around her. "My God, it feels good to hold you."

"And it feels so good to have your arms around me – to have you feeling strong again."

Jake kissed her hair. "How do you stay so beautiful after all the hell you've been through the last few months?"

Randy turned her head up and they kissed lightly.

"Being loved *keeps* a woman beautiful." She traced her

fingers over his lips. "As far as making love again, that's your decision, Jake. You say you're strong enough, but you need to be sure. I'm fine with just being able to sit here and talk like this."

"Truth?" he asked.

"Truth."

"Well, my beautiful wife, the truth is—and you'll find this hard to believe, coming from me—I've been worried I'll disappoint."

"You? You can't be serious!"

"Oh, yes I can. You know what being with you means to me. And it's been a long time."

Randy sat up straighter. "Jake Harkner, do I have to get Gretta over here to try things out first?"

"Well, Cole might object, but I wouldn't."

"You *devil*! Don't tell me you're worried if things are still working right, because I can see right now that you haven't changed a bit."

Jake grinned the familiar grin that always undid her. "It's taken a while to wake things up, but in all seriousness, *I am* a little worried." Jake pulled her to him, meeting her mouth in a hungrier, deeper kiss. He moved his lips to her eyes, her hair. "I think we should make a trip to Echo Ridge, where we don't have to worry about grandkids running in and out and the other constant traffic."

"I think that's a wonderful idea! But that's almost a two-hour ride from here. Are you sure you feel up to it? It will be cold."

"Not that cold. We're having a typical February warm-up like we always do before more snow gets dumped on the mountains. And who cares if we get snowed in up there? I can't think of anything better than spending a month or so alone with you, lying in bed watching a fire in the fireplace."

Randy smiled and settled against him. "As long as you're sure you're strong enough. I will say, you look wonderful, and you've gained back a lot of your weight."

"How could I *not*? If you keep stuffing bread and fried chicken and pie down my throat, I'll get a belly like other old men have."

"You aren't built for a big belly, and you're the one who kept telling me to bring you more of that bread. And you aren't old. Old men don't live through what you lived through."

"*Mean* old men do."

"You aren't a mean old man."

Jake smiled sadly. "I know a few people who'd disagree with that. Trouble is, most of them aren't with us anymore." He reached up to pull some of her hair over her shoulder, the back of his hand brushing against her breast, the fondled her breast gently as he kissed her again.

"*Lo nuestro sera eterno, Randy. Tu y yo estaremos unidos eternamente.*"

Randy knew the meaning of his words. *You and I are forever.* He met her mouth again in the kind of kiss they hadn't shared since the night before he left for the Mitchel place, sure he was headed for death. The kiss lingered as he felt her breast again.

"Tell me something, Mrs. Harkner," he said as he nuzzled the side of her neck, a touch that always waked up deep desires.

"What?"

"I think the last word we used for making love was despicable." He kissed her earlobe. "Can you come up with anything new?"

Randy smiled. "I think the last word was salacious. We could add the word scandalous. Other than that, I am out of words." Randy rested her head on his shoulder again. "And somehow you manage to mix the most beautiful lovemaking into all of those deeply naughty words."

Someone knocked on the door and, before Randy could answer it, Lloyd and Evie came inside, both laughing, only to stop short at catching their parents sitting together in Jake's big chair.

"Oh, my," Evie exclaimed.

Lloyd laughed even harder. "Sis, I think we came at a bad time."

"You sure as hell did." Jake looked at Randy. "See what I mean? If we're going to finish this conversation and tend to other things, we need to go to Echo Ridge, where no one will barge in on us."

Evie held up a cake. "I made a cake for you, Daddy. Chocolate, from that chocolate powder mother brought home from Chicago. I have to say, I love chocolate mixed with sugar. We *have* to try to find more in Brighton. I'd go all the way to Denver for it." She hurriedly set the cake on the kitchen table and headed back to the door. "We'll leave you two alone now."

"No. Stay." Randy got up from Jake's lap.

"You didn't ask *me* if she could stay," Jake joked.

"Mother, I'm so sorry—"

"Don't be ridiculous. Come back to the kitchen with me, and we'll cut the cake. Your father is in the best mood he's been in since – well – you know. And he's feeling good physically."

"Looks to me like he's feeling more than just good," Lloyd joked.

Jake just shook his head as Lloyd moved closer, studying him intently. "You really okay, Pa? Anything you want to talk about?"

"Not with you, you party crasher. How's Katie? "

"She's fine. Don't change the subject."

"Okay." Jake grinned. "We were talking about

disrespectful, despicable, scandalous, salacious sex, and how I need to get back to it."

Lloyd shook his head. "Okay then, let's *do* change the subject, since it involves my mother."

Jake chuckled. "Don't tell me *you* don't do disrespectful things with that beautiful woman you're married to."

Lloyd shrugged. "We're having a little trouble dealing with her getting pregnant again, but we'll work it out."

"You mean *you* are having trouble with that. I'll bet Katie isn't. Don't ignore her needs, Lloyd, or your own. She loves you. Make sure she knows how much *you* love *her*. Women like a lot of attention, which brings me to the fact that I want to take your mother up to Echo Ridge. It will be good for both of us."

"Okay, but two problems. It will be cold up there. The last thing you need is to come down with pneumonia again. And I don't think you should ride a horse yet."

Jake frowned. "As Sadie Mae would say, you aren't the boss of me."

Lloyd chuckled. "I am until you're strong enough to duke it out with me."

Grinning, Jake looked him over. "Son, sometimes I worry that day will never come again."

Lloyd shook his head. "Knowing you? It will come, all right. But if you try taking care of trouble on your own again, I'll fucking chain you to a wall and leave you behind while the rest of us take care of it. Got that?"

"I got it, all right. Just don't leave me out when you *do* need to take care of trouble. I promise to be good."

"Yeah, well, save your guns for teaching the boys the right way to use them. And you should know that I took Ben hunting this morning, and he damn well shot a rabbit with a shotgun—one-handed—all on his own."

"Honest to God?"

Lloyd nodded. "You know how a shotgun kicks, but he

managed it. The men are cleaning the rabbit now, so Katie's mother can cook it. Ben wants Annie to come over and eat some with him. Those two are getting to be quite a pair, in case you weren't aware of it."

"Oh, I'm aware of it all right," Jake answered with a grin of his own.

"I hope it's okay with you, but I gave Little Jake one of my older .45's yesterday and let him practice shooting it. The kid handles the damn thing like he's already been using one for months. He's either a natural, or he's been practicing behind our backs."

Jake frowned. "I'm not real sure that's something to be glad about, considering whose blood runs in his veins."

"That same blood runs in my veins, remember? And I didn't turn out so bad."

Jake smiled sadly. "You sure as hell didn't."

"When do you want to go up to Echo Ridge?" Lloyd asked.

Jake glanced at Randy. "The sooner, the better."

Lloyd shook his head and stood up. "I'll have Rodriguez and Teresa go up later today while the weather is good and air out the line shack. It's been closed up all these months. Teresa can take clean towels and bedding, and they can build a fire to dry the place out good. I'll send a couple of the men with them so they can clean up around outside, cut some wood and stack it."

"Watch out for ornery grizzlies. A few might already up from a long winter's nap and out looking to fatten up."

"Well then maybe you and Mom shouldn't go up there yet."

"I'll take my rifle. And my guns."

Lloyd gave him a warning look.

"I don't intend to take your mother to Echo Ridge in early spring without being able to do something if there's trouble. And I'm damn well strong enough to pull a trigger, Lloyd."

Lloyd smiled wryly. "You sure you're strong enough for other things?"

Jake frowned. "Son, if you had to go months without making love to that gorgeous woman you have at your house, how strong would *you* have to be to do what needs doing?"

"I'd *find* the strength."

"You bet."

"Strength for what?" Evie asked as both men walked to the table.

"Baby girl, just serve the cake," Jake told her. Someone knocked at the door, and Jake yelled, "Come join the crowd! Seems like there's always one at this house."

Cole and Gretta entered, and Gretta strutted up to Jake. "Well, well, look at you, all up and dressed and looking strong and handsome as ever." She stood on her toes and kissed him on the lips.

"Hey, you're kissin' the wrong man," Cole objected.

"Just checking to see if he's back in the land of the living," Gretta joked, "and I'd say the way he kissed me just now, he's back, all right."

"He's taking my mother up to Echo Ridge tomorrow," Lloyd told her. "What does that tell you?"

Gretta's laughter filled the house and drifted outside to where Ben and Annie approached, with Young Jake, Stephen, Katie, Sadie Mae and Tricia. Jake sat down to the table, and in minutes, the house was its usual bedlam, as Evie and Katie discussed tomorrow's Sunday dinner with Randy. Soon, the Donavans arrived with more of the grandchildren, all wanting to see grandpa and how well he was doing today. Then Teresa came in to see if Randy needed her to do any cleaning.

"Rodriguez, he is at the bunkhouse cooking for the

men," she told Randy. "Vance and Charlie want tacos for lunch."

"Will you and Daddy be back from Echo Ridge by the next?" Evie asked her mother as she poured Jake some coffee. "That's a whole week from tomorrow."

Randy looked at Jake, thinking how good his color was. Sadie Mae and Tricia were climbing onto his lap and giving him kisses. Sadie Mae made him kiss one of her dolls, and Jake met Randy's gaze with that helpless look that said, "*Rescue me!*"

Randy smiled. "I think we'll be up there a while," she told Evie. "We need some time alone, maybe a couple of weeks. We have a lot to catch up on."

"Mother! Are you saying what I think you're saying? Are you sure he's well enough?"

"Oh, he's well enough, all right." Mother and daughter shared a laugh as everyone ate cake, even though they hadn't had lunch yet. Young Jake bragged to his grandfather about how well he did practicing with Lloyd's .45.

"You and I need to talk about that," Jake told him. "Make sure you handle that gun safely. And don't practice with it when there are other kids around. And make sure it's unloaded when you're done. Don't *ever* point it directly at someone, even if you think you're sure it's unloaded. Understand?"

"Sure, grandpa. I know all that."

"Maybe so, but you can't be too safe. I'll talk to you more about that later."

Ben stood with his good arm around Annie and excitedly told Jake about shooting the rabbit with a shotgun. Jake praised him for how far he'd come and teased him about Annie. "See what I mean about using that good arm?" he asked.

Ben blushed and pulled Annie even closer as Jake set

Tricia on her feet and handed her a doll. "Button, you're wearing me out with all that energy. I wish you could give some of it to me."

Tricia put little hands to each side of his face. "There. I'm giving you my energy, Grampa."

"Thank you!"

"Me, too." Sadie Mae took a turn putting her hands to his face.

"Okay, everybody," Randy announced. "I thought we were just going to share a little cake with Evie and Lloyd. We love all of you, but this is a little much for Jake. Let him go back to his chair by the fire and sit down."

"She just wants him to herself," Lloyd joked. He began herding the grandchildren out the door. "Come on. Ben. You and Annie are supposed to eat that rabbit for lunch over to my place."

Ben, Annie, and each grandchild gave Jake a hug and told him they loved him before Lloyd herded them and Katie out of the house. "Pa, you finish your cake and get some rest," he said on the way out.

"Lloyd, I'm sixty-three, not ninety-three."

"You'll *feel* ninety-three if you do too much too soon."

"Go take care of that beautiful woman on your arm. And have the men clean up the Runabout and attach the canopy. Pick out a good, strong horse to pull us up to Echo Ridge, but tie Thunder to the back of it, and a decent riding horse for Randy, too."

Lloyd paused in the doorway. "Why Thunder? You shouldn't ride yet, Pa."

"Something could happen that I have to ride fast. You know you can't predict anything out here, especially this time of year. Besides, it's time I started riding again. And something could happen that your mother needs a horse, too. Once you're up there, make sure the men cut plenty of firewood."

"I know what to do and what supplies you'll need. Don't worry about it. I'll go talk to Rodrigues and Teresa. And I'm posting a couple of extra men up there whether you like it or not. We built that extra line shack a little below the cabin so men would have a place to stay and keep watch when you and mom go up there."

Brian came inside just as Lloyd and Katie left. "Is it me? What did I do to chase everybody else away?"

"Just a little too much company all at once," Randy told him.

Brian, stethoscope around his neck, approached Jake. "I'd better give a listen to that lung, Jake. Are you smoking again?"

Jake leaned back in the chair. "Cigarettes are the only thing that soothe my restless soul, Brian, but I'm down to only a couple a day. Of course, I could switch to whiskey, but if I did that, you'd meet a Jake Harkner you never knew before, and believe me, it wouldn't be pretty." Jake drank some coffee and waved off his son-in-law when Brian started to listen to his breathing. "I'm feeling better than I have in a long time. In fact, Randy and I are going up to Echo Ridge in a couple of days."

Brian frowned. "I'll let an exam go for now, but I'm coming back to check you again before you leave. Sometimes after a big trauma, these moments of feeling better are fleeting and a person relapses, which already happened to you once last month, if you will remember, so you be careful."

"Brian, I'm fine. Really. It's time I started taking care of your mother-in-law instead of her taking care of me. And can I take a moment to eat this cake now?"

"Yes." Smiling, Brian reached for Evie. "Come on, honey. You can come back later." He kissed her, then turned to Jake. "Try getting some mid-day sleep."

"I will."

Evie kissed her father's cheek. "Enjoy your cake, Daddy. And take care of yourself."

"Evie, do you know how tired I am of haring those words? I'm a big boy. Besides your mother orders me around like a prison guard. I think she's still mad at me for leaving without telling her."

"You just don't realize how much everybody loves you," Evie told him. "And if mother is still mad at you, I don't blame her. I still want to sock you myself, but I pray for you instead."

Jake gave her a hug. "Don't waste your prayers on me, baby girl. Save them for the rest of the family."

"It all starts with you, daddy. Remember that." Evie kissed him once more and headed for the door with Brian, who called back teasingly to Jake, "Don't forget you'll need your rest if you're going to Echo Ridge, Jake. Don't overdo yourself once you get up there."

"Can you think of a better way to die than in your wife's arms?" Jake answered.

Brian laughed and closed the door.

Jake looked over at Randy, who stood on the other side of the table, arms folded.

"What just happened?" Jake asked. "One minute we were alone, and the next, all hell broke loose."

"*Family* just happened."

There came a light knock at the door. Jake opened it to see Tricia and Sadie Mae standing there shivering into their little wool coats. Sadie Mae was crying.

"What are you two doing back here?" Jake asked.

Both girls bent their heads back to look up at their grandfather. "We told our mommies we wanted to play over here," Tricia told him. "They said no, and you needed to sleep."

"I wanna' be here," Sadie Mae sniffled. "Please,

grampa?" Sadie Mae asked. "We'll be real quiet so you can sleep."

Jake grinned and ruffled Tricia's bright red hair, then patted Sadie Mae's cheek. "I don't *want* to sleep. I want hugs from the two prettiest girls in Colorado. Go over to grampa's big chair and sit there with me. I'll read you a couple of stories." Jake glanced at Randy as the girls ran inside and took off their coats. "That's the 'why' that Kraemer asked me about," he told Randy, referring to the girls.

"I know, Jake," she answered.

Jake saw Evie and Katie watching from outside. He gave them a wave. "They can stay," he shouted to them before closing the door. He headed the girls toward his chair and sat down while they took off their coats and laid them on the love seat.

"Will we hurt you if we sit on your lap?" Tricia asked.

"No, you won't hurt me. Pick out a couple of your favorite story books from the table in the corner over there."

Outside, the rooster Jake hated crowed.

"Outlaw missed you," Sadie Mae told Jake. She wiped tears from her cheeks. "When you were sick, you never went outside. Did you miss him?"

Jake chuckled. "That devil out there? Heck no. And the only thing that rooster missed was flapping his wings at me and daring me to a fight."

"And Outlaw would win, I bet," Sadie Mae answered. "He would leave claw marks on you like he did that time you tried to collect eggs and you said all those bad words about Outlaw."

"And you squealed on me to your mother," Jake told her. "That was supposed to be our secret."

Sadie Mae giggled. "You're scared of Outlaw, aren't you, grampa?"

"Yes, I am. That rooster puts the fear in me. I wouldn't try collecting eggs again if I was starving to death. That's *your* job."

"You won't hurt Outlaw with your loud guns, will you, grampa?" Tricia asked. Both girls climbed into Jake's lap with books in their hands.

Jake sobered. "No, Tricia, I would never hurt that rooster."

Both girls hugged him and kissed his cheek, telling him their kisses would heal the scars there. Jake opened one of the books and began reading.

Randy thought how the girls' kisses wouldn't heal those outer scars, but they helped heal the deep, deep inner scars.

# CHAPTER 50

*February 14 . . .*

"Lloyd, what happened to you? I've been worried." Katie pulled the covers back as Lloyd climbed into bed. "You stayed away longer than you said you would after taking your folks up to Echo Ridge."

Lloyd lay back with a sigh, putting an arm over his eyes. "Things just took longer than I expected. I decided to visit a few of the other ranchers and then ride into Brighton and order some supplies. They'll bring them out to us."

"I wish you would have found a way to tell me. I was worried . . . and lonely."

Lloyd looked at his wife with concern. "Lonely? You have a passel of kids, and your parents, and Evie, and – "

"That's not the same." Katie blinked back tears. "Lloyd, ever since we lost Gabriel, you've been different. The first month made sense, but then that trouble with the settlers started, and then the shooting and your father coming home to all that tragedy with the boys – " Katie wilted onto the pillow beside him. "That awful gunfight, and your father nearly dying – you taking care of him every day for so long and then having to catch up on other things and - " She sighed. "Lloyd, since the baby died, you've acted like I hardly exist. I know how much you have on your mind, but—"

Lloyd turned over and moved on top of her. "But I've been a lousy husband?"

Katie pushed some of his long hair behind his ear. "Something like that. I completely understand you've been through an awful lot, Lloyd, and why you felt you should help with your father, but you need to share it all with *me*. I know your parents mean the world to you, and you're worried about the ranch, and we had that awful snowstorm. But it warmed up and everything melted and . . . and now your father is much better, and - Lloyd, I'm right here, and I need you as much or more than anybody else on the J&L. I *love* you. I *need* you."

Lloyd kissed her lightly. "Baby, it's not just worrying about my father and snowstorms and meetings with other ranchers that has kept me away more than I should be. I'm just—I'm worried about another pregnancy, Katie. I'm scared of losing you."

Katie studied his dark eyes. "You're so much like your father. He would give up anything, deny himself anything, *do* anything to keep your mother or anyone else in the family safe. But you have to remember that I'm completely healed. I'm not being held or abused by outlaws or something. I'm your *wife*. It's been six months! I'm completely healed, and yes, we lost Gabriel, but we've had healthy babies, too. I want more, and I want *you*."

"We can't take the risk."

"It's *not* a risk! It's something that's I *God's* hands. You can't fight or shoot your way out of this. Don't forget how many times your mother was hurt by things you father did that he thought was best for her. All it did was hurt her and leave her lonely. He understands that now. Talk to him if you think it will help, or to your mother, or Evie – "

"I can't. It's our private business."

"What about Gretta?"

"*Gretta?*" The suggestion lightened Lloyd's mood. He laughed and rolled onto his back again.

"Well, she *knows* about those things," Katie told him. "Sometimes she actually talks sense. Maybe she knows about how to keep from getting pregnant."

"Katie, Gretta would probably say something that would make me want to run over here and jump right between your legs."

"Then maybe you *should* talk to her."

Lloyd's laughter turned to a soft smile, and he turned on his side, resting his head on his hand. "You trying to tell me something?"

Katie traced a finger over his dark brows. "Half the time you sleep in another room, Lloyd." Her eyes teared. "The only time you get into bed with me is when you've worked so hard all day that you're too worn out to do anything but fall to sleep. I need you here with *me,* and for more than to just listen to you snore. And you're all man. I know you have needs. Don't forget that *I* have needs, too."

Lloyd brushed at a tear that slipped down the side of her face. "Katie, I've been fighting the terror of you dying in childbirth ever since we lost Gabriel. What with running this ranch and worrying about my father's health - it wears me out. Sometimes I want to turn to whiskey, but I know that's the worst thing I could do."

"Then maybe getting something else out of your system would help keep you away from drink." Katie leaned over and kissed him again. "Honey, your folks have had a lot of visitors, and that rancher that came over the other day brought his twenty-year-old daughter with him. I saw how she flirted with you. You were laughing and smiling. And my heart broke into a million pieces when you walked off with her to the barn. You're so handsome, and young girls think you're rich and - "

"Katie, you can't be serious!"

"Well, you did walk off with her."

Lloyd ran a hand into her hair. "Honey, she was asking about Tommy Tyler. He's good looking and single and just about her age. She wasn't flirting with me. She wanted to get to know *Tommy*. He was working in the barn, so I took her over there."

"Really?"

"Really. Ask Tommy if you don't believe me."

Katie threw her arms around his neck. "I thought you didn't want me anymore. I can't seem to lose my baby weight, even after all these months, and—"

"Wait! Wait! Wait!" Lloyd pulled away and kissed her tears. "After all we've been through since we got married, do you really think I'd look at some other woman?"

"I don't know."

"Katie, I would never hurt *you* that way. You're the mother of my children. And you saved me from the hell of grief after I lost Beth."

Katie studied his handsome face, his dark eyes. "Then *show* me how much you love me, Lloyd, by making love often like we used to do. I miss that. The way we are living now is not a marriage. And you *are* losing me, just by throwing away the intimacy we always shared. You used to tell me you couldn't keep your hands off of me. I know you think that the way to keep me from having so many babies is to stay out of our bed. But that's not happiness and joy, Lloyd, and you are a viral man with needs. I'm so scared you will end up turning to some other woman. Maybe I have made it easier for you because I'm not the slim, energetic young woman you married. I'm always running after the kids and don't always have time to fix my hair and wear nice dresses. Maybe you don't find me attractive anymore."

Lloyd frowned and sat up. "Katie Donavan Harkner, you are the most beautiful woman on the J&L. And that's saying a lot when you figure how pretty my mother an Evie are. I see how men look at you, and sometimes I want to put my fist in a man's face for what I know he's thinking. You fill out a dress in ways that give a man all kinds of ideas. You have hair like fire and those green eyes sparkle like emeralds – and your lips are so pink and full. They make my mouth water, let alone these full breasts that feed my babies." He rolled back on top of her. "But it's not just your beauty. I fell in love with you for how *strong* you are. And smart."

"But my weight – "

"I love every inch of you." He kissed her again. "When I married you, I damn well knew it's not easy being married to a Harkner, but I had this gut feeling you could manage it, and Stephen needed a mother. You've been all of that and more, and you've given me a beautiful little girl and two great sons. I love you so much. Pa has always said a good woman is hard to find, but I found one in you. I'm afraid of getting you pregnant again. I've never quite gotten over watching Beth die in childbirth, and that thing with Gabriel tore me up. Don't you know how bad I want you?"

She sniffed back tears. "No, I don't anymore. You've been so distant. You haven't given me nearly the attention you used to give me. I don't see desire in your eyes, and the few times we *have* made love, you are always in a hurry. You always come outside of me. You said that way I won't get pregnant, but I don't want you that way, Lloyd. I want to feel you inside of me longer. I want to feel your *life* inside of me, too."

"Katie, I'm trying to protect you."

"You *aren't* protecting me. You're breaking my heart, Lloyd, just like your father breaks hearts when he thinks all he's doing is protecting. How many times did he leave your mother, thinking it was best for her? And how much did she cry because of it? She *needed* him, and I need *you*. I talked to Evie, and she said we have to love each other in all ways and leave things in God's hands." She smoothed back some of his hair again. "Lloyd, if God wants us to have another baby, then I'll get pregnant again. And if it's not to be, then I won't. But I need you in *all* ways. I need you here in this bed with me every night. And I want to give you more babies, because some day you're going to need a lot of little Harkners around here to help you run this place when you're too old to do it."

Lloyd sighed. "Let's hope I have another twenty or thirty good years left in me."

Katie sniffed back tears. "Of course, I hope that, but the fact remains that someday it will be just us – you and me – running the J&L. We have to face the fact that the day is coming when Jake and your mother won't be with us anymore. I know it kills you to think about that, but it's a fact of life. We have to be strong and together, like your parents have always been. I admire how much they love each other. I want that for us."

Lloyd kissed her eyes. "I've tried to stay away because being *without* you would be worse than going crazy with wanting you," he told her. "Can you understand that?"

"Yes, but you should have talked to me more, Lloyd. I know with all that's been going on, talking about babies and intimacy have been the last thing on your mind, but – "

"No. Not the last thing." Lloyd kissed her lips. "It's on my mind constantly – so much so that it's the reason I've tried to have as little sex as possible."

"That's not your choice, Lloyd. It should have been *our*

choice, and I would have told you I'm not afraid of another pregnancy. I would have told you that the way you have ignored me has shattered my heart. I fell in love with a beautiful man – beautiful in looks and in spirit. I married him because I'm crazy about him and I want him to make love to me as often as he wants. We need to trust God, Lloyd. He created man and woman to want each other in all ways. I get my strength from you being part of me. And I know you feel the same. I want to get back to that. If I get pregnant, then I'm *supposed* to get pregnant. We can't go the rest of our married life like this, Lloyd. I'm well and strong now, and I'm healed, and -"

She didn't get the chance to finish. Lloyd met her lips hungrily, pushing up her night gown at the same time. He grinned wryly. "You little trickster," he told her as he reached down to remove her panties. "You aren't wearing any underwear."

"Because I hoped I wouldn't need it. I need my beautiful husband."

"Don't call me beautiful." He smothered her with more kisses as she opened her legs. "Men aren't beautiful."

"*You* are."

"Then that makes you ravishing, with that hair red as the desert rocks and those exotic green eyes." He kissed his way down to her nipples. "And these breasts I love to taste."

The talking ended. He kissed his way back up to her neck, her lips, exploring secret places that aroused her until she was begging him for more. Her gown came off, and he pushed himself inside her with pent-up needs that made everything feel like the first time. He ran his hands into her thick mane of fiery red hair as he took her with wild passion, pushing deep. He knew already that tonight he'd take her twice, probably three times, maybe more. It had been too long since he'd fully drawn the deepest pleasure from this woman who meant so much to him. He relished her moans of ecstasy, realizing his own passionate needs in return. He couldn't fight this need any longer.

"I'm sorry, Katie," he whispered. He pushed deep, and she met his thrusts eagerly. They hadn't made love this deeply in a long time.

Katie was right. This wasn't just his choice. This voluptuous woman needed his attention. And he needed her in all the ways a man enjoyed a woman.

"I want to make up for lost time," he groaned as he grew hard again. "Let's do this all night."

"Oh, Lloyd, I've waited so long for this."

Lloyd let up on kisses for a moment. "Katie, I can prove that even though I haven't been here for you physically, I'm always thinking about you."

"What do you mean?"

"Stay right there." He rolled off of her and reached out to a chair where he'd hung his winter coat. He took an envelope out of the pocket and handed it to her, moving between her legs. "Read it."

Katie frowned with curiosity and opened the envelope, able to see what was inside by the light of a lamp she'd left on when she came to bed. She gasped at what was inside. "A Valentine's card!" she exclaimed.

"I bought it in Brighton."

Katie's eyes teared. "Oh, Lloyd, I forgot it's Valentine's Day!"

"I was worried I wouldn't get back in time. I didn't give it to you right away because I wasn't sure you would even be awake when I got home."

Katie threw her arms around his neck. "Lloyd, you remembered!"

"Of course I did."

"But I didn't. I don't have anything for you."

"Oh, yes you do. Having you right here underneath me is all I need."

*"I love you in the spring when all is bright and new ... "* Katie read. *"And in the warmth of summer, in the blossoms I see you. I love you in soft autumn, your lips they do inspire . . . And you're beautiful in winter, when we're wrapped together by the fire."*

"Do you think it's silly?" Lloyd asked her with a smile.

"No! It's beautiful! *You're* beautiful!"

"There you go again with that beautiful stuff. The men still won't stop teasing me about Peter Brown's wife calling me a Greek God."

"Oh, but you are!"

"Then you are a Goddess."

They laughed together. They kissed. And in seconds he was inside her again.

*The air I breathe.* Lloyd understood now what his father meant. Trying to stay away from Katie had only made him want her desperately. There truly had been moments when he felt he couldn't breathe without her. He drew strength from pushing himself deep into her very soul. *That's where you enjoy the real beauty of a woman,* Jake told him once. *Deep inside, where no other man can touch her.*

When was that? He couldn't remember, but the man was damn well right. The Valentine's card fell to the floor.

## CHAPTER 51

Randy shivered into her coat. There was a light layer of snow on Echo Ridge, and much more on the higher peaks to the west. Horse Creek was partially frozen, and in another month it would swell with spring runoff from the heavy snows on mountain peaks. She sat on a large, flat rock she'd covered with a quilt.

Smoke wafted from the chimney of the cabin. She'd built a good fire before she decided to walk to her favorite look-out point on the ridge while Jake slept. The trip here had tired him out more than he expected. He'd ridden Thunder most of the way and insisted he was fine, but she could see he wasn't fine at all. Still, there was no arguing with him, and when they reached the cabin, he claimed he was just going to lie down for a while. His nap ended up lasting into the night and he was still asleep when she got up this morning. She was relieved to notice his breathing seemed rhythmic and clear. He needed the rest after the most exercise he'd had in months, so she left him in bed.

She stared out at the grand landscape that was the northern end of the J&L. So peaceful. So beautiful. A picture only God could paint. After several minutes, her thoughts were interrupted when Jake came out of the cabin wearing boots and denim pants, and a sheepskin jacket over his shirt. He was carrying a rifle.

"How long have you been out here?" he yelled as he walked toward her.

The bright morning sun lit up his face, and he looked tall and strong again. The sight of him so healthy caught her heart so that she put her hand to her chest.

"About a half hour."

He walked closer. "Randy, I told you there are hungry grizzlies roaming around this time of year, some females with babies in tow. You know what that means. You should have waked me."

She stood up and greeted him with a hug, resting her head against his chest. "I was keeping watch. If I saw a bear I had time to run back to the cabin."

"Good God," Jake scoffed. "Do you know how fast a bear can run?"

"Thank God I've never had to find out." Randy chuckled and looked up at him. "My darling husband, you have to stop worrying all the time. You know Lloyd has men posted all just below us. Relax and enjoy this beautiful morning." She faced the valley below and took hold of his hand. "Look out there! It's beautiful! Breathe in this fresh air." She pulled at him. "Come sit on this rock with me and drink in the scene before us, the view of the J&L we have always loved."

Jake clung to her hand and held her in place for a moment, looking around warily and studying a stand of pine and some shrubbery. Seeing nothing, he walked with her and sat down on the rock, leaning the rifle against the side of it. "Promise me you won't walk out here alone again. Grizzlies can be sneaky, Randy. We don't need any more disasters."

"All right. I promise." Randy met his gaze and smiled. "You look so healthy and rested."

"I *should* be rested after sleeping so long. I didn't intend for that to happen." He leaned close and kissed her. "We were supposed to make love last night."

"I have no doubt that we'll manage that in time. Right now, I want to know you're okay emotionally, Jake, after what happened, and all your pain, and seeing your mother."

Jake pulled a blade of high grass from the ground and put it between his lips to chew on it. "I'd rather have a cigarette, but I'm trying to cut way back. Maybe chewing on this will help."

"Answer me, Jake."

He sighed deeply. "Is it true you socked Cole that night?"

"Yes. I split his lip, and I'll never forgive myself for it. I've apologized to him ten-fold. He's the best friend you've had since Jess York died." Randy ran her hand along his thigh. "I was so angry that morning. It's *you* I wanted to hit, but you weren't there. Sometimes I *still* want to hit you."

Jake grasped her hand and turned to face her squarely. "Have at it. I deserve it."

Randy smiled and touched the still-pink scar across his right cheek. "Don't tempt me."

"I *am* tempting you."

Randy leaned in and kissed the scar. "You know I won't. Besides, hitting you would be like hitting a piece of wood. It wouldn't phase you a bit."

Jake snickered and grasped her face in his hands. "I'm sorry for what you've been through, Randy—all the sickness and worry."

"You've had to take care of me other times. You were so patient and understanding after that . . . " She closed her eyes. "After what happened with Brad Buckley." She grasped his wrists. "Jake, your body can't take one more bullet wound or one more beating. Just please, please promise me you won't go riding off alone like that again. I thought sure I'd lost you this time."

He sighed. "I promise. And I'm sorry I missed Valentine's Day. I think it was yesterday. I'm not exactly in any shape to ride into town to look for a card."

"Don't be silly. I don't care about that. You sitting here looking so good and getting well is my Valentine's present." She touched her necklace. "Let alone this beautiful diamond. This is my birthday, Valentine's, Mother's Day and Christmas present for the rest of my life."

Randy held his gaze. "And here we sit, in this beautiful spot where we've shared so much love. For a while I was afraid we would never be together like this again."

Jake took the stem of grass from his lips and closed his eyes, then rested his forehead against hers. "Randy, when I saw my mother, I wanted to go to her, but she told me God wasn't ready for me yet . . . that I should go home to you. Ever since then I've felt a peace I never felt before, as though I have finally rid myself of that terrible guilt. And when I was lying wounded in that creek, I thought I saw you. Later, when I felt your breath on my lips and heard you telling me to breathe, that's all I needed to want all this to end." He studied her lovingly. "I'm more at peace than I've been at any time in my life, mainly because I saw my mother as vividly as I see you right now." He moved an arm around her, and they both sat gazing at the scene below – the homestead a little dot in the distance, patches of white snow, glittering ice, green and yellow and brown grasses, brilliant silvery aspen, and deep green pine.

Randy waited quietly, deciding it was best to say

nothing. They sat there several long seconds before Jake continued.

"She was so beautiful, just like I remembered her," he said nostalgically. "Evie looks so much like her that it almost hurts sometimes for me to look at my own daughter. And seeing my mother makes me feel closer to that God Evie's always talking about, because I know my mother is with Him and no longer suffers any pain. And she has Tommy with her."

"Your mother's spirit lives deep inside you, Jake, and that's why a goodness shines through all the dark things you've done. Accept the love we all have for you, and don't be afraid to love back. And I'm not talking about loving others, Jake. I'm talking about loving *yourself*. You have to trust God to take care of the others you love. He has already done that, many times over, so stop thinking you have to go to extremes to protect what you so desperately need and love. We are all here and we aren't going anywhere. No one in this family will ever leave you, especially not me."

Jake pulled her into his arms. "I'm going to tell you something else I'd never share with anyone else."

Randy rubbed his arms lovingly. "That's why we're here together alone."

Jake sighed. "When Evie, uh, when she sings that favorite hymn of hers – *Amazing Grace*. You think that doesn't touch me, but it does. One line . . . *My chains are gone. I've been set free*." He paused and cleared his throat. "After seeing my mother and feeling assured she's all right . . . that's kind of how I feel. Like I'm free of those chains of guilt over not being able to help her. Free of the chains my father put on me."

Randy couldn't answer right away for fear of breaking into tears and maybe interrupting his thoughts. She just grasped his hand and kissed it. Saying something so personal was not Jake Harkner.

Jake drew a deep breath then and cleared his throat again. "Boy, you sure have a way of getting things out of me when we come up here."

"That's why I thought we should come."

"That newspaper man back in Chicago was so right," Jake said, keeping her close. "I *am* a dying breed, Randy. I'll try to abide by this new West, but it's not easy. There was a time when a man had to be judge and jury or die – or watch a loved one die. But not anymore. I've hung up my guns."

*Have you, Jake? Have you really?* She wanted to believe him.

"A rifle and shotgun for hunting," he told her. "I'll teach the boys a few things about handguns, but I won't wear my .44's all the time. Plus, it's time for Lloyd to take over. I see a lot of strength in him and Katie. Someday they will be running this place while you and I sit our achy bones in rocking chairs and just watch. Lloyd and Katie are the future, with Evie and Brian's help, and Ben's. Hell, the whole family. We won't be needed."

"I don't want to think about that, Jake. I just got you back into the land of the living."

"I just want to get used to the idea that the future of this place lies with Lloyd. The way things are changing, I might have been right about the homestead turning into a little town. The grandkids will marry, and most of them will settle right here."

They sat there quietly a little longer. "And it all started in that little supply store in Kansas," Randy said nostalgically.

"With a wanted man who didn't now a damn thing about love and family."

"You see? God truly is in control of your life, Jake. He's

brought you through some really bad times, and now he's shown you that he's taking care of your mother and Tommy. It's time for you to trust Him and not those .44's."

"I know. I'm trying."

*God help him.* "Are you hungry?" Randy asked aloud.

"Yes." Jake stood up, and she let out a little scream when he picked her up in his arms. "For *you*."

"Jake, you shouldn't be doing this! You aren't strong enough."

"Oh, I'm strong enough, all right. When it comes to making love to you, I can *find* the strength. Besides, you're still too skinny. You aren't much heavier than a child." He knelt a little. "Pick up that rifle."

Randy obeyed, hanging on to the rifle while he carried her to the cabin. "I was extremely disappointed when I woke up alone in that bed," he told her. "From now on you are not allowed to get out of bed without my permission."

"Oh, I'm so afraid," Randy mocked.

Jake carried her up the steps and managed to open the door, then kicked it shut behind them. He knelt again, this time near the table. "Set the rifle on the table."

Randy managed to do so. "It's heavy," she told him.

"I should teach you to shoot that thing for when you go off alone like you did just now. Please don't do that again." He carried her over to the bed and dropped her on it. "Woman, get your clothes off."

Randy laughed. "Pull my boots off. They have snow on them. I'll get the bed wet."

Jake pulled off his jacket, then her boots. "It will get wet, all right, but from perspiration, not from snow." He walked over to stoke the fire in the fireplace. "I don't know about you, but I'm damn cold and need warming up." He came back to the bed and pulled off his boots, then undressed. "Why is your coat still on?"

"Because I'm cold, too. I have to warm up before I get naked."

An already completely naked Jake moved onto the bed and started stripping off her clothes. "I'll warm you up quick enough. There is a beautiful body somewhere under all this, and I aim to get to it. I also intend to stuff food down your throat for the next two weeks and take home a fat wife." He grinned when he realized she wore only a nightgown under her coat. "Well, Mrs. Harkner, this will be easier than I thought." He pulled the nightgown up and over her head, and she sat there naked, too.

Randy ignored the quick stab at her heart and memory when she saw the white scars on his chest, his lower left side, his arm, his shoulder, the scar across his cheek, and most touching of all, a scar in the shape of a cross right over his heart. *Don't think about it*, she told herself. *He's here and alive and fully a man for you again.* "Are we going to do something salacious?" she asked, wanting to keep the moment light.

"That depends on me finding out just how long I can keep up."

Randy smiled lovingly. "Well, don't overdo yourself. Just lying naked beside you will be wonderful. Really. You don't have to make love to me, Jake. We have the rest of our lives to make love."

Jake smiled the handsome smile that had always made him irresistible to her. "And I think it's time we found out, now that I'm healed, if everything is working right." They both scooted under the covers and pulled quilts over themselves.

"I'm just glad you didn't decide to practice with Gretta," Randy joked.

Jake laughed – that deep, full laugh that said he was fully happy and at peace. "My God, I love you." He moved on top of her. "Like I told Brian, I can't think of a better way to go out of this world than lying naked in bed with my beautiful wife."

"Please don't let that really happen," Randy teased. "You're too big and heavy. I'd never get you off me."

"You might not get me off you anyway."

Randy smiled, reaching around his shoulders as he kissed her deeply.

"By the way, we need to get that shower installed upstairs," Jake told her between kisses.

"I'd *love* that."

"You'll have to buy plenty of soap. The good, slippery kind."

Randy laughed. "I brought some home from Chicago. But if we put in a shower, you had better not embarrass me with remarks about what you like to do in it."

"I wouldn't think of it."

"Oh, yes you would." Randy frowned. "Maybe we shouldn't have one installed after all."

"Another rule? I can't make remarks about the shower?"

"Something like that."

"Have I ever followed any of your rules?"

Randy smiled. "Never. Not even one time." She felt his hardness against her belly, and he kissed her, a long, deep kiss that told her he was indeed ready for lovemaking.

She was soon lost beneath him. He hadn't lost his touch, and she groaned with long-neglected desires. When he pushed inside her, she arched her head back . . . and there they were - the famous .44's - hanging on the bed post. He'd brought them along only for quick protection if a grizzly decided to push its way through the door in the middle of the night and come after food inside the cabin. He also kept his rifle against the wall on his side of the bed at night.

*God, help him hang up those guns like he said he would.*

Randy hated the term "dying breed," and it made her heart ache to realize that's exactly what he was. She could only hope for a final peace, a peace they could enjoy for many more years yet.

Jeff's book was titled *Jake Harkner: The Legend and the Myth*. Perhaps he would become a legend, but the man making love to her right now . . . this man who owned her, body and soul . . . was no myth.

"Who do you belong to?"

"Jake Harkner."

"You bet."

## MY STRENGTH . . .

You are my strength, my joy, my breath, my safe place.

I need nothing more . . .

# OUTLAW HEARTS

To learn about the Harkners from when Jake and Randy first met, read the entire *Outlaw Hearts* series:

<u>Outlaw Hearts</u> *(Their dramatic meeting, and Jake's years as a wanted man)*

<u>Do Not Forsake Me</u> *(Oklahoma and Dune Hollow – How Jake finds and adopts Ben)*

<u>Love's Sweet Revenge</u> *(Lloyd's near-fatal shooting at the cattlemen's ball in Denver – Jake's trial —The barn fire and Randy's ordeal with Brad Buckley)*

<u>The Last Outlaw</u> *(Jake's venture into Mexico to rescue Gretta's daughter, Annie)*

<u>A Chic-A-Dee Christmas</u> (a short Christmas story in an anthology titled *Christmas In A Cowboy's Arms*—a sweet story about Sadie Mae and a cougar attack on a Christmas tree hunt)

*Blaze of Glory*

I plan more stories, next about Jake's son Lloyd, and about "Big Jake's" namesake - grandson, Little Jake, as a grown man living with his grandfather's legacy.

DEATH CAME KNOCKING . . .

Death came knocking,
   But I opened the door, and it ran away,
   For it saw that I was angry
   And would not welcome it.

                    Rosanne Bittner

# ABOUT THE AUTHOR

Rosanne Bittner has been writing almost forty years, with seventy-four published novels as of this book. Her first love is American history and America's Great West—its magnificent landscape and its exciting history. She has traveled the West almost her entire forty years of writing, visiting the majority of the locations involved in her stories. Learn about all her other books by visiting her website at www.rosannebittner.com. She also keeps an active blog at www.rosannebittner.blogspot.com, and you can find her on Facebook, her Facebook Street Team, and on Instagram and Pinterest. Rosanne also writes Native American stories based on real history and real events. Her stories are well-researched, and she is known for her very realistic plots and characters. She has been called an "emotional powerhouse" because of the high emotion and in-depth character study in her stories. More than all else, Rosanne writes unforgettable love stories that stay with readers for years. Another continuing love story involving the same couple over many years is her 7-book <u>Savage Destiny</u> series, about the Cheyenne and the settling of Colorado.

Made in the USA
Las Vegas, NV
09 December 2021